Praise for *New York*

Catherine
Anderson

"A major voice in the romance genre."
—*Publishers Weekly*

"Catherine Anderson is an extraordinary talent.
She has a voice that is gritty and tender,
realistic and romantic, and always unique."
—Elizabeth Lowell

"An author who excels at crafting
emotionally powerful romances that celebrate
the importance of family and love."
—*Booklist*

"Emotional and heartfelt, her stories
make you believe in the power of love."
—Debbie Macomber

"Ms. Anderson never fails to keep you intrigued."
—*Rendezvous*

"No one can tug your heartstrings
better than Catherine Anderson."
—*RT Book Reviews*

Coming soon from
Catherine Anderson
and Harlequin HQN

Endless Night

Catherine Anderson

sweet dreams

HARLEQUIN®
entertain, enrich, inspire™

ISBN-13: 978-0-373-77800-3

SWEET DREAMS

Copyright © 2012 by Harlequin Books S.A.

The publisher acknowledges the copyright holder of the individual works as follows:

REASONABLE DOUBT
Copyright © 1988 by Adeline Catherine Anderson

WITHOUT A TRACE
Copyright © 1989 by Adeline Catherine Anderson

PLEASE RECYCLE

Recycling programs
for this product may
not exist in your area.

This edition published by arrangement with Harlequin Books S.A.

For questions and comments about the quality of this book, please contact us at CustomerService@Harlequin.com.

® and TM are trademarks of Harlequin Enterprises Limited or its corporate affiliates. Trademarks indicated with ® are registered in the United States Patent and Trademark Office, the Canadian Trade Marks Office and in other countries.

www.Harlequin.com

Printed in U.S.A.

CONTENTS

REASONABLE DOUBT   7

WITHOUT A TRACE   245

REASONABLE DOUBT

To Robyn and Sarah
And to my mother, who inspired me

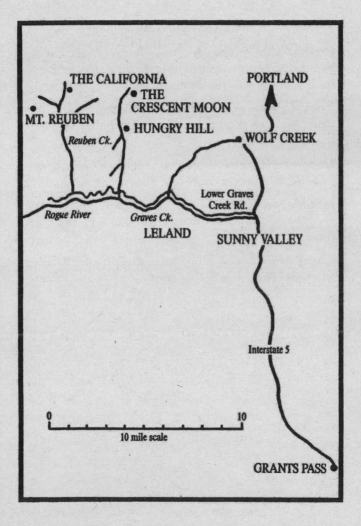

THE CALIFORNIA

PORTLAND

MT. REUBEN

THE CRESCENT MOON

Reuben Ck.

HUNGRY HILL

WOLF CREEK

Rogue River

Graves Ck.

Lower Graves Creek Rd.

LELAND

SUNNY VALLEY

0   10

10 mile scale

Interstate 5

GRANTS PASS

CAST OF CHARACTERS

Breanna Van Patten Morgan—Ten years ago she had run away from her doubts, but now she was back, and she was finished running.

Tyler Ross—A man of many talents and no past, who always seemed able to be in the right place at the wrong time.

Dane Van Patten—Obsessed with dreams of hidden treasure, Breanna's cousin had always loved secrets.

Jack Jones—Tyler's "partner" allowed himself to trust very few people, and Breanna Morgan wasn't one of them.

Chuck Morrow—A powerful man with a lot to offer when he chose, but a very dangerous man to refuse.

PROLOGUE

THE COLD IN the room cut bone deep, dank as a grave. A lantern perched on a wooden shelf, its flickering sphere of light overwhelmed by the shifting shadows that played upon the earthen walls. Four men stood near the door, three together, one alone, the air between them crystallized with tension.

The heftiest of the threesome unrolled his T-shirt sleeve and lifted out a pack of cigarettes. When he tapped the pack against his ink-stained forefinger, the sound echoed around him. He smiled as he reached for his lighter. With a flick of his thumb, he rasped flint against steel and dipped his head toward the spurt of orange flame. The glow from it rippled over his face, emphasizing his coarse features and cold, flat eyes.

"It's like this," he whispered, exhaling smoke. "You get rid of her, or I do. It's your decision."

"How?" Desperation rang in the lone man's voice. "What do you suggest? That I tell her to leave the second she gets here? She won't go. She inherited the cabin in the will. It's hers and the mining claim's filed in her name."

"If you'd filed before she got here, the claim would have been yours. We could have taken the cabin by default. You screwed up. How you undo it is up to you. The way I see it, if she stays, it's her or us."

"Just what the hell do you mean?"

Letting his cigarette dangle from the corner of his mouth, the older man leaned against the wall. Lifting his hand to his throat, he made a slashing motion across his Adam's apple. "That clear enough for you, pretty boy?"

"You aren't serious! A move like that would bring every cop in the country down on our heads."

"Not if it's done right. No one knows we're here, remember?"

"You miserable bastard," the younger man hissed. "How much time do I have? She doesn't scare easy."

"We can hold off production a few days. Meanwhile, we'll watch her so she doesn't poke around and find our equipment. Sound reasonable?"

"Reasonable? You don't know the meaning of the word."

CHAPTER ONE

HYPNOTIC REGRESSION. THOSE were the only words to describe the feeling that washed over Breanna Morgan as she climbed out of her silver Honda and gazed at her grandparents' small cabin. In the dusky light, its yellow logs and tin roof looked postcard perfect against the tree-studded backdrop of Hungry Hill. Flashbacks buffeted her, some sweet, some nostalgic, others painful. She stood rooted until her mind could assimilate the shock.

With a determined lift of her chin, Breanna strode to the aluminum driveway gate and swung it wide. The night wind whispered, a decibel louder than the gurgle of Graves Creek, following the stream's course as it twisted and turned through the canyon to spill into the white water of the Rogue River five miles west. Above Breanna, a clapboard sign dangled by one corner from the arbor that formed an entry arch. Its rhythmic, forlorn squeaking underscored the surrounding gloom. Glancing at the encroaching laurel and oak trees, she drew in a deep breath and slowly exhaled. After spending most of her twenty-seven years in the mountains, as a child playing in the surrounding woods, as an adult doing wildlife studies, the remote location of *The Crescent Moon* mining claim shouldn't bother her.

But it did. Vague unease wrapped itself around her and refused to let go.

Turning back toward the Honda, she saw her black dog, Coaly, had exited the car. He seemed bent on exploring everything, and that was a mighty big order when miles of Oregon forests stretched in all directions.

"Come on, old man," Breanna called as she slid back behind the steering wheel. "It's time to get settled for the night."

The mostly Labrador mutt led the way down the drive, his incongruous plumed tail waving like a flag over his back. Some of his excitement spilled over to Breanna. She had always loved it down here. Once she settled in, maybe a little of the magic would return. It was a perfect environment for writing, much better than living in town with all the distractions that neighbors inflicted.

Parking near the retainer wall steps to facilitate unloading her hatchback, Breanna fished in the pocket of her faded jeans for her cabin key as she slid out of the car. Coaly ran circles around her for a moment, then veered away to sniff the foundation of the old barn. As she ascended the steps to the overgrown yard, Breanna could see the ravages of neglect everywhere. Weeds flourished in her grandmother's rose beds beside the house. The cement edges of the stone walkway were beginning to crumble. She didn't know what her cousin, Dane, had been doing during his visits here these last seven years, but it was clear he hadn't been caretaking. No wonder their grandmother had given the cabin to Breanna.

Four paces up the walk, Breanna froze, her gaze riveted on the front door. It hung awry on its hinges, swinging slightly as if someone had bumped against it only seconds earlier. The door frame was split and gouged where the sturdy dead bolt had been forced inward. Myriad emotions rushed through her. Disbelief turned to outrage, and both were quickly smothered by fear. Intruders caught in the act could be dangerous. Standing here, she blocked the only exit as effectively as a cork in a narrow-necked bottle.

The door swung slowly shut, then yawned open again,

creaking on its hinges. Breanna jumped. Then she realized it was only the wind. Coaly lumbered up the steps behind her, tongue lolling, tail whipping against her leg as he passed. With no apparent presentiment of danger, he bounded onto the porch and gave the swinging door a nudge with his nose.

Trusting her dog's keen sense of smell, Breanna relaxed a bit. He'd be raising a ruckus if anyone was in there. Straining her ears for any unusual sounds, she advanced on the cabin. As she stepped onto the porch, her well-trained eye zeroed in on a footprint in the soft dirt next to the walkway. She leaned over to study it. A man's boot, judging by its size, one with a waffled sole. A hiking boot? It gave her an eerie feeling looking at it.

"Coaly, wait up."

The canine's response was a happy bark as he frolicked into the dark entry hall. Pausing on the threshold, Breanna pushed the door wide. No growls from Coaly yet. That was a good sign. She'd need her flashlight, though. It was black as a tomb in there. Hurrying back to the Honda, she dug into the glove box until her fingers curled around the cylinder of plastic.

"Coaly?"

Breanna switched the flashlight on as she entered the short entry hall. Glossy log walls burnished with age, just as she remembered. Gramps's hand-carved coatrack hung to her right. On her left was a— She came to a dead stop and stared. A white face glowed back at her. For an instant that seemed like eternity, she couldn't move. Her blood pounded in her ears, a loud, rhythmic swish that deafened her. Then she recognized her own distorted image, reflected by an old mirror. She laughed, the sound squeaky and tremulous. If she didn't stop this, she'd have cardiac arrest before she reached the living room.

"Coaly? Come here, boy."

The hall spilled into the main living area. She eased forward, then fell back, waving her arms. Cobwebs. She sputtered, shining the light on her shoulder. Gray wisps clung to her sun-streaked brown hair. She brushed them away, then played the light over the river rock fireplace, the battered kitchen table, the lime-green gas stove. A thick layer of dust covered the sheets on the studio couch and sofa. More cobwebs were draped from rafter to rafter.

"Brother! Talk about a hard day's work; this is it." Her voice rang hollow in the room. The heavy smell of aged pine mingled with moldy dampness, making her shiver. "Gives me the creeps to think of sleeping in here."

First things first. For now, her major concerns were dealing with the broken lock on the front door and clearing a place to stretch out for the night. When she pushed through the curtained doorway to the bedroom, the tarnished brass bedstead gleamed back at her. It was the only valuable antique in the house; she'd been half-afraid it would be gone.

But when she came to think of it, nothing seemed to be missing. Breanna returned to the living room, flicking the light around. Gran's oil paintings of the creek hung above the oak mantel. The mahogany tables stood in their respective corners, the tops littered with Gran's odds and ends. A thimble. A short piece of fishing line. A garden trowel. Nothing disturbed, nothing stolen. A slight frown settled on Breanna's brow. It didn't make sense. Usually if you found your front door kicked in, your house was either vandalized or stripped of its valuables.

"Maybe someone got stranded out here and needed shelter," she said to Coaly. "Polite houseguests. They even left the sheets on the furniture."

The dog didn't respond with his usual bark, but she could hear his claws clacking on the planked floor. Training her flashlight on one of the paned windows, Breanna sighed. Night was closing in fast. She wouldn't sleep a wink unless she could lock up tight. Her earlier feeling of unease had escalated into a full-blown case of edginess. No phone, no electricity. Worse yet, no lantern. Where was it?

Fanning the light along the rafters, she spotted the old Coleman hanging on a hook above the stove. Red clay dust coated its base. It had probably hung there untouched since Gran's first stroke seven years ago. She could almost see her grandmother in the kitchen, flour streaking her apron, her salt-and-pepper hair swept back with tortoise-shell combs. The cozy picture accompanied her as she returned to the Honda to get her can of kerosene.

Forty-five minutes later, Breanna jammed a chair securely under the doorknob and knelt before the hearth to light a fire. Now that the car was unloaded, she could try to relax. Flames licked up the crumpled tufts of old newspaper she had found on Gran's closet shelf, blue tendrils curling hungrily around the sticks of kindling. Mesmerized, she stared at the smoldering newsprint. Then she noticed the date on the right-hand corner.

August twenty-third, ten years ago. Only a few days before the—

Her throat tightened and she grabbed the poker, shoving the newspaper into the flames. Why on earth had Gran kept papers that old? And from that particular month?

Forcing the tension out of her shoulders, she glanced around. The yellow glow of flame and kerosene light cast the rooms into flickering shadow. How many times had she sat in this very spot, knees hugged to her chest, eyes transfixed on her grandfather's face as he told stories about John Van Patten's ghost and his legendary gold? Those were the memories she should dwell on, the wonderful ones that were the essence of her childhood.

Smiling, she rose to double-check the door. If someone wanted in, her makeshift barricade might slow him down,

but that was the best she could hope for. Breanna tugged
on the knob to be sure the chair was angled under it to the
best advantage, still wondering who had broken in. The
most likely explanation was treasure hunters. Gramps had
sounded so convincing when he talked about the Van Patten gold that most people in this area thought the story was
gospel. Even her cousin, Dane.

Dane.

She hadn't spoken to him in years, but it wasn't beyond
the realm of possibility that her cousin had given the house
one last search before Breanna moved in. It would be just
like him to come down here on the sly, thumping the walls
for a hidden panel, checking the stones in the fireplace to
make sure none were loose. Yes, it could have been Dane.
On the other hand, it might not have been. Goose bumps
rose on her arms.

As she reentered the living room, she noticed smoke
escaping through the fire screen. Hurrying to the hearth,
she grabbed the poker and shoved it up the flue to check
the draft lever. Wide open. The chimney was blocked. Just
what she needed. "I don't believe this!"

Coughing and waving her hand to clear the air, she
stepped to a French window and threw it wide. Then,
kneeling on the hearth, she again seized the poker and
shifted the wood so it would burn more swiftly. Dousing
it with water would only create more smoke.

The wood was laurel, deadfall from Hungry Hill. Its
scent and the searing of hot smoke in her nostrils cata-
pulted her mind into the past—to another night, another
fire. *August, ten years ago.* Her knuckles went white as she
tightened her fingers around the brass handle of the poker.
Images flashed with Technicolor clarity, faster and faster
until they came together in a hot, kaleidoscopic amber
glare. Sweat popped out on her forehead, triggered by the
panicky shiver of nausea that still swept over her whenever

she thought about it. Arson, death, suspecting someone she loved. Guilt roiled within her. She wasn't sure which ate at her the most, believing Dane capable of such treachery or keeping silent about her own inconclusive suspicions.

Memories of that violent night lingered in Breanna's thoughts as she turned out the lantern and unrolled her sleeping bag on the sofa. She sank wearily onto a cushion, drawing her legs beneath her and propping an elbow on the couch arm. Her nerves were strung so taut that she couldn't lie down and rest.

The open window made her feel vulnerable. It would be so easy for someone to creep up on her. At least she had Coaly. She gazed out at the shadows in the moonlit yard. Just shadows, not an intruder. A rafter creaked above her. The lantern gave a final sputter, sending a prickle of alarm up her spine before she realized what had made the sound.

Seconds dragged into minutes, minutes into hours. Nothing but the usual noises. Breanna pulled the sleeping bag close, watched the window, blinked herself awake when her eyelids drifted shut. As exhausted as she was, she didn't dare sleep. An owl hooted. The sound of its call faded into silence, mournful, lonely. It was the last thing Breanna was aware of as she slipped into an uneasy doze....

It seemed only moments later that birds were singing her awake. She slipped off the sofa to stand at the open French doors, gazing out at the golden shafts of sunlight that spilled through the oak leaves. *Home,* she thought. *This is how I remember it.* The sweetness of Gran's roses perfumed the June morning, lightly blended with honeysuckle and the lingering fragrance of withered lilac blooms. Coaly slept on the lawn, warmed by a circle of sunshine.

Turning, she directed a speculative glance at the dusty stove. Breakfast would be short and simple. Her work was cut out for her if she wanted this place livable by nightfall.

BY EARLY EVENING, Breanna had given the last screw on her new front door lock a final twist. She had been busily working since morning, scrubbing the cabin, unpacking her things, driving to town for a lock and wood to replace the splintered door frame. She stood back to survey her handiwork with a sense of satisfaction. Not only had she accomplished a lot, but staying occupied had diverted her thoughts from last night's uneasiness.

Tossing her screwdriver into the toolbox, she leaned her head back and stretched. As tired as she was, it comforted her to know she would be able to sleep tonight, safe behind a locked door. Then a troubled frown pleated her forehead. Dropping her outstretched arms, she glanced over her shoulder. If she had felt it once today, she had felt it a dozen times. Eyes following her, making her skin crawl.

Was someone out there? Or had her nerves shoved her imagination into overdrive? She scanned the thick brush that bordered the creek. Nothing, not a sign of movement. Smiling at her own silliness, she bent to close her toolbox. Even if someone was there, it was probably a local from Wolf Creek or Leland. Sunday was a day for campers.

"Nice evening, isn't it?" a deep voice boomed.

Breanna gave such a start that she slammed the lid of the toolbox on her thumb. Pain ricocheted up her arm. She sprang to a standing position and turned with a muffled cry. A dark-haired man wearing jeans and hiking boots was striding up the steps. His shirt was such a brilliant red that she couldn't believe she had missed seeing him a moment ago.

"Where did you come from? Don't you know it can be dangerous, sneaking up on someone like that?"

He paused midway up the walk to study her, his steely blue eyes alert to her every move. "I wasn't sneaking. I'm sorry. I didn't mean to startle you."

She gave a shaky laugh and dropped her gaze to his

boots. Hiking boots, suede with red laces and waffled soles. She felt the blood drain from her face as she focused her attention on him. If this was her intruder, she could be in serious trouble. He was well over six feet tall with a good two hundred pounds to back up his height, every ounce hard, lean muscle. A camera hung from a braided strap around his neck, a Leica, the type only a professional photographer or serious hobbyist might carry.

"Well, for not trying, you sure did a good job of it. I about jumped out of my skin. I didn't hear you drive up. Are you on foot?"

He nodded. "I'm Tyler Ross. I have a cabin about a mile up the road. Been down by the creek working and when I saw you moving in, I thought I'd better stop by and check on things. You do realize this place is a mining claim? It belongs to the Van Pattens."

"You say you were working? Doing what? How long have you been watching me?"

"I wasn't exactly watching you. I just noticed you up here." He shrugged one shoulder, an offhanded gesture that belied the distrust she saw in his eyes. "I'm a photographer. I was getting a few shots down in the orchard."

"In my orchard? Of what?"

"Deer. A doe and fawn."

Breanna tensed, watching his face for any sign of deception. His eyes met hers without wavering. If anything, she read suspicion in them, not guilt. This time of evening, deer usually emerged to feed. The apple orchard would be a likely spot to get pictures of them. "You say you live up the road?"

"Look, I didn't mean to frighten you—"

"I'm not frightened." Her voice rang a little too sharply. A flush of heat spiraled up her spine. "Well, maybe I am, just a little." She managed a smile and extended her hand. "I'm Breanna Morgan, Alicia Van Patten's daughter."

Expecting him to relax, Breanna kept her hand extended, but he ignored it.

"Then you're related to Dane Van Patten?"

Why the question sounded like an accusation she didn't know. "Yes. He's my cousin. Is there a problem with that?"

"No, of course not."

Feeling ridiculous with her hand held out, she dropped her hand just as he reached out to shake it. By the time she could react, he was drawing back.

A sudden smile creased his tanned cheeks. "We'll get this right sooner or later. I'm pleased to meet you, Miss Morgan."

"Likewise, I'm sure." She placed her palm across his. His callused fingers tightened around hers in a firm grip, pleasant, not crushing, the kind of handshake Gramps had called trusty.

"It is Miss, isn't it?" He loosened his hold slowly. "Or should I say Ms.?"

"Miss is fine."

With a nod toward her porch, he said, "I see you've fixed the lock."

"You knew it was broken?"

"Noticed it late yesterday afternoon. I planned to repair it, but I haven't been to town since to get a dead bolt and molding. Nothing disturbed, I hope?"

Tipping her head back to watch him, she said, "There were a few things stolen, but nothing I can't replace."

She braced herself for a reaction to the lie, a twitching muscle, a flicker of surprise, but all Ross did was nod. He either had rock-steady nerves or was innocent, she wasn't sure which. While she studied him, she caught herself admiring the striking blend of his irregular features. His nose was a bit too large, jutting sharply from between his thick eyebrows with no indentation at the bridge, but it suited him, enhancing his high cheekbones while it offset the squared angles of his jaw.

"So, Miss Morgan, how long do you plan to stay?"

His eyes caught and held hers, a much deeper blue than her own, smoky, darkened with flecks of cobalt and outlined by a sweep of black lashes. Magnetic, direct, the kind of eyes that hid secrets well. She would be wise not to forget that.

"For good. My grandmother passed away recently and willed me the cabin. One stipulation was that I file on the claim and keep the assessments done so it can stay in the family. Her biggest fear was that strangers would take it."

"You mean you plan to live here?"

"Why shouldn't I?"

"On a permanent basis? Mining, part-time or full-scale, is heavy work."

"I'm not afraid of work. And I come from a long line of miners. My grandfather worked in the *California* mine for a number of years."

He glanced toward Mount Reuben. "The *California*, that's up Reuben Creek, isn't it? Funny name for a mine in Oregon."

"My grandfather claimed it was named for a Californian, and other miners said it ran so deep, it went clear to California. I don't think anyone knows now for sure."

"So you're going to be a prospector? Having no electricity will get old in about a week. Same for no indoor plumbing. It'd take a lot of mettle to stick it out down here." The breeze lifted a lock of his ebony hair, waving it across his forehead. "Take some friendly advice. This is no place for a woman alone. You'd be asking for trouble."

"I avoid trouble."

"I hope so. Wouldn't want you getting hurt."

Breanna's earlier distrust mushroomed again. She

tensed and shot him a glare. "Hurt? I played in these woods as a kid, know them like the back of my hand."

"It's not as peaceful down here as it used to be."

The night wind picked up, cool, raising goose bumps on her arms. "Is that so?"

"Look at your door. If that's not trouble's calling card, I don't know what is. If you plan to stay, I wouldn't go wandering if I were you. And I'd steer clear of those old outbuildings. You don't want to end up a statistic."

"You have an interesting way of turning a phrase, Mr. Ross. I could almost believe you're trying to scare me."

"Maybe I am."

"Why?"

"Could be I'm a concerned neighbor. I realize it's a dying breed, but there are still a few of us left."

Shoving her hands into her jeans pockets, she nudged a pebble on the walk with the toe of her sneaker. "Well, I don't scare easy."

"I hope I haven't offended you."

"Not at all." Breanna gritted out a smile she felt sure looked set in concrete. "I do have a lot of work to do, though, and it's nearly dark."

One of his eyebrows shot up, but he didn't argue. "I'll get out of your hair then. Nice meeting you." He turned and struck off down the walk.

"The pleasure was all mine," she replied evenly. Then, as a parting shot, she called, "Oh, and watch out for my dog. He's not one to be friendly with strangers. I'm afraid he's an incurable biter."

Ross slowed and glanced back at her. "A little black fella?"

"Not so little."

Another smile curved his mouth. "He and I already tangled down by the creek. The only thing he seemed interested in biting was my lunch. Be seein' you, Miss Morgan."

She stood there watching until he disappeared around a bend in the road. "Not if I have my druthers, you won't."

Silence settled around her like a cloak. Sighing, she nudged the pebble with her shoe again, then kicked it. She wasn't quite sure what to make of Tyler Ross, but for now he was her number one suspect. It would take a big stretch of her imagination to believe his visit this evening had been sheer coincidence, especially after the ominous little warnings he had given her. The word statistic conjured up ugly newspaper headlines.

Shifting her gaze to the weathered old barn, Breanna mulled over their conversation. A treasure seeker, perhaps? Maybe he was one of a group. She could almost see them, armed with maps, metal detectors strapped to their shoulders. Ross didn't look the type, but one could never tell.

Her eyes trailed to the boot prints near the porch that she had found last night. Waffled soles. Did Ross's hiking boots leave a similar impression? Unfortunately, he hadn't stepped off the walk onto soft dirt so she could check. Even if he had, and she could be certain the prints were his, it would prove nothing. He had admitted to having seen her broken door. He might also have walked onto the porch to examine the damage.

Exhaustion weighed like an anchor on Breanna's shoulders. A flash of black at the corner of the barn drew her notice. Coaly. Dirt flew from beneath his paws. He was probably after some animal. She gave a sharp whistle and waited for him to reach her. An early night sounded tempting. First a bath, then a quick dinner, and the last order of business was bed.

After gathering fresh clothes and toiletry articles, Breanna struck off for the creek with Coaly tagging behind. The bathing hole was a deep pool, surrounded by a privacy screen of thick foliage. On the opposite bank, the eroded earth was rust red, with gnarled tree roots reaching like clutching fingers into the stream. She stripped near a bush, dumping her clothes in a pile, then carried her bathing things to the diving rock, a low bank of shale that curved out into the water. As she poised to dive, she hesitated.

Eyes. Instinctively she hugged her breasts with one arm and crossed her lower body with the other. Then Coaly came into view, tail wagging, nose to the ground. That was her cue to stop being paranoid. She lifted her arms and pushed off the rock, slicing deep into the water.

Breanna emerged in a spray, gasping for breath. She had forgotten how icy Graves Creek was. Doing a breast stroke to the rock, she grabbed her shampoo, did a quick job on her hair, then seized the soap. This would be one quick bath.

Coaly, drawn by her splashing and sharp gasp of surprise, came bounding onto the rock, barking furiously. Breanna tried to reassure him, but he seemed convinced she would go under and never come up. In his frenzy he managed to muddy her towel, knock her razor into the pool and slip partway off the rock to douse his hindquarters.

Breanna heaved herself out of the water, fended off the dog, and extracted her towel from beneath his feet. The fabric was nearly as wet as she was and smelled of…dog. By the time she had used her clean clothes to dry off, and then struggled into them, she had had it with dogs, and even without using the doggy towel, she felt pretty sure she was wearing enough dog hair to pass as one if someone didn't look close.

And someone *was* looking. It hit her as she finished tying her sneakers. Coaly, elated to have her safe on shore, paused in his prancing to curl his lip, his liquid brown eyes glinting.

CHAPTER TWO

AN EERIE CREAKING noise drifted to Breanna from the brush. It had no sooner stopped than Coaly barked, throwing his ears forward. Then off he went into a thick growth of manzanita. Apprehensive about what he might find, she held back for a moment. When no snarling erupted, she struck off after him. Ten feet into the foliage, she found her pet sniffing the ground. Pushing him aside, she spied footprints. Waffled soles, like the impression she'd found by her porch.

Impotent rage. Now she knew exactly what it meant. Coaly, hot on the scent, plunged through the brush toward a low-hung copse, but Breanna had seen enough. It had to have been Ross. Graves Creek wasn't exactly teeming with people.

Returning to the stream for her things, Breanna then strode for the cabin. She made short work of getting ready for bed, then sat on the edge of the mattress to brush her wet hair, glaring at the floor. Ross was cool, she'd give him that. He hadn't batted an eyelash when she baited him. Well, she wasn't leaving, if that was his game plan. It would take a whole lot more than silly warnings and lurking in the brush to make her break her promise to Gran and leave the place to claim jumpers.

Going to the kitchen, Breanna hugged her arms around her against the evening chill. Her long flannel gown did little to warm her, especially with her hair hanging wet on her shoulders. Putting a pan of soup on the gas stove to heat, she cast a determined glance at the fireplace. Cleaning the flue was the next chore on her list. Next time she bathed, she could dry her hair by the fire. She would need a chain, though, to knock the blockage loose. If she remembered right, Gramps had kept some in the barn.

Her lips thinned to a grim line. If Ross showed his face tomorrow when she was armed with a chain, she'd be sorely tempted to throttle him with it.

EN ROUTE TO THE BARN the following morning, Breanna was brought up short by the low rumble of a powerful car coming around the bend. A blue Corvette? A fancy automobile like that was as out of place down Graves Creek as a San Francisco trolley car. She knew instantly who must be at the wheel. Less than two months ago her mother had mentioned how well Dane seemed to be doing at the accounting firm, and that he had recently purchased a fancy new sports car.

Breanna walked toward the approaching vehicle, debating how to handle this meeting. Dane undoubtedly resented the stipulations in Gran's will that gave Breanna first option of owning the cabin. With much less enthusiasm than she would have liked, Breanna watched her cousin climb out of the driver's seat. The sunlight glanced off his blond hair as he straightened his gray sport coat and gave one leg a shake to get a wrinkle out of his slacks. Same old Dane, fussing and primping.

"Hello, Dane. It's good to see you." The lie left an acid taste on her tongue.

"Hi, Bree."

His eyes met hers, large, sky-blue Van Patten eyes, right down to the thick fringe of his gold-tipped lashes. Looking into them, Breanna could no more deny her kinship with him than she could her own brother. Memories of their childhood drifted into her mind, of long, lazy days of

summer when they had run wild together, catching sala-
manders in the creek, romping in the hayloft, sharing secrets. What had happened to them that they could stand
here today, eyeing one another like enemies?

"It really is good to see you," she repeated, truly meaning it this time, hoping he'd do nothing to spoil it.

"So you said." His tone was curt. "I wish I could say
the same. When I drove in, you were headed for the barn.
What for?"

"Some chain. I have to sweep the chimney."

"Yeah. Well, who promised you a rose garden?"

"Dane, there isn't much point in being antagonistic."

"Isn't there. I've put my sweat into this place these last
seven years. Have you? No, you just get it handed to you."

"It was Gran's decision, Dane. I tried to make her
change her mind and she refused."

"Because you were her favorite, always were."

"Oh, come on. Be fair. Of the four grandkids, I was the
only one who could really make a go of this place. You're
an accountant, Jason's a lawyer, Deanna's a teach—"

"You could have refused, Breanna. The word no *is* in
your vocabulary. I've heard you say it enough times."

"Are you questioning my right to be here?"

"You swore you'd never come back. Then, bingo, you
walk in and take over. Why, Bree? That's all I want to
know."

"I was seventeen when I said that. I realize now that I
have too many memories here to let the place go to strangers."

"Are you implying I'd let claim jumpers come in? Watch
what you say. My mood isn't the best."

The thin thread of Breanna's patience snapped. Before
she could stop herself, she gestured toward the neglected
yard. "The truth is that you don't give a fig for the claim,
Dane. Look at it, then tell me Gran should've left it to you.

For seven years she paid you to keep it up—out of her social security, mind you—and in all that time you squeaked by, doing as little work as you could. The walks are disintegrating. The outbuildings are rotting away. The fences have tumbled down. For the time you've spent here, you've done precious little sweating. What have you been doing, anyway? Lounging under a tree, daydreaming?"

"What I do down here is none of your business unless it somehow affects you, which it doesn't. Too bad I can't say the same. You come sailing in, taking over, to hell with the gossip it will cause. It doesn't even occur to you that I've stuck it out, lived through the stares and nasty whispers until people started to forget." A grimace crossed his face. "All that is beside the point. What bothers me worst is you don't stop and think how I feel. I've spent years searching, never giving up on the gold. With my luck, you'll stumble over the treasure and keep it yourself. It isn't fair, but you don't care, do you?"

"You know better than that. If there is a treasure, and I stress the *if*, I'd divide it equally among all us kids." Breanna felt the color wash from her face. "It isn't the treasure at all, though, is it? That's not really what's troubling you."

"Don't be ridiculous."

She didn't miss the way his gaze shifted, as if he were afraid she'd read too much in his eyes. "It's the fire," she said softly. "Admit it, Dane. What really concerns you is that my return may start people talking again."

"And why not? You're not stupid, Breanna. We got off by the skin of our teeth on a fake alibi. Don't you realize how shaky our position is? Another investigation could land us both in jail."

"Not if we've nothing to hide." Breanna shoved her hands into her jeans pockets, watching, analyzing his expression. She knew him so well, perhaps too well, this man who had been her childhood chum. "And we don't. Do we, Dane?"

The question drifted into the air; hung there unanswered. Dane's sudden pallor alarmed her.

"Dane." Breanna stepped forward, lifting a hand to touch his arm. "Dane, I love you like my own brother, you do know that? If there's something you haven't told me, you can trust—"

He jerked his arm away. "I'm so sick of you suspecting me. What kind of a person are you? We used to be best friends, and you believe I'd murder somebody? You know better."

"Yes...yes, I do. And knowing you is what has kept my mouth shut. But you're hiding something. I see it in your eyes. What happened that night, Dane? What *really* happened?"

He stepped back, leveling a finger at her. "Fair warning. Don't go stirring up gossip. You got it? And don't go poking your nose where you shouldn't. That goes for the gold *and* the fire. Is that clear? You screw around with me, and I'll—"

"You'll what?" Every muscle in Breanna's body tensed. "You'll what, Dane? I want to hear it. Don't threaten me. It won't work this time. You're not the only one who's fed up. You're hiding something from me. I'm going to find out what it is."

"There's nothing."

"And I think you're lying."

"You think I murdered a man?"

Breanna couldn't speak. She could only stare at him.

"That's it, isn't it?"

"Yes! Does that satisfy you? I think you lit that fire, Dane. I think you killed Rob Thatcher." The words came with such difficulty that she trembled. Ten years, and she had finally accused him to his face. She hadn't planned on that. A sob ripped its way up, ragged, hollow, turning her throat raw. "I think you were involved. When I woke up that night, you were just returning to camp. You *said* you'd been out in the bushes, but you had been running. You were sweating and breathing hard."

"Sure I was running. For God's sake, the whole damned mountain was on fire!"

"How far did you go into the bushes? A mile?"

"I was scared. That's why I was out of breath. Panicky."

A surge of anger swept through her. "If I knew for sure that you were lying...if I had any proof whatsoever, I swear to heaven, ten years ago or not, I'd turn you in."

"Oh, is that right? You remember one thing, *Saint* Breanna. We were *both* camping on the mountain that night. If it hadn't been for Morrow giving us an alibi, we'd have both hung for it. So go ahead, tell the whole world. When you put a noose around my neck, you'll put one around your own as well."

Breanna knocked away his accusing finger. "I told you, don't threaten me. One thing keeps me silent, just one thing, and that's not knowing anything for sure."

"And you never will." His voice grated as he spoke.

"That remains to be seen, doesn't it? I need to get supplies in town. Maybe I'll do a little research, too. Go to the library, read the old news stories. Will I find something, Dane? Something I didn't notice then?"

"Let me give you a little advice. If you ever decide to tell the cops we weren't with Chuck all night, that I had left camp, you remember one thing. You'll be stepping on toes. You might end up real sorry someday, *real* sorry."

"For someone with nothing to hide, you sure rile easily. Get off my land, Dane. Now, before I forget you're my cousin."

"Gran wouldn't want me to feel unwelcome here, remember?"

"Maybe Gran didn't know you. Maybe none of us really did. Get out of here."

"Oh, I'm going," he said with a laugh. "And, uh, take care of yourself. It's rugged country. Fact is, I'd think twice about staying. A lot of folks around here might not like having an arsonist for a neighbor."

Breanna had an unholy urge to draw back her arm and hit her cousin. Dane's gaze dropped to her tightly clenched fist. "What's happened to you?" she whispered. "There was a time I trusted you with my life. Now you threaten me? Me, Dane? Look at me. Really look. I'm not your enemy."

Something other than anger crept into his eyes, another emotion, long lost, almost forgotten.

"Take care of yourself." He looked over his shoulder. "No matter what you might think, I never meant to hurt anyone. I sure as hell never meant to hurt you." His voice dropped so low that she could barely discern the words. "Leave here, Breanna. Please. Don't stay here."

"Why? What are you saying?"

He clamped his mouth shut and shook his head, his expression pleading. Then he turned and strode toward his car.

"Dane!" Breanna started after him.

Just then she saw a streak of black coming from behind the lean-to garage. It was Coaly, running low to the ground, neck extended, going so fast he was almost a blur. The dog skidded to a halt, lifting his muzzle to bark, circling Dane. Breanna wasn't alarmed. Her pet usually greeted strangers in a threatening manner and her cousin had never met Coaly before.

"It's okay, Coaly," she called.

Her words didn't have their usual calming effect. 1 dog drew closer to Dane, sniffing, snarling, his eyes ing. Dane stood stock-still.

"Call him off, Bree."

At the sound of Dane's voice, the dog crouched, then leaped forward. Too late, Breanna managed to scream. "No!"

Coaly cannoned into Dane's chest and knocked him backward against the automobile fender. Man and dog rolled in the gravel. Dane yelled, fingers entangled in the animal's black ruff, arms shoving him away. Breanna couldn't believe what she was seeing. As cantankerous and protective of her as Coaly was, he had never launched a flying attack before. His fangs snapped the air.

"Coaly, no…no…!" Breanna rushed to drag the dog off her cousin. Coaly was so intent upon biting that he nearly turned on her before he recognized her touch. "Bad dog." Never before had she hit her pet, but now she raised her hand. "You bad, bad dog!"

"Don't!"

Breanna hesitated. Blood streaked Dane's cheek. His expensive jacket was torn at the lapel.

"Don't," Dane repeated more quietly. "He's just trying to protect you. Don't punish him for it."

"But he…"

Dane staggered to his feet, keeping his face averted. He turned toward his car, straightening his coat with a shrug of the shoulders. "Think about what I said, Bree. You shouldn't stay here."

"Dane, how bad are you hurt? You're bleeding. Dane?"

He stopped beside the car, fishing in his slacks for his keys. Breanna wanted to go to him, but didn't dare release Coaly. Dane threw open the door and swung himself into ⸺ A moment later he was reversing up the driveway ⸺ en the Corvette disappeared around the ⸺ was still standing there.

⸺ onds passed before she could straighten ⸺ gers to release Coaly's collar. Then, as she ⸺ ack to the barn, she saw something green on the ground, right where Dane had stood. A neatly folded twenty-dollar bill. He must have pulled it out with his keys. She hurried to pick it up, snatching it from under Coaly's nose.

"You start eating money, fella, and your compulsion to devour paper could get expensive." Breanna stuffed the twenty into her pocket. The next time she visited her folks, she'd leave twenty dollars with her mom to pass on to Dane's. Better that than seeing Dane herself to return it. "Come on, troublemaker," she called crossly to her dog.

As she walked up the drive toward the barn, she held off scolding Coaly until she calmed down. Lifting her eyes to the mountain, she paused. It was beautiful, silhouetted as it was against the powder-blue sky. The burn area was on the other side of the ridge. By now, any significant clues would be overgrown with new trees, grass, underbrush. After all these years, was it worth it to dredge it all up again?

Yes. Once and for all, she wanted to get to the bottom of it. Rob Thatcher had lost his life in that fire, one that had been deliberately set. Whether it had been premeditated murder or a prank gone awry, she had to know if Dane had been in any way involved. There was something her cousin had never told her, something he *couldn't* tell her.

Breanna propped her hands on her hips. Perhaps Dane had found the entrance to *The Crescent Moon*. The Van Pattens had stopped working it after the second collapse at the opening, and that was before Gramps was born. It was too dangerous, Gramps had said. Over time, with the help of several rock slides, even Gramps had forgotten exactly where *The Crescent Moon*'s entrance was supposed to be, and he had forbidden Dane to look for it. Had Dane disobeyed? Had he found the underground tunnels that honeycombed the property?

A lump of dread congealed in the pit of her stomach. What if Rob Thatcher had also found the entrance? She couldn't believe Dane would hurt someone over a fictitious treasure, but maybe she had never really known him. Her stride lengthened. As soon as she finished cleaning the flue, she was making that trip to town.

As she drew near the barn, Breanna remembered her dog. "And you! You're on my blacklist, old man. Dane is family, understand? You act like that again, causing a big ruckus, and I'll have to chain you. I can't have you making trouble."

She had the distinct feeling she wasn't alone as she walked up the entrance ramp. Turning, she checked behind her, but there was no one in sight.

THE WOMAN'S VOICE TRAILED across the orchard, clear as a bell as she climbed the rickety ramp into the barn. The two men watching her glanced uneasily at one another. "Call Ross. We gotta get her out of there. The last thing we need is her snooping around and finding our equipment."

"You warned him."

"Call him," the older man growled. "Tell him to get down here on the double."

BREANNA GAVE THE HEARTH a final sweeping and carried the last bucket of ash out of the cabin to dump it behind the garage. On a scale of one to one hundred, she rated chimney sweeping at about zero. She was black from head to toe. A bath was in order before she drove to Grants Pass, no question about it.

"Hello there."

Breanna whirled, nearly upending her bucket. Tyler Ross was walking up the drive. "Well, well," she said. "Fancy meeting you here." Taking quick stock of his fresh brown shirt and denims, she added, "Not crawling in my bushes today, I see?"

His eyes touched on her face. Breanna couldn't see her

reflection in them, but she didn't need to. She knew her face was soot-streaked.

"Have I caught you at a bad time?"

"Not at all. Last night was a bad time. Today's a mere irritation."

Oblivious to her sarcasm, he gestured at the bucket. "Cleaning the fireplace?"

"The chimney." Her nose itched. She resisted the urge to scratch. "Mr. Ross, let's get down to brass tacks, shall we? I know you were spying on me last night, and to say I'm furious would be an understatement."

"I thought I explained—" He broke off, apparently at a loss. "Look—uh—I dropped by to apologize. I'm afraid I got off on the wrong foot with you last night, and I didn't—"

"The wrong foot? If you think an apology can undo it, you're very much mistaken. You violated my privacy."

He raked a hand through his hair. "Come again?"

He was either a consummate actor, or he hadn't the faintest idea what she was talking about. "Last night, down by the creek. You spied on me while I bathed."

"Someone was spying on you while you bathed?"

"Not someone…you. I found hiking boot tracks all through the brush. And please don't insult my intelligence by denying they were yours."

"Why would I deny it? My prints are all up and down the creek."

"They are?"

"I traipse all over down there." His voice rose. "Listen, it wasn't me. I drove to Wolf Creek right after leaving here. If you want to check, ask Charley at the gas station. I filled up before I went to the store. Are you okay? Did they hurt you?"

"They?"

"The men."

"What makes you think it was more than one?"

Irritation flickered in his eyes. "A figure of speech. Are you all right?"

Uncertainty stilled her tongue. He looked so sincere that she found it difficult to believe he was lying. Charley. It would be easy to check his story. Surely he realized that. "I'm fine. Angry, but fine. I'm sorry for jumping to conclusions if it wasn't you. I guess I put two and two together and came up with five. You do have on hiking boots."

"So does anyone else down here who has good sense." His eyes dropped to her sneakers. "Present company excluded, of course."

A smile tugged at the corners of her mouth.

"I'm batting a thousand, aren't I? Look, Miss—could I call you Breanna?—I stopped by to apologize for being so negative last night. After I had time to mull it over, I realized I didn't even welcome you back to the neighborhood. I'd like to do that now."

He proffered her his palm, his gaze meeting hers so directly that she would have felt petty refusing the handshake. She peeled off her sooty glove. "Thank you. A welcome is a nice change of pace after the last two days."

"That sounds discouraging. Problems?"

"Nothing I can't handle. You know how it is when you're moving. Murphy's Law and all."

She eased her hand from his.

"You know, I don't live but a mile from here by road. If you need anything, anything at all, I'd be happy to help."

For the second time since meeting him, she found herself admiring the handsome blend of his features. "I appreciate the offer."

"I'd like to know you'll take me up on it. Don't get me wrong, but what I said last night still stands. It's not safe down here nowadays. A woman alone…well, it worries me. I'd rest easier, knowing you'll come pounding on my door if trouble pops up. And please stay out of that barn. The floors in there are about to rot through. If you fall and bust a leg, you could lie there for days before anyone found you."

She had to agree. The floors in the barn had seemed a little weak. "I'll bear that in mind."

With a nod at her bucket, he said, "Well, it's obvious you're busy. I'll be on my way so you can finish up."

Breanna wiped the soot off her watch crystal to check the time. "You're right. I'd better get cracking if I'm going to town."

Striking off up the drive, he lifted a hand in farewell. "Catch you later."

"Yes, later."

Breanna strode to the ash pile and dumped her bucket, then gazed toward the brush along the creek where she had seen Ross's footprints. Worrying her bottom lip between her teeth, she turned toward the house. Then she realized what was bothering her. Tyler Ross had mentioned the barn. How had he known she'd been in there? And why did he care? Breanna shrugged and went on into the house.

Before bathing, she wanted to check the flue. A small fire would come in handy. She could dry her hair more quickly by the heat of the flames. She hurried to the bedroom closet where Gran had stacked the old newspapers. Pulling one down, she crumpled a sheet as she returned to the living room. Tossing it onto the freshly cleaned grate, she tugged out another.

Just as she was about to crumple it, she noticed a circle of ink around a tiny news story. Frowning, she smoothed the paper and sat down on the sofa to scan it. A fatal car accident on Mount Sexton, a man whose name she didn't recognize, a resident of San Diego, California. A single-car wreck. No alcohol level in his bloodstream. The police assumed the lone driver had lost control in a curve and plunged through a guardrail.

Puzzled, Breanna crumpled the paper and tossed it into the grate, following it with another sheet. Why had Gran circled a story about a stranger? Breanna stared at the front page. August sixteenth, the year of the Reuben Creek fire. Recalling the date of the newspaper she had used on her first night back, she returned to the bedroom. She lifted the entire pile off the shelf, throwing them onto the bed. Shuffling through them, she checked date after date. All were August releases.

Sifting through them, she searched for headlines about the fire, hoping to save herself a trip to the library. That seemed strange. Gran had saved papers up through August twenty-fifth, the day before the tragedy. After that, nothing.

Glancing at her watch, she started. If she was going to bathe before going to town, she'd have to hurry. She'd need to make copies of the newspapers on file at the library, speed to the courthouse for maps, buy No Trespassing signs, then go grocery shopping. And she wanted to be safely locked in the cabin tonight when the sun dipped behind the mountain.

EIGHT O'CLOCK. BREANNA looked at the darkening sky. She had a good thirty minutes of light left. She had made record time going to town. Despite a dead end at the courthouse, which had forced a detour to the mini-storage facility where Gran's papers were stored, she had obtained everything she needed, including copies of maps of *The Crescent Moon*, which the court clerk had maintained didn't exist. She was pleased she had time for a walk before dinner and bed. A little exercise would help her sleep.

Her sense of accomplishment faded a bit as she strolled with Coaly through the lower orchard. She had photocopied several reports of the fire, but hadn't yet had time to study them. Later. For now, she and Coaly deserved a romp. Dragging in a breath of air, she broke into a jog. After making three circles around the orchard with Coaly at her heels, Breanna headed upstream toward the house.

The orchard made a lovely picture this time of evening. No wonder Ross took photos here. The old barn, weathered gray with age, sat to the left. As Breanna passed it, a thumping noise echoed through the dusk. She swung around to stare and saw a flash of movement angling from the barn across the road to disappear into the shadowy woods. A man? Gramps's tales of John Van Patten's ghost filtered into her mind. One of his favorites had been that he had seen John inside the barn one evening.

Sheer, black fear surged through her for an instant and her knees turned to water. Then sanity flooded back. Of all the ridiculous—*I don't believe in spooks,* she scolded herself. *And even if I did, this particular one would never hurt me.* Breanna watched the woods. Her unwelcome visitor had vanished. As much as she hated to admit it, she preferred the idea of John Van Patten's company. Ghosts came and went without reason, but flesh and blood specters didn't appear in a remote area like this without motive.

She might find something if she followed the man's trail. Her tension rose a few more percentage points at the thought. Not in the dark. Whoever her uninvited company had been, she wasn't chasing after him. Nope, not this lady. She'd do the smart thing, which was to go home and lock the door. Tomorrow she'd get busy on those fences and tack up the No Trespassing signs.

CHAPTER THREE

THE DOOR TO Tyler Ross's cabin was opened with such force that it hit the interior wall and resounded like a rifle shot. Tyler jumped, slopping hot water from the kitchen kettle onto his hand. He swore under his breath, grabbed a towel off the counter and swiped at the water.

"What in hell's wrong now?"

Jack Jones stomped into the room, trying to shake mud and globs of pine needles off his boots. "What isn't?"

"Do you mind? I don't have a maid to do the floors."

Jack lifted his dark head, brown eyes glaring. "That broad's a pain in the butt. You were nowhere to be found, so I went into the barn to make sure she didn't mess with any of the listening devices when she was in there, and she damned near caught me. Had to make a quick exit through the woods, ran into a tree, fell in a stream. I wish we could arrest her and get her out of the way until this is over."

"Do it. I'll come with you. She'll be safe that way, at least."

"Don't start that again," Jack hissed. "I told you. If we make a move on her, she could blow the whistle. It's not much longer now. We can't screw things up this late in the game."

"And I told *you*...I'm not convinced she's in on it."

"You can't be sure of that."

Tyler walked to a window and gazed at the trees along the road. "Call it a gut feeling."

"I don't trust gut feelings, not with women. Your hormones are doing your thinkin' for you."

It was an accusation Tyler couldn't deny. The Van Patten woman was pretty with those vulnerable eyes of hers. If Jack was right, she could probably smile like an angel and knife you in the gut, never changing expressions. "Okay, I concede the point. She appeals. But, Jack, what if I'm right? What if she isn't involved? She could end up dead if she makes a wrong move. That scares the hell out of me."

"*You* ending up dead is my worry. I'm tellin' you, watch your back. She's tied into this. She has to be. Just do your job, man, and make like her shadow, beginning tomorrow morning. Keep her busy. Keep her entertained. *And keep her out of that barn.* It's no skin off my nose if you take advantage of a few fringe benefits, but don't forget who and what she is, not for a second."

Tyler turned toward his boss. "Fringe benefits? You know that's not my style." Bracing a hand against the wall, he sighed. "If she's clean and something happens to her, maybe you can live with it. I'm not so sure I can."

"Sometimes that's part of the job."

BREANNA QUICKLY DISCOVERED the most difficult thing about hanging No Trespassing signs was the fence repair they necessitated. She had been working since seven, it wasn't yet ten, and she was already worn out from digging and hauling sand from the creek. Planting posts that stood up straight was no easy chore. The morning was half gone, and all she had to show for it were three leaning railroad ties. She had helped Gramps do this a dozen times, but knowing how and doing it alone were two different things.

She had just stepped back to survey her last attempt at a vertical line when she heard a vehicle approaching. A dusty red pickup appeared around the curve and slowed. Putting a hand up to shade her eyes, she tried to see the driver, but the windshield reflected the sun. The truck pulled onto the shoulder and the engine sputtered to silence. The driver's door swung wide and denim flashed as a man climbed out.

Tyler Ross. On the one hand, she felt glad to see him, even a touch excited. She wasn't completely immune to a nice-looking man. But could she trust him? If he was a treasure hunter, his friendliness could be a ploy.

He gave her crooked fence posts a long, rather puzzled look as he passed them. "Havin' some problems?"

With her hands riding at her waist, she regarded him with a weariness she was unable to hide. She knew she must look a mess in her dirt-smudged pink blouse, with her hair falling from its clasp. She lifted one arm, checked it for dust, then swiped at her cheek. "A few, yes."

He dug in his heels to descend the bank. "Need an extra pair of hands?"

At this point Breanna felt so hot and dusty that several extra pairs would have been welcome. There were limits to pride, and she had reached hers. "That's a slight understatement. What I need is a whole crew. Supposedly, my cousin was caretaking here. As you can see, he did his best work sitting on his laurels."

He came to stand beside her. Another look at her posts had him laughing. "Looks like we had high wind."

"It might help if I had a level or a plumb."

"Maybe we can jury-rig something. I don't have anything pressing to do. I'll pitch in if you'll pay off with lunch. Fence building is a two-person job."

Breanna gave him a thoughtful glance. It couldn't hurt to give him the benefit of the doubt, at least for the duration of the job. "You're on."

Coaly came charging from behind the barn, his barking interspersed with snarls. Tyler cast an unconcerned glance over his shoulder as he strode toward his truck. "I'm fresh out of roast beef, you old codger." The dog cocked an ear and slowed to a walk. Tyler paused to give him a pat.

It was a rare stranger that Coaly liked. In her book, the dog's unreserved acceptance of Tyler on the property was an imprint of approval. "It looks like you two are old chums."

"He just likes me because I gave him chocolate chip cookies." Flashing her a quick, completely artless grin, he added, "And my napkin. And my sack. Sure he's not part goat?"

"I've had cause to wonder." She met his gaze. *Windows to the soul,* Gramps had told her. *When you size a man up, honey, look him dead in the eyes.* Approaching the truck, she asked, "Have you ever set posts?"

He pushed back his sleeves and raised a challenging eyebrow. "You're asking a born and bred Oregonian if he's ever set a post? You're lookin' at the best posthole man this side of the Cascades. You don't have any rope, I'll bet." He rummaged in a large toolbox. "Luckily, I always carry some. We'll stretch a length between two posts and rig up some kind of plumb line."

Dubious as she was, within ten minutes he had one rope tied off level and had made a makeshift plumb from another piece, with a rock looped in its end.

"This'll work," he assured her. "Won't be perfect, but it's better than a kick in the rump, right?" He positioned the plumb. "Okay, you hold the post straight, and I'll shovel and pack."

Grasping the upended tie, she held it in position. Tyler moved with loose-limbed grace for so tall a man, precise, quick, well balanced. Muscle rippled in his arms and shoulders, clearly visible under his shirt. She relaxed a bit. He made short work of fence building. Maybe she would have perimeter posts to keep out trespassers, after all.

She felt silly now for thinking he wanted her out of here.

A man didn't go this far to be neighborly if he didn't want you around. "I really appreciate your help."

He glanced up and caught her scowling. "Penny for them? What's bothering you?"

Inclining her head toward the barn, she said, "I had company last night. Some man. Saw him run out of my barn and take off into the woods. That's why these fences are so urgent. I want to put up some No Trespassing signs."

"A man, you say? Did you get a good look at him?"

"No. Have you any idea who it could have been?"

He helped her brace the post while he stomped the encircling ground. "Sure you're not jumping at shadows?"

A tingle of irritation crept up her throat, but she quickly swallowed it back. She couldn't blame him for being skeptical. *The Crescent Moon* wasn't exactly a metropolis; the story sounded a bit farfetched. "I guess it could have been the ghost," she said lightly.

"The ghost? What ghost?"

His wary glance at her made her smile. "My great-great-uncle, John Van Patten. You haven't heard of him? How long've you been living down here?"

"Three years."

"And you've never heard of John Van Patten? He found the mother lode, you know, then died without telling where he hid it—a very selfish man, from all accounts. And now a selfish ghost. Get too close to his treasure and he appears to frighten you away."

"Uh-huh. Next, you'll gladly sell me the Brooklyn Bridge, right?" He chuckled and stepped on the blade of the shovel, burying it to its hilt. "One thing's sure, though. Ghost or man, he's not too smart. If a brisk wind comes up, that barn'll topple like a card house."

"It's not that bad. I went in yesterday and the floors didn't give way."

"Well, I'm telling you, don't trust them. I went in there

once to see if I could find a wrench to adjust my tripod. Those planks gave with every step. Stay out of there. Okay?"

Breanna decided to be gracious. "I'll be careful. But it *is* my barn, you know. There are things in there I'll need now and again."

"Tell me what and I'll get them for you."

"And have my fence builder disabled? Not a chance."

Tyler laughed. Easy, relaxed laughter. It cleansed the last traces of uneasiness from Breanna's mind.

Three fence posts later, Tyler was as dusty and sweaty as Breanna had been upon his arrival. The afternoon sun glared down on them, mercilessly hot, making Breanna's nose feel parchment dry. "How about a lemonade break in the shade?" she suggested. "I'll make some sandwiches."

He wiped a shirt sleeve across his forehead, squinting down at her. "You won't have to twist my arm on that offer."

IT TOOK A VERY CAREFUL balancing of the tray to walk from the cabin to the barnyard without spilling liquid from the pitcher onto their sandwiches. Tyler was sitting in the shade of the fruit cellar, his back braced against the shake siding, arms propped on his upraised knees. "Man, that looks good."

She placed their tray on the ground, cast Coaly a glance to warn him away, then poured Tyler a brimming glass of lemonade and handed it down. "Better be. It's fresh-squeezed."

He tipped back his dark head and took several long swallows. Breanna filled another tumbler and lowered herself cross-legged beside him, proffering the pitcher. "More?"

"Mmm-mmm," he replied, putting his glass to the spout. She gave him a refill, then settled back against the shakes, taking slow sips while he made short work of a sandwich. It had been a while since she had fed a man, two years, in fact, since her breakup with Richard. She had forgotten how big their appetites were. She felt almost guilty reaching for her share on the tray, but was too hungry to resist. "Does that revive you a bit?"

"Delicious. And there's nothing like lemonade to quench the thirst." Tyler looked over at her, trying his best to remain objective. She was a pretty woman; straight nose, a sensitive mouth, her sun-streaked brown hair escaping the twist of braid atop her head in wispy curls. Her eyes were cornflower blue, expressive and easy to read, the kind that gave a guy's heart a twist if he had any conscience at all. His stomach tightened. "Tell me something. Do you really believe in ghosts?"

She shifted her gaze to the barn. After a thoughtful moment, she swallowed and replied, "To say I didn't would be to call my grandfather a liar. He saw John Van Patten with his own eyes. Gramps never fibbed. He exaggerated sometimes, but never fibbed."

Tyler watched her closely. "Aren't you scared?"

"Oh, yes, terrified." Her smile dimpled her cheek, so mischievous that he nearly laughed and ruined her punch line. Her voice, when it came, was low and impish. "I don't have a bridge to sell you. How about a good used car?"

Now he did laugh, the kind of laugh that came from deep inside and erupted without effort. If she was a criminal, it wasn't any wonder she was still on the loose. With her personality as a front, nobody would ever believe— The thought jerked Tyler up short, and he sobered. He was doing exactly the opposite of what Jack had told him, letting down his guard, trusting her. If he wanted the last laugh, he'd better watch his step.

Breanna saw the sudden seriousness cross Tyler's face. She wondered if she had said something to upset him.

Swallowing the last bit of her sandwich, she asked, "Is something wrong?"

"No. Why?"

"You look like somebody stepped on your grave."

"Not as yet." His eyes met hers, searching, then veering away. He glanced at his watch. "Could you hold off on the rest of this until I can help? I do have a couple of errands to run this afternoon."

"I don't expect you to do the entire fence for me," she protested.

"Hey, what are neighbors for? They used to have barn raisings. We're having a fence raising." He gave her a slow wink. "Besides, there are fringe benefits."

His smile told her she was the attraction. "Oh, really? What might those be?"

"The fantastic lemonade and good sandwiches, of course." He rose to his feet in one fluid movement, hauling her up with him. "We'll hit it for another hour, then call it a day. You're getting sunburned."

"I tell you what. I'll accept more help on the fence if you'll come to breakfast tomorrow morning. I'd like to repay you for all the work."

"I'll be here. What time?"

"Sevenish?"

"Sounds great."

Two hours later, Breanna put away the last of the lunch mess and dried the dishes, stowing them in the cupboard. Tyler had just left. She wiped the table, then rinsed the rag and folded it neatly over the antique pump handle. Then she stepped to the window to gaze out at the rose trellises framing the glass. All in all, it had been a good day, exhausting, but nice.

Only one thing troubled her. Off and on she'd noticed a certain reserve in Tyler's manner, subtle, but there, almost as if he held a part of himself in check. Not once had he offered any information about himself, nothing about his family, his marital status or if he had children. She guessed him to be in his mid-thirties. A man that old had to have a past. Yet Tyler gave nothing of his away, not even by a slip of the tongue. It was fanciful, but she had the impression his identity began and ended with Graves Creek. Perhaps she would get to know him better over breakfast tomorrow.

Stifling a yawn, Breanna went to the bedroom to retrieve her newspaper photocopies she'd made at the library. She stretched out on the sofa, determined to stay relaxed. If she planned to investigate the fire, she had to stay objective.

She read until the cabin's interior was swathed in shadows. Read, reread. And found nothing new. But discouraged though she was, she felt better because she was actively seeking answers. If she kept searching, the truth would come out sooner or later. When it did, perhaps Dane would be as relieved as she was to have it in the open.

Digging in her cooler, Breanna pulled out the fresh vegetables she had purchased yesterday. A salad with slices of roast beef from the deli sounded just right after a hot day. After a sponge bath at the sink, she would settle herself in bed with a cup of herb tea and her glitzy novel. She deserved a bit of pampering if the sore muscles in her back were an indicator.

THREE A.M. BREANNA squinted at the luminous hands on her travel alarm clock, unsure why she was suddenly awake. She flopped onto her back and groaned. The dog. He was whining, running from window to window. Throwing her legs over the side of the bed, she staggered to her feet. "All right, already, I'm coming."

Coaly's low snarl brought her up short. She knew that growl. Someone was outside. Clammy sweat filmed her palms as she braced herself against the bedstead to look out the French windows. The fruit cellar blocked her view of the orchards beyond.

"What is it, boy? What do you hear?"

Breanna tiptoed to the kitchen, peering out the paned glass at the moonlit drive. Nothing. She glanced down at the dog. His growl deepened, as if to assure her he knew what he was talking about. There was somebody out there, no question of it.

"I've had all I'm going to take of this nonsense. What the devil's going on around here?" She hurried toward the bedroom. "A man in the bushes, a man in my barn. Well, I think it's time I found out why." Tossing off her nightgown, she bypassed underwear, dragged on her jeans, zipped up, and leaned over to shove her feet into sneakers. "Don't look so worried, I'm just going to look. I won't get caught."

Coaly whined again. Breanna had to agree with him. It was risky going out there, but she couldn't continue living here with her nerves stretched like a tightrope, either.

"Nope, you can't go. You'll bark." Yanking on her green blouse, she quickly buttoned it. "Now, you stay." Leveling a finger at the dog's nose, she said, "Quiet, understand? You raise a fuss and you'll give me away."

Coaly's whines trailed off into miserable squeaks. She gave him a consoling pat. "Hey, old man, trust me to take care of myself, huh? If all else fails, I can outrun him."

As quietly as she could, she slipped out the front door, straining her ears for noises. A faint clanking sound rang in the night. *Someone on the other side of the fruit cellar.* She sneaked to the retainer wall steps. Fearful images crept into her mind, but she quickly banished them. This was her property, and if she didn't come out and check on it, no one else would.

If she darted across the drive she could make it to the outhouse, where she would have an unobstructed view of the barnyard. Not giving herself time to chicken out, she bounded down the steps, stooping low as she crossed the opening.

"Whoa, did you see that?" she heard someone bark.

"What?" a fainter voice asked.

"I thought I saw something."

Breanna did a third-base skid behind the outhouse, her heart pounding. She hadn't expected someone to be so close. Especially not two someones. Thirty miles out in the middle of nowhere, she had envisioned at most a lone prowler. *Ouch.* A sharp rock gouged her ribs. She crawled to her knees, grasping the rough wall of the outhouse to help herself up. Inching her head around the corner, she searched the moon-silvered darkness. A hollow thumping sound drifted to her, like footsteps on a wooden floor. A shadow moved from the front of the barn, cutting through the field toward the road. A man. All she could distinguish about him at this distance was that he wore dark trousers and a white shirt.

Another man appeared on the road, a mere shadow in his dark clothing. He stood waiting until the other man reached him, then gestured toward the outhouse. The fellow in the white shirt stepped across the road, pivoting to see her cabin. There was something familiar about his walk, the way he kept his legs stiff and held his arms curved out from his body. She had seen him before. But when? Where? Breanna flattened herself against the planks, suddenly afraid.

The sound of their low voices drifted faintly through the night toward her and from their tone, she felt they were arguing. She glanced uneasily at the house. Coming out here had been a dumb move. A lone prowler was one thing; two were quite another. If they spotted her, she could end up in big trouble.

Remembering Tyler Ross's warnings, Breanna dashed behind the garage and ran its length, carefully skirting the ash pile. At the far corner of the lean-to she paused to get her bearings. If she worked her way through the brush to the upper clearing, she could cut across and double back to the house with the building blocking her from the men's view. Tensing for a burst of speed, she pushed off and plunged into a thick growth of waist-high manzanita. Every snapping twig resounded like a rifle shot. She knew they couldn't fail to hear her. The branches scratched her arms, but she was so frightened that she barely noticed.

The bushes hindered her. Her spurts of speed were taken in lunges as her hips and legs pushed through the maze. Throwing a glance behind her, Breanna sent up a silent prayer she wouldn't see anyone following. She burst into a tiny clearing, and the sudden lack of obstacles increased her forward thrust. She saw something on the ground in front of her, but it was too late to stop. Before she could register the fact that it was a man, she stepped right on top of him.

"Son of a—!"

A whoosh of expelled air cut off the rest of his exclamation. Her shoe sank into his flesh with a sickening squish. And then, to her horror, the man pushed up, catapulting her into a helter-skelter somersault.

"I don't believe you, Jackson!" he grunted.

She tried for a tumbling tuck, but gymnastics had never been her forte. Landing in an ungraceful back flop, she hit a clump of manzanita, plunging through it to the ground.

She didn't know if it was the impact or the sheer incredulity she felt that dazed her, but she couldn't move. The network of branches above her formed a crisscross pattern, so the man's silhouette as he peered down looked like an apparition out of a horror movie. There were small protrusions over his ears and a piece of wire looped around the side of his face to his mouth. *Headphones.* Her every nerve leaped and shuddered.

"I swear to God, Jackson," he whispered, "you'd screw up a sexy dream if we gave you half a chance. Can't you do anything right? Why the hell are you running? Do you want the broad coming out here?"

Jackson? The man leaned farther forward to offer her a hand.

"Get on a loudspeaker, why don't ya? Tell everyone we're out here. You damn near broke my back."

The urge to scream was so strong that Breanna held her breath. She stared at the extended hand. Just another few inches and he would touch her chest. And when he did, it wouldn't take him long to realize she wasn't his friend Jackson. With a trembling arm, she reached up and grasped his palm. Prepared for his startled reaction, she took full advantage of it. With all her strength, she gripped his fingers and pulled. He pitched forward and, as he did, Breanna slammed her right foot against his chest. With a mighty heave, she launched him over her into the manzanita. He landed with a grunt, then yelped with pain.

Springing to her feet, she vaulted the bushes. Her legs felt numb. She staggered into a run, her head resounding with the crashing noises behind her. *Dear God, he's chasing me.* She'd made it halfway across the orchard before she realized the sounds were growing more distant, heading in the opposite direction toward the creek. Whirling and looking behind her, she saw the distinct shapes of three men diving for cover at different angles. Her eyes fastened on one in particular, a tall, broad-shouldered one.

Tyler? Breanna stared in disbelief. No, it couldn't be. An unnatural quiet filled the night. Breanna hugged herself and turned in a full circle. *They're all around me.* She had known fear in the woods before, but never such an icy, eerie dread. In the distance, a coyote wailed, long and low, the last notes of his moon call rising to a mournful crescendo. Panting in terror, she threw one more glance at the brush and turned to flee.

The cabin wasn't that far, but it seemed to take forever to reach it. She clawed her way over the retainer wall, pulling herself flat on the ground for a few feet until the black shadows from the oak tree shielded her. Even then she didn't feel safe. There could be more of them in the yard. She stumbled forward, flattening herself against the cabin to guard her back. *Please, God.* Crab-walking, she inched sideways toward the corner.

Then someone grabbed her hair.

For a wild, frenzied moment, Breanna fought, flinging her head, flailing her arms. Then she realized her attacker was a rose-entwined trellis. Thorny vines snaked around her. Her hair was caught in the trellis slats, tangled in the thorns. She threw herself away from it. Her skin tore. Her scalp exploded with pain. But all she could focus on now was getting inside.

With a sob that cut through the silence around her, she pelted forward, careening around the corner, shooting for the porch. The door jammed, and she shoved on it with all her weight till it gave way and spewed her into the entry hall. Breanna slammed it shut behind her, pressing against it with her back, quivering legs braced before her. Whimpers erupted from her that she couldn't control. Reaching behind her, she grasped the dead bolt and shoved it home.

Coaly leaped at her, whining, licking. She collapsed to her knees, wrapping both arms around him and making fists in his thick wavy fur. He was solid, warm. She clung to him and sobbed. Then hysterical laughter bubbled in her chest. She clamped a hand over her mouth. She had to get ahold of herself. *Think. Panic won't do a bit of good.*

Taking long, deep breaths, she willed herself to calm down. When strength returned to her legs, she rose and ran to the living room. Her skin crawled at the thought of someone staring at her through the uncurtained windows, but she forced herself close enough to double-check the latches. If someone tried to come in, at least he would make a racket breaking the glass. At the table she sank into a chair, staring first at one window, then the next, glad the embers of the fire didn't put off much light.

What will I do if they break in? How many of them are there? Do they know I'm here alone?

Tyler Ross had told her to come to him if there was trouble. Should she make a run for her car? Or would she be safer right where she was? A vision of the tall man running through the bushes sprang to mind. She didn't want to believe it had been Tyler, but what if it had?

No, if she was going to get help, the wisest course would be a police station. The nearest one, as far as she knew, was thirty miles away in Grants Pass. Breanna looked out at her car. Without a phone, it was her only link to the outside world. In the moonlight, its silver paint glowed like phosphorus. If she went anywhere near it, she'd be spotted. They might try to stop her, and that was a chance she couldn't bring herself to take.

The haze of panic slowly cleared from her mind. There were five men on her property, possibly more. The question was, why? She walked over to a front window. The guy in the manzanita had been hiding to watch something. It hadn't been her, obviously, or he wouldn't have stayed where he was so she could step on him. She had a clear view from here of the upper and lower orchards. From where the man had been lying, it was a straight shot to the barn and the road.

Prowlers didn't spy on prowlers. The police would think she was crazy if she went to them with a story like this. Nothing was out there but a ramshackle barn, an old fruit cellar and an outhouse. Why would anyone be out there? That would be their first question. And it was one she couldn't answer. She could almost see the skeptical look on their faces if she started talking about ghosts and hidden gold. And what if it were someone who blamed her for the fire, as Dane had said...? She certainly didn't want to talk to the police about that.

Returning to the table, Breanna sat down again and propped her elbows on its edge, cupping her chin in her hands. Before she went to the authorities and made a complete fool of herself, she had to have something concrete to tell them.

She had no idea how long she sat there, so tense that her muscles ached. Her body felt as if it were on fire and at the least movement, pain shot up her back into her shoulder. She twisted, trying to feel what she had done to herself. Her fingertips came away sticky with blood.

She folded her arms on the table to pillow her head, still staring watchfully at the windows. With her nerves stretched so taut, she knew she wouldn't sleep. A minute in dead of night lasted an hour, an hour a lifetime.

Morning might never come.

CHAPTER FOUR

BREANNA WOKE TO the sound of knocking. Blinking in confusion, she pushed herself up from the table, recoiled at the pain in her back and stared at the window. Sunshine. What a welcome sight. Coaly raced to and fro, barking at the door.

"Who is it?"

"The Fuller Brush man," was the good-natured reply.

Tyler. Breanna got up from the chair, weaving on her feet, and dragged her tangled hair from her eyes. She didn't know what to do. Images from yesterday slipped into her mind, but those were quickly pushed out by flashbacks from last night.

"Yo? You in there?"

"Yes, I'm coming."

Quick glances out the windows showed nothing had been disturbed in the yard. She went to the entry and drew the dead bolt. Tyler stood on the porch, casually dressed in jeans and a chambray shirt, his dark hair tousled by the breeze. Coaly squeezed past her, greeting him with an enthusiasm Breanna was far from sharing.

"Oh, it's you."

"Breakfast, remember? I do have the right morning?"

"Yeah, I guess you do."

"My God, what happened to you?" He took a step toward her. "You're hurt."

Breanna didn't think she could possibly look that bad until she glanced down at herself. Her arms were scratched.

Her jeans were torn. There were drops of blood on her left tennis shoe. From the horrified expression on Tyler's face, she knew the rest of her looked even worse. "I'm all right... I think. Just took a spill."

"Do you have a first-aid kit?"

"Yes."

He grasped her elbow, taking care not to touch lacerated skin as he steered her down the hall. "Let's get it. Some of those cuts should be cleaned before they get infected. I thought we agreed you would come to my place if anything went wrong?"

She lifted her other arm to survey the damage. "I can handle it. It's just a few scratches."

"A few scratches? You haven't seen the back of you yet. Were you afraid of bothering me? When a person's hurt, they should be able to count on neighbors. Look at you. You've let this go so long, your blouse is stuck to you."

Somehow she had ended up on the defensive. She lowered a shoulder, trying to see. "It can't be that bad. I just took a tumble in the brush."

"Manzanita is a tad sturdier and sharper than regular brush. You're sliced up like a salad tomato."

She braked to such a sudden stop that Tyler nearly ran over her. His chest bumped into a sore place on her back, making her stiffen. With her heart slamming so hard she felt sure he could hear it, she glanced back at him. "How did you know it was manzanita?"

Tension crystallized the air between them. Her breath caught in her throat as she waited for his answer. If he knew where she had fallen, then he was also the man she had seen running in the brush. There could be no other explanation.

"It doesn't take a genius to figure it was probably manzanita. Nothing else would cut you up like that."

Dogwood and rosebushes could cut a person, too. Maybe not so deeply, but they could still penetrate the skin. She swallowed, the sound a hollow plunk in the pit of her stomach. "Tyler, I think maybe you should leave and come back another time when I'm feeling better. I can handle this myself."

After a long moment, he replied, "If you're not feeling up to guests, that's okay. But at least let me clean those cuts before I go." Settling his hands on her hips, he propelled her to the kitchen table and drew out a chair, turning it so that she could sit astride with her arms propped on its back. His voice was firm. "Where's the first aid?"

There didn't seem to be any way to get rid of him. "In the bedroom, on the closet shelf."

His boots tapped briskly across the room. She heard him rummaging. A moment later, he returned, carrying a white case.

"Tyler, I saw you last night."

Looking down at her scratched face, with those big blue eyes shimmering, Tyler knew he was in for a hard haul. He was never at his best with no sleep, and he had spent all last night pacing, waiting, dreaming up reasons to come check on her, each of which Jack had vetoed as too flimsy. Unless he lied flat out, he'd have to be damned evasive, and right now he didn't feel too witty. She was a bright lady, at this point a suspicious one, and he knew she would pick up on his least slip of the tongue.

He shot her a glance, his mouth curving up at one corner in what he hoped was a perplexed grin. Snapping the kit open, he said, "And so?"

"You mean you aren't going to deny it?"

"Why would I? I was here planting posts. You sure you didn't bump your head?" She made as if to stand and he shot out a hand to touch her shoulder. "First things first. Let's tend that back."

"I'm crazy to let you do this, but I hurt too bad to argue."

"Take a chance on me," he advised. "I'm a good risk."

She glanced over her shoulder to find him contemplating her blouse, a pair of scissors in one hand. "Do you know anyone named Jackson?"

"Should I?" He paused and a slow grin spread across his face. "It does ring a bell. Michael?"

"Somehow, I don't think that's the same Jackson, unless he took a break from making hit records to come out here and liven up my evening." She threw him another questioning look that he deflected by bending over her. "I hope I don't regret this." Dipping her head, she pulled her long hair forward. "I would have sworn it was you I saw diving into those bushes last night."

"And why would I dive into bushes?" He set the plastic kit on the table. *One round from her. Now fire back.* "Do you want to pull your blouse down, or should I cut a bigger hole?" He grasped her collar as if to peel the cotton off her. She reacted just as he hoped, clinging to the blouse, losing her train of thought. He felt her pulse skitter under his knuckles where they touched the side of her throat.

"A bigger hole, of course. In case you haven't noticed, the blouse is ruined anyway."

"Don't wiggle. These aren't exactly what you'd call man-size scissors and I may be clumsy with them. It looks like you did the diving."

Breanna felt the warmth of his large hands where they touched her arm and back, gentle, so careful. In spite of herself, she relaxed a bit. "Coaly woke me up out of a dead sleep last night. When I went out to investigate, the place was crawling with men. I tripped over one and fell. That's all."

"You're lucky that was all."

Releasing her hair, she twisted her neck to see his face. "Tyler...was it you? Tell me the truth."

He leaned forward to put the scissors on the tabletop, the hard flatness of his midriff brushing her arm. "This is a deep cut, lady. It's going to hurt like hell when I pull this material loose. I'm really upset that you didn't come directly to my place when this happened. I think I'll try soaking it with peroxide."

"You haven't answered me. Was it you?" His reply was to uncap the bottle and pour ice-cold peroxide down her spine. She gasped and bolted upright. "Oh!"

"Hurt?"

"No, no, I'm fine. It's just cold. Are you or are you not going to give me a direct answer?"

"No." He bent over her, prying the material away. "There's that," he muttered, soaking a cotton ball. He bent to look through the hole he had cut in her blouse. "You look like a road map."

"No, it wasn't you? Or no, you won't give me an answer?"

"I've just discovered why doctors put people to sleep on the operating table. I'm trying to concentrate back here. Why would I be running around on your property in the dead of night? Give me one sane reason."

"I can give you a couple. Gold, for starters. Are you a treasure hunter? Is that it?" Before Breanna realized what he was up to, he grabbed the scissors and she felt the blades snipping again, this time right up the center back of her blouse. "What are you doing?"

"What do you think I'm doing? Alterations?" He made a final snip through her collar and the cotton garment fell forward. "No, I'm not a treasure hunter."

"Tyler, if I'd wanted to take off the blouse, I would have in the first place."

"Can we argue about one thing at a time? You're leap-frogging so badly, I can't keep track."

Breanna, struggling to keep her blouse in place, threw him an incredulous glare. It seemed to her that he was the one scrambling their communication. And he was doing a good job of it. "Are you going to answer my question?"

"Which one?" Just before he shoved her head forward, she saw his eyes dancing with mischief. "You see, right now, only one thing seems important to me. Your back. So be still while I take care of it."

"It *was* you. Otherwise you'd just say it wasn't." Even as the accusation trailed off her lips, she doubted the truth of it.

He dabbed at a particularly painful scratch, making her wince. "Breanna, use your head. If I was sneaking around your place last night, I wouldn't bat an eye at lying. I guess the reason I'm not denying it is because I'd like you come to your own conclusion. Do you really think it was me?"

She looked up, into his eyes. What he said was true. If it had been him, he wouldn't hesitate to lie about it. "No, I guess I don't, not really, or I wouldn't be sitting here with my back to you when you're armed with a pair of scissors."

He chuckled at that, then began cleaning scratches again. "Imagination, I guess. Scissors in the back? You're right about one thing, though. It was probably treasure hunters. I've never heard of the ghost, but I've sure heard about the Van Patten gold. It's almost legend." He doused her with another measure of peroxide. "Or it might have been poachers. Did you think of that? There are a lot of deer down here."

"I didn't hear any gunshots. And the man I tripped over had a radio unit of some kind. Sophisticated for poachers, don't you think?"

"Not in this day and age. Anyone with a pickup in this country usually has a CB and hand units. As for shots, they could have used bows."

"Poachers," she mused. "I don't know, Tyler. I suppose it could have been. They had lookouts. Maybe they were watching the road for cars. But why were they in my barn?"

"They were in your barn?" He grew quiet for a moment. "Maybe they were looking for rope or some rags to wipe their hands. It's messy, skinning a deer."

"That could be."

He capped the peroxide, returning it to the kit. "It was foolish of you to go outside. You could have been seriously hurt. What would you have done if they chased you?"

"I could have lost them in the woods."

"In the dark? Someone would have gotten lost, all right, more likely you. This is no place for you to be living alone. There's too much that can happen that you can't handle on your own."

She jabbed a thumb over her shoulder. "See that type-writer over there? I make my living on it, writing books about wildlife. I've spent a lot of time in the woods get-ting material for my books. I don't get lost in the woods, Tyler, at night or any other time."

"You're angry."

"Yes! If you had prowlers, you'd go out and check. No one would think that strange. But let a woman do the same thing and she's taking unnecessary risks. I don't under-stand the thinking behind that." She stood up, clutching her destroyed blouse to her chest. "It's a double standard. As for leaving here, I can't. It's out of the question. It's Van Patten land, and it's going to stay Van Patten land."

He smiled slightly. "Listen. Your back should be okay now. Why don't I come back later? We'll deal with the rest of this then."

"That's just it. I don't need your help to deal with it."

He lifted a staying hand. "Get some rest. You'll feel bet-ter when you've had some sleep. After last night, those No Trespassing signs are more important than ever. You can't expect to finish those posts alone. Not the shape you're in. And if you're bent on staying here, fences are a must." He opened the door, pausing to look back at her. "Catch you later, say noonish?"

With that, he was gone. She stood there for a moment, annoyed, confused, frustrated. Then she sighed and bolted the door behind him. A man didn't terrify you at night, then take care of you come morning. He didn't prowl on your property one moment, then post No Trespassing signs for you the next. Maybe he was right. She needed some sleep. Her body felt like a battlefield. Her head ached. Sand gritted under her eyelids. Heading for the bedroom, she sprawled across the bed, tugging the corner of the spread over herself. *Just a short nap,* she promised herself. Then she was going to check that barn to see what the big attraction was.

SMOKE SPIRALED FROM Jack Jones's cigarette. He watched it thoughtfully. "And on that basis, you expect me to risk blowing this case?"

Tyler slammed his fist on the table, jarring the radio equipment. "Dammit, Jack, why won't you trust my judgment? I remember a time when you risked your life on it."

"You've been out of the business too long. You're rusty." Leaning forward, Jack smashed out his cigarette in the ashtray. "You didn't get personally involved back then. And you knew a snow job when you saw one."

"It isn't a snow job." Tyler stood up so suddenly that his straight-backed chair tipped. He reached out to catch it, then shoved it none too gently against the table. "Her willingness to tell me what happened supports my theory. I tell you, she's completely in the dark."

"Tyler…" Throwing his head back, Jack let out a tired sigh. "Look, give it a couple of days. If you can get something solid, some real proof, I'll get her out of there so fast it'll make your head swim. I don't want the girl hurt, you know that. But my first responsibility is to this case.

I can't jeopardize all our work on supposition. Do you realize how many false leads we followed before we finally pegged this location?"

"Can you risk an innocent person's life on poor judgment?" Tyler placed both hands on his hips. "All right, if you want proof, I'll get it."

"And you'll clear it through me before you make a move." Jack's tone made it clear it was an order, leaving no room for argument. "These people are sharp. That's how they've stayed in operation so long. It's not beyond the realm of possibility that Breanna Morgan is the slickest little con artist in the business. And just you keep that in mind."

AT ELEVEN, BREANNA locked Coaly inside the cabin while she went to check the barn. The dog whined when she shut the door on him, but because she had seen him digging holes under the foundation, she wasn't about to take him with her. With her luck he would scare up a skunk.

She had the strangest feeling when she walked up the ramp into the old building. At first it seemed the same inside, dark and gray-walled with age, but when she studied it closely, there seemed to be something different, something not quite right. As she paced down the corridor that stretched by the feed room and stalls, an inexplicable chill ran over her.

When she reached the end of the passage, the tack room seemed tiny. She remembered it as being a much larger room, almost airy. Now it seemed cramped, with barely enough floor space for a few bags of grain. She knew everyone remembered their childhood haunts as being larger then they really were, but she hadn't been that young when she left. The impression that the barn had shrunk made her feel claustrophobic. The slightest sound made her jump, and she found herself checking behind as she paused to peer into doorways.

The floorboards creaked under her weight. Tyler was right; it wasn't safe in here. Old fruit jars. A box of discarded clothing. A pile of rusted tin cans. Breanna kicked one and sighed. It was just an old barn, smaller than she remembered. She had gone through some nasty experiences in this place. Maybe that was what made her skin crawl. She strolled slowly through. Even the corridor seemed narrower. She remembered Gran's milk cows moseying through here with plenty of room to spare.

The loft. It would be a perfect hiding place. She went to the ladder and gripped its sides. The rungs groaned in protest as she ascended them. Either they were much weaker than they had been ten years ago, or she was heavier. She reached the top and peeked over. Just hay. And not much of that. No sign that anyone had been in it either, not recently. She had played in here enough times as a child to know how hay looked if someone walked in it. She sighed and climbed back down. So much for being a sleuth.

Something on the floor by the door caught her eye. She moved toward it, bending over to see in the dim light. Her eyes widened as she realized it was a crisp twenty-dollar bill. Brand-new. She folded it and slipped it into her jeans pocket. If her prowler had dropped it, it served him right. He owed her that much and more for the trouble he had caused.

As she straightened, her sore back panged her. Why couldn't he have dropped a hundred? That might have made up for her fall in the manzanita. She stepped into the adjacent stall, surveying the shelving, a pleased smile on her face. It was nice, the way money kept dropping into her hands around here. Of course, she mustn't forget to return Dane's.

The gold pans. Another pang, this time one of sadness,

ricocheted through her, but she quickly squelched it. She would miss Gran, but memories of her were enough to last a lifetime.

"Well, I guess this was a shot in the dark," she mused aloud.

No sooner had she spoken than Breanna heard footfalls right next to her. Or at least that was where they seemed to be located. She froze and cocked her head. In the wall? The hair on the nape of her neck stood up. Under the floor? It could be Coaly snooping outside. No, he was in the house. Some other animal, then?

"Who's there?" she croaked.

The moment she called out the sounds ceased. Then Tyler's voice rang out from the front of the barn. "Breanna?"

She hadn't realized she'd been holding her breath. It gushed out of her. "In the back." She stepped into the corridor, then flinched, batting at a curtain of cobwebs that stretched across the left corner of the doorway. It swept across her face and into her hair, clinging like sticky cotton candy. The musty smell was suffocating and she shuddered. "Oh, yuck. It's all over me." Wiping her mouth with her arm, she added, "You're early."

Tyler sauntered down the corridor, a silhouette against the bright sunlight behind him. He paused to glance around. "Must be I'm telepathic. I thought I told you the floor was rotten in here. You shouldn't take chances, you know. This thing is really old."

"The floor isn't too bad. It's the cobwebs that are the pits." She sputtered, trying to get the taste out of her mouth. "And the acoustics. I thought I heard somebody in here."

"Oh, yeah? Pretty popular place, this old barn." He stepped past her to give the stalls and tack room quick once-overs. "Not many places in here to hide."

It was so good to see him after her footstep scare that she couldn't quite remember why she had been so annoyed with him earlier. It reassured her to realize that the footsteps she'd heard couldn't possibly have been his. He had called out from the front only seconds after she heard the noises in the back.

"Probably a rat in the wall," Tyler commented dryly. "You ever seen a barn rat? They can sound like three-hundred pounders with fangs a foot long."

"It did sound like someone walking." Remembering her own suspicion that it could be a rodent, she added, "But I suppose a small animal could sound pretty loud. It sort of echoes in here. And I've heard John Van Patten can be a noisy fellow."

"I'm beginning to see you've got a writer's imagination," he teased. "Apparitions in the barn, spooks in the bushes, and—" he curled his hands into claws and moaned, low and spooky "—ghosts who guard their treasures."

He looked so silly that Breanna couldn't quite manage anger, though his making fun did rankle. Joking with him about the ghost didn't make her prowlers any less real. "Look, Mr. Ross. Can you explain this?" She dug into her jeans pocket, fishing out the newly found twenty to wave it under his nose. "Do you think a ghost dropped it? Or maybe a rat? Or maybe I'm imagining it." She gave the bill a sharp tug. "The real thing, see? Dropped by a flesh and blood prowler."

His gaze was riveted on the greenback, and he started to reach for it.

Breanna jerked it away. "Nope. Finders keepers, losers weepers. My barn, my twenty."

With that, she strode past him down the corridor to the door. Tyler stood watching her, his mind clamoring. She wasn't involved in counterfeiting, or she would never have flashed that money at him. He had to get his hands on it, have it analyzed, and get it to Jack Jones. The question was, how?

She walked down the ramp, turning to look back at him, her hair shimmering golden in the sunlight as she cocked her head. "Come on, or are you gonna stand there till you fall through my rotten floors?"

He moved to the door, leaning a shoulder against the frame. Her eyes shone up at him like beacons, clear as stained glass. For the first time since meeting her, he could allow the feelings she stirred within him to surface. Jack was dead wrong. Tyler's gaze dropped to her lacerated forearms. Thinking of what could have happened last night made his knees weak. Then anger at Jack hit him, hot and liquid, pulsing through him until he felt his neck flushing. Rusty, was he?

"Hey," she said softly, "I'm only giving you a hard time to get even."

Too late, he realized his face had mirrored his thoughts. He made himself grin, which didn't prove too hard. Looking at Breanna Morgan was great incentive, mainly because of her infectious smile. "I guess it upsets me when you make light of something so dangerous. If you fell through in here, no telling how far you might drop. This is a tall foundation."

"I concede the point. The old mine tunnels run under some of these buildings. Who knows? There might even be one under here."

His nerves leaped. She had a clear, musical voice that carried too well. "So you'll follow my advice and stay out of here?"

"Yessir. The floors *are* a tad creaky. I felt uneasy walking in there a couple of times. Satisfied?" Breanna watched his dark face, waiting for him to lighten up. Then a thought hit her. "Tyler! You know what? When I heard that noise, it sounded like it was coming from under the floor. Do you realize what that…?" Excitement tightened her throat, and she had to pause. "The mine could run under there. And if it does, it could explain— Tyler, what if somebody is down in *The Crescent Moon*?"

Tension shot through Tyler like a bolt of high voltage. "Like who? The ghost?" He strode swiftly down the ramp. She was talking so loudly that she was a regular broadcasting system. He put a finger to his lips to shut her up, did some quick thinking and whispered, "If someone's down there, let's not warn them we know."

Her eyes widened with delight. "Then you agree it's possible?" she whispered back.

Feeling as if he were in one of those bad dreams where everything happens in slow motion, Tyler steered her toward the house. It was like herding a flock of ducks. "Sure it's possible."

She braked. He walked into her. He felt like screaming. "Watch it, I'm sore," she complained. "What's your hurry? It *is* my mine. If somebody's in there, I don't care if they're scared out. Do you realize how dangerous it could be? Why, if there was a cave-in, I could be sued." She reared back to look at him. "I've got to find the entrance to that mine, Tyler. If it's accessible, I need to blast it closed, board it up and post warnings." She broke off, a strange look clouding her eyes. "Of course, it could be just an animal."

"More likely," he agreed. "Possibly a bear using it. But it's more fun the other way."

"It's been closed because of cave-ins since before I was born. If someone's found it, we're talking dangerous, really dangerous. Come on. I'd rather be safe than sorry. Let's go look at my maps."

"Maps?" Tyler wanted to kick himself for being so transparent, but his interest zoomed in on the word like a telephoto lens. Jack wanted maps. Jack didn't have maps. Why Jack didn't, raised a question Tyler couldn't resist asking. "Where did you get them?"

"Well, there weren't any on file that the clerk could

find. So when the courthouse was a dead end, I went to the storage building where we have Gran's things and went through her papers. I don't know how accurate they are. I think Gramps drew them. But they show the tunnels in close proximity to where they probably are."

"I wonder why it isn't filed. You'd think any underground mine would be on record, for safety if nothing else."

"That's what the clerk said. But the file on *The Crescent Moon* was an exception. All the other documents were there, but no maps."

"Sounds unorganized." Tyler slowed to let her precede him up the steps. *Suspicious, that's how it sounds, but I can't say so.* He had to see those maps and get them to Jack if he possibly could. To do that, he needed a darned good reason for seeming so interested. "Breanna, on second thought— Don't laugh...."

She glanced back at him. "About what?"

"Well, it just occurred to me that we could possibly find the treasure." He paused to let that sink in, then added, "If your uninvited treasure hunters don't get to it first."

"If there *is* a treasure."

"Your grandfather said there was, didn't he? And he never fibbed, remember?"

"Well, he *believed* there was. Me, I've never thought the story held water. I watched Dane going crazy after it too many years, finding nothing."

"But the underground chambers have been closed since before you were born. *Think*, Bree. No one could have found it if it was in the shaft. I want to see those maps. That gold should be yours, not some treasure hunter's. If the maps aren't to scale, I've got a friend who's a licensed surveyor. He might be able to revise them."

Leading the way into the house, Tyler stood back, watching as Breanna tucked the twenty from the barn into the side pocket of her purse. He almost whooped with relief when she headed for the bedroom.

"I'll be right back. I've got the maps in the closet."

Tyler waited for the curtain to drop behind her, then stepped softly to the counter. *Quickly, quickly.* His fingers were just reaching…almost there…and he heard her coming back. He began whistling and leaned his hips against the sink hoping he looked more casual than he felt.

"Here we go," she said. "Come look. They're really fascinating."

The maps. Riveting his gaze on them, he cautioned himself not to appear overanxious. *Talk about a lucky break! Those maps are it,* he thought. They could be certain there were no undiscovered entrances to *The Crescent Moon* if they could get copies and study them.

Casting one last glance at the purse, Tyler made a silent vow. No matter what, later he had to get one full minute alone with that handbag.

DANE TRIED TO STILL his hands, but they trembled as he strapped a bundle of money and set it on the pile. Too much pressure, not enough sleep. He narrowed his eyes and gazed at Chuck Morrow, who stood beside him. He was so nervous that he felt sick.

"I thought I made myself clear," Chuck said in that soft, menacing way he had. "You were told to get rid of her. You haven't."

"I—I just need a couple more days. Give me some time. I've got a plan I'm working on. Believe me, she'll leave after tonight, I promise."

Chuck shook his head. "She almost caught us last night. I saw her out behind the shack, spying on us. She's a bright girl, Dane, too bright. At this point she doesn't suspect. And I want to keep it that way. But we can't curtail work forever."

"She won't find out, I swear it. Come on, Chuck, who would ever dream an operation this scale is down here? According to records, the place doesn't even exist. Marcy took care of that when she lifted the maps."

"Cute kid, Marcy." Chuck bundled a stack of twenties, gave them a pat, then turned, lifting an eyebrow. "Too bad her brakes went out and she went over that grade. Damned shame, wasn't it? On the other hand, it does solve one problem. She can't spill her guts. Now, Breanna, she's another story. She finds out about this, and she'll squeal like a stuck hog. I can't let that happen. You get rid of her, Dane. Understood? Or I'll do it myself."

"How? Like you got rid of Marcy?"

"You have no proof of that. It was an accident."

Dane gripped the edge of the workbench. "Breanna's my problem, Chuck. I'll handle her."

"Then do it!"

CHAPTER FIVE

THAT SAME EVENING, shortly after Tyler left, Breanna refolded the maps of *The Crescent Moon* and stretched out on the bed for another nap, promising herself she would clean up their dinner mess later. A smile settled on her lips as she nuzzled her head into her pillow. Sore and exhausted as she was, she had thoroughly enjoyed Tyler's company as they studied Gramps's drawings of the shafts. Tyler had a rare appreciation for the ridiculous that had kept her entertained. Expecting him back in the morning to work on the fence posts gave her something nice to anticipate. Hanging one arm over the side of the bed, she stroked Coaly's silken head as she drifted off to sleep.

It seemed to Breanna that she had just closed her eyes when someone called her name. She stirred, stared at the ceiling and listened. Had she been dreaming? No, there it was again, a low, keening wail. "Bree-ee-a-a-n-n-a… whoo-oo-oo…Bree-ee-anna…"

The eerie call brought her bolt upright in bed. She glanced at her alarm. Midnight? She swung her legs over the edge of the mattress and stood.

"Coaly?" She tiptoed to the bedroom curtain. "Coaly, where are you?"

A low growl drifted to her from the living room. She paused, then pushed through the curtain. The interior of the cabin was dark. The fire had burned low. She inched across the floor.

"Bree-ee-a-a-nna…"

Freezing, she stared in disbelief. Outside the French door stood the shadowy figure of a man. His arms rose, so slowly that they almost appeared to float. Then his head burst into light, blinding her. She blinked and threw up an arm to shield her eyes. Coaly lunged at the window, snarling, clawing the wood. Breanna squinted into the brightness.

She couldn't be seeing what she thought she was seeing. *John Van Patten, The Crescent Moon ghost.* The burst of light on his head was a miner's light. He wore old-fashioned slicker pants, heavy boots, a red flannel shirt. There was no question. It was either John Van Patten or someone who had gone to great lengths to look like him.

"Get ou-ou-t," he moaned. "Get ou-ou-out. Or die… Get ou-ou-out."

Fear of the unknown writhed inside her. She didn't believe in ghosts, but it was difficult to remember that when one stood before her. The miner's light suddenly went out. The shadowy shape drifted sideways, beyond view from the window. She saw another burst of brightness shortly afterward, then heard the ghost calling to her again, first by her bedroom—light flashed by the windows—then near the front door. "Bree-ee-aa-aa-nna."

A scream clawed at her throat. Her entire body dripped perspiration. She turned, her movements jerky as a puppet's, staring at the door, knowing even as she did that a spirit could come right through it, locked or not. Coaly ran down the entry, sniffing, snarling. The fact that he didn't bark alarmed Breanna all the more. Even the dog sensed something abnormal.

Before she thought it through, Breanna acted, racing for the dead bolt. Since a closed door was useless, the least she could do was get a good look. There was no point in running away or hiding, so she threw the door open, stepped out, pulled it shut, launched herself over the porch and landed, not on the ground, as she'd intended, but on an escaping Coaly, who seemed as eager to nab the spook as she was. The next few seconds were a riot of confusion. Breanna heard Coaly yelp, felt herself falling, and then hit the side of the fruit cellar. Someone screamed. For a moment, she thought it was herself, but the four-letter words that followed soon convinced her otherwise.

Stunned, Breanna sat crumpled on the ground for a moment, fighting to get her breath, which had been very effectively knocked out of her in her collision with the cellar. She heard her "ghost" curse again. Then Coaly launched what was, by the sound of it, a vicious attack. Breanna pushed herself up on her knees and staggered to her feet. "John Van Patten" streaked past, literally a flash of light because his headlamp was still on, Coaly snapping at his heels.

"Coaly!"

If John Van Patten was man and not ghost, Breanna didn't want her dog hurt. After last night, she knew there could be a group of intruders, and Coaly could find himself surrounded. She bounded after him. Coaly, because of his color, was hard to see, but "John Van Patten" was an easy spook to follow. He not only glowed like a beacon, but he was yelling, fighting off Coaly. Breanna broke into a run. To her relief, she saw the miner's light zoom up the barn ramp, beam bobbing. Then the "ghost" paused, turning back to emit one last "Whoo-ooo-oo" at her before he disappeared into the barn and slammed the door shut. Coaly, unable to pursue, barked and snarled, hurling himself at the offending barrier.

By the time Breanna arrived at the barn to collect her dog, Coaly was off the ramp and circling the building, piercing the night with a volley of barking. With the "ghost" trapped inside, the thought of pursuit occurred to her. But she wanted no repeat performance of last night.

She seized her dog's collar and ran for home, dragging the protesting canine with her.

Less than a hundred feet away, Tyler Ross and Jack Jones saw everything. Tyler, relaxing now that Breanna was safely back in her house, turned to his superior. "Explain that one. Somebody's trying to get rid of her. Seems a strange thing to do to a co-worker."

Jack grunted with disgust. "Dammit, Ross, get your head on straight. You see, but you don't see. If they wanted to get rid of her, they'd think of something a little more persuasive. What is it about this broad that's got you blind to what's happening?"

Staring toward the cabin, Tyler's reply was to shake his head. He could be wrong. "Explain the twenty, then. She flashed that at me, no qualms whatsoever. She found it in the barn, dammit. You know it's counterfeit."

"Do I? And on the other side of the coin, what if it's genuine? What if, Ross? That's our job, you know, the what ifs? Say you've made a slip. She's suspicious, thinks you're on to them. She could flash a good bill, knowing you'll pull a switch. You have it gone over, it's clean. End of your suspicion. I tell you, she's poison. Hell, she even left it in a side pocket of her purse, making it simple for you. Use your head. It's bait."

Tyler felt sick. He remembered her slipping the twenty into her purse, right in plain sight, then leaving the room. What if? It looked bad. He had to admit it. Until he got hold of the twenty, no one could know for sure. Until then, he had to be careful, very careful. "I'll get it tomorrow. I'm supposed to help her plant fence posts in the morning. I'll pull the switch then."

"Believe me. She'll probably give you an open invitation," Jack replied.

"What about this ghost business, though? If she's one of them, why would they do this?"

"I don't have all the answers. Maybe she's horning in on this one fellow's cut, taking over his territory. You take a pack of wolves, give them slim pickings, and one always turns on another. Survival of the fittest. Don't give this group too much credit."

BY NINE O'CLOCK the following morning, Breanna had not only convinced Tyler they should postpone fence building in favor of finding the entrance to *The Crescent Moon*, but had led him over the hill behind the cabin to look for it.

"The way I see it," she informed him cheerily, "is that my ghost last night has heard the legend. John Van Patten is only supposed to appear when someone gets close to the treasure. So, this guy capitalized on it, trying to scare me away. My guess is he's found the old entrance, and now he's afraid I will. Don't get me wrong, I don't believe there's a treasure. But *he* believes there is. If I want any peace, I've got to find that shaft and blast it shut."

"So you don't plan to search the tunnels?"

Breanna stopped climbing to look back down the trail at him. "Well, we might walk through."

"Bad idea. It could cave in on us." Tyler looked beyond her to the rock slide. Was the old entrance up there? The closer they came, the more nervous he felt. Was Breanna setting him up. Or was she as innocent as she seemed? "I think caution should be our byword, don't you?"

She shrugged. "It hasn't caved in on the ghost. Why would it give way on us?"

As they approached the rock-strewn hillside, Tyler prepared himself for the worst. He kept close to Breanna. If counterfeiters leaped out from the brush, a certain lady Tyler knew would be between him and their guns. His stomach wrenched at the thought. How could he have been so wrong about her, so completely taken in?

Smoothing the map, Breanna studied it with a frown.

"What do you think? Could this be it?" Expecting Tyler to check the map with her, she glanced up in puzzlement to find him scanning the woods around them instead. "Tyler?"

He leveled steely eyes on hers. "What?"

"Do you think this slide could be near the entrance?"

"It looks likely to me."

Perplexed by the strange expression on his face, Breanna carefully stowed the map in her hip pocket. Yesterday he had seemed so anxious to explore, now he was dragging his heels. "Well, unless you want to forget it, let's get cracking and search it out."

Tyler stood back, watching her weave her way in and over the rocks. "If it's a caved-in entrance, your ghost can't be using it."

"Unless there's a narrow opening." She rounded on him, propping her hands on her hips. "He could use a narrow opening, then conceal it with rock. Are you going to help?"

Reluctant and unable to hide it, Tyler advanced on the slide, rolling up his sleeves. He'd have to work with one eye on her, one eye on the brush, and both ears strained for noise, which wouldn't be easy with boulders clunking. He studied her in amazement. She was a sturdy girl with a well-rounded figure that was amazingly toned for a writer. She threw rocks even he might think twice about. "Do you take extra iron or what?"

She glanced up, perspiration filming her forehead and dampening her hair where it formed a widow's peak. "I told you, I'm not afraid of work."

Her tone implied he was. An unbidden smile twisted his mouth. "I know, you come from a long line of miners."

"Hey, don't laugh. There's no harder work. Gramps was one tough fellow. At eighty he could outdo men half his age. A very smart man, too, for one with no education."

"Well, until this moment I would have said you had inherited his brains. Now I'm not so sure." Tyler heaved a rock. "This is a lot of trouble to go to on a maybe."

"Yeah? And if you don't act on maybes, what do you go on? Sitting and contemplating never got anything done."

Tyler straightened. Every couple of seconds, a medium-size boulder flew past him. He saw a small bulge of muscle pop up on her arm as she strained, and he raised an eyebrow. Most women would be babying those scratched arms and that lacerated back. Criminal or not, she was quite some lady.

Two hours later, Tyler led the way down the mountain, unafraid to turn his back on the woman behind him. They had found nothing yet, no trace of an entrance, and, more importantly, no counterfeiters waiting to ambush them. If Breanna was acting, she had moved one hell of a lot of rock to make it convincing. As the trail widened, he slowed so that they could walk abreast. "We'll take a break, then come back," he assured her. "Some of your lemonade will hit the spot." She didn't return his smile. "Disappointed?"

"Yeah, I am."

"Hey, it's not that important." Before he thought, Tyler draped an arm around her shoulders. Once it was there, he didn't want to move it. "It's just a pipe dream, something to chase away boredom."

"To you, maybe. I *have* to find it, Tyler. My gran made me promise I'd keep the claim. I can't break my word. And if I want to stay, I've got to get rid of whoever's bugging me. The mine theory seemed the most likely place to start." A shadow crossed her face. "I have another reason, too. One that's not quite so clear-cut, more a crazy hunch."

"That sounds serious."

"It is." Her eyes rose to his, wavered with uncertainty. "Probably silly, but— It's about my cousin, something that I've been wondering about."

"Tell me about it."

Her lips parted. He held his breath, waiting, hoping.

"I—can't," she whispered. "I wish I could, but I just can't."

When they reached the cabin, Dane's Corvette was parked in the driveway behind Breanna's Honda. Breanna dived for Coaly and nabbed him by the collar. She saw that the cabin door stood ajar.

"Well, it looks like my company invited himself in," she remarked to Tyler. Stepping to the fruit cellar, she opened the door and pushed an unwilling Coaly inside, dropping the lock bar with a click. "It's my cousin, Dane. And Coaly doesn't get along with him."

"Maybe I should leave," Tyler suggested, hoping she'd veto the idea.

"Nonsense. You're my guest. There's no reason you shouldn't be here."

Breanna's irritation mushroomed into full-blown anger when she found Dane in her bedroom, busily looking through the collection of papers on her closet shelf. He didn't even bother to look guilty when he saw her. "Dane, what do you think you're doing?"

Dane, unaware that Tyler was in the other room, threw the maps and photocopies in Breanna's face. She stepped back in surprise, and her cousin advanced on her. "The question isn't what I'm doing, lady, it's what you're doing. First I see you up the hill, looking for the old mine entrance. Then I come in here and find all this. Why are you collecting all these news stories?"

Breanna's retreat ended when she backed into the wall. Fury twisted Dane's face. His eyes were wild, crazy. "Dane, stop it."

"Answer me!" He shot out a hand and grabbed her hair, making a fist in it. Tears sprang to her eyes. "Answer me, damn you! Why are you doing this? Back off, Breanna. I'm warning you. Back off."

Then Tyler came through the curtain. With a low snarl, he pushed Dane away from Breanna, then squared off, fists clenched at his sides. Dane staggered backward, catching his balance by grabbing the bedstead. "You're the one who'd better back off, buster," Tyler warned. "You got something to say to the lady, say it, but keep your hands off her."

Dane straightened, smoothing the lapels of his jacket. "And who, might I ask, do you think you are, Ross? This is family business. Butt out."

Breanna stepped between the two men. "Wait a minute, fellas. Let's not turn a disagreement into a brawl." Turning to Tyler, she managed a smile. "I appreciate your concern, Tyler, but Dane just lost his temper there for a moment. Right, Dane?"

"No, that's not right," Dane hissed. Glancing down, he ground one of her photocopies beneath his heel. "You see that? Keep poking your nose where it doesn't belong, and next, it'll be you. Do you understand what I'm saying? Quit snooping. Back off. Forget the fire. Stay away from the mine. You're in way over your head. Pack up your stuff and get out of here while you still can."

Leaving that threat to cloud the air, Dane shoved his way past Tyler and left the bedroom. The entire cabin shook as he slammed the front door behind him. Breanna tensed and squeezed her eyes closed.

"What was that all about?"

Ignoring Tyler's question, she knelt to gather up the papers, infuriated all the more when she saw Gran's old newspapers lying in one corner of the closet, crumpled and torn. If ever she had doubted Dane's involvement in the arson, she didn't now. His reaction to those papers was testimony against him. She rose to her feet, clutching the photocopies to her chest.

"I think Dane may have set the Reuben Creek fire," she blurted, "because someone had found *The Crescent Moon.*"

Tyler stooped to pick up Gran's old papers. Breanna saw him note their age. He read for a moment, then tossed them onto her bed, turning back to raise an eyebrow at her. "That's a pretty serious accusation."

"And ten years too long in coming." Setting the photocopies back in their place, Breanna clutched the edge of the shelf, fighting back tears. "You don't have to get involved in this. It's not your problem. It's mine. I don't know if you're familiar with that fire. A man was killed." She looked over her shoulder at him. "If Dane was the arsonist, he murdered him."

The bedroom went dead quiet. After a long moment, Tyler reached for the photocopies. "May I?"

Sighing, Breanna nodded her permission. "There's nothing, no clue. I've already read them."

"Who knows? Maybe someone uninvolved will see something that's been missed."

Following him to the kitchen, Breanna said, "Don't use that word. I wasn't involved, period. Not in any way."

Tyler pulled back a chair. "I didn't think you were."

Dragging her hair back from her eyes, she heaved a tired sigh. "I'm sorry. I guess I'm too sensitive. We were accused of setting it, you know, Dane and I."

"No, I didn't know."

"You will once you've read those papers. I'm going to go get Coaly. I'll be right back."

Tyler waited until she went out, then bounded to his feet. The purse, where was it? Not on the counter. *Damn it all.* He ran for the bedroom. There it was, on the closet shelf. He grabbed it, stuffed his fingers into the pocket and pulled out a—grocery list? He pushed it back. A bank deposit stub? Where was the money?

He heard Breanna talking to the dog, drawing near to

the porch. Tossing the purse back on the shelf, he dived through the curtain, raced across the living room and landed in the chair. When she walked into the room, he stretched and yawned, smiling up at her.

AN HOUR LATER, TYLER ROCKED back in his chair, folding his arms across his chest. His eyes searched Breanna's.

"Well?" she demanded.

"You want the truth? I see nothing conclusive to implicate Dane. Or you, for that matter. You had an alibi, an airtight alibi, given by Chuck Morrow." He shook his head. "There has to be another side to this story. You don't strike me as the type to make accusations unless you're mighty positive you're right."

"That was my biggest problem. I wasn't sure, so I kept my mouth shut. A man was killed, and I said nothing."

"I don't understand. According to the paper, Dane couldn't have set that fire."

"And the paper is all lies. At least about the alibi. We weren't with Chuck all night. We ran into him when we were escaping the fire. Chuck lied to the police to get us off the hook." Breanna propped her elbows on the table, covering her eyes with trembling fingers. She could scarcely bear the memories, the screams that echoed inside her mind, the vision of Rob Thatcher caught under a tree, burning alive. And with the memories came guilt that cut through her like a knife. She couldn't bring herself to tell all of it. But some of it she had to tell. It was too heavy a burden to keep locked inside her any longer. "Oh, Tyler, why didn't I simply tell the truth?"

"Only you can answer that. Did you suspect Dane then?"

"Yes and no. I woke up after the fire started, and Dane wasn't in camp. By the time he got there the fire was all around us—" She broke off. She didn't want to verbalize the rest, couldn't. "It was all a blur for days after, the trees falling, the fear, the realization we might die. I wasn't thinking. I was just running."

"Go on."

"Then the next morning the police came. They accused us of setting the fire. Arson, they said, started with gas cans placed around the hippie commune. The hippies weren't too popular in these parts. Lots of people, kids and adults, had made threats. Dane and I were just in the wrong place at the right time." She dropped her hand to look at him. "I was terrified. Murder! Rob Thatcher was pinned by a fallen pine and couldn't escape. I envisioned the electric chair. At seventeen, it's pretty scary when police accuse you of anything, let alone killing someone. We swore we didn't do it, but the police were convinced otherwise. They didn't believe anything we said. And they took us to juvenile hall. I think Dane was even more frightened than me."

"I can imagine. That would scare even an adult."

Breanna forced herself to remember. "It's like a fog, those first few days. I was no sooner in custody than they put me in the hospital for treatment. Smoke inhalation. Just a day, for observation. By the time I was released, Chuck Morrow had come forward, saying we were with him all night, that we couldn't have set the fire. Dane and I—we—we were so scared, we said it was true."

"Chuck was a friend, I take it? According to the paper he was quite a hero, risking his life to save women and children that night."

Tension clogged Breanna's throat. "I've never understood that part. Chuck is—a snake. He'd never put himself out for anybody."

"He did for you, for Dane."

"And demanded his pound of flesh, believe me. A few days after I got home, Chuck started coming around."

"You lived here?"

"Only for a month in the summer. And we visited a lot. We were staying here then, Dane and I, like we did every year."

"And Chuck demanded his pound of flesh?"

She nodded. "Little favors at first, then bigger ones. Dane seemed scared to death of him. That's when I began getting suspicious. I remembered Dane being out of camp. I realized Dane was scared Chuck would go to the police about something. It occurred to me Chuck knew something, something Dane had done that he wasn't telling. But I wasn't sure, and without being sure, I couldn't accuse Dane. Now I regret that. I think—no, I guess suspect is a better word—that Dane has something hanging over his head, something eating at him, even though it's been ten years."

"You had a reasonable doubt. I don't think there's anything so wrong in your not having gone to the police, considering the circumstances."

Breanna straightened in her chair. Her chest tightened. "I knew right from wrong. And I've had to live with my decision ever since."

"And you're on a guilt trip? Breanna, give yourself a break. You were young, scared, confused. If you had gone to the police, what would they have thought? You could have been charged with a very serious crime at that point. I think it's understandable. Not wise, perhaps, but understandable. What kind of favors was Morrow asking of Dane?"

Breanna glanced up at him. There were some things she couldn't yet bring herself to discuss; not with Tyler, not with anyone. "Nothing important."

"So, here we sit with photocopies. Am I to understand you're looking for proof against Dane, that you've returned to set a wrong right?"

"No, I didn't come back with that intention." Breanna

told him about Dane's first visit, his warnings. "It seemed suspicious. It set me to thinking. Dane's so paranoid about the treasure, so afraid I'll look for it. And he gets absolutely furious if I mention the fire. I know he's afraid of something. And I want to find out what. It's almost as if it all ties in together. I know it doesn't make sense, but it's as if the fire and the mine are all the same in Dane's mind."

"You're right. It doesn't make sense." *Or does it?* Tyler studied the woman sitting opposite him. Now that she had told him this, the possibilities were endless. Dane Van Patten with a secret. Morrow holding it over his head as blackmail. It had never occurred to Jack or to himself that Dane Van Patten's involvement could be due to coercion. A fire, a death, a kid with a secret. If Breanna had acted unwisely out of fear, why not Dane? "If I were you, I'd let the past be buried, Breanna."

"Dane could have been my ghost last night." She laughed softly. "I know it sounds idiotic, but he's obviously getting desperate. He wants me out of here so badly, he might do something like that to scare me away. Don't you see? I can't forget it. Dane won't let me."

Tyler rocked back in his chair again. "Has it occurred to you he might go even further, that he could be dangerous?"

Her eyes widened. "Dane? No, not Dane. You saw him at his worst today. Dane could never hurt me. And if he hurt someone else, I'm sure he never meant to."

"I saw him trying to bully you around. Sorry, but I think he's capable of violence. It's not worth it, Breanna. I think you should do as he said. Pack up and go."

"I won't give him the satisfaction. No, if it was Dane here last night, he'll have to get more inventive. I'm not breaking my promise to Gran because a ghost is haunting me and Dane made vague threats."

"Vague? I thought he was pretty blatant."

"You don't know him like I do. Believe me, Tyler. Dane would put his life on the line for me. I know he would."

Tyler hoped she was right. Oh, how he hoped she was right.

BECAUSE BREANNA INSISTED, Tyler returned with her to the rock slide to do more searching for the entrance to *The Crescent Moon*. He was more relaxed on the second trip up there, more certain of Breanna's motives. She was off base, thinking the mine and the fire were tied together, but for one guessing in the dark, she was close to the truth. The mine was intertwined with crime, all right, but it had nothing to do with the fire.

The entire time they worked, he tried to think of ways he might get Breanna's twenty from the barn out of her purse. If he could distract her, he would be able to snatch it and pull a switch. To do that, he had to stick to her like glue until the opportunity presented itself.

After moving what seemed like mountains of rock, Tyler and Breanna found the wooden frame of a mine opening. "Well, nobody's going in through that," she quipped. "Not without several sticks of dynamite."

Tyler nodded, staring at the cave-in. Rock filled the opening. The day wasn't a complete loss. Now he knew for certain the counterfeiters had only one entrance, the one under Breanna's barn. Jack would be pleased to hear it. "Well, that scotches the theory of a bear under the barn," he said lightly. "We're back to rats."

Breanna laughed. "I guess we are, at that. It's a relief in a way. I can stop worrying that Dane found it. It was pretty scary, thinking he might have hurt someone, trying to keep the old mine a secret."

"I'll tell you what. How's about a late lunch in Grants Pass?" He glanced at his watch. "We've got time. What do you say? My treat. We can make a laundry run while we're at it."

"I don't know, Mr. Ross. You might regret the offer. I'm so hungry after all this work, I might bankrupt you. One thing I don't have is a delicate appetite."

"So make it two lunches. I'm willing to pay that price for your company."

As they walked down the trail, Tyler rested his arm over Breanna's shoulders once again, this time intentionally. An ache of protectiveness tightened his chest. Judging by Dane's threats, he knew he had to get that counterfeit twenty to Jack fast. Breanna's life could be riding on it.

CHAPTER SIX

FORTY MINUTES LATER, Tyler pulled Breanna's Honda to the far right lane of Interstate 5 and entered Grants Pass at the town's north end. As they passed the gigantic statue of a caveman at the city's entrance, he said, "Now, that's my kind of fellow. See that club he's got? Those things saved prehistoric man a lot of lunch tabs when it came to wooing the ladies."

She arched an eyebrow at him, thoroughly enjoying the easy camaraderie that had been established between them during their drive. "Neanderthal are you? You didn't by any chance go to school here?" She pointed to a busy parking lot on their right. "Pull in at the Ninety-Nine Market and I'll get us some laundry soap."

Tyler braked the Honda and shifted down to make the turn. Pulling to a stop, he shoved in the clutch and reached for his wallet. "Here, use this," he said, handing her a twenty.

"I'll spring for the soap. You're buying lunch."

"Well, take it for a roll of quarters then."

She took her wallet from her bag. Flipping it open, she withdrew a ten and exchanged bills with him.

His eyes sharpened as she fitted his twenty into her billfold. "Why don't you just take the twenty, Bree, and leave your purse? It'd be less to carry."

"I might want something else. Be right back."

The moment Breanna turned to walk away, Tyler heaved

a sigh. With any luck, she wouldn't spend the twenty from the barn, and he could snatch it later.

The store was crowded with customers. Breanna found the laundry soap, then selected two candy bars from the display rack as she passed. The opportunity to tease Tyler about her gargantuan appetite later was too tempting to resist. She stood in line, stepping forward as the clerk finished each transaction. When her turn came, she set her purchases on the counter and pulled out her wallet.

"That's four forty-nine," the clerk told her.

"Oh, and I need quarters. Can you spare a roll?"

"Sure." The woman took a red cylinder of coin from the left section of her drawer. "That makes it fourteen forty-nine."

Handing her a twenty, Breanna opened her grocery bag.

"A brand-new one," the blonde said. "I don't see many."

Breanna, busy fishing for her candy bars so she could hide them in her purse, replied, "Yes, it is, isn't it?"

The clerk counted change into Breanna's outstretched palm. When she finished, she lifted curious green eyes, her eyes friendly. "You have a nice day."

"You, too."

As Breanna approached the Honda, she smiled to herself. After lunch, when Tyler was full, she'd offer him a candy bar. Sliding into her seat, she said, "Okay, I'm ready to eat you into bankruptcy."

He flashed her a grin and pulled out into traffic.

FOUR HOURS LATER, BREANNA parked outside the cabin and cut the Honda's engine. The sun dipped behind the mountain, streaking the gray-blue sky with cottony pink. She sat there a moment, absorbing the evening sounds, the swish of pine boughs, the songs of the crickets, the occasional chirp of a bird preparing to roost. She heard Coaly barking from inside the cabin, eager to be let out, but she stole another few seconds of quiet. Leaning her head against the rest, she closed her eyes.

Tyler. What a lovely day it had been. Even doing the laundry with him was fun. There had been only three dryers available, so Tyler had suggested drying their white things together. It had seemed a practical idea until the clothes came out sparking with static, her nylon lacies sticking to his briefs and undershirts. When all the clothes were folded, two pairs of her bikinis were missing. She felt fairly sure Tyler would pull on a pair of shorts one morning next week and find her lavender Tuesday panties inside the garment with him. A mischievous grin slanted across her mouth. It was one way to make a man remember you. And he was supposed to help her dig postholes again in the morning. She found herself looking forward to that with as much anticipation as she might have to a dinner date.

Glancing at her watch, she sat upright. No more time for loafing she decided. She still had to unload her laundry, let Coaly out for a run, and take a bath before dark.

TYLER PARTED THE DOGWOOD leaves, gazing down the hillside as Breanna left the cabin. She had a blue terry robe draped over one arm, and clutched her toiletry items in the other. Glancing at his watch, he noted the time. *Seven-thirty.* He had to enter the house, find the twenty and be gone within ten minutes. That creek was too cold for her to lounge around in. A quick scrub, and she'd be out and headed for home. He watched her crisscross through the brush along the creek, checking to be certain no one was there. Someone was watching her, all right, but not for the reasons she suspected.

He waited for her to disappear, then ran out of the bushes, crossed the road and leaped the picket fence that bordered one side of the yard. Pulling out his wallet, he withdrew a plastic credit card and crept to the French doors. Coaly appeared, pressing his wet nose against the glass. *Don't bark,* Tyler prayed. The dog let out a single "Woof," then wagged his tail.

Sliding the plastic card into the door seam, Tyler jiggled the lever lock, lifting it free of its catch. The doors swung open, and he stepped inside, nabbing Coaly by the collar. "No way, pal. If you get loose, the game's over."

Breanna's purse sat on the table. Tyler slid his hand into the side pocket. The grocery list, the bank stub, a tissue blotted with lipstick. Voilà, the twenty. He took it, replacing it with a bill of his own. As he slid his wallet into his hip pocket, he noticed the maps and photocopies lying on the table. His hand hovered over them, then he vetoed the idea. She'd probably let him take them later to have them drawn to scale. No sense in making her suspicious. Just in case, though, he gave the map another quick study.

A growl from Coaly made Tyler leap and toss the papers back on the table. Footsteps. In three strides, he stepped outside and pulled the windows closed. No time to lock them. He vaulted the fence, zigzagged across the asphalt and dived into the bush.

THE NIGHT WIND WAS PICKING UP. Breanna shivered, knowing how chilly the water would feel. She stepped into the copse and shimmied out of her clothes. Draping her robe over a limb, she carried her bathing things with her to the diving rock. She missed Coaly. With him nosing around, no one could sneak up on her. She had checked the brush, though. She was probably safe enough, and without Coaly along to liven things up, she wouldn't smell like a dog after her bath.

The pool felt like ice when she dived in. Clenching her teeth, she surfaced and began scrubbing. She had just finished rinsing her hair and was rubbing the soap from her lashes when she heard a creaking sound, similar to what she had heard that second night when Coaly had growled.

Pulling her hair back, Breanna stared at the copse beyond the bathing hole.

The brush still swayed where someone had disturbed it, but she couldn't see anyone. Alarm coursed through her, growing in intensity until her nerves jangled. Not only was no person there, but her clothes weren't there, either.

She gaped in disbelief. Even her towel was gone.

"Tyler?" That scoundrel. She sank in the water to her collarbone, smiling expectantly. She envisioned him dangling her jeans, teasing her. "All right, Mr. Ross, the fun's over. I'll freeze if you don't cut it out."

The scenario was so clearly etched upon her mind that alarm coursed through her when Tyler didn't step out of the brush. Silence weighted the air. Tyler might tease, he might give her a scare, but he wouldn't drag it out like this while she was treading neck deep in icy water.

After several minutes had passed, Breanna could bear the cold no longer. *Modesty be damned,* she thought. She couldn't stay in there and freeze to death. She seized handholds on the diving rock, hauling herself from the pool. Water poured off her as she gained her footing. Hiding her body with her arms, she ran along the rock, reached shore and dashed into the bushes.

Acutely aware of her vulnerability, she didn't stay long in the brush. Working her way through the foliage, she kept her ears strained for the sound of approaching footsteps. Then, taking a deep breath, she ran into the open. Rocks and stickers gouged the soles of her feet, but she didn't slow down as she wove her way between the outhouse and garage and sprinted across the drive. When she reached the retainer wall steps, a horrible thought hit her. The cabin key was in her jeans. She was locked out of the house.

That realization had no sooner sunk in than Breanna froze on the walkway in midstride. Her clothes lay on the porch, slashed to ribbons. The thief had taken a knife to them. Her pulse rate accelerated as she drew closer. If this was a joke, it wasn't funny. It was sick.

Fear and anger knotted inside her, the ferocity of both blocking out all else. She grabbed her tattered jeans, slipping her fingers into the pocket. *The key. Thank goodness.* With trembling hands, she inserted it in the lock, gave it a twist and burst into the cabin, shoving the door closed behind her.

Making her way to the bedroom, she grabbed a towel off the shelf and dried. Then she dressed, searching the floor of the closet for her other shoes. Her earlier fear ebbed, crowded out by rage. Someone was trying to terrify her. There could be only one motive, to force her to leave.

"Well, it won't work," she vowed, shoving the bedroom curtain aside as she went to the kitchen.

Coaly sat back on his haunches and uttered a sharp bark. She shot a glance outside. About twenty minutes of light remained. "No dinner yet, fella. First, we do some investigating."

As she reached for her flashlight, Breanna noticed that her papers were scattered. A tense silence enveloped the room. *Someone has been inside the cabin.* Knowing her home had been violated disturbed her more than the incident by the creek. How had someone come in without forcing the door? The key in her jeans, of course. She reached for the flashlight. "Come on, Coaly. Let's go see what we can see."

With anger as turbofuel, Breanna returned to the bathing hole, armed with her flashlight. Coaly dived into the copse, sniffing the ground where she had seen the brush moving. More interested in where her prankster had gone than where he had been, Breanna made a wide circle around the undergrowth, fanning her light on the ground. What she *didn't* see made her uneasy. There were no footprints coming out of the foliage. She stooped to get a closer look, walking the perimeter three times. Nothing.

Her throat tightened with irrational fear. For a man to enter and leave the brush, he would have to make tracks. The story of John Van Patten's ghost crept into her mind. *I found the mine entrance today,* she thought. *He appears when someone gets close to his treasure.* Breanna tightened her grip on the flashlight. She couldn't allow her imagination to run wild. *A ghost wouldn't leave footprints, though.*

Before searching further, she checked the horizon to be sure she had plenty of twilight left. No way was she getting caught out here after dark. Entering the brush, she trained her light where Coaly was sniffing. There, confined to a two-foot area, were some very real tracks. Boot tracks, similar to the ones she had seen before. Breanna knelt and touched her finger to a print. Definitely not Tyler's boots. His soles had slanted ridges in the rubber. These had a squared indentation, with the pattern angling triangularly outward from the center.

So she had checked Tyler's boots without realizing it. Ah, yes, she remembered looking at his tracks the day he helped her plant fence posts. It disturbed her that she was subconsciously observing him as if he were her enemy. She passed a hand over her eyes, disgusted with herself. Then relief swept through her. Considering everything that had happened, it was normal to be wary. At least these prints proved that Tyler wasn't her prankster.

Coaly ran to a grassy bank inside the copse. Sniffing a tuft of grass, he snarled. His strange behavior piqued her curiosity and she followed, picking up a trail of tracks that led to the slope and ended there. Coaly walked the bank, his nose skimming the ground in erratic patterns. Had her thief climbed up it? Breanna drew closer, leaning forward to shine her light. There were no footprints.

"I wish you could talk," she muttered to Coaly. "He

was in here, that much is obvious, but how did he get out without leaving tracks? Human beings don't evaporate into thin air."

It was a question Breanna couldn't answer. As she left the copse, she trailed her light behind her. Sure enough, there were her own tracks, even in the grass. The ground was moist here, so close to the creek, and her weight left its imprint.

Coaly ran ahead of her, then halted to bark. She slowed her pace. He was trying to tell her something. Did he know where the man had gone? "What is it, boy?"

Coaly wagged his tail, then struck off for the barn at a dead run. Breanna followed him. When the dog reached the building, he stuck his nose to the ground, sniffing at the foundation.

"Oh, for Pete's sake. I'm people hunting, you silly beast." Coaly responded with another round of wild barking, running the length of the barn, then back again to do a full circle around her. "He isn't in there," she scolded.

As she turned to walk away, Coaly startled her by lifting his nose to the sky and howling. It was such a mournful cry that she paused to look at him. A shiver of dread crept up her spine. She remembered the noises she had heard under the barn floor, recalled the cave-in at the entrance. No flesh and blood person could be in there. But Gramps had seen John Van Patten in the barn.

Supposedly, she reminded herself. *Gramps was an old man, Breanna. His eyes were bad. Get ahold of yourself, and stop this nonsense.*

Flipping off her light to save the batteries, she made a beeline for the cabin. She didn't believe in ghosts, but facts were facts. Someone had come to the creek, stolen her things, slashed them and moved them to her porch, walking a hundred and fifty feet without leaving footprints in soft ground. Ghost or man?

She wasn't sure anymore.

CHAPTER SEVEN

BREANNA SAT ON the porch with one foot propped on her knee. In the bright morning sunlight, she had pulled out dozens of tiny stickers that had imbedded themselves in her soles as she ran barefoot in the brush. As she plucked the last of them from her skin, she thought of last night. If her wild musings about ghosts were any indication, it was time she took a break and got her mind off her troubles.

"I thought I'd find you hard at work."

She glanced up with a start to see Tyler climbing the steps. "Hi. You're bright and early."

He carried his camera in one hand, strap dangling. "What d'ya have there? Slivers?"

"I made the mistake of walking barefoot in the grass."

Giving her foot a final inspection, she drew on her sock and shoe, deciding then and there to tell Tyler nothing more. She knew what he would say if he heard about her clothes being stolen and slashed. One word. *Leave.* Since she had no intention of doing that, another argument seemed senseless. At the worst, it might be some misguided local with a grudge left over from the Reuben Creek fire. And besides, scare tactics had never hurt anyone.

"You gonna be able to work? Or are your feet too sore?"

She groaned. "It's almost too pretty to work. Today's a day to loaf, don't you think?"

His steel-blue eyes rested on her face. "I agree. Too pretty to work."

Heat sprang to Breanna's cheeks and she glanced away.

It was the first time he had even hinted he was attracted to her, except with his jokes about lemonade and lunch, and she felt awkward, uncertain how to respond. "How about panning? Do you enjoy it?"

"For gold? Never done it. Sounds fun, though."

"Then let's do it."

"I'm game."

After Tyler had put his camera on the table and she had shut Coaly in the cabin, she led the way to the barn. She preceded him up the ramp and stepped into the dim corridor. "I spotted the gold pans in here the other day. We'll have to scrub them, but they looked usable."

"Careful," he cautioned. "Walk close to the walls where the floors have more support." He paused with her to look inside a stall. "Wood stain," he commented wryly, stepping into the room to check out the garbage pile. "Pop cans. Ah, here we go, Breanna. Someone dined on beer and Vienna sausage in here."

"Probably a picnic in the hayloft. Kids from town, hiding out from their folks."

He followed her into the next stall and plucked a pan off the shelf after she did, dusting it on his jeans. "Well, are you ready to teach me the ropes?"

"Just don't get gold fever," she warned. "It happens, you know."

"You sound like we might actually find something."

"Sure we will. But it's called getting color."

"Getting color. I'll remember. Won't do, me sounding like a greenhorn when I'm in the company of a pro."

Laughing, she walked toward the door. "I'm no pro. Now, Gran, she was a miner. I swear, she could get color out of a kid's sandbox. It takes me a bit longer."

"Well, I'm looking forward to learning. I've always wanted to pan, but I didn't know where to start."

Turning at the bottom of the ramp, she said, "We start

by finding a cache in bedrock. Or a turn in the stream is good, where the water hits the bank and eddies for a bit."

"Why's that?"

As they walked toward the house, she elaborated. "Gold usually washes downstream with erosion, then settles. You've seen hollowed places in bedrock that catch dirt? Well, that's a likely spot for gold. You put some soil in your pan, and slowly wash the dirt out over the edge. The color settles because it's heavier. It takes a knack, but you'll catch on."

THE DAY WITH TYLER WENT peacefully. They knelt together on the rust-red bank, working their gold pans for hours, breaking only for a quick lunch at the house. They conversed infrequently. A companion who shared her love for tranquillity was a new experience for Breanna. Most of her acquaintances either chatted constantly or brought along a transistor radio and drowned out the more beautiful symphonies of the forest.

The lack of conversation between them troubled her, though. Again she was plagued with questions about Tyler, information most people volunteered. She suspected he was from Grants Pass, but he had not yet confirmed that. She knew his name, and that was all. And because he was so closemouthed, she felt reluctant to share information about herself. She had already told him far too much, her suspicions of Dane, her guilt about the fire. Tyler was a quiet man, but this went beyond that. She wondered if he was hiding something.

It seemed a shame. She sensed something special between them, a rare compatibility, but he held back from her, stifling its chance of growth with a curtain of silence.

"This is therapeutic," he said, holding up his glass vial to examine the gold dust he had collected. "How much do these hold?"

"An ounce. When they're filled, you can take them in and get cash." She gave her pan a final swish, then shook her hands, wiping her palms on her jeans. "It may be therapeutic, but this water's so cold, I think it comes off snow."

"Not snow, just good old mountain springs. No water on earth like it, is there?"

"There's nothing on earth to compare to this place. Gran called it God's country and I think she was right. Now that I'm here, I don't know why I waited so long to come back."

"Sometimes, things we run from get bigger and bigger. It's hard to turn back and face them."

"Yes...hard." She looked over at him, and their eyes locked. Shadows lurked in his. Something troubled him; she knew it, felt it, heard it in his voice. "Tell me, do you speak from experience? Are you running, too, Tyler?"

He lifted an eyebrow. "What gave you that idea?"

She gazed across the creek. "You never say anything about yourself. It's like—well, as if your life started here along the creek and you left everything else behind you."

He laughed. "I don't have any secrets. What do you want to know? I'm thirty-six. My marriage ended in divorce. No kids. And I'm a photographer. I love chocolate, hate liver, and onions don't agree with me, but I eat them anyway because I have very little willpower. Anything else you'd like to know?"

"Where did you grow up?"

"Right over the mountain. You guessed right, I was a Grants Pass kid, graduated from G.P.H.S., played football for the Cavemen. My folks still live there when they aren't vacationing. My dad's retired."

"Well, I guess that's a pretty fair accounting of yourself." She looked into his eyes again. The shadows were still there. She realized he had told her everything—and nothing. "I grew up in Grants Pass, too. But for nine years, we might have gone to school together."

"So you're twenty-seven?" He shook out his gold pan and set it on top of hers, smiling. "Married, divorced? You've never said."

"I was engaged. It didn't work out. My work, you see. It's a little odd, a woman traipsing off into the hills for days on end."

"Not odd, different. No harm in that." He rose and offered her a hand up. "As much as I hate to call it a day, it's about that time. I need to get my camera and do some traipsing of my own. Can't buy the bacon without working now and again."

She tipped her head back. The expression on his face held her spellbound. He reached out and touched her hair, threading his fingers through it. The blue of his eyes clouded with sudden tenderness. Then his hand tightened. He pulled her slowly toward him, stepping to meet her. When his mouth touched hers, his lips feathered so softly they were like butterfly wings, gentle, questioning, experimenting. She felt breathless. There was a rightness between them she had never dreamed could exist.

When he pulled away, Breanna felt a sense of loss she couldn't explain, a feeling of *almost*, as if he had abruptly put an end to something he felt he shouldn't have begun. A troubled frown drew his brows together.

Bending to get the pans, he said, "I've enjoyed today. It's nice being with you."

"Maybe we can do it again sometime."

"I hope so." He smiled and placed his left hand on her shoulder, giving it a squeeze as they walked up the bank. "We'd better build fences first, though. I'll come back in the morning."

"You don't have to, Tyler. I can get them done. I hate to interfere with your work schedule. I know what it's like, free-lancing."

"I want to help. That is, if you don't mind the company."

"Not at all. I'll look forward to it."

After he'd retrieved his camera from the cabin, Tyler struck off through the orchard. Breanna leaned against the retainer wall, watching until he disappeared. Tomorrow seemed an eternity away on the one hand, too soon on the other. Something special was happening between them. And that frightened her. She knew what her secrets were and why she couldn't share them. But what were Tyler's?

TWILIGHT FOUND BREANNA hunched over her typewriter, squinting to see in the dimness of the cabin. When she glanced up at the windows and saw how late it was, she pulled the dustcover over her machine. If she didn't take her walk now, she wouldn't get one before dark.

As she descended the steps, she called Coaly, groaning when the dog appeared from behind the barn, his muzzle caked with red dirt. If he didn't stop his infernal digging under that foundation, he'd end up sprayed by a skunk or bitten by a snake. Breanna scolded him and headed toward the bathing hole, walking aimlessly until she passed the copse. Unable to resist, she made another circle, looking for tracks she might have missed last night.

When nothing caught her eye, she headed downstream. It wasn't until she drew abreast of the orchard that she realized she was hoping she'd find Tyler working. She didn't, of course, but once the thought had entered her mind, she was curious to see his photo blind.

Keeping to the creek bank where she could see, she watched for footprints. Not far from her starting point, she spied disturbed earth. Making a sharp right, she ran up the rocky bank and pushed through the brush. After several feet, she came to a small clearing that offered a perfect view of her upper orchard and barn. A smile settled on her mouth. It was an ideal place to sneak pictures of deer. She saw where Tyler's knees had pressed into the dirt. He had so frequently parted the brush that it was permanently separated. Imagining him here gave her a warm, comfortable feeling.

Turning to leave, she spied a small, black object in the grass. Stooping, she picked it up. It was round and made of plastic with a mesh face, about the size of a quarter. She knew very little about audio equipment, but it looked like a tiny microphone of some kind. Did Tyler take videotapes, accompanied with sound? She slipped the disc into her pocket.

The light was fading fast. She worked her way out of the blind and cut across the orchard. With every step she took, she had the sensation of being watched. She did a complete circle a couple of times to look around her. Dread filled her as she scanned the woods and brush. A film of cold perspiration broke out on her brow, and she quickened her pace.

Halfway through the orchard, she turned toward the mountain where the deserted *California mine* tunneled for miles into the earth. She could almost see the night sky as it had looked so many years ago, tinted rose red with fire. Her ears echoed with the shrill screams of horror that had haunted her dreams ever since. Taking a deep breath, she closed her eyes for a moment, remembering the fire, Rob Thatcher's torturous death, her own frenzied attempts to save him. So long ago, but it seemed like yesterday.

As she neared the barn, other memories pelted her, memories of her last day here ten years ago when Chuck Morrow had cornered her in the loft. Waves of nausea rolled in her stomach. Images of him flashed before her. Her footsteps slowed. She turned haltingly, her eyes widening with alarm as she stared sightlessly at the barn. Sudden realization hit her. Chuck, with his cocky swagger—the prowler in the white shirt with the muscle-bound walk. Now she knew why she had felt so afraid when she had seen that man. It must have been Chuck Morrow, and on a subconscious level she had recognized him.

Breanna broke into a run.

By the time she let herself in the cabin door and shoved the dead bolt home, she had to find the lantern in the dark. Holding a lit match to the lantern's fragile mantel, she adjusted the white glow, then hung the Coleman on a rafter hook.

"There," she said aloud to her dog. "That's better."

Coaly curled up on the braided rug before the hearth, watching her crouch beside him to light the small fire she had laid earlier in the day. It was a fairly warm evening, but the crackling of the cheerful flames might chase away the gloom that seemed to hover.

She rubbed her forehead, staring at the multicolored twists in the rug beneath her. How like life those intertwined strands were, all knotted and kinked so that nothing looked as though it could ever be put straight again. She hated remembering the fire and the events that followed, but it seemed the longer she stayed here, the more she thought of it. Ten years had brought her full circle.

Stretching out beside Coaly, she reached up to the end table to turn on her transistor radio. Some music in the room might make her feel less alone. A throbbing drumbeat came over the air, sensual and intense. She closed her eyes and slowly relaxed, allowing thoughts of Tyler to slip into her mind.

The radio station's disc jockey broke in on the music. "A quick news update, folks, and then back to the beat. The Josephine County sheriff's department made an official statement today, warning all local merchants to be on the lookout for counterfeit bills. And keep your eyes open. The woman who passed a fake bill yesterday still hasn't been apprehended."

Breanna groaned and sat up to flip off the radio. She

wasn't in the mood for news, not right now. She got up and let Coaly out for a run, watching the fire while she waited for him. About five minutes passed. Then she heard the dog barking. She hurried down the entry hall, opening the door. It sounded as if he was out near the barn.

"Coaly!" Breanna stepped onto the porch, listening. "Coaly, come here, boy!"

She had just turned to fetch the flashlight when she heard a sharp yelp. A few moments later, Coaly scurried onto the porch, favoring one hind leg. "Oh, Coaly!" She closed the door after he'd hobbled inside, kneeling to check him. He whined when her fingers grazed his right haunch. "What happened, boy?"

The dog lifted one ear and stared at the door. The hackles rose on his back. Breanna stood and slid the dead bolt home. Walking back up the hall, she studied the paned glass windows. Inky blackness coated the squares. The cloak of night beyond the room was impenetrable. Did the light from the lantern seem bright from out there? Could she be seen?

She shrank back into the shadows. The log walls closed in on her. Her heart thudded like the suspenseful drumbeats in a horror movie. Coaly dragged himself to his feet, still snarling. He limped to the living room, glaring at the end windows. There was someone out there. She knew her dog. He didn't react like this to other animals.

After several minutes, Coaly finally relaxed. His limp seemed less pronounced, too. Breanna ran her hands over him again, anger welling inside her when he flinched. Kicked, surely, or hit with something blunt. She couldn't feel any punctures on his skin. Smoothing his soot-black fur, she rested her cheek atop his head for a moment.

"Sleep won't come easy tonight," she whispered, giving him a pat. "But I suppose we should turn in."

She turned off the lantern, waiting for it to sputter out

so she could see the yard. Nothing moved. Going to the bedroom, she undressed in the darkness, groping for her nightgown. Tugging it on, she folded back her bedding and slid between the cool sheets. Lying on her side, she watched the windowpanes above her, uncomfortably aware of the fragility of the glass partition. What if she slept too soundly? What if Coaly didn't hear the soft fall of footsteps if someone approached the house? What if, before she could react to the noise, a hand shattered the glass and reached in?

TYLER REACHED FOR A SANDWICH. He took a large bite and chewed slowly, watching Jack examine the twenty-dollar bill from Breanna's purse.

"There's no question," Jack finally agreed.

"So what's our next move? Can I get her the hell out of there?"

"Nope."

"Why? You said get proof, and I got it, dammit. What more do you want? Blood? Hers, to be specific?"

Jack strode to the kitchen, pouring himself a mug of coffee. "Tyler, I've got new information on her."

"What?"

"She passed some bad stuff in town yesterday."

Tyler tossed the remainder of his sandwich on his saucer. "Come again?"

"You heard me. She passed a bad twenty when you two were in town yesterday." Jack turned, leaning his hips against the counter. "It's a positive ID. The clerk described her and the Honda."

"It's a mistake!" Tyler leaped up from his chair. "It has to be."

"No mistake. I'm sorry, old friend." Jack gazed into his cup for a moment, then shook his head. "You know, Tyler, it's possible she's been coerced. If it could happen to Van

Patten, it could happen to her. I'm not saying she's not a nice gal, just that she's in one helluva situation. If she turns federal witness, we can get her off with a light sentence."

Tyler walked to the window, staring out at nothing. "I tell you, Jack, she's not involved. I don't know how she got hold of another counterfeit bill, but she's not involved."

Silence settled in the room. Jack scuffed the floor with the heel of his boot. "I wish I could be sure of that." After a moment, he looked up. "You fallin' for her?"

"No." The denial came fast, the truth more slowly. Tyler sighed. "Oh, hell, I don't know. What's love?" He laughed and shook his head. "I like her. We're friends, we have a lot in common. And I sure don't want her hurt."

"Friends," Jack said with a snort. "Sounds like a terminal case to me."

"Yeah, well, you're a century behind. Nowadays, men and women *can* be friends."

"We can't tip her off. You do understand that?"

"Yes, I understand, Jack. I don't like it, I think you're wrong, but I understand."

"If she isn't tied in with them…" Jack sighed, the sound heavy, tired. "My advice to you is to convince her to leave, without compromising our position."

"I've tried that."

"Give it another shot. Morrow's an odd one, unpredictable. I believe he could be violent. If she's innocent and steps on his toes, she could be in trouble."

CHAPTER EIGHT

WHEN BREANNA OPENED the door the next morning to let Coaly out for a run, she saw a piece of meat lying on the ground next to the porch. She gaped at it for a long while, holding Coaly back so he wouldn't try to eat it. Gingerly she lifted the meat between two fingers. A fine white powder coated the blood-red grain.

Afraid to let her pet wander the yard alone in case there were other pieces, she followed him closely, growing angrier with every step. Unless she missed her guess, this meat was poisoned. And it had been left by the porch for her dog.

Calling Coaly back to the cabin, Breanna shut him inside with her, then stepped to the nearest window to examine the meat in a stream of sunlight. White granules. She took a sniff. The trace of sweetness seemed vaguely familiar. A loud knock on her front door startled her.

"Who is it?"

"Your favorite fence builder. Who else?"

She let out her breath in a shaky sigh. Of course, it was Tyler. Who else would it be? "Come on in. It's not locked."

She heard the door being dragged inward, then the thunk of his boots as he stomped them clean on the entry rug.

He walked into the living room, holding up her lavender bikini underwear, his face alight with laughter. "For some reason I thought of you the moment I got dressed this morning, and I haven't been able to get you off my mind since." His smile faded. "My God, what's wrong? You're white as a sheet."

She held up the meat. "I just found this on the porch. There's a white film on it, Tyler, and I think it might be poison."

He strode toward her, tossing her lacy underwear toward the sofa. Snatching the piece of steak from her, he stepped to the window to examine it. "Wash your hands. Do you have any plastic wrap?"

Breanna indicated a drawer and ran to the sink, pumping on the rusty handle. Water spewed into the washbasin she held under the spout. "What is it? Will it go through the skin?"

Tyler took a smell. "White arsenic."

"Arsenic? Are you sure?"

"Not positive. It's mixed in with something else. I'm not sure what, but it smells like powdered milk."

"Powdered milk, of course! I knew I recognized it. Tyler, arsenic would kill Coaly. Someone tried to poison him."

Tyler scrutinized the dog. "As little as six one-hundredths of a gram can be fatal for a person, so, yes, if he ate all this, it would probably kill him. Are you sure he didn't get any?"

Breanna couldn't help wondering how he knew so much about arsenic. "Yes, I'm sure." Drying her hands, she tried to smother the fear rising in her. "Tyler, why would anyone want to kill my dog?"

He opened her drawer and pulled out a sandwich bag, depositing the meat in it and running his fingers along the Ziploc seal. "God, I don't know." Stepping past her to the sink, he pumped more water to scrub his hands, then took the towel she held out to him. "I'm going out to check the property, just to make sure there's nothing else out there."

She swept her hair back from her face. "I'll put some coffee on and get dressed."

Tyler spun on his heel and left the cabin without a backward glance. Once outside, he let loose a string of low curses. If he could have gotten his hands on the people responsible at that moment, he would have strangled them. As he walked around the yard, his anger turned to fear. They were growing desperate to get Breanna out of the way. What they might do next was anybody's guess. He had to convince her to leave. Fast. And he was forced to do it without telling her why.

By the time Breanna had finished dressing, Tyler was sitting on the lawn, basking in the morning sunlight. She poured them each a mug of coffee and went to join him. For a long while he said nothing, just stared at the road with a scowl on his face. She studied each separate angle of his features. The blade of nose jutting from his thick brows already seemed familiar to her. When he smiled, she knew exactly how his lips would quirk up at one corner in that lopsided grin of his. But for all that, she had no more idea what he was thinking than when she'd first met him.

"Breanna, I think you should leave here," he said at last, glancing over at her. "I know you hate to go, but it really would be best. Surely you see that."

"But—" She shook her head. "I can't leave."

"That's poison on that meat in there." He leveled steely eyes on her. "Somebody just tried to kill your dog. It's not safe for you to stay here."

She set her mug on the grass and hugged her knees, gazing at the undergrowth on Hungry Hill. "Tyler…I can't leave. Try to understand. Maybe from your viewpoint it looks foolish, but from mine there's no choice. When my grandmother was dying I promised her I'd come here, and I promised her I'd stay."

"What kind of a grandmother would ask that?"

Sudden, white-hot anger surged through Breanna. "What does that crack mean?"

"Exactly what it sounded like. Deathbed promises! They're the worst kind of blackmail, manipulating a person from the edge of the grave. She would never have wanted you to stay here at the risk of your safety, not if she was any kind of grandmother."

"My safety isn't in question here. The threat was to Coaly."

"Oh, and he's expendable?"

"No, he's not expendable. What's your problem? You've no right to talk to me this way."

"Oh, I don't? Maybe I care what happens to you. Maybe I'm making it my right."

"Is that so?"

"Yes, that's so."

She dug her nails into her knees and refused to look at him. "I'll take care of Coaly. I'll watch him."

"End of problem? That doesn't take care of the who. Somebody's getting nasty, real nasty. What will they do next? You think you're pretty tough right now, but what happens when the next threat's to you?"

Before she thought, she said, "There's already been a threat to me. You don't see me running, do you?"

The ensuing silence was so frigid that she felt certain a loud noise would shatter it.

"What kind of threat?"

"Nothing. It wasn't important."

"Breanna, what kind of threat?"

"Nothing! You don't have to know every little thing."

"Maybe I want to."

"And that's your problem, Mr. Ross, not mine."

He bounded to his feet, slopping hot coffee down his

leg. She saw him flinch. The denim of his jeans was soaked and steaming.

"Are you burned?" she asked anxiously.

"I'm burned, all right," he replied in a clipped tone. "I want to know what happened. Are you going to tell me? There's no crime in caring what happens to you."

"Oh, Tyler, it's not that. It's just—well, if I tell you, it'll make you all the more upset."

"So, upset me."

"It was nothing, really...."

"Bree-aann-aa?"

"Well, it really wasn't. I went down to take a bath and somebody stole my clothes."

"And? Don't stop. I can see in your eyes there's more."

"Well, when I made it back to the—"

"Made it back?"

"Well, yes, I was naked. It wasn't easy, especially without shoes."

He knelt again, being more careful of his coffee this time. "The stickers, ah yes, I remember. So you ran up to the house in your altogether?" A glint entered his eyes. "What else?"

"Well—um—when I got up here, my clothes were on the porch." In a much lower voice she added, "Slashed."

"What?"

"Slashed," she repeated, a bit more loudly.

"Slashed? With a knife, you mean?" He was talking a little more loudly, too, she noticed. Almost yelling. "Let me get this straight. You were in the creek naked. Someone stole your clothes, slashed them with a knife and left them on your porch?"

"Of course I was naked. You don't take baths with your clothes on."

"You are being deliberately obtuse. I can't believe something like that happened and you never told me about it! My

God, don't you realize—? Breanna, it could have been *you* someone took a knife to! Why the hell didn't you tell me?"

"I didn't tell you about it because I knew you'd act just like you're acting." She stood and glared down at him. "It gives you more ammunition to convince me I should leave. Well, I'm not. This is my land, and nobody, not you or anybody else, is going to run me off it."

With that, she stormed off to the house. Tyler stared after her for a moment, then sat down on the lawn, so angry with himself that he could have screamed. While he sat there, he did his best to calm down. From her viewpoint, things weren't nearly as serious as they were from his. She knew nothing of the counterfeiting. Given that fact, he could understand her thinking. He could also see why she was angry. Just who did he think he was? He had no business pushing her around, no business preaching to her, no business caring the way he cared....

He clenched his teeth. As Jack would say, he had a job to do. And he was dangerously close to losing all objectivity. He was spouting off, losing control, forgetting who he was and what she might be.

She wasn't leaving. Not that it was any big surprise. His only option now was to try to protect her. To do that, he needed to be with her. And to be with her, he had to make up with her. A humorless grin twisted his mouth.

When Tyler knocked on the door, Breanna was seated at the table braiding her hair. As she twisted it atop her head, she called "Come in!" through the hairpins she clenched between her teeth. She liked the effect, sort of a hiss.

He walked to the end of the hall, resting his shoulder against the logs. "I'd like to apologize."

She pulled one hairpin from her teeth, jammed it in her hair and slurred, "I'm listening."

"I'm sorry for sounding off. I shouldn't have. It's just

that I—well, I'm worried, that's all, about what might happen."

Taking the last hairpin out of her mouth, she finished fastening her braid. "Just as long as it's clear. I'm not leaving."

"Believe me, you made it perfectly clear."

"You won't pick at me about it anymore?"

"I don't promise that. But I won't pick at you anymore over this."

She said nothing.

"Look. How about dinner out tonight? A peace offering. Do you accept?" Coaly sat between them, tail wagging, eyes darting to each of them as they spoke. Tyler glanced down at him. "You can't disappoint him. Think how he'd miss me if you stay mad forever."

She smiled. The truth was she would miss Tyler, too. "Dinner sounds nice. One thing, though. Don't say anything derogatory about my gran again. You can say a lot of things, but never about my gran."

"Is that what got you so boiled?"

She shrugged one shoulder. "It was what started it. And once I get started, I sort of escalate. I'm sorry. I guess I overreacted."

"I didn't intend to slam your grandmother. I just think if she were here, she'd be telling you to leave, too. I'm sure she never meant to lock you into an impossible situation."

Breanna shot him a warning glare.

"And I'm equally sure she was a wonderful person," he added quickly.

"Yes, she was. The best grandmother ever."

"Not the best. *Mine* was the best." His eyes began to twinkle. "Truce? How's eight o'clock sound? We'll go to the Wolf Creek Tavern. Over dinner, maybe we can plan some kind of strategy to put a stop to this nonsense."

"That sounds a whole lot more acceptable to me than chucking everything and running."

"Somehow I kinda figured that." He leaned around the corner and lifted the plastic bag of meat from the counter. "I have a friend who can analyze this. I think I'll get it checked."

"You have a friend who analyzes poisons?"

"Yeah, a chemistry teacher at the high school. I grew up with him. See you at eight, then?"

She nodded. "I'll be ready."

Just before the door closed, he called, "Keep close tabs on Coaly in case I missed something out here."

CLOSE TABS, BREANNA DISCOVERED, meant keeping Coaly locked in the house with her while she worked. His whining nearly drove her mad, but she toughed it out, typing, dabbing white ink over her mistakes and muttering. By eleven her nerves were jagged. When she heard someone pull into the driveway, she gave such a start that she jumped up and bruised her knee on the edge of the table. Limping to the window, she looked out. A blue Ford pickup sat beside her Honda, and she glimpsed a man climbing the retainer wall steps. A moment later, a knock came on the door.

Breanna stepped into the entry hall. For a moment, she considered calling out before she opened up, but that seemed so timid that she discarded the idea and turned the knob. She had no sooner done so than she wished she had erred on the side of caution.

Chuck Morrow stood on her porch. Ten years had turned him to fat around the middle, but otherwise he seemed unchanged. His deadpan brown eyes slid over her. He smiled the same sneering smile. And, as before, he managed to make her feel violated just by looking at her. Breanna's stomach lurched.

"What do you want?" she asked.

Her heart leaped when he put a boot on her threshold and braced a shoulder against the jamb. Instinctively she stepped back, wedging herself between the door and the wall to keep Coaly in the house.

"I just came to chat." He spoke barely above a whisper, his tone low and suggestive.

She tightened her hold on the knob. "Get lost, Chuck."

"Forget that. It's time we got down to business. Dane tells me you've been snoopin', reading all the old news stories about the fire. That true?"

"What's it to you?"

"The way I see it, you know all you need to know. I put my neck on the chopping block for you, lied for you. I don't like it too good, you coming back and rehashing everything now. The way I see it, if you screw around and get yourself arrested again for that arson, I'll be sent up as an accomplice. That would make me mad. And you don't want to make me mad."

Breanna looked him straight in the eye. She knew he was trying to frighten her, bully her, the way he had before. That was Chuck's style. He tried to control people, using their fears as leverage. It had worked ten years ago. He was hoping she'd react the same way now, either by leaving or acquiescing to his demands. But she wasn't a kid anymore. She was a woman who could see Chuck Morrow for the lowlife he really was.

"To be quite frank, I don't care one way or another if you're mad, Chuck."

"You better care, missy. You owe me. Maybe I'm here to collect."

Anger tightened her throat. "I beg your pardon?"

"If I was to go to the police, even now, and tell them you weren't with me that night, that only Dane was, why you'd be in jail so fast your head'd spin. Way I see it, you wouldn't like that, being locked up. I'm doin' you a big favor. Seems like you'd treat me nice and make it worth my while. Some excitement a couple of times a week, maybe, a little TLC. Keep me happy, make me feel appreciated for puttin' myself out for you."

Breanna tipped her head toward him. "So it's excitement you want, huh? Why, Chuck, you've come to the right lady for that. I'll give you more than you ever dreamed."

She leaned a little closer, winked coyly, and opened the door for Coaly. The dog cannoned out of the door like a bean from a slingshot, snarling viciously. Breanna nabbed him by the collar just in the nick of time, halting his forward thrust. Chuck sprang backward, his attention riveted on the dog. "Is that exciting enough for you, Chuck, or would you like more?"

It gave her no end of satisfaction to see the man scramble to get away from her. "You're crazy. You're a crazy woman!"

"More woman than you can handle, that's for sure. Now you get your slimy little carcass off my place! Is that clear? And don't come back. You do, and I'll let Coaly loose next time."

"That damned dog's a hazard, that's what," he muttered, staring at Coaly. "I thought he was dead. He *will* be. That's a promise you can bank on, sister." He staggered down the steps, jabbing a finger at her. "Sic him on me and I'll shoot the little monster."

Chuck leaped into his truck, gunned the motor and reversed up the drive. A cloud of red dust rose in his wake. Breanna sank onto the porch. Her legs felt like half-set Jell-O.

She stroked Coaly's head, looking into his eyes. A sweeter, gentler dog there never was, yet in the last week she had seen him launch three vicious attacks. He had always been protective. He had always been a growler. But, contrary to what she had told Tyler at first, he had never bitten anyone before coming here. Now, all of a sudden, he had turned mean. There had to be a reason. Could he sense danger here that she couldn't?

Adding up all the facts, she had very little to go on, but it was enough. She had seen Chuck on her property late at night. He had by his own admission been speaking to Dane. And, as he left just now, he had muttered that he thought Coaly was dead. Like it or not, she had to face it; Chuck Morrow was at the root of her troubles.

And she knew from experience that any trouble Chuck Morrow stirred up was bound to be ugly.

CHAPTER NINE

AT FIVE-THIRTY, BREANNA headed for the creek to wash her hair before her date with Tyler. After her last bath, she felt too nervous for anything more than a quick shampoo. This time if anyone crept up on her, she would be fully dressed and able to run.

As she worked her way through the brush, she heard Coaly yelping back at the cabin. She would have liked to bring him along, but it was too risky. Finding the poisoned meat this morning, and hearing Chuck's threats since then, she didn't want him wandering while she wasn't watching.

Kneeling on the diving rock, she unfastened her braid. Her reflection shimmered on the surface of the water, and she turned her face to see it at a different angle. Her blue silk dress would do nicely for dinner, she decided. Her strand of pearls and white heels would—

Her heart leaped into her throat. A face shimmered beside hers on the water. Not a human face, though. The other reflection was straight out of a child's nightmare, black, featureless, with great, gaping holes where the eyes should have been.

For a moment fear paralyzed her. She couldn't move, couldn't scream. By the time she'd collected her wits, it was too late. A hand slammed into her back, launching her headfirst into the water. The blackness of the bathing hole surrounded her. Water seared her throat; burned into her lungs. She flailed her arms, clawing for the glow of sunlight above her.

Breaking the surface, she thrashed about, aiming for the rock, but her attacker still stood upon it, one arm extended toward her, a scythe clutched in his hand. She stared at the long, curved blade, at the gleam of its sharp edge. The man's intention was clear; if she left the water, he meant to kill her.

It *was* a man. Even as she struggled for air, she realized the face she had seen had been human, after all, disguised in a black ski mask. He wore a black overcoat to conceal his body build. She stared up at him. Who was he? And why was he doing this?

The weight of her clothes and shoes was dragging her down. Breanna kicked frantically, making figure eights with her arms to stay afloat. She knew she couldn't stay in the deep pool long. If the cold didn't overcome her, exhaustion would. The man strode along the diving rock back to shore, then stepped into the copse. He had no sooner disappeared into the trees than Breanna swam toward the opposite bank. She could find a handhold in the tree roots and escape into the woods.

She had only moved a few feet toward the bank when a rock splashed beside her. Glancing back over her shoulder, she saw the man had emerged again. He stood at the water's edge, his arm drawn back, the scythe a gleaming arc over his head. He didn't speak, but the threat was clear. If she went anywhere near the far bank, he would come after her.

She was trapped.

The man stepped back into the brush, but she could still see his silhouette. He stood there, watching, waiting. Her blood thrummed in her temples. Even in the freezing water, she could feel sweat break out on her brow. The current tugged at her legs. She fought to keep her chin up, paddling backward, praying her toes would touch bottom. The man leaped from the brush, moving to aim the scythe at her. He wanted her in deep water? She took a mouthful, choking, fighting to get her chin high. Oh, God, he wanted her to drown!

Could he hit her? The stream wasn't that wide. He wouldn't have to throw the scythe far. She imagined the blade sinking into her skull, imagined dying there in the bathing pool where she had played as a child. As long as she stayed in the center of the stream, he didn't threaten her. As terrifying as drowning was, Breanna preferred that to being gaffed like a fish. Again the man stepped back into the copse, barely visible.

He waited like a sentinel standing guard. She realized he was going to wait until she sank....

Stay calm, she thought. "Who are you? What do you want?"

No answer. She trod water, her chin bobbing against the ripples. Her shoes felt like lead weights on her feet, heavier and heavier with each kick. Exhaustion was setting in quickly and still the man stood there. She began to feel cold. *Oh, God, so cold.* It seemed to her that hours passed. She knew she had to find something to hold on to soon to keep from sinking. But she couldn't. The man's profile was clearly visible against the patches of light behind him, a black hulk, staring, not moving.

Shudders began to rack her. Spasms followed. Then after a while, even that passed. Numbness settled in. Her arms and legs felt like stiff rubber.

As dusk settled over the mountains, she panicked. "Go away!" she pleaded. "Go away, whoever you are! Go away, do you hear?"

She couldn't be sure, but she thought she heard low laughter. Why? Who could hate her so much that he would enjoy seeing her die?

Later, when the sky had lost nearly all its light, Breanna heard footsteps approaching in the brush. A low creaking noise drifted toward her.

"Bree? Yo? You down here?" Tyler's familiar voice boomed, ricocheting back and forth along the creek. Nothing had ever sounded quite so good to her. "Bree? You down here?"

"Tyler?" Her voice came out in a wail. "I'm in the creek."

He emerged from the tangle of undergrowth, becoming recognizable as he drew nearer. Neatly pleated gray slacks, a white shirt, a tweed jacket. Breanna sobbed and windmilled her numb arms, swimming clumsily forward against the current.

"Breanna, what the hell?"

"Watch out! Behind you! He's behind you!" Her feet scraped bottom, and she staggered toward him. "He's got a scythe, Tyler."

Whirling, Tyler crouched to defend himself and the woman behind him. No one was there. He relaxed slightly, then Breanna's sobs reclaimed his attention. He turned to look at her. What he saw scared him. Her face had a blue cast to it. Her lips were purple. But what concerned him most was that she wasn't shivering. Her body temperature must be dangerously low.

"He's in there. He'll kill us."

She ended the sentence with a low whimper and fell sideways in the stream, too weak to stand. He swore under his breath and waded out to her, lifting her to carry her to shore. Water cascaded from her clothes, soaking him from the chest down. Shifting her slightly, he shrugged out of his jacket and wrapped it around her. "It's all right. If someone was there, he's gone, sweetheart. Damn, you're like ice. How long have you been in here?"

Breanna tried to hug his neck, but her arms were deadweights. She pressed her cheek to his shoulder, so glad for his warmth that she began to cry.

"He came—behind me—out of nowhere, pushed me in. Wouldn't let me out. I was getting so tired."

"My God!" he whispered, pressing a wonderfully hot mouth to her forehead. "I'll kill the bastards for this."

Breanna shrank as close to him as she could get. She was so exhausted, so cold. Knowing he was there, that she was safe, seemed like a miracle. And she *was* safe with Tyler. Just the way he held her told her that.

He carried her to the cabin and shouldered his way through the door, heading directly for the bedroom. Pushing the doorway curtain aside, he stepped in and lowered her feet to the floor, holding her by her arms for a moment to be sure she could stand. There were towels folded on the open shelving. He grabbed one and began peeling her clothes off of her.

Breanna felt no trace of embarrassment, only relief. Limp relief. Her awareness centered on him—the deft touch of his hands, the warmth of them against her skin, the solid wall of his chest holding her upright. She was barely conscious of her nakedness as he dropped her shirt to the floor. Next, he tugged her jeans over her hips, set her on the bed and peeled them down her legs, taking her shoes off with them.

"I thought I was going to die."

He lifted her to her feet again, rubbing her briskly with the towel, taking care not to touch the manzanita scratches on her back. In the dusky light she could see the worry in his eyes. "The main thing is to get you warm. Did he hurt you?"

"N-no."

"How long were you in there?"

"T-two hours, I th-think."

"I swear to God, if I ever get my hands on the creep, I'll kill him."

"T-Ty...I—I'm s-so c-cold."

"There, you're halfway dry, at least." He lifted the bed covers to deposit her beneath them. "I'll go light a fire."

While he was gone, Breanna huddled between the sheets and longed for his warm arms. She was shaking convulsively now. She heard the clatter of kindling and the rustle of paper, then a soft whoosh of flame when Tyler struck a match to it. Amber patterns of light danced on the doorway curtain. He returned to the room, rifling through her stacks of clothing on the shelves until he found one of her flannel nightgowns.

"My l-logger socks. Th-there on the bottom shelf, the g-gray ones with r-red tops. My feet are so cold I can't f-feel them."

"Honey, don't try to talk." He stepped toward her with the gown. "Sit up and I'll get this over your head."

She held the sheet to her breasts, releasing it with one hand while she shoved an arm down each sleeve. That alone was quite a feat, considering how badly she was shaking. The soft flannel felt dry and warm. Tyler pulled one of her feet at a time from beneath the covers, slipping the socks over her toes.

"Oh, Tyler, I'm s-so c-cold, so h-horribly c-cold."

Huddling on her side, she cinched her arms around herself, clinging to what little heat she had left. Tyler's shoes thunked on the floor, and she heard the change jangling in his slacks as he pulled them off. He untucked the other pillow and threw back the covers. She felt the mattress sink with his weight.

"Come here, sweetheart."

Breanna tried to speak, but the moment she did, her teeth clacked. He drew her head to the hollow of his shoulder. Both his arms encircled her, one around her back so that he could rub her side, the other over her hip to massage the backs of her thighs. She rolled toward him, desperate for his heat.

"You're chilled clear to the bone. It's lucky I came when I did. I can feel the cold coming clear through your gown."

Breanna had given up talking.

"Much longer and…" She felt a tenseness sweep through him. "The shaking's a good sign," he whispered. "Your body's trying to warm itself. Damn, Bree, you're so cold it's scary. Hypothermia is no joke. You don't feel numb anywhere besides your feet, do you?"

"Y-yes." Her teeth immediately chattered and she clenched them shut again.

"Where, Breanna? Your legs? Your arms?"

It took an effort to nod.

Tyler swore under his breath and sat bolt upright, flipping around onto his knees. His hands dived under the covers to strip off her socks, then he clutched the hem of her nightgown. Her eyes flew open when he slid the cloth up her body.

"No arguments," he muttered. "It's coming off."

He seized her by the shoulders, sat her up and tugged the gown over her head, tossing it aside. When he lay down again, the shock of his hot skin against her cold breasts made her breath catch. His arms encircled her. It seemed to her his hands were everywhere, rubbing her buttocks, the backs of her thighs, her shoulders, rubbing so hard, so vigorously that her skin burned.

"T-T-Ty-ler!" she protested.

"Hush," he whispered, draping one of his legs over hers to run his foot up and down her calf. "It's okay, it's okay."

"B-but it h-hurts. It b-burns."

"I know. It'll stop after a while. Shh, sweetheart. Just get close so I can get you warm."

Breanna turned her face into the curve of his neck, breathing in the musky, steamy heat of his skin. *Tyler*. She drifted, sinking ever deeper into the swirling heat that radiated from him. And without realizing it, without knowing exactly when, she finally stopped shaking and slept.

MUCH LATER, SHE WOKE, blinking in confusion, her face pressed so snugly into the hollow of Tyler's shoulder that her lashes fluttered against his skin. Her lips had parted in slumber and when she explored with the tip of her tongue, she tasted saltiness. *Tyler's chest.* Her mind cleared and she stiffened. *God, he's wrapped around me like a sarong.*

"Don't panic. We've been like this for hours." His breath was warm on the top of her head, his lips feathering against her hair. "You've been snoring like a little buzz saw."

She lifted her chin. "I don't snore."

He laughed and rolled with her, coming up on one elbow, his broad chest canopied over hers. "You most certainly do, Miss Morgan. But it's a very appealing snore."

Breanna swallowed and her larynx plunked in the base of her throat like a pebble hitting a still pool of water. Every fractional inch of movement, hers or his, stimulated her nipples. The muscle in Tyler's jaw ticked. She could see it going a mile a minute in the silver moonlight, a shadow, then gone. His eyes met hers, shimmering pools of gray.

"Feeling better?"

"Yes," she replied in a strained whisper.

"Is all the numbness gone?"

"Yes."

He smoothed her hair from her cheek, his touch so light, so slow that she was sure her heart stopped beating for a second. And it seemed to her that his face had drawn closer.

"I was so scared," he whispered. "So scared. I've never felt so…" His face tightened, his gaze delving into hers. A long silence followed, wrapping around them like a warm cocoon. "Bree?"

"Yes?"

Gazing up at his dark countenance, at the now-familiar

line of his jaw and his squared chin, Breanna knew what he was asking. Her reply was to touch his cheek, trailing her fingers to his mouth. For a long moment they looked into each other's eyes. Then he lowered his head, brushing her lips with his.

An indescribable sweetness unfurled inside Breanna. It was too late to ask herself questions. Perhaps her narrow escape from death was making her reckless. Maybe it was waking in his arms, feeling his body pressed against hers. All she knew was that she needed him. For now, there was only the moonlight—and Tyler.

He came to her as if in a dream. A slow, languorous dream that slowly built in intensity. Their bodies melded as if they had been made for each other. No shyness, no awkwardness, no sense of strangeness. Only an indescribable pleasure that lifted them on its swells to higher and higher peaks. Joined with him, she felt a sense of completeness she had never experienced before.

Afterward, he held her, stroking her hair, pressing gentle kisses to her forehead. She relaxed against him, feeling blissfully content. The way he touched her made her feel treasured, and that, more than anything he could have said, told her that what had happened between them was as special to him as it was to her.

He curled around her and slept, his dark face buried in the drapery of her hair upon the pillow. She ran light fingers down the length of his muscular arm. His name whispered like a lullaby in her mind until she fell asleep.

WHEN BREANNA WOKE AGAIN, Tyler was no longer beside her. It was still dark beyond the window, but the doorway curtain danced with golden firelight. The inviting crackle of burning logs enticed her from the bed. She found her nightgown and logger socks, slipped them on, then tiptoed to the curtain, lifting it to peek out.

Tyler sat before the hearth, one arm resting loosely on an upraised knee. He wore only his slacks, and the dancing amber of the firelight burnished his skin to bronze. Sensing her presence, he glanced around and lifted an arm to beckon her to his side. Breanna needed no further invitation. When she lowered herself to the rug, he cuddled her close, tracing circles on her arm through her flannel sleeve.

"I've been sitting here daydreaming about murder," he told her with a low laugh. "I wish I could have caught that son of a bitch."

"Didn't you see him?" she squeaked. "He had to have left right when you showed up."

"No, I didn't see a soul. Of course, I wasn't looking for anyone except you on the way down. Which direction did he come from? Do you know?"

"He came up behind me and pushed me in."

"Can you identify him?"

"No, he was wearing a black ski mask and overcoat." Catching her lower lip between her teeth, she stared into the fire. "I can't be sure who it was."

"Something's troubling you. What? This is no time to keep secrets, Bree."

She lifted her face. His hovered a scant inch away, cast into shadow by the firelight. For the first time since she had known him, his eyes didn't have that shuttered look. They ached with readable emotion, his fear for her underscoring all else.

"It's just that—" Breaking off, she sighed, took a bracing breath and averted her gaze so she needn't look at him. "Chuck Morrow paid me a visit today. He was rather unpleasant and I can't help but wonder…"

"If it could have been him? My God, Bree, why would he—?"

"Ten years ago, we had a very similar conversation and

I ran away. I think he hoped the same tactics would work again."

"What kind of tactics?"

She leaned against his warmth, drawing strength from him. His arms crisscrossed around her. He rubbed her skin through the sleeves of her gown, massaging her, patting her, his every touch a comfort. "Remember, I told you Chuck came around asking favors? Of Dane? Well, he made demands on me, too. He tried to make me sleep with him. He said he'd tell the police the truth if I didn't do it."

"Oh, damn," Tyler moaned, "that rotten bastard."

"I—I was so scared by then that I went clear up into the loft with him. Dane begged me to do whatever he said. And then he threatened me if I didn't. He was more terrified of Chuck than I was."

"How did Dane threaten you?"

"He said they'd tell the police *I* set the blaze."

"And what did you do?" His hands clenched on her arm. "Up in the loft, Bree. With Morrow?"

The memories flashed in Breanna's mind, ugly, horribly real, as clear as yesterday. "I couldn't bear for him to touch me. He kissed me...pushed his tongue in my mouth. I'd never been kissed like that before."

"Of course you hadn't."

"It made me feel sick. I realized, almost too late, that jail would be preferable to having his hands on me and I ran."

Tyler lifted a hand to her hair, stroking it. "What kind of man would use leverage like that on a young girl?" His whisper was ragged. "Ah, Breanna, no wonder you ran from the memories for so many years. Who would blame you?"

"Dane," she whispered. "We were never friends again. I couldn't forgive him for standing down at the door of the barn, watching to be sure Gramps didn't come. He didn't care about me, Tyler, or about Rob. All he cared about was himself."

Silence fell over them for a moment, then he said, "I have a feeling Dane has paid dearly for hurting you, Bree."

"How has Dane paid? The only thing he lost was my friendship and I don't think he misses it. Dane has everything, fancy clothes, an expensive car, a beautiful home and family."

"If Morrow tried to blackmail you, don't you suppose he's asked similar favors of Dane over the years?"

The thought made her shiver. Knowing how low Chuck Morrow could stoop, it was entirely possible. "What kind of favors, though? What could Dane give him that he would want?"

A tense silence followed. "Who knows?" Tyler replied. "I just have a feeling. How was that fire set? I know I read about it, but I can't recall."

"Cans of gas, stashed in the brush around the hippie commune. Someone put a dynamite cap over the mouth of one, set the fuse and ran. When the fumes in the one can exploded, the resulting fire set off the others."

"A person would need a permit to get a dynamite cap."

"Not if you were the grandson of a retired miner."

"You really believe Dane did it, don't you?"

A faint memory invaded Breanna's mind. *Gas.* She had a vague recollection of driving to town with Dane in Gramps's Jeep, filling the back with red cans. The muscles in her stomach tightened. When had they done that?

She pressed closer to Tyler, suddenly cold. "Oh, Tyler, I don't know. Dane was a good kid. Not mean. He might have set a little fire…as a prank…but I can't imagine him trying to light the whole mountain. He knew how tinderdry the woods got."

"You may never know the truth," he told her. "Morrow—he didn't hurt you when he came this time?"

"No, I handled him. I don't expect him back anytime soon."

Quiet settled over them, the minutes passing, the warmth of the fire and Tyler's presence soothing her. Breanna stared at the orange embers. *The gas.* Why couldn't she remember? Had it been for Gramps, for Chuck Morrow? Was it the gas used to set the Reuben Creek blaze? Her head began aching again. She had to find out, she had to. The only way to do that was to arrange a meeting with Dane and ask him flat out. Even if he wouldn't tell her, she knew him well enough to read him. If the questions scared him, then she'd know....

"Bree, don't get angry." Tyler's hand tensed, pressing hard against her arm. "I have to say it one more time. *Leave.* Go stay in town, at least for a while. Please. You could have been seriously hurt tonight. Let me drive you to town, your parents' place...anywhere."

"Oh, Tyler. I know you're right. And I'm scared, really scared. But now it's even more important than before that I stand my ground. Don't you see? I ran before. I've lived with it for ten years, never escaping it. If I don't see it through this time, I'll be running from the truth for the rest of my life. Try to understand."

"I do understand. I hate to admit it, but if it were me, I'd stay, too." He sighed. "Okay, lady. You want to stand your ground and fight back? I just volunteered for the infantry."

She smiled. "What does that mean?"

"It means you have a new roommate. Mind? No more baths alone, no more staying alone here nights."

"I *should* say thanks but no thanks. It's an awful imposition on you."

"What are friends for? Besides, you couldn't pry me away from here with a crowbar, not after tonight. I say we check out that brush by the creek come daylight, find out where our friendly scythe carrier came from. Seems like the first move to make. Agreed?"

"Agreed. Oh, Tyler, I'm glad you're here."

His mouth moved next to her ear, whisper light. "Me, too."

She tipped her head back to look at him. "You know, there is another possibility we haven't considered. Last night by the creek it could have been the ghost."

"Old John, guarding his treasure? Come on, Bree, you're just upset, strung out. You can't believe that."

"What if he did find the mother lode?" she whispered. "Is it so farfetched?"

"Honey..."

"I know I'm upset. It did frighten me. It's just that he seemed to come out of nowhere and disappear the same way. You didn't see him, did you?"

"No, but there's so much brush, you can hide quite easily. Remember the evening I met you? I was right at the edge of the property and you couldn't see me. Tell you what. We'll save the ghost theory as a last resort, until after we check the brush. I'm fairly sure we'll find evidence that your friend was a real live creep, not a dead one."

Breanna hoped he was right.

CHAPTER TEN

DAYLIGHT FOUND BREANNA and Tyler circling the copse. Tyler walked from the brush to the diving rock, studying the footprints, his face creased in a scowl. "I don't understand it," he said, propping his hands on his hips. "We can see where he stood in the copse. His tracks come out to the rock and go back. So why the hell isn't there any sign showing what direction he came from? It doesn't make sense."

Sinking to a log, Breanna braced her elbows on her knees. "It does if you think ghost."

"Oh, come on. He didn't disappear into thin air. There's a perfectly reasonable explanation. We're just overlooking it."

"What is it then?"

Tyler strode back to the copse, staring at the circle of prints that led to the bank and vanished. The trees there weren't big enough for climbing. "I don't know. It'll come to me. But it wasn't a ghost, that's for damned sure."

Breanna rose from the log, brushing bark from the seat of her jeans. "You're right. I know you're right. But the kid in me is getting spooked. This is the second time!"

"Bree, say it was John Van Patten? Hell, I'm open-minded. Let's say he haunts the place, guarding his treasure trove. If he did, you'd be the last person he'd harm. You're a Van Patten. He'd want you to find it."

"That's probably true."

Their eyes met, and Tyler started to laugh. "I can't believe this. I'm actually standing here talking about spooks as if they're real. Come on, let's go to my place and pack my things."

She threw one last glance at the ground as they left, hoping against hope she'd spy something both of them had missed.

Tyler slowed his pace so Breanna could catch up, draping an arm across her shoulders. "I tell you what. Let's go on this assumption. Say it's treasure seekers, like you suspected before, acting out the ghost legend to scare you away. The only way to put a stop to it is prove there's no gold, right?"

She nodded, not quite sure what his line of reasoning was.

"Okay, so let's do it," he said.

"Do what?"

"Prove, for once and for all, there is no gold. We'll go all out, use the maps, rent a metal detector, dig all over God's creation. And we'll tell everybody we see that we're looking. If it's treasure hunters doing all this, when we find nothing, they'll give up and leave you alone."

"Mr. Ross, I hate to burst your bubble, but whom do we ever see to tell? I mean, it's a good idea, but this isn't exactly a metropolis out here."

"We can start tonight in Wolf Creek."

"Wolf Creek?"

"Yeah, yesterday's dinner, remember? We'll go tonight. Talk loud. Tell everybody we meet. And then tomorrow, we'll go to town, get a metal detector, make a big deal out of it. The treasure hunters will hear. Rumors travel like wildfire."

"I suppose it might work. Okay, let's try it."

A smile settled on Breanna's mouth as she fell into step with Tyler. She wasn't sure treasure hunters were her problem, not after the things Chuck and Dane had said, but going along with the idea would assure her of Tyler's company. After last night, she was running a little short on bravado. With Tyler along as her backup, tonight would be an ideal time to ask Dane about that gas they had bought years ago, too. She would find a pay phone and give her cousin a call. If he wasn't home, she could leave a message with his wife, Nan, saying she would be in Wolf Creek most of the evening and needed to see him.

WHEN TYLER OPENED the front door to his cabin and led Breanna inside, she hid a smile. Natural wood tones and leather. It pleased her that he liked down-to-basics living. It gave them something else in common. The kitchen area was clean. A four-place set of brown earthenware dishes shone on the open shelving. The top of the gas cooking range was scrubbed and shining white. His small dining table was positioned in the center of the rectangular room, flanked by the kitchen and the small living area, which boasted a leather sofa, a matching chair and a neatly made bed.

Coaly flopped just inside the door, and Tyler motioned her toward the ranch-style sofa. "Grab a seat."

Breanna chose a straight-backed kitchen chair instead, drawn by the array of radio equipment that crowded half the tabletop. Citizen band? She didn't know much about shortwave communication, but the paraphernalia spread out before her looked too sophisticated for a simple CB base unit. Propping one elbow on the arm of her chair, she leaned forward. An unpleasant odor drifted to her. Next to the radio she spied a brimming ashtray.

"Tyler, I didn't know you smoked."

"I don't. Oh, that's Jack's."

"Jack?"

"Yeah, my partner. He comes down to work now and again."

"Oh, I see." She pushed the ashtray to one side and refocused her attention on the radio. "Do you mind if I turn this on and talk?"

Tyler glanced up from where he was taking jeans off a shelf. "Yes, I do. Please don't touch it."

His tone was so curt that she jerked her hand away from the power button. "I wouldn't break anything."

"It's for emergency use only." It was so unlike him to speak harshly that all she could do was stare. He must have seen how hurt she was; he shrugged offhandedly and turned away from the shelf where he was gathering clothes. "Someday when we're not pressed for time, maybe I'll teach you to operate it. Would you like that?"

"Are we in a hurry?"

"Dinner out, remember? If we're going, we have to get cracking." He sighed and strode toward her. Tossing down a pair of jeans near the radio, he placed his hands on the chair arms to lean down and kiss her forehead. "I'm sorry, Bree. It's expensive equipment, that's all. I have the frequencies all set and the antenna just so. With no phone, it's a lifeline in case of emergency. You can understand, can't you?"

"That's fine. It's yours. I respect that."

He cupped her chin in his hand. "Accept my apology?"

The sincerity in his expression was irresistible. A smile tugged at the corners of her mouth, and his answering grin brought it to full bloom. "Accepted. With my luck, I'll be the emergency."

"Come help me pack," he said, taking her hand to pull her from the chair.

Breanna stowed his things in a bag while he finished selecting an assortment of clothing off the shelves.

"I'm taking you dancing tonight," he announced. "You do dance?"

"I'll dance you under the table."

"Oh, no, I'm not talking fast stuff." He cast her a teasing grin as he walked to the closet. "I mean romantic dancing."

"Oh, that kind." She picked up a pair of socks and put them in the bag, then strolled toward him.

He opened his closet, and Breanna's eyes widened. On the inside panel of the door, in a very carefully arranged order, was a host of pictures. Her own image stared back at her, some frontal shots, some full-length of herself walking across her orchard. Below them, he had printed *Breanna Van Patten Morgan* on an index card in bold, black letters. There was even a picture of Coaly, with *Bites* scrawled on the bottom edge of the photograph.

Tyler had no sooner opened the door than he tensed. It was so obvious that he had forgotten the gallery of photos that it almost struck her as funny. Almost. It was so strange a collection and so painstakingly displayed that it sent a chill over her instead. Why? What had possessed him to take all those shots of her and her dog?

Her gaze flew to a cardboard poster that stood just inside the closet. Pictures of her claim? Breanna couldn't believe what she was seeing. The layout was extensive, done almost like a map, each photo labeled. Tyler...

He took some clothing off hangers and pushed the door shut with a loud click. The muscle in his jaw ticked as his eyes met hers. "I was fascinated with the subject matter."

Fascinated? He had clearly marked off her land, almost as if he had staked it out. But why? And when?

"Breanna..." He looked down at her for the longest time, then sighed in defeat.

"Why did you take all those pictures?"

"I needed an exact layout of the property for my observations. I use the orchards all the time for my animal studies. You know that. You use maps, don't you?"

"Yes, but—why did you need an exact layout of me?"

"I've wanted an exact layout of you since the moment I first saw you."

"You expect me to believe that?"

"I'm asking you to," he said simply.

"And what if I don't buy it?"

"I know it seems a little peculiar, Bree, but why wouldn't you buy it? I've got no reason to lie, do I?"

"Tyler..." She watched him carefully, trying to gauge his reactions. "I—I'm beginning to care for you, you realize that? You wouldn't use me to cover looking for the gold?"

She relaxed when his gaze didn't waver from hers. "No, Bree, I'm not looking for the gold. The gold? You don't believe that."

"But Tyler, the pictures. Why did you put them on a poster like that?"

He sighed and ran his hand over his hair. "Well, when I put them up, I barely knew you. I took the pictures on a lark, then when I developed them, I thought I might as well use them, so I did a layout. Sometimes I work with a partner. Not often, but I have been doing that here the last couple of months. And since I quite often use the blind in the orchard, I didn't see any harm in doing a spread for him, so he'd know how the land was situated in relation to the cabin." He shrugged his shoulders. "The pictures of you were so he'd know you if he saw you. And the ones of Coaly are pretty self-explanatory. I didn't want Jack getting his leg chewed off."

Now that he had explained it to her, it all made perfect sense. Only moments ago, he had mentioned Jack, his partner. The ashtray was further proof the man worked with him. Tyler was a photographer, after all. He probably snapped pictures of just about anything if the mood struck him, much as she did with her writing, doodling notes and sketching stories.

"Oh, Tyler, I'm sorry. I don't know why I'm acting this way."

He toyed with a stray curl at her temple, his wrist warm

against her cheek. "Don't say you're sorry. You had a rough time last night. I understand that. You're not yourself."

"That's no excuse for—" She laughed softly. "I'm sorry."

He touched a fingertip to her mouth. "I just said don't say you're sorry. You know, we'd better hurry. As it is, I'll barely be unpacked before it's time to get ready to go to Wolf Creek."

Breanna nodded and reached for his satchel on the bed. "Do you have everything you need?"

His gaze rested on her for a long moment. "Everything," he said softly.

THE WOLF CREEK TAVERN was a relic of the past, a huge white building in Colonial-style, with tall columns rising from the veranda to support a graceful, full-length balcony. Because of the periodic shutdowns for repairs over the years, Breanna had never visited the inn. She caught her breath in awe when they entered the central hall, gazing appreciatively at the red oak graining on the wainscoting and doors.

"Gorgeous," she whispered.

"I'll second that." Tyler's gaze trailed from her upswept hair to her blue silk dress, warming with appreciation. "You look fantastic."

He looked pretty good himself. In his black slacks and charcoal-gray shirt, he was easily the most attractive man she had ever known. And the nicest one. While they waited for the hostess, he gave her a mini-tour of the ladies' parlor and the men's sitting room on the ground floor, entertaining her with stories about famous people who had frequented the place.

"Ah, here comes the hostess," he said, interrupting himself and taking Breanna's arm. "Now comes the best part, the food."

They stepped back into the central hall, following the waitress to a large, rustic dining room. After they were seated, Tyler ordered coffee, then smiled at her. "The manicotti here is out of this world."

It sounded good to her, so she agreed with a nod, then glanced over her shoulder to check the door, half expecting Dane to appear.

"Looking for someone?" Tyler asked.

"Yes, as a matter of fact. I called Dane's while you were getting gas. I need to talk to him. I told his wife we'd be in town most of the evening, so I'm kind of hoping he'll pop up."

"We should be easy enough to find." Tyler smiled. "In Wolf Creek there aren't too many places we could be. Right?"

When the waitress returned, Tyler placed their order and chose a wine. Before the woman left, he asked, "By the way, is there a rental outfit in Wolf Creek? We'd like to get a metal detector."

The waitress's brown eyes filled with curiosity. "No. You'd have to go clear to Grants Pass, I imagine."

"We're treasure hunting. You know of the Van Patten place, down Graves Creek?"

"Anybody who's lived around here long knows the Van Patten place. Why?"

"There's supposed to be a fortune in gold buried down there." Inclining his head toward Breanna, he added, "She's a Van Patten."

"Sounds exciting," the woman said enthusiastically.

Breanna couldn't help but notice that Tyler's good looks were stimulating a lot more interest in the waitress than his talk of buried gold. Of course, natives of Wolf Creek were accustomed to tales of stashed treasure.

"How sure are you that there's something there?" the waitress asked.

"About as sure as you can get." Tyler left it at that, lifting an eyebrow for emphasis.

"Well, I wish you all the luck."

"Just keep it under your hat," he said in a stage whisper. "We don't want word getting out. You know?"

After the waitress had left, Breanna leaned forward over her steaming cup of coffee. "Now, why did you say that? I thought the idea was to spread the word all over town?"

"That *is* the idea." His eyes twinkled with devilment. "Don't you know the quickest way to get a woman to repeat something is to ask her not to?"

"Oh, those are fighting words, Mr. Ross."

He winked at her over the rim of his cup.

AFTER A DELICIOUS MEAL, Tyler led Breanna through the parking lot to the car. As he opened the passenger door for her, she glanced up to find him looking at her with a strange, almost sad expression on his face. The iridescent glow from the light poles in the parking lot glistened on his dark hair.

"Is something wrong?"

He smiled and ran his knuckles along her cheek. "No. I was just thinking how much I enjoy being with you, that's all."

At a loss for words, she slid into the seat. He closed the door and came around to the driver's side, climbing behind the wheel. "Now where?" he asked.

"Not home?"

"This early? I promised to take you dancing. And it sure couldn't hurt to pass the word at one more place about our treasure hunt."

Trying to recapture her earlier lightheartedness, she teased, "Wanna print up a notice and pass it out?"

"No, I think telling one more woman ought to do the trick."

Breanna groaned at that remark, then burst into laughter.

DANE VAN PATTEN ROLLED DOWN his window to get some fresh air. Chuck smoked one cigarette after another, filling the Corvette with smoke. The smell of chicken-fried steak from a nearby café's exhaust fans wafted through the night air, mingling with the scent of pine from the surrounding hillsides.

"There she is," Chuck whispered, leaning forward to peer through the windshield as a car pulled up near the café. "With some man, dammit."

Dane tensed, focusing on the parking lot across the highway. "It's too far away. I can't tell who the guy is. What should we do? Wait?"

"Hell, no! We don't wait. If she's suspicious, I want to know it."

Dane opened his door to climb out. "Did it ever occur to you that maybe I didn't lose the money at her place? That it might have been some other woman fitting the same description?"

"That's what we're fixin' to find out, isn't it?" Chuck slammed his door and circled the front fender of the car.

"And if it was her? If she's on to us, then what?"

"Use your imagination."

THE SMALL CAFÉ WAS QUIET and its jukebox supplied Breanna and Tyler with the music they needed for dancing. Beyond that, nothing mattered. Tyler scooted two tables aside to provide them with floor space and wrapped both arms around her, nudging hers around his neck. Body to body, hardness cradling softness, they swayed, oblivious to everything around them. Breanna found herself forgetting all about Dane.

Tyler bent his head, pulling Breanna closer. As his eyes drifted shut, a dozen images of her flashed behind his lids. His arms trembled, and he cinched them tighter. Time was closing in on them, and he felt as though he were sinking in quicksand. Each second with Breanna might be the last. If she was involved in the counterfeiting, she would never forgive him when Jack started making arrests. And he couldn't blame her. He had committed the unforgivable sin, done the one thing he had always sworn he'd never do. He was intimately involved with a suspect. When the truth came out, she'd never believe he hadn't intended it this way, that he hadn't used her, trying to get information. And how could he convince her otherwise when he wasn't sure of his motives himself?

Raising his lashes, he studied the curve of her cheek, the soft fullness of her mouth. Like hell, he wasn't sure of his motives. He'd fallen in love with her. And that wouldn't make his job any easier. Was he out of his mind? If Jack was right, she might be a liar, a con artist, a thief, even a killer. How could he forget that, even for an instant?

She opened her eyes, and he found the answer to his question when he looked into those deep pools of soft blue. When he was with her he forgot everything, everything but the tenderness she evoked in him. Maybe Jack was right, but Tyler didn't think so. Even her agreeing to the treasure hunt was testimony to her innocence. If she were a counterfeiter, the last thing she'd want would be someone snooping around on the property.

A slight frown drew her brows together. "What are you thinking?" he asked.

"Oh, just how nice this is, how I wish—"

"What? Tell me, Bree, what do you wish?"

"That it didn't have to end, that the night could go on forever, just like it is right now."

"Well, I can't make that wish come true. But we could

do it again." His throat tightened around the words. "Next week, maybe?"

She pressed her cheek to his shoulder. "I'd like that."

The bell above the door jangled and Breanna turned her head to see who had come in. *Dane.* And right on his heels came Chuck Morrow.

"What is it?" Tyler followed her gaze, and she felt his body snap taut. "Your favorite personality. What luck."

"You know Chuck?"

"By sight. I haven't had the dubious pleasure of making his acquaintance."

Dane spotted Breanna. He froze in midstride when he saw Tyler, then continued walking. Chuck didn't seem nearly so big with Tyler in the room. Tyler dropped his arms and a chill ran over her. She'd felt much more secure pressed against him, not so alone and vulnerable.

"Hello, Dane," Tyler said in a low voice.

"Ross." Dane gave a polite nod. "Uh, Bree, that first day when I was at your place, did I by any chance drop something?"

"Oh, yes, you did, but that wasn't what I wanted to talk to you about."

Dane's eyelid twitched. He threw a quick glance at Chuck, who stood nearby, legs spread, arms akimbo, his chest puffed out to show off the physique he didn't have. In his white T-shirt, with one sleeve rolled back over a pack of cigarettes, Chuck resembled a potbellied hoodlum from a sixties movie. Breanna gave him a wide berth when she went to the table to get her purse.

"I have twenty right here," she told Dane, digging her hand into the side pocket of her bag where she had stowed the bill she had found in the barn. She handed it over, forcing herself to smile. "Dane, is there someplace we could talk a minute?"

"I don't want just any twenty," Dane whispered. "I need the one I dropped."

Breanna laughed. "Oh, that should be simple enough. You had your name on it, right?" Then she realized Dane was serious. "Um, wait a sec. I put yours in my wallet, I think." She sifted through the currency in her billfold, handing Dane the worn twenty that was left. "There, is that the one?"

"No. Here, let me see that." Dane grabbed her purse and pulled out her wallet. Leafing through the money inside, he said, "Dammit, it isn't here. Lord, you spent it, didn't you?"

"What's the problem here?" Tyler asked her.

"Dane dropped a—"

Chuck interrupted, smiling and rubbing his chest. "It's nothing really. Dane here, he'd lose his head if it wasn't attached." Glancing at Breanna, Chuck's smile broadened. "He had a real important number written on it, that's all. You sure you don't have it?"

"Just what are you looking for?" Tyler stepped to Breanna's side, so close she felt his arm pressing against hers. His voice soothed her.

"Dane dropped some money down at the cabin," she explained. "I guess there was an important number written on it, and I spent it."

Breanna stared into Dane's eyes, knowing even as she said the words that she was repeating a lie. He wanted the twenty, all right, but not for any phone number. Her cousin returned her purse and one of the twenties. She tightened her hands on the soft leather, shifting her gaze to Morrow. As she did, she inched closer to Tyler, thankful for his presence. Something was wrong here, very wrong. "I'm sorry, Dane. Tyler and I went to town the other day. Not knowing it was special, I didn't keep your money separate. I planned to leave twenty with my mom so she could pass it on to yours."

Chuck cocked his head. "You don't happen to remember where you went shopping, do you?" He laughed, holding up a hand. "That's a dumb question. What good would it do now?" Patting Dane's shoulder, Chuck shrugged. "Tough luck, old man."

Breanna's gaze wavered and she pressed a hand to her throat. "If it will help, we went to the Ninety-Nine Market...for soap."

The color washed from Dane's face. Then he grinned. "Like Chuck says, my tough luck. Um—Nan said you wanted to see me? What about?"

Breanna had no time to think. She acted on pure instinct. "Oh, nothing important...just to visit. I—I thought it might be fun if you and Nan—you know—it would have been like old times if we could have spent an evening together."

Chuck stepped closer. "That's good to hear. When Dane first got the message, he thought maybe you were still—" Breaking off, Chuck's gaze moved to Tyler. "But, nah, you wouldn't be that silly. Not after our talk yesterday, right? After me explaining everything so clear to you?"

Breanna flinched when Chuck raised his hand to place it on her shoulder. It was a seemingly friendly gesture, but she knew the meaning that underlined every word he spoke. Dane had suspected her true motive for wanting to see him, that she had wanted to grill him about the fire. Chuck was letting her know his threats of yesterday still held. If she continued to pry into what he considered none of her business, he would be angry. Her stomach lurched as his fingers tightened, digging into her flesh. Pain radiated down her arm, and she lifted her chin in response, refusing to be intimidated.

"Speaking of being like old times, isn't this just?" Chuck gripped her shoulder harder. "We go back a long ways, don't we, babe?"

Something flashed before Breanna's eyes. The next second, she realized it had been Tyler's hand. He clamped his fingers around Chuck's wrist. "The lady is with me, Morrow."

"Oh, the jealous type, are you?" Chuck released Breanna, shaking his head. "No need, man. Me and Bree, we're just friends. Right, Breanna? She owes me a dollar for every hair on her head. When she was a kid, I pulled her out of one scrape after another."

Tyler's answering smile was deadly. "Touch her again, and you'll get what she owes you, all right. Breanna's told me all about her *debt* to you."

Chuck's face stiffened. His brown eyes shot to Breanna's. "Oh, is that so? My, my, aren't we getting cozy."

"That's right," Tyler said softly. "Real cozy. So cozy, in fact, that I'll make this fair warning. Bother her again, and you'll tangle with me, not her. Is that clear?"

Chuck stepped back, lifting both hands. "Hey, man, no quarrel. I didn't realize…"

"You do now."

Chuck's eyes were riveted on Breanna. Their murderous gleam frightened her. "Yeah, I'd say I do. The writing's on the wall. Come on, Dane. I get the feeling we're not too welcome here."

Breanna was shaking with aftershock by the time Dane and Chuck pushed out the door of the café. Tyler's arm circled her shoulders, warm, hard, indescribably comforting. "You okay?"

"Yes, fine." Pressing trembling fingertips to her shoulder, she forced a smile. "I'm not sure you should have done that, but thank you, Tyler. He was hurting me."

En route through the parking lot, Tyler asked, "Why shouldn't I have done that? If I interfered where I shouldn't have, I'm sorry."

"No, it's just—he didn't like it, me telling you. He's

mad now. And Chuck mad is like a rattler when it's shedding. He strikes blind."

Once they were in the car, Tyler flipped on the dome light and turned sideways in his seat. With a grim scowl on his face, he gently peeled her dress back to look at her shoulder. Glancing down, she saw ugly red marks coming up where Chuck's fingers had bruised her. Tyler feathered his thumb across them, then bent his dark head to press a kiss there.

"You don't have to be afraid of him," he whispered. "If he ever so much as touches you again, he's going to think he's a mud hole I'm stomping dry."

"If you're around," she interjected.

Tyler touched her cheek. "Oh, I'll be around, lady, you can count on that. If you want me, that is."

The question in his voice was so subtle that she could have ignored it. Tyler, always the gentleman, never putting her on the spot. An unbidden smile curved her mouth. "I think it would be fair to say you have a standing welcome."

During the ride home, Tyler held her hand, releasing it only to shift gears. She twined her fingers into his, tightening her grip without realizing it until he looked over at her.

"What is it?" he asked softly.

"You'll probably think I'm crazy, but I think there was something fishy about that little scenario back there."

Tyler was quiet a moment. "Like what?"

"That story Dane gave me. He was lying. He didn't have a number written on that money. Tyler—" She turned slightly. "Remember your saying Chuck may have been asking favors of Dane all along? Do you think Dane's gotten mixed up in something illegal?"

"Something illegal?"

"I—Tyler, I remembered something this morning. Right before the fire, I went with Dane to buy gasoline, lots and lots of gasoline. But I can't remember why. Or who it was for." She lifted her free hand and passed it over her eyes. "It's all so foggy. But what if we bought it for Chuck? Tyler, what if that gas was used to set the Reuben Creek blaze?"

"Couldn't you have bought it for someone else?"

"Maybe a neighbor. Or for Gramps. But I—"

"Honey, slow down." He raised her hand, pressing his lips to the inside of her wrist. "I told you earlier, you're strung out. You're not yourself. Why don't you think about something nice for a while? Like our treasure hunt, hmm? I know last night rattled you, but I'm here now. Relax. Forget the ghost and the fire and Dane. You're shaking."

"All right, I'll try."

He leaned forward, flipping on the radio. Static filled the car as he adjusted the dial, then KAJO boomed loud and clear, the disc jockey's cheerful voice resounding all around them. "And now, folks, we interrupt the music for a quick news update."

Breanna shot her hand forward, turning off the radio, her pulse hammering so wildly she felt dizzy. "Oh, my God, Tyler! It just hit me. Oh, my God, how dense can I get? The other night I heard part of a newscast. About a woman who passed a counterfeit bill! I didn't think it was impor— Oh, Tyler, it was me!"

"What?"

"It—it was me! That twenty Dane dropped. It was counterfeit. That's why they were acting so pecul—"

"Breanna, stop it!" he snapped. "You've got to calm down." Reaching to reclaim her hand, he gave it a comforting squeeze. This was one line of reasoning he couldn't let her pursue. "That's the wildest—well, it's just plain ridiculous, that's all. Dane and Chuck? Come on. Counterfeiting is big-time, not Wolf Creek stuff at all. You're going clear off the deep end here, lady, and scaring hell out of me in the process. I'm really starting to worry about you."

"You don't think it's possible?"

"Of course I don't think it's possible." He flashed her a smile. "Come on now, loosen up. Counterfeiting?"

She found herself laughing with him. "I guess it is sort of far out, at that."

"Like clear into the twilight zone. Where's a good place to rent a metal detector? You know of one?"

Breanna cleared her mind, focusing on Grants Pass. "Well, probably most any equipment rental place carries them."

TWENTY-FIVE MINUTES LATER, Tyler pulled the Honda into her driveway. As he brought the car to a stop, she grew rigid in her seat. A dim glow of light flashed within the old barn.

"Tyler, did you see that?"

"Did I see what?"

"There were lights in the barn."

"Nah, it was just the reflection of our headlights."

"It wasn't, I tell you." She shifted in her seat to look at him. "Someone's in the barn."

"Honey, if there *is* someone in there, it's probably kids from town."

"You think so?"

"I know so, and you're not going in there looking for trouble. You're going directly inside and straight to bed. We've both had about all the excitement our nerves can take for one day."

They climbed out of the car and walked up to the house. Tyler unlocked the door and stepped aside, holding it open for her. She waited in the living room while he lit the lantern on the mantel. He rasped a match and golden light sprang onto the walls. It cast his sharply carved features into shadow.

"I think I'll take Coaly out for a short run," he said, turning from the hearth. "Why don't you hit the sack?"

"I think I will. I must be more tired than I realize."

Breanna went to the bedroom and slipped from her dress into her nightgown. Sighing, she pulled back the bedclothes and sank onto the mattress, thinking of Dane and his strange behavior. Was she overreacting? Or was Tyler making light of something serious?

The cabin door was dragged open and she heard Coaly's nails tapping on the floor. Tyler parted the curtain, stepping to the foot of the bed to remove his shoes. When he stretched out beside her, still fully clothed, she smiled and turned to him. "I have a new bedmate, too, hmm?"

He drew the covers over them. "Just to sleep. You're so nerved up, I thought you might like a little company." He curled an arm around her, pressing a kiss on her forehead. "Want me to leave?"

"No," she whispered drowsily.

His hand traced light circles on her back. "Go to sleep. You'll feel better come morning."

For a long while she lay there awake, listening to Tyler's even breathing. Then, at last, her eyes grew heavy and she snuggled close, drifting off into slumber.

TYLER SLID ON HIS BELLY through the brush, stretching out beside Mike Jackson in the blind. Mike slipped off his headphones, smiling. "Hey, man, I didn't expect you here."

"Yeah, well, there's been a new development. The Van Patten woman is definitely clean. I need to see Jack. Call him and tell him to get down here. I can't make a move without his say-so, and time's running out. I want her out of here, yesterday if not sooner."

"Gotcha." Mike reached for his handset, keying the mike. "You got your ears on, Jones? This is The Deer Hunter calling Indiana Jones."

Tyler closed his eyes, not sharing Mike's enthusiasm for the silly call names everyone was using in case someone broke in on their frequency. This was no game of intrigue. Breanna's safety was at stake. Losing patience, he grabbed the handset from the younger man, keying the mike himself. "Jones, this is urgent. Get down here, stat."

Jack's voice rasped back, broken with static. "Gotcha. I'll—b—down—about—ten—minu—"

Tyler swore. "Make it five, Jones. Five, not a second longer. I don't have time to wait."

IT SEEMED TO BREANNA that she'd only been asleep a few seconds when Coaly's whining and scratching at the door woke her. She sighed and reached for Tyler. He wasn't there.... His pillow felt cold to the touch, so she knew he had left some time ago. She sat up, listening for movement inside the cabin. The only sounds came from Coaly and, if his anxious crying was any indication, Tyler had gone outside.

Throwing back the covers, she slipped out of bed and tiptoed through the curtained doorway. "Tyler?"

He didn't answer her. Coaly pawed excitedly at the door, but Breanna ignored him, leaving him inside when she stepped out onto the porch. Tyler had probably just gone to the outhouse, which wasn't a bad idea. The moon was bright, so she could see quite well from her position on the top step; it gave her a clear view of the upper orchard and the front of the barn.

Proceeding down the pebbled walk, she wrapped her arms around herself to ward off the chill air. As she approached the second flight of stairs, a movement caught her eye and she turned to look at the barn. A man stood at the top of the ramp, cast in shadow by the doorway. He bent low, as if to lift something, straightened, then disappeared into the corridor.

Remembering the light that she had seen earlier and Tyler's explanation for it, Breanna's first thought was that the teenagers were still inside and something awful had happened. The loft was high and enclosed on only three sides. A fall from the ladder could have seriously injured someone.

Hurrying down the retaining wall steps, she struck off for the barn, not even thinking about the nettles in the field grass until she stepped on some. She hated to go clear back for her shoes, so she plucked the stickers out of her soles, then wove her way more carefully, trying to stay on trodden ground.

A humming noise greeted her as she slipped inside the barn, so low and indistinct she couldn't identify it. An engine of some sort? Perhaps an airplane overhead or a car on the road?

She braced her hands against the walls, groping her way down the dark corridor. The humming noise grew louder with each step. Horrible pictures flashed through her mind of Tyler carrying an injured youngster out the back exit to a waiting vehicle.

"Tyler?" she yelled. "Tyler, it's me, Breanna. Where are you?"

She had scarcely finished speaking when the humming noise stopped abruptly. Total silence fell around her. Freezing where she stood, she peered into the black abyss that yawned ahead of her, listening for the sound of a vehicle driving away.

"Tyler?" she squeaked.

What if it hadn't been Tyler she had seen coming into the barn? Her heart tripped a beat. Just the thought of meeting Chuck out here made her blood run cold. *Don't even think that way, Breanna. Of course it was Tyler you saw. He's out here someplace. It stands to reason it was him. He probably went out the back door as you came in the front, that's all.*

It was so dark that she couldn't be certain exactly where

she stood, but she knew she had walked at least halfway down the passage. There were rooms in front of her and behind her. Inching backward, she held her breath, her ears straining to hear above the pounding of her pulse. Her palms rasped against the splintery boards and the planked flooring beneath her creaked with each footstep. She tensed, ready to run. *Dear God, what if it wasn't Tyler?*

Right on the heels of that thought, hands clamped down on her shoulders like steel vises.

CHAPTER ELEVEN

WHEN TYLER SPOKE her name, Breanna's knees turned to jelly and she sagged in his grasp, so relieved that a sob of laughter escaped her lips. "Tyler."

He clamped an arm around her waist, hurrying her to the doorway. His heart was slamming every bit as hard as hers. "What the hell are you doing in here? I was in the blind when I spotted you heading for the barn."

"I saw you go in and I was afraid something had happened. You must have gone out the back as I went in the front. What were you doing out here? When I found you gone, it scared me."

He guided her to the cabin, never breaking stride. His fingers bit into her waist, hard, relentless. "I was out taking pictures. I just stepped in there to make sure those kids had left. No sense in sitting forever in a blind, just to have someone spook the animals."

"In the dark? Where's your camera?"

"I have infrared lenses," he informed her. "I dropped everything when I saw you. I'll go get it all come morning."

She could feel some of his camera equipment jabbing her in the shoulder as they walked. He seemed upset. Had her hollering spoiled his photo session?

"Did you get any good shots?" she ventured.

"Mmm-hmm, a couple."

"What of?"

"A mother raccoon and her babies."

He propelled her up the steps to the porch and threw

open the door. Coaly tried to run outside, but Tyler nabbed him by the ruff. He pushed Breanna into the entry and pulled the dog along, none too gentle with either of them. Coaly yelped.

Breanna spun on her heel, hugging herself while he lit the lantern. When the white glow illuminated the room, she leaned back her head to gaze up at his taut features. His eyes met hers, glassy and expressionless. He looked pale and beads of perspiration glistened on his brow.

"Tyler, what's wrong?".

"Nothing's wrong. I'm just tired, that's all."

"Being tired excuses you for being cranky with the dog?"

As if a hand had passed over his face, his expression changed. He sighed and ran trembling fingers through his hair. "I'm sorry, Bree, I didn't mean to hurt your dog. You just gave me a scare, that's all. When I heard you calling for me, I was afraid you'd been hurt."

He seemed so sincere that Breanna's anger faded, and she glided across the room to put her arms around him. He stepped back abruptly and caught her hands before she could slip them beneath his jacket. "Let me get out of this shirt. I got into some foxtails and I'm itching to death. I wouldn't want you getting them all over you. Why don't you put some coffee on for us?"

"At this time of night?"

"Make it weak."

As she went to the kitchen, she saw him stop at the end of the sofa and shove something down behind it before he proceeded into the bedroom. A moment later, he reappeared, donning a fresh yellow shirt. She couldn't help wondering what he had slipped out of sight behind the couch. Curiosity bubbled up within her.

"You sure do something for flannel," he told her warmly.

Breanna lit the burner and moved the pot onto the flame.

"Bree?" He touched her hair as he said her name and his tone was such that she lifted her chin to look at him. The tenderness in his eyes warmed her clear through. His fingers sifted through her hair, sandpapery and warm on the nape of her neck as he drew her against him. He encircled her with both arms, drawing her close to rest his chin atop her head. They stood like that for minutes on end, saying nothing.

The coffeepot hissed over the flame and he reached to turn it down, then propped his back against the warming oven, spreading his booted feet so she could lean against him. "You look like a little girl in that nightgown with your hair all tumbling down," he whispered.

"Do you speak from experience? Do you have a little girl?"

He ran his hand down her back. "My wife didn't want children."

"Why?" Breanna loved youngsters so much that it was incomprehensible to her that anyone could dislike them.

"My work. It was so demanding that our family life suffered." He laughed humorlessly. "I finally changed fields, but it was already too late. She was in love with another man—a nice, boring accountant with hay fever."

"Oh, Tyler, I'm so sorry."

He smiled. "It happened years ago. No need to be sorry."

The coffee began to perk. He checked his watch to time it. When it was finished, they broke apart to sit at the table.

"What kind of work did you do then?"

He took a sip of coffee before answering her. "Systematic inquiries. It took me into the field a lot."

Breanna had no idea what he meant by systematic inquiries, but she imagined him going into offices, reorganizing their operations to make them more efficient. "And your wife missed you?"

His eyes filled with laughter. "Not too much. I was finding wads of tissues around the house a long time before I caught the sniffler who was leaving them." He shrugged. "To be fair to Karen, I have to say she hung in there a long time. She just wasn't the type to be alone. No career, no interests. Her life revolved around me. I'm not saying that's bad, but—" He flashed her a smile. "Enough of that. It's past history."

Lifting her mug, she suggested, "To the future?"

As he raised his cup to hers, she noticed how exhausted he looked. Had he been losing sleep a lot lately, doing night photography? Before meeting her, he had probably slept in the daytime if he worked at night.

"Let's go back to bed," she proposed, reaching to shut off the lantern.

He nodded, shoving away his half-emptied mug and yawning. The grin he flashed her fell short of being convincing. "I've never turned down a proposition like that yet."

"I think you need an eight-hour battery charge, Mr. Ross."

"Amen. I'm beat."

Breanna pulled him to his feet and led him to the adjoining room, drifting apart from him at the foot of the bed. The lantern glow was fading, obscuring him in shadow. She heard the thunk of his boots, the rustle of his shirt. Then the mattress sank beneath his weight.

Breanna curled on her side, gazing at his profile. She saw his lashes drift closed, heard his breathing change almost as soon as he grew still. Minutes passed. She tried to relax, but it was no use. The coffee, she reflected.

She finally gave up on sleeping and slipped quietly from the bed. Tyler wasn't the only one who could work in the middle of the night. Now would be as good a time as any to do some proofreading.

As she stepped through the curtained doorway, her eyes

dropped to the shadowy outline of the sofa and she remembered Tyler shoving something behind it. Hunkering down, she groped along the wall until her fingers bumped into smooth leather. Running her hand over the bulky shape, she recognized what it was. Tyler's camera case. She could feel his Leica inside it. He couldn't have been taking pictures with infrared lenses. He had lied to her....

The realization washed over her like ice water. Her mind stumbled, then stopped short. If he hadn't been taking pictures, then what had poked her in the shoulder when they were walking? She turned to peer through the curtain. Her knees cracked when she stood, and the sound startled her. She suddenly knew what had been under Tyler's jacket. If her conclusion was correct, the last thing she wanted to do was wake him.

Creeping back to the bedroom, she found his jacket and shirt discarded in a corner. There was nothing wrapped in them and no sign of foxtails, either. She knew he wouldn't have hidden anything in her open shelving. There was only one other place to look. She stared at the sleeping man on the bed, listening to his breathing, not knowing what she'd do if he woke up and caught her.

Dropping to her knees, she inched her way to the bed and fanned her arm under it. Her fingers bumped into cold metal and leather. She traced the shape, then recoiled. *A gun. Oh, God!* Now she knew why he hadn't let her hug him earlier. The story about foxtails in his shirt had only been an excuse to keep her away from him until he could hide the revolver.

"Bree?"

Tyler's voice jarred her so much that she gasped and brought her head up, cracking it on the metal bed frame. The springs groaned above her. Large hands encircled her waist. A sudden, breathtaking fear flooded through her.

Tyler must have sensed it, for he lifted her to her feet

and wrapped both arms around her. "Breanna…I'd never hurt you. Don't you know that?"

She had so many doubts racing in her mind that nothing seemed certain to her right then.

"You found the gun, didn't you?" he asked.

Should she admit that she had? Breanna drew away from him. "Why? Why do you need a gun?"

"I always carry a gun when I'm working at night. You never know when you'll run into a snake."

Her chest constricted. He hadn't been working. His camera behind the sofa testified to that, unless his work was something entirely different from what he'd been pretending. In the moonlight, his face was a shadowy caricature of the one she knew; harsh, frightening, his features etched black against the bronzed planes of skin.

"You found my camera, too, didn't you." It was more a statement than a question. He motioned her to sit on the bed and when she stood there, frozen in place, he pressed her down onto the mattress, lowering himself beside her. "Okay. Let's talk."

"Talk?"

He leaned forward studying her, his eyes silver, penetrating.

"What's going on around here?" she demanded. "Why are you wandering my property at night carrying a weapon? Tyler, answer me, or I'm going straight to the police."

"That would be a very bad idea," he said softly.

She stared at him, her stomach churning. The set of his mouth told her he was prepared to use force to stop her. The true Tyler Ross had just stood up to take a bow.

"There are things I'm not at liberty to explain to you," he said gently. "I have commitments that I can't walk away from, as much as I might like to, commitments that I made before I met you. That's all that I can say."

"What kind of commitments? I detest guns, Tyler. I refuse to have one in my house."

"Then I'll leave it unloaded."

"You said you were working! You weren't taking pictures out there. So what *were* you doing? That's all I want to know."

"I can't tell you that."

His tone rang with finality. A slow rage boiled up inside her. Had it been Tyler she had seen running in the brush that night, after all? Whatever it was Chuck had been doing in her barn, Tyler had been in on it. Oh, he had been clever, convincing her it had been poachers or treasure hunters. What a fool she had been! And ever since that day he had pretended an interest in her, keeping her occupied, trying to get her involved in treasure hunts, covering for his friends so she wouldn't find out what they were doing. *Oh, God, he even made love to me!* The truth hit her like a rush of cold air. Tyler had been using her.

On the tail of that thought, Breanna realized that everything he had ever told her was suspect. Every smile, every offhanded shrug, every explanation he'd given her for the strange goings-on, all of it had been lies. Even tonight when she'd been upset about Dane's behavior, his concern about her had been a sham. He had very artfully distracted her, bringing up the treasure hunt.

Suddenly it was all so clear, so sickeningly clear. Tyler was committed to something all right; to *Chuck Morrow.* He was a counterfeiter.

Pain twisted her heart as she studied him. "Was it you with the scythe, Tyler?"

A sad smile curved his mouth. "You know better than that. Deep down, you know."

"Lies, it's all been lies, hasn't it?" she whispered. "Tyler, I think it would be best if you left now. You can come get your things tomorrow."

He sat there on her bed like an immovable rock. "Breanna, don't misunderstand this, but I can't do that. I'll sleep on the sofa if you like, but I can't leave you alone here. It's not safe. At least you know I won't hurt you."

"Do I? I think I know precious little. I don't like being lied to, and I like being used even less."

He averted his face, gazing at the floor.

"There's something here on my land that you want, isn't there? You know who spied on me down by the creek. And you're involved in it somehow. Maybe not directly, but you know who did it." It was on the tip of her tongue to accuse him of knowing Morrow, too, but fear held the words back. She didn't want to find out she was right. "Leave, Tyler. And lock the door on your way out."

He dropped his head into his hand, ruffling his hair with tense fingers. "I can't blame you for thinking what you're thinking, Bree. But let's get a couple of things straight. What happened between you and me…that has nothing to do with anything else, nothing. I would have felt the same way at any other time, in any other place. As for the guy with the scythe, if I knew who he was, he'd be mincemeat." He turned to look at her. "How can you think, even for an instant, that I'd let someone harm you? I know you're upset. I know this looks bad. But surely you know me better than that."

"I don't think I know you at all."

He rose from the bed, pulling two blankets and an extra pillow from the closet shelf. "Don't pass judgment on me until you know all the facts." He glanced down at her. "Think how it was between us last night. How could that be a lie? You're jumping to conclusions…all the wrong ones. I may not be able to explain myself satisfactorily now, but I can tell you this. I'm no criminal. There's no need for you to go to the police."

"Don't you dare throw last night at me!" she cried,

jumping to her feet. "As far as I'm concerned, it never even happened. Is that c-clear?" When her voice broke, she threw up an arm to hide her tears, trying to step around him. He grabbed her bruised shoulder to stop her and she flinched. "Don't touch me!"

"I'm sorry.... I forgot you were sore there."

"It isn't that. Just please, please don't touch me."

He tossed the blankets onto the bed, reaching an arm around her waist to pull her against him. She couldn't bear him to see her face, so she burrowed her head into his chest. "Take your hands off me. You disgust me, do you hear? Lying is one thing. I might forgive that. But I'll never forgive you for using me."

"I didn't use you."

She laughed. "Oh, I see. It's true love, right? I've swallowed everything else you tossed me, hook, line and sinker. Why not one more time?"

"I can see you're in no frame of mind to listen to reason."

"Reason? I think you've reasoned with me far too much."

"Breanna, please..." His voice flowed over her, warm, gentle, filled with concern. "Whatever else you think, don't misunderstand last night, please. I admit, I made a mistake—"

"A mistake?" She tipped her head back. "Oh, Tyler..."

He rasped his knuckles across her cheek, catching her tears. "When I say it was a mistake, I only mean it in the sense that it was bad timing. I should have waited until all this was settled."

"All what?"

He sighed and closed his eyes. "Listen, I'll sack out on the couch. Okay? That far enough away for you?"

"Do I have a choice?"

His gaze delved into hers. "No, not really, I guess you

don't. Neither of us does." He pressed a quick kiss to her forehead before she realized what he was going to do. "Good night, Bree."

He brushed past her to pick up the blankets. She swiped at her cheek with her sleeve, watching him. At the doorway, he paused, turning to look back at her. "Sometimes you have to go on gut instinct. What does your intuition tell you about me?"

"If you're not involved in anything illegal, then do as you preach. Go on gut instinct about me. Trust me and tell me what this is all about."

He smiled. "I can't tell you anything more than I've told you. As for the instinct, I already used it. You don't know it yet, but I believed in you when no man in his right mind would have." He nodded toward the bed. "Don't mess with that gun. It's loaded and it has a hair trigger. And don't leave the cabin without waking me. If nature calls, I'll walk down with you."

Breanna climbed back into bed. Sleep still refused to come to her and she could tell by Tyler's breathing that he, too, was restless. Sometime later, she slipped out of bed to get a drink of water. As she swept the curtain aside to tiptoe past the sofa, his dark head turned on the pillow. Even in the dim shaft of moonlight from the window, she could see him watching her.

"Where are you going?"

"To get a drink."

He settled back, but she felt his eyes following her as she went to the sink. The room was so quiet that every time she swallowed, the sound echoed. As she walked back to her room, her skin prickled. She was a prisoner in her own house.

"Good night, Breanna."

She could have sworn his tone was underlaid with laughter. She climbed back into bed and glared at the ceiling.

She heard Coaly plop onto the floor, positioning himself in the doorway between herself and Tyler. Even the dog loved and trusted him. Curling onto her side, she wrapped her arms around herself, watching the moon. This was either the first time Coaly had misjudged someone or Tyler was telling the truth, at least in part. Doubt crowded into her mind. Was she jumping to the wrong conclusions? If she was wrong, if Tyler, Dane and Chuck weren't involved in counterfeiting, she'd never forgive herself for running to the police with wild stories, getting Tyler in trouble for something he hadn't done. She knew what it felt like to be falsely accused. There had to be a way for her to find out for sure. All she had to do was think of it.

In the other room, Tyler gazed out at the moonlight, too, his thoughts centered on the woman beyond the curtain. Without Jack's okay, he couldn't remove Breanna from the premises. And now that she had found his gun, he didn't dare leave her alone long enough to persuade Jack to give that okay. One minute with his back turned, that was all she would need.

That thought brought him upright. Swinging to his feet, he went to the kitchen, opened her purse and took her car keys. He couldn't risk her getting away from him. If she made it to a police station, the local authorities would swarm in and ruin everything. Tyler didn't so much care at this point if the crooks got away, but he did care about the men he worked with, and didn't want any unsuspecting police officers hurt, either. As important as Breanna was to him, he couldn't risk dozens of lives. Since he couldn't get her out of here, he'd protect her as best he could and hope to God that Jack didn't waste any time bringing this mess to a close.

Tyler dropped the keys in his slacks pocket and returned to the sofa. From here on in, he was on his own.

CHAPTER TWELVE

WHEN BREANNA WOKE up in the morning, she had a solution to her problem. Or at least to part of it. She could find out if her hunch about counterfeiting was correct by making a simple phone call to the Grants Pass police. How she had come up with the idea was a mystery to her, unless she had concocted the plan in her sleep, but it really didn't matter as long as it worked. And it would. She felt sure of it. If she could just escape Tyler long enough to reach a phone.

That turned out to be the catch. Tyler didn't let her out of his sight. When she made her morning sojourn to the outhouse, he accompanied her and waited outside. Later, when she walked down to the creek for her bath, he sat on the boulder with his back to her and kept up a steady conversation to assure himself she was still there.

By nightfall, Breanna's nerves were not only frayed, but the tension between herself and Tyler was nearly unbearable. There had been no opportunity for her to use a phone, even though they had driven into Wolf Creek to continue spreading the rumor about their gold hunt. Their stops at the grocery store, the gas station and the café were brief, and Tyler stayed by her side every second. Breanna had never spent such a miserable afternoon.

But the worst part about the dragging hours had been the constant ache in her chest, an ache that sharpened every time she glanced Tyler's way. She didn't know when and, God help her, she didn't know why, but somehow she had fallen crazy in love with him. She stressed the crazy every time the realization hit her; insanity was her only excuse. Their relationship, if by any stretch of her imagination she could call it that, was a shambles. She felt helpless, frustrated and angry. How could Tyler look so happy all the time?

"What lovely things are on the agenda for tomorrow?" she called through the curtain as she undressed for bed that night.

The clank of the coffeepot resounded and she heard the pump handle squeaking. "I guess we'll go get a metal detector."

Breanna shrugged. There was no point in getting the metal detector, but no point in arguing about it, either. She slipped into her nightgown and turned to get his bedding off the top shelf. With no undo ceremony, she elbowed her way through the curtain and tossed it onto the sofa. "Don't let the bedbugs bite."

He turned from the stove, placing his hands on his hips. "Am I to understand that you're going to let the sun go down without us settling this?"

She nodded toward the dark windows. "It's already down. And even if it weren't, in this situation it's beyond my control. Only you can rectify the problem. Good night, Tyler."

"Great attitude. If it isn't rectified *your* way, it can't be rectified."

She returned to her room and jerked back the bedclothes with a snap. "Good night, Tyler…."

"Good night, Breanna."

She climbed into bed and pulled the quilt up to her chin, staring at the ceiling. She wouldn't let him put a guilt trip on her. There was a gun under her bed that was still unexplained. He had been up to something last night and he wouldn't tell her what. Oh, no, she wasn't the guilty party here. And she wouldn't let him make her feel that she was.

She heard him making his bed. In a moment the lantern light faded. "If you wake up first, the coffee's ready. Just light the burner," he told her.

Breanna didn't bother to reply. Better just to pretend she was already asleep. Fat chance of that. The way she felt, she'd lie here awake all night. She curled onto her side and tried her best to relax. It seemed to her as if hours passed before she finally grew drowsy and drifted off.

FIRE....

At first, Breanna thought she was dreaming. The amber glow flickered through her closed eyelids and she heard the crackling of the flames. Fear clutched her and she tossed fitfully in her sleep, trying to stave off the images she knew would come. It was the nightmare, just as she had experienced it a thousand times, and she didn't want to give in to it. *Forest fire.*

When she opened her eyes, she knew something was terribly wrong. The fire wasn't a dream. It was real. The flames were outside, beyond the paned windows. She rose to her knees in bed and stared through the glass, horrified. Her fruit cellar was burning. Flames snaked up the siding toward the shingled roof, hungry, hot, eager. Breanna screamed.

"Bree…" Tyler tore through the curtain, making a dive for his gun. He was already crouched beside the bed when he saw what she was screaming about. "Oh, Lord…"

"My house…" Her voice faded to a moan. "Oh, my God, there's no water! It'll catch the cabin."

She leaped out of the bed, and his arm lashed out, catching her around the waist before she could get beyond the curtain. "You stay right here until I'm dressed."

"Dressed? Dressed! You're worried about clothes when my place is burning down?"

He shoved her toward the bed and slipped into his shoulder holster, pulling his shirt on over the top of it. "You're damned right. I don't know who's out there and, believe it or not, *you* are more important to me than this hulk of logs!"

When he ran through the living room, hopping first on one foot and then the other to drag on his boots, Breanna was right behind him. Coaly barked excitedly when they went outside, but Tyler shoved him back as he closed the door.

"A shovel, where's a shovel?" he roared.

Breanna stood staring at the outside of the door. A skull and crossbones were painted on the wood, glaringly white, with LEAVE scrawled below it. When Tyler turned and saw it, he hissed, "Those bastards."

Breanna rounded on him. "You know, damn you! You know who did this, don't you? Oh, God, Tyler, I'll never forgive you if my cabin burns, do you hear? Never...."

"Where's a shovel?"

"In the lean-to!"

He jumped over the retaining wall and ran into the lean-to, returning in moments with two shovels, one of which he thrust at her. "Smother the flames with dirt. It's the only chance we've got."

Breanna dug her blade into the hard soil, heaving on the handle. "I trusted you. I trusted you!"

Tyler's face looked grim as he bent to his work. He threw twice the dirt she did, but she was still panting with exhaustion by the time they had extinguished one corner of the cellar fire. She sagged, leaning on the shovel handle.

"Watch out!"

Tyler cast his tool aside and dived toward her. For a moment she didn't know what madness had come over him. His shoulder slammed into her midriff and carried her backward. They hit the dirt with jarring impact, and he began slapping at her legs. Breanna glanced down and saw flames shooting up her nightgown.

The moment was both nightmare and reality. She was back on the mountain the night of the forest fire, seeing Rob Thatcher's panicky face, hearing his screams. Only this time, she was the victim, and her own screams were piercing the night. Her first instinct was to run, and that was exactly what she tried to do. Tyler was all that prevented it and she fought him wildly.

"Let me go!… Oh, my God, please, let me go!…"

"Breanna…dammit, hold still."

His arms clamped around her and hysteria whirled in her mind. She was pinned by Tyler, just like Rob Thatcher had been pinned by the fallen tree. And the fire would consume her. Her arms were anchored to her sides and her legs were vised in the crook of his. All she could do was scream in helpless rage as he rolled with her.

Rolling…screaming…rolling. The sky became the ground and the ground the sky.

"It's out, Bree!" he yelled. "Honey…do you hear me, it's out, it's *out*! You're okay. My God, Bree, stop screaming like that….Breanna, stop it. Breanna—"

Whack. Her head snapped back and she blinked. Tyler's face came into focus, illuminated by the nearby flames, his expression frightened. She pressed a palm to her cheek. Even in the flickering light, she could see the anguish on his face. "Bree, say something, say anything. Are you burned? Answer me."

He tried to lift the charred hem of her gown and she grabbed hold of the still-warm flannel to hold it over her knees. "Don't touch me!" she sobbed.

His gaze swiveled from her to the fire and back, as if he couldn't decide which required his attention the most. With an oath, he ran back to the cellar and began shoveling again. Too numb to move, she sat there, watching him battle the blaze. When at last it was out, he staggered back to her and sank to the ground, resting his forehead on his knees.

"Are you okay?" he asked.

For the life of her, no words would come out of her mouth. She turned to look at him, her eyes coming to rest on his soot-streaked face. There was blood on his cheek; she realized she must have scratched him when they were struggling.

"Tyler, I'm sorry," she whispered. "I don't know what came over me. I know you were only trying to help me."

"Do you?" he asked hollowly. "You sure had me fooled. I would have sworn you thought I was trying to barbecue you."

"I..." The words to explain died in her throat.

"Come on, let's get you inside and see if you're burned." He helped her up and led her inside.

"I'm okay, Tyler, really I am," she argued as he reached to peel off her nightgown.

"I want to *see* that you're okay." Her arms were snagged in the sleeves of the gown and when she instinctively tried to cover herself, she foiled his attempts to get it off. "Breanna."

His tone brooked no nonsense. She sighed in defeat and let him tug the sleeves off her wrists, then crossed her arms over herself. He tossed another log onto the fire to give them more light, without exposing them to whoever lurked outside, and sparks sprayed up the chimney. When he turned back to her, she felt a flush of shame creep up her neck.

"For God's sake, I've seen everything there is to see. Turn around." He hunkered down behind her, and her skin tingled beneath his gaze. His light touch on the backs of her thighs did nothing to dispel her tension. No matter what he said, being naked when they were making love had been an entirely different thing than standing here, all passion gone, him studying every inch of her. His fingers grazed her back and she flinched. "Do you have any ointment?" he asked.

"In the bedroom, but I don't need it. I wasn't burned, I tell you."

"You might not know it right now, the state you're in. I'll put on ointment, just to be safe." With that, he stomped to the other room. When he returned, Breanna had her nightgown clutched to her breasts, which earned her a disgusted snort from Tyler. "Turn around," he said tonelessly.

"Really, there aren't any—"

"Just humor me, okay? I don't want this beautiful skin scarred, that's for damned sure."

He dabbed a glob of cream onto her bottom and rubbed it in. He was none too gentle, which made her glad she didn't have any blisters. "Well, if I did scar, it's where no one would ever see."

"It's where *I* would see."

"You're mighty sure of yourself," she retorted. "The way things are right now, there's no guarantee you'll ever lay eyes on it again."

"I'm *damned* sure of myself," he came back.

"Sometimes I think God poured cement between your ears instead of brains."

"The way I see it, you're the one who's a little dense. You see to the end of your nose, and that's it."

He stopped applying cream and stood, striding into the bedroom and returning with a fresh nightgown, which he tossed at her in a wad. With that parting shot, he went to the sink and pumped the basin full of water, then dipped the point of his elbow into it. She pulled on her gown, jerking it down over her hips as she ran to him.

"You're burned!"

He clenched his teeth, easing his forearm into the cold

water, inch by painful inch. She watched helplessly, realizing that he had left his own injury untended until he had cared for hers.

"You got burned putting out my gown, didn't you?"

"No, I was playing with matches." He stiffened when she tried to look. "Just get back. It's not that bad."

"You're furious with me and I don't blame you."

He swung his dark head around. "Right now, Breanna, I'm furious with the whole damned world! I'd like to kill the idiots who did this, number one. I'm mad as hell that I'm caught in the middle of it. And every time I remember you fighting me out there, I want to shake you until your teeth rattle. I might be guilty of a lot of things in your eyes, but how could you believe I'd hurt you? Do you have any idea the things you said to me out there? Just leave me alone for a minute."

Breanna closed her eyes. She couldn't remember what she had said, but she could guess. "Tyler, let me explain."

"You don't need to. It's picture clear."

"I'm t-terrified of fire." She licked her lips, averting her face. "Rob Thatcher—he died slowly, pinned under a tree. I—I didn't mean anything I said personally. I have bad dreams, that's all, about burning...."

"You were clear on the other side of the mountain. You were, weren't you? You didn't see Rob Tha—" He broke off. The silence in the room crackled with tension. "Why didn't you tell me?"

"I couldn't." Tears blinded her for a moment. She blinked them away. "I knew the fire was near the commune. There were—women—lots of little kids. I went to try to help. And we came across Rob. He—he wasn't even hurt, not that I could see. Just pinned. Dane and I couldn't lift the pine, it was too big."

"My God...."

Breanna took a quick swipe at her face. "He was hysterical, of course. He knew the fire was deliberate. We were there. He said the—the most awful things. Accusing us, screaming he'd kill us, damning us to burn in hell. He was still screaming when Dane dragged me out of there. I can still hear him. Still, after all these years, like it just happened."

"Breanna…" Tyler straightened and reached for a towel. "Come here."

"No, no, I'm going to doctor that arm. Come sit down at the table."

His eyes challenged her for a moment and then he sighed, walking over to the chair. He rested his forearm on the table's edge, looking up at her as she approached him with a tube of salve. "I wish you had told me all of it."

Breanna's fingers trembled as she smoothed the ointment onto his skin. "It's blistered. You'll have a scar."

"I'm sorry," he said softly. "I should have realized you would be scared of fire. I'm really sorry."

Heat flooded her cheeks. "Tyler, please—I told you, it's said and I don't want to talk about it."

"Some things need to be talked about. You can't bury something like that. It eats away at you like a cancer."

"Would you shut up?" She stared down at him, the words hanging there between them. "Just, please, shut up…."

"No." His gaze probed hers. "You can get angry. You can hate me for it. But you can't bottle it up any longer. Something else about that night is tearing you apart inside. I can see it in your eyes. What, Breanna? You can't leave it unsaid."

"Watch me," she told him as she capped the tube. "Right now, I've got no time to talk about a fire that happened ten years ago, even if people around here still believe I set it. The one tonight needs taking care of first. You saw that message on the door. Someone set that fire on purpose, to drive me out of here. Well, I'll tell you this. It won't work. I'll be damned if I'll leave now."

"And what if it's the cabin they burn next? What are you gonna do, pitch a tent?"

"Very funny. And yes, if they burn my cabin, I'll pitch a tent. If you know who did this, I want their names. I'm going to the police."

"We'll discuss that come morning."

"No, we'll discuss it now, because I'm getting dressed and driving to town. Enough is enough."

"No, Breanna, you aren't. I can't let you do that."

"You what? Did I hear you say that you can't *let* me do that? Correct me if I'm wrong, but since when do you have the right to tell me what I can and cannot do?"

"Since right this minute."

She laughed and took a step back.

"Don't jut your chin out at me like that. You're not going to the police and that's final. I can't explain why, but I'm not letting you go."

"You…?" She sputtered, trying to form sentences and saying nothing. "*You* aren't letting me go? *You* and whose army plan to stop me?"

"Don't be ridiculous, Breanna."

"We'll see who's being ridiculous."

He sat relaxed in his chair. "I'm warning you, Bree, I have to do what I have to do. Please don't force my hand."

"Please and a threat, all in one breath? A second ago, you wanted me to bare my soul. I can't believe you." She took another step back. "I'll tell you this. Don't you dare put a hand on me, because if you do, I'll file charges against you, just as quick as anyone else."

"You don't mean that," he told her softly.

Breanna hugged herself, staring at him. He was right; she didn't mean it. But she *wanted* to mean it. And a part of her hated him for dividing her loyalties this way, forcing her to choose between him and everything else that mattered to her.

"My cabin could have burned down tonight. I should have gone to the police when I first saw those men on my property. I won't be that stupid this time. Now I'm going and that's final."

He stood up and began unbuttoning his shirt. "I'm telling you I won't let you go to the police."

She wheeled and went to her bedroom, rifling through her clothes. He came to stand in the doorway, the curtain swept behind his shoulder. When she had her things gathered together, she placed her hands on her hips. "I'd like to dress."

"Go ahead."

"Very funny. Please leave and give me some privacy."

He didn't move. She had her blouse in her hand and she threw it down on the bed. "You have no right to stop me."

He sighed and closed his eyes for an instant. "Breanna, you aren't leaving this cabin."

"Why, will it ruin things for your friends?"

The muscle along his jaw rippled with anger at that remark. "Yes, it will."

"So, you admit it?"

"I admit nothing. You asked me a question and I answered it as honestly as I could. Someday, you'll see that I tried never to lie to you."

"Give me one good reason why I shouldn't go to the police."

"Because I asked you not to," was his simple reply.

"You ordered me."

"I'm sorry. I should have asked you." He shoved his hands into his jeans pockets and pressed his shoulder against the doorjamb. "I was asking for a fight when I didn't and I'm sorry."

He studied the toe of his boot, making scuffing sounds

on the floor. She stared at the top of his head, wishing that she could read his thoughts. He straightened and let the curtain fall. Taking a step toward her, he put the heels of his hands on the brass bedstead, leaning forward with one knee slightly bent.

Breanna picked up her blouse again, then let it fall. "I don't understand you; I don't understand you at all. If you care anything for me, how can you let this happen? If this place had burned, I would have lost everything."

He looked out at the fruit cellar's charred siding. "It didn't happen, though, that's what's important."

"It didn't happen? Is that all you can say?"

"Yes."

"Really? Or is it just all you choose to say?"

His eyes met hers for an endless moment. That look was so intense and delved so deep, she felt as if he'd touched her. "Breanna, I know it's asking one hell of a lot. But please will you trust me for just a couple of days?" He held up a hand. "Before you answer, remember what I said about gut feelings. Think about it for a moment. Not about the gun, not about Chuck and Dane, but about me and who I am to you. I know it looks bad. I know it seems to you I'm being impossible. But if you'll just give me two days, I'll tell you everything."

"Tyler..." Her chest filled with an awful ache. How could she say no when he looked at her with such pleading? "Oh, Tyler, this isn't fair...."

"When you were in the creek, who took care of you? Tonight, who put the fire out? When you fell in the manzanita, who tended your back? I'm not saying you owe me. God knows, I can't blame you for thinking everything you're thinking. All I'm asking is that you take a long, hard look at me and ask yourself if you can't give me a period of grace." He gripped the bedstead so hard that she could see his knuckles turning white, even in the dim light. "Please,

Bree, a lousy couple of days? I swear I'm not involved in anything illegal."

Full circle; she had come full circle. Her common sense told her to go directly to the police. Her heart was torn with doubt. Looking at Tyler, how could she believe he was guilty of working with Chuck? Of harassing her, trying to harm her?

"Oh, Tyler, you don't know what you're asking." She sank onto the edge of the bed. "Remember when you told me it wasn't so awful that I didn't go to the police with my suspicions about Dane and the fire? A reasonable doubt, you said. It was understandable, not wise maybe, but understandable? Now you're asking me to do it again, to turn my back on what I know is right and wait. The biggest mistake of my life, and you're asking me to repeat it. Do you have any idea how it's haunted me all these years? I know something's going on around here that shouldn't be. If I'm going to be true to myself, I *have* to go."

Again his eyes locked with hers. "I'm asking you to be true to me. Wait for two days, only for two days. That's all I need to put things right. After that, I'll drive you to the police myself, if you still want to go."

The muscles in her stomach knotted. She brushed her fingers across the nap of the bedspread. "Can I think about it?"

"Sure. I know it's a lot to ask."

"And if I say yes, will you let me help you?"

"Breanna, trusting me will be more help than you know."

Trust. It seemed to Breanna she had operated on blind trust all her life. If he just needed "two days to put things right," she owed him that much. But she still planned to make that phone call to the police to see if her hunch about the counterfeiting was correct. She would try to get a description of the woman who had passed the fake twenty in Grants Pass and see if it matched her own. And she would get information on how to identify a counterfeit bill if she saw one. Yes, she would give Tyler his two days, but she would do it despite the facts this time, not because she didn't know all of them.

"I'll give you till tomorrow to decide," he said.

"Yes, tomorrow," she whispered.

CHAPTER THIRTEEN

Chuck Morrow slid a partition back and began unloading a crate of money, stacking neatly strapped bundles on the waist-high pile of currency. "The shipment's got to go tonight. We can't hold off any longer. If this stuff doesn't hit Frisco by the weekend, we can't get it laundered for another month. And I'm not sitting on it that long."

"Just give me one more day. I'll get her out of here, I swear it," Dane pleaded. "Come on, Chuck, please. She's family. I can't stand by and see her get hurt."

"Look, pretty boy, I gave you time, plenty of time. If she's dumb enough to stay after that fruit cellar fire last night, that's her problem. I'll burn her out if they're not gone by dark."

"Oh, that's right up your alley, isn't it?" Dane cried. "If someone's in your way, a little gas and a match will take care of them."

"Damned right," Chuck retorted. "And don't you forget it."

Though Breanna's decision to give Tyler his two days' grace was already made when she woke up that morning, she still held off telling him. She knew it was ornery, but watching him squirm gave her a perverse satisfaction. He hadn't made the decision an easy one for her, after all, by being so closemouthed. The way she figured it, trust was a two-way street, and he wasn't holding up his side of the bargain. When she went to the bathing hole, Tyler followed. She smiled as he stationed himself on a rock, turning his back to her.

"Looks like I traded Coaly for another form of guard dog," she commented as she undressed.

Ignoring her sarcasm, Tyler replied, "Sure is a pretty day."

"Peachy."

"Ah, come on, Bree. Look at this sunshine. It's fantastic."

Breanna gazed at his back, wondering how many topics of conversation he could dream up to keep her talking. Her replies were his only way of being certain she was still behind him.

Her silence spurred him to ask, "Don't you love this time of morning?"

"Yes, Tyler, I love it."

She especially loved the way the sunlight glistened in his black hair, she thought, sliding the soap up her arm. Sinking to her chin, she watched him lean forward to pick up pebbles and toss them aimlessly into the river. Maybe she did owe him the two days he'd asked for, she thought with an impish grin, but she didn't owe him an easy time of it.

"You know what I'd like to do?" he asked. "I'd like to take off right up the side of that mountain, just you and me."

She saw him cock his dark head to listen. Her grin widened.

"We could sleep under the stars. Cook on an open fire. Forget the whole world exists. Wouldn't you like that, Bree?"

Breanna stood motionless in the water and made no reply. Tyler's shoulders straightened.

"Breanna, are you okay?"

Seconds ticked by.

"Bree, answer me."

It was all she could do not to giggle and give herself away.

"Damn!" He leaped off the rock and whirled. When he saw her, he relaxed. "Why the hell didn't you answer me?"

"Just checking something," she murmured demurely.

"What?"

"I thought you were talking to make sure I didn't leave—and I was right."

He lowered himself to the rock, facing her this time. A twinkle of amusement entered his eyes. "Oh, you were, were you? And now what? Here I planned to be a gentleman and let you bathe in privacy."

Breanna smiled sweetly, unperturbed by his veiled threat. "And now you're afraid I'll swim off? Tyler, you're jumpy. If I did swim off, what would I have to wear?"

The laughter in his eyes faded. "Has it come to that? Do you really want to leave?"

"If I did, would you let me?"

"Why should we open that can of worms unless you want to go?"

"I have the feeling that you would force me to stay here if I tried to leave. Am I right? I'm not sure what it is you're so afraid of, but I'm a threat to you now, aren't I? You haven't said it, but I may as well be your prisoner."

"Breanna…" He tossed the handful of pebbles onto the rocks and brushed his palms clean. "Isn't the word prisoner a bit strong? Is that how you feel about me? Because you found my gun, you no longer *want* to be with me?"

She sighed in exasperation. "You are a master at twisting things, did you know that? And it's always in your favor. You answer a question with a question and turn it around until I'm sounding like the bad guy here instead of you."

"Oho, so now the truth comes out. Because I have a

gun, because I fibbed to you one lousy time, I'm the bad guy. Thanks for the vote of confidence. Thanks one hell of a lot!"

Breanna stared at him in disbelief. He *was* a master at twisting things. And where did he think he got off by looking wounded? "Confidence inspires confidence, Mr. Ross. You do a lot of asking and no giving."

"And just what have *you* contributed to our relationship? Tell me that!" he fired back at her.

Breanna lost her footing and took a mouthful of water. She sputtered and coughed. "At least I told you everything about myself. Do you know what you could do with that information? You could destroy me, my cousin, our families. And I trusted you with it. But when it comes to your precious secrets, you clam up."

He turned his back to her. "Just shut up and get dressed. There's no point in our having a huge fight about something I can't change."

"You see? I rest my case." Breanna strode angrily from the water to grab her towel. "I must be out of my mind to give you two days, absolutely out of my mind."

He swiveled on the rock. "You mean you will?"

She made a circle with her hand. "Two days, Mr. Ross, not a peep show."

A boyish grin creased his face. "Breanna, you're a gem."

"Yes. Well, two days isn't very long. And that's it, not a second longer."

He leaped from the rock, ran down the bank and grabbed her by her shoulders to give her such an exuberant hug that he nearly dislodged her towel. "Two days is all I need. You're beautiful. Have I told you that?"

"I'm wet, that's what I am. Turn your back so I can dress." Just as he started to turn, Breanna clutched his arm. "Tyler, did you hear that? That creaking sound?" Chills swept over her. "There in the copse."

He cocked his head. "It's a limb groaning, that's all. See the trees swaying."

"You sure?"

"Of course I'm sure." He presented his back to her, chuckling to himself. "Of course, it could be the ghost. They make noises. Listen...." He glanced back at her, lifting an eyebrow. "Chains rattling, doors creaking. Hear 'em?"

She rolled her eyes and gave him an exasperated push. "Get out of my way. At this rate, we'll never get to Grants Pass."

Two HOURS LATER, Breanna held a quarter up to the coin slot on a pay phone and dropped it in. With a shaking finger, she punched out the number of the Grants Pass police, then turned to watch the front of the service station to be sure Tyler didn't walk up on her. He had instructed the attendant to fill her gas tank, then he'd gone around the opposite side of the building to use the men's room. She only had a matter of minutes before he returned.

When a female dispatcher answered the phone, Breanna said, "Hello, my name is Sharon Wilson. I own a small store in Canyonville, a grocery store. And—um—I heard something on the news about counterfeit bills being passed in the area."

"Yes, we had one incident. Have you had a problem, too?"

"No—no—nothing like that. No, the reason I called was more as a preventive measure. I didn't catch the description of the woman who passed the bill and I was hoping you could tell me what she looked like. You can't be too careful, you know, and Canyonville isn't far from Grants Pass. I'd like to be able to tell my clerks what to be watching out for and I'd like to have some idea of the woman's appearance."

"What was your name again?"

"Sharon Wilson."

"Just a moment, Ms. Wilson." Breanna heard paper crackling. "Ah, yes, here it is. Female Caucasian, slender, medium height, middle twenties, with long, frosted brown hair and blue eyes." The dispatcher laughed softly. "That only describes half my friends. Ah, here we go. She drove away in a foreign car—the lady didn't know what make, but it was silver gray. Does that help?"

Breanna leaned weakly against the wall of the booth. She longed to tell the woman the blond streaks in the suspect's hair were not from a frost job, but the absurdity of that thought stymied her. "Yes, that helps immensely."

"Now, as for what to look for. Counterfeit money can easily be detected, but you really should bring your workers in so an officer can instruct them as to what to watch for."

"Oh, well, it may not be possible for all of them to come in. They're on different shifts. Aren't there any simple ways to tell?"

The dispatcher sighed. "Well, one of the easiest ways is to take a suspicious bill and lay it alongside a good one. First check the red and blue fibers in the paper. Counterfeiters can't exactly duplicate the paper used by the U.S. Bureau of Engraving and Printing, not even with the new photocopying techniques some are using. Next, look at the front and back for distinct print. It the portraits look dull, if the numerals are blurred on the edges, you could be in trouble. The serial numbers should be clear, evenly spaced, and counterfeit bills often have the same digits on every reproduction. Like I say, it's hard to help you over the phone."

"Oh, you've helped immensely. I really appreciate it."

"It would be better if you could come in. Once you know what you're looking for, you could educate your employees."

"I just might do that. Thank you so much."

Breanna hung up and hurried back to her car. The station attendant turned to smile at her, giving her windshield one last swipe with a blue towel. "Say, do I know you from someplace?"

"No." *Oh, God.* Breanna opened the passenger door and climbed inside, slamming it behind her. She bent forward so her hair fell over her face. *I don't believe it. They've got an APB out on me. I'm wanted.* A sharp rap on her window made her jump. She looked up to see the attendant peering in at her.

She cracked her window. "Yes?"

"Aren't you Jason's sister?"

"Oh, yes." She laughed with relief. "Do you know him?"

"Yeah, real well. You're Bree, aren't you? Deanna's the married one with the short hair. I didn't use to be able to tell you two apart."

"Yes, I'm Breanna. And your name is?"

"Jim. Jimbo to Jason. We played basketball together in high school." Tyler walked up just then and the station attendant flashed Breanna a farewell grin, walking to the front of the car. "I filled you up and topped it off. Your oil is fine."

Tyler handed him a twenty and Breanna's eyes were immediately riveted on it. *Oh, please, don't let it be counterfeit.* The man stepped to the island till and made change, then came back to count it into Tyler's palm. "Thanks. Stop in again. Bye, Bree. Tell Jason I said hi."

"I will," she called.

Tyler slid into his seat and buckled up. "An old friend?"

"Of my brother's."

"Well, we're ready for that treasure hunt." He started the car, shifted into first and pulled into the traffic. "Do you feel okay? You're kinda pale."

"No, I'm fine," she lied.

"Are you sure?"

Breanna pulled back her hair from her cheek, meeting his gaze for an instant. *Counterfeiting.* It was incredible. "Yes, I'm sure."

And she was. She stared straight ahead at the road, amazed at how calm she felt. Two days or a hundred, she would give Tyler the time he requested. She had no choice. She was in love with him.

FROM THE OUTSET of their gold hunt, the detector beeped every time Tyler went near metal of any kind. Since the treasure hunt was his idea, Breanna didn't feel the least guilty when he spent more time digging than he did using the rental equipment.

"Hurrah," she teased. "A bottle cap. If any treasure hunters are watching, this should impress them."

Next they found an old belt buckle.

"Don't laugh," Tyler warned. "I'm getting blisters doing this and we've only just begun."

"Must we?" She squinted into the glaring afternoon sun. "I can think of other things I'd rather do."

His eyes ran appreciatively over her figure. "So can I."

He sighed when the detecting device shrilled another signal. Breanna exchanged tools with him again, then took stock of their surroundings for a more exciting spot to search, preferably one in the shade. "Tyler, if we're going to go through with this stupid charade, shouldn't we be systematic about it?"

"Meaning?"

"Well, if there really were some gold, Uncle John would have buried it near something that he could have used as a marker, not out here in the open."

"Good thinking. Trees, maybe?"

"Or a big boulder, like that one in the upper orchard."

"I'm game," he agreed. "Let's go."

Breanna gasped with amazement when the metal detector went crazy near the rock she had suggested.

Tyler glanced at her, barely suppressing an excited smile. "You don't suppose old Uncle John is whispering clues over your shoulder?"

"Dig! It has to be something big to set the detector off like that."

He stuck the shovel into the dirt. He had removed about eight inches of topsoil in a two-foot circle when the metal blade grated against something. Breanna's body went rigid. He made a wider hole and tested the earth with a chopping motion. The blade still clinked.

"Whatever it is, it's gigantic," he declared in a low voice.

"Could it be a chest?"

He raised an inquisitive eyebrow at her. "I didn't think you believed any of those old stories. Now look at you."

"Well, could it be?"

"It's sure big enough. A good three or four feet long and a couple of feet wide. It's going to be a hell of a strain to lift, if it is a chest."

"Especially if there's gold in it," she added.

The more Tyler dug, the more certain both of them became that they had discovered something significant. The object was large and rectangular.

"I can't believe this," Tyler said. "I think we've really found something."

Breanna knelt beside him, placing her hands on her knees and leaning forward, watching as he cleared away the earth around the iron. "Want me to dig awhile?"

"Sweetheart, I like your hands just the way they are. I'm fine." He stopped digging for a moment to wipe the sweat from his brow with his handkerchief. "Do I get a free dinner out of this?"

She giggled. "If there's gold in there, Mr. Ross, I'll take

you to the finest restaurant you can find. Do you know the price per ounce right now?"

"It's up, isn't it?"

"Better than it's been for quite some time."

"You know, if this *is* gold down here," he reflected, "you should have a nugget made into a necklace, as a keepsake. It's not every family that has a history like yours. It would be quite a conversation piece, like having a family crest."

Tyler bent over the shovel again. It seemed to take forever for him to dig out the soil around the buried object so that they could each get a grip on an end and lift it. When the moment arrived, she could barely contain her excitement. Tyler was as anxious to see the contents as she was; she could see it in his eyes. He motioned her into the hole, stepping down when she did.

"Oh, I wish Gran was here to see this, Tyler. She'd be so excited." Coaly jumped into the hole with them, trying to dig, and she shooed him out, bending to grab her end. "Silly dog."

"Ready? Now, if it's too heavy, don't strain to lift it, Bree. I don't want you getting hurt."

"I'm stronger than I look."

"Not that strong. Okay, one, two, three, heave...."

He turned slightly red in the face, but managed to raise his end about a foot. Breanna couldn't budge hers. Panting from the exertion, she said, "You'd think he would have put handles on it."

"You know, I don't see how he even planned to open it. It's welded solid."

"Yeah. Do you suppose it's upside down?"

"I doubt it. Maybe it's just sealed." He placed his hands on its corners again. "Let me try by myself."

"No way, Tyler. You'll hurt your back." She grabbed her handholds and strained upward. No sooner had she done so than something showered on her feet and the iron container grew lighter. Glancing down, she saw that her sneakers were covered with dirt.

Tyler looked at her over his end of the box. "Bree, I just figured out what this is."

"What?" she breathed.

"A trough. We have just spent an hour and a half digging up a damned old water trough."

After all his hard work, she knew she shouldn't laugh, but his expression struck her as so funny that a giggle escaped. To her relief, she saw him grin. A second later, they were both laughing so hard that they'd dropped the trough and sat down on it to catch their breath.

Sitting there beside him, the thought occurred to her that it really wasn't that funny. Their laughter bordered on hysteria; it was an outlet for the tension they had both been under these last two days. Behind her eyelids, Breanna felt tears burning.

"I don't believe this," he told her between chuckles, draping an arm around her shoulders to pull her against him. "I nearly ruptured myself getting this thing out of here. And all that's in it is dirt. Coaly thinks he's finally made a soul mate of me."

Breanna sighed, holding her palm over her aching stomach, smothering another giggle. His arm around her felt so right, the possessive pressure of his hand so good. Her common sense told her to pull away, to keep a wall between them, but another part of her argued that anything so wonderful couldn't be wrong.

"Look at the bright side. There could be some gold in the dirt." Another laugh rippled up her throat. "Now I'm glad Gran wasn't here. She'd never let us live this down. That trough has probably been lying there for years and years, sinking deeper and deeper."

He reached to rub something off her chin, then glanced at his dirty hand. "I think I just made it worse." His eyes rose to meet hers once again. "You know, all the gold I need is right here."

Breanna's chest grew tight with emotion. Even the way he touched her, so lightly, as if she might break, broke down her defenses against him. "Oh, Tyler…"

She thought he might kiss her, but her turmoil must have shown in her expression. "I love you," he murmured. "I know I haven't done a good job of showing that I do. But I do love you."

"Love doesn't mix well with secrets."

A shadow crossed his face. "I know. That's me, the fella with bad timing. I guess I've no right to say it, do I?" A humorless smile curved his mouth. "I'm sorry."

"Don't be. I'm glad you said it."

"Maybe when all this is over, we can talk. Until then, I guess we're on hold."

"Not entirely."

"No?"

There was an eagerness in his eyes that made her smile. "I gave you the two days, didn't I?"

"Yes, you did." His hand tightened on her arm. "I guess that should tell me something, shouldn't it?"

"Yeah, that my timing is as rotten as yours."

"We both need a bath," he said, wiping her face again. "You're a mess. What do you say we go down and take one at dusk?"

"Together?"

His mouth claimed hers with an infinite gentleness that told her how much he truly cared. A tender caress, underscored with a hesitancy that erased any lingering doubts about her decision to give him the two days. Breanna leaned into him. There were no answers to the questions that plagued her. Tyler just *was*, and nothing beyond that made any sense.

CHAPTER FOURTEEN

ON THE WAY back to the cabin from their bath that evening, Breanna and Tyler walked with their arms around one another, hers around his waist, his draped over her shoulders.

"When I was little, I loved it here," she said with a sigh. "At night, Gran would make fudge or hot chocolate and we'd sit around the fire while my grandfather told stories."

Tyler traced circles on her arm, as if he couldn't get enough of touching her, even now. "I make a mean batch of fudge. I like to drop-test it and eat the balls. How about you?"

"Yeah, except that I could eat the whole pan that way before it was done. I have to make a double batch if I expect to get any to keep."

He laughed and tightened his arm around her. As they drew close to the cabin, she heard Coaly whining. Handing Tyler her soiled clothes, she said, "Go on in. I've got to take a walk."

He glanced toward the outhouse, then at his watch. "Okay, but hurry." Giving her a quick kiss, he ran up the steps. "How's about I make some fudge? Sound good? We'll build a fire."

"Sounds great." Breanna smiled as she angled across the drive, pleased that he trusted her enough to let her go alone.

Just as she reached the outhouse, a hand clamped down on her arm. "Bree."

Her heart missed a beat. "Dane, you scared me out of a year's growth."

"I'm sorry," he whispered. "Keep your voice down." He pulled her behind the lean-to, then released her to lean against a corner post. In the moonlight, she could see he was pale. "Breanna, I'm in big trouble, the worst I've ever been in. But this time I'm not gonna drag you down with me. You've gotta get out of here, tonight. You understand? Grab your things, get in the car and go. Right now. Before it's too late."

She put a hand on his arm. "Oh, Dane, what is it? What's happened?"

"I...set the fire. I never meant to hurt anybody. I swear to God it was just a prank, Bree. You gotta believe that."

"I do, Dane, I do."

"It was Morrow! Thatcher and a guy named Darren, they were working with him, growing and selling marijuana, and they cheated him somehow." Dane's voice shook. "I didn't know that then. Chuck talked me into setting a small fire, just as a prank. You know how we all hated the hippies. I thought that was why, to scare them. I had no idea, no idea. I swear to God, Bree."

"Go on, Dane." *Darren, Joseph Darren.* He had been killed in a car accident. Breanna remembered the name from the news story Gran had circled. A hippie from San Diego. She was beginning to see the picture now. After ten years, it was all becoming clear.

"I put a gas can by one of their sheds and used a dynamite cap of Gramps's to set the fumes off. It had a long fuse, so it gave me plenty of time to run. And then it blew. But it blew like an atomic bomb. The whole damn mountain went up, Bree. Morrow had stashed more gas all around, in bushes, behind trees. And the explosion just kept setting cans on fire."

Breanna closed her eyes.

"And I did it!" Her cousin's voice rose to a shrill pitch. "I set the cap off. You and I even bought the gas."

"You and I?"

"Yeah, two days before that. Remember, when we filled all those cans for Chuck's generator? And we loaded them in Gramps's Jeep?"

Breanna swallowed her nausea. *Oh, God, please no.*

"I bought the gas on Chuck's charge card. He had my signature on the receipts. It was my cap that was used to set the fire. Don't you see? He had evidence against me. He could have sent me up with what he had on me. When Thatcher died, it wasn't just a prank anymore, Bree, it was murder."

"All right, I understand." Breanna hugged his waist to hold him steady. "Dane, it's okay, it's okay."

"No, it—it isn't okay. You don't understand. Rob didn't just *happen* to get pinned by that tree! Remember all the wild things he screamed at us? Accusing us? He thought we knew! He thought we knew!"

"Knew what?"

"Chuck drugged him, put something in his beer. Then carried him up there, downed the tree and used the winch on his truck to lift it and pin Rob under it. He murdered him, Breanna, burned him alive. Only he framed me for it, just in case it came out the fire was arson."

Breanna stood speechless, clinging to Dane, her eyes riveted to his face.

"Morrow used it against me over the years. Just little favors, at first, dirty work, never anything serious. But the deeper I got, the bigger the favors got and the more I was involved, until there didn't seem to be any way out for me. I just did what he said, so he wouldn't ruin my life."

"Oh, Dane…" She pressed her forehead against his shoulder. "If only you had told me. You should have trusted me. We could have gone to the police. I would have testified for you. Why? Why didn't you tell me?"

"It's too late for that now. Chuck's crazy. I mean really

CATHERINE ANDERSON

crazy. He's got to make a shipment. You won't leave. He's talking murder, Breanna. You've got to get out of here. I've tried to talk sense to the rest of them, but they won't listen." He took in a bracing draught of air. "It was the twenty I dropped that did it, that's what clinched it. Chuck was turning them against me anyway, because I've been getting suspicious. I found out about…well, this girl named Marcy, she did Chuck a few favors, knew too much. And then she had a wreck. I suspected Chuck of tampering with her car. And he's been out after my ass ever since. Some of the money came up missing, counterfeit money. The guys Morrow's tied up with now, they think I stole it. Morrow's set me up again. This time to get rid of *me* because *I* know too much."

Breanna couldn't stop trembling now. "Oh, God, Dane…"

"He's taken a stash and hidden it. I don't know where. But that twenty I dropped, the one you found, it came from him. He deliberately gave it to me, knowing I'd spend it without realizing it was hot. Only I didn't. I dropped it. And it came over the news that a woman had passed it, a woman who fitted your description. The others put two and two together and figured I gave you the money. You don't screw these guys over and get away with it."

Breanna groaned. "Dane, they might kill you. You can't go back."

"If I don't, they'll get suspicious. But you've got to run, Bree." Dane gripped her shoulders and moved her away from him. "You understand? This is my way of making it up…all those things I did to you. I had to come tell you."

"Dane…"

"I know I don't deserve it, but trust me, just once more. Go inside and tell Ross what's happening. He doesn't know things have turned sour and he's got to know it. If he doesn't, I won't be the only one who gets hurt. You understand?"

"Tyler," Breanna whispered. "He's a part of it. I've known for a couple of days."

"God, no! Ross? He's an agent. I wasn't sure at first, not until he moved in with you. He's a G-man with the Treasury Department. Since Morrow pulled that stunt with the scythe down by the creek, Ross has been guarding you."

"No...." Breanna shook her head. "No, Dane, that couldn't be true. He and I...we..." Her voice trailed off and a hundred memories flashed into her mind. Damning memories. "He's been watching me? You mean it was part of his job?"

"Breanna, right now the last thing I'm worried about is your feelings. He's a cop. None of the others know it, but I trailed Ross one afternoon and saw him meet some other fellows in the brush, down by the creek. They're Feds. It stuck out all over them."

Strangely enough, she didn't feel so much frightened now as empty. Just empty, horribly empty. "All right, Dane, I'll go tell him what you've said. But I want you to come with me. This doesn't have to be the end for you. You never meant to hurt Thatcher. You haven't done anything *that* wrong, not yet, not if you stop now."

"I can't. They'll know something's up." Dane cocked his head, then shoved her away from him. "Go! Morrow's coming."

She looked toward the creek. She heard the footsteps, too. "Dane, please..."

"Bree, one more thing! The mine—there's another— Oh, damn, run! Run, Bree. I can see him coming."

Breanna saw a flash of white in the bushes and turned to go, more afraid for Dane than she was for herself. She knew her cousin had committed the unforgivable sin by confiding in her. They'd kill him for sure if they found out.

She reached the cabin and let herself in as quietly as she could. Tyler was wiping the stove when she stepped into the living room, and he turned to smile at her. "My God, what's wrong?"

"Everything."

He clenched the dishcloth in his fist. "What are you talking about?"

"You're with the Treasury Department. Everything, it was all a lie."

"Not everything."

"Oh, yes, everything. Why? Was it a fringe benefit of the job? Do you sleep with every woman you protect?"

Anger flashed in his eyes. "Who the hell have you been talking to?"

"It's true, isn't it? You were assigned to watch me. Weren't you?"

"Yes, but—"

"No buts. When you moved in here, it was part of your job, wasn't it?"

"Breanna…" The guilt on his face answered her question.

"Looking back on it, I think you even thought I was part of it all for a while, didn't you?" She wiped her moist palms on her jeans. "Answer me!"

"Yes," he admitted. "Breanna…it hasn't all been a lie. I believed—"

"Just shut up!" she hissed. "You *used* me. You wormed your way into my confidence to learn all you could about Dane, about the hold Morrow had over him. It's all so clear now. How could I have been so stupid? My cousin's going to die, and you don't even care. Anything for your precious investigation!"

"Breanna, you weren't stupid. What you told me that day, I've never repeated. The only thing I told Jones was

there was a chance Dane *did* have something to hide and
that Morrow might be using it to coerce him. I swear it."

"They're going to murder him. You could have stopped
it! Don't tell me you didn't know about Morrow, Thatcher
and Darren. You've known. And you stood back, watching Dane go under. Tough luck, right? Well, let me tell you
something. Dane's a good person. He's made some mistakes, but only because he didn't have anywhere to turn.
Of course, you wouldn't understand that, would you? All
you think about is getting the job done."

"You're hysterical. Who's Darren?"

"You're right, I'm hysterical. You did nothing to help
Dane. Why? Doesn't a human life count for anything with
you people?"

"I'm getting confused here. I began to suspect Dane
was being coerced, but—"

"You're confused?" There was an awful stillness in her
chest. "You ought to be me, then you'd know what confused is."

"I think you'd better calm down," he said softly.

"I'm calm enough." She blinked tears from her eyes.
"Dane told me to tell you we'd better get out of here. Mor-
row has set him up, stolen some of the money. They…"
Her voice faltered, then she regained control and finished
Dane's message in a stilted monologue, telling him every-
thing. "I think they're going to kill him."

Breanna lifted her hands in a helpless gesture. "I tried to
persuade him to come with me. But Morrow was coming."

She started to cry, softly, brokenly, and Tyler came to
her, wrapping both arms around her. "Breanna, it'll turn
out okay. It's not as bad as it seems right now. You'll see."

She stiffened and drew away from him, wiping her
cheeks. "Get me out of here. Maybe if I'm gone, he'll have
the sense to run."

Tyler doused the lantern and strode quickly to the bedroom. As he reentered the living room, he strapped on his shoulder holster and donned a yellow jacket. "Forget packing. Breanna, are you sure Dane's the only one who knows who I am?"

"That's what he said. And I think he's beyond lying."

"I'll notify Jones of that, then. Thank God Dane had sense enough to keep his mouth shut."

"How will you notify anyone?" She no sooner asked the question than she knew the answer. "Oh, on your radio. I was incredibly naive, wasn't I?"

In the fading glow of the lantern she saw him shake his head. "You just trusted. There's no sin in that."

If there wasn't, why did she feel so humiliated? Tyler groped in his jeans pocket for the car keys, then led her onto the porch. Coaly scampered in front of them, down the steps and around the fruit cellar.

Just as they reached the car, Coaly charged off, barking furiously. It was a frenzied, wild sound. Breanna whirled. In the dark, the black dog was scarcely more than a shadow, but she saw him streak up the ramp and into the barn, in hot pursuit of something. *No, not something, someone.*

Almost immediately there came a bout of vicious snarling, then a shrill yelping that ripped nightmarishly across the drive. She sprang into a run. The dog was screaming with pain, and each cry cut clear through her. She saw Tyler coming from the other side of the Honda, also running flat out.

"Bree, no!"

"Coaly? Coaly!"

Breanna was up the ramp in two strides and into the corridor before Tyler could reach her. He clamped his arms around her, dragging her backward. "No, Bree, for God's sake, no!…"

Just then the barn fell deathly quiet. Breanna froze in

Tyler's arms, staring into the black bowels of the passageway. "Coaly?"

Tyler's hand swooped down over her mouth and stayed there, pressing so hard that it almost suffocated her. He stepped back with her. She could feel his heart pounding against her shoulder blade and realized, too late, that the counterfeiters were inside the barn with them.

A gun went off and she heard Dane's voice. "No, damn you! Leave her alone!"

The bullet splintered the wood right beside them. Tyler swore under his breath and dived with her toward the door. They rolled partway down the ramp, then thudded off it onto the ground, hitting so hard that Breanna got the wind knocked out of her.

Crouching over her, Tyler whipped out his gun. She heard a click and knew he had pulled back the hammer. When she looked up, she saw he had his right wrist braced against his left palm, arms extended and locked. He remained like that, his eyes riveted above them on the yawning doorway.

"Run," he whispered. "Straight up the drive to the car."

Breanna caught her breath and rose on the balls of her feet. "Tyler, we can't risk the car...not after what Dane said about Darren and the girl."

Tyler thought furiously. She was right. "Cut through the woods to the road. I'll catch up with you. My place. There'll be other agents there to protect you. Tell them to douse the lantern. If no one's there, turn on the radio, leave the frequency where it is and call for help. If I don't make it, someone else will."

If you don't make it? Breanna's heart sank. "But..."

"Go," he ordered, "before you end up getting me killed."

She leaped forward into a full-length run. Behind her, she heard the report of a gun, then another, the shots increasing quickly to a volley.

Never in all her life had she run so hard. All she could think of was reaching the radio to call for help. Nothing would stop her. When her foot hit a chuckhole, sending her into a headlong sprawl, she jumped up again, ignoring the pain of a twisted ankle.

It was her fault, all her fault. Tyler had called out to her, trying to stop her from going into the barn, but she'd run on ahead. *Stupid, stupid, stupid.* If he died back there, it would be her doing, as surely as if she'd held a gun to his temple and pulled the trigger.

Oh, please, God... The unfinished prayer echoed and reechoed in her mind as her legs ate up the distance to Tyler's cabin.

She had reached the last bend in the road before the cut-off, when Tyler caught up with her. He grabbed her hand and dived with her into the ditch alongside the graveled shoulder, covering her body with his. "We need to get out of sight. They're not far behind." She heard him reload his weapon.

"Breanna, I love you. I want to be sure you know that, just in case. I love you, Bree...."

"Oh, Tyler, I'm sorry. They were hurting Coaly and I ran in there without thinking. I'm so sorry...."

"Hush!"

Headlights came around the curve, bathing them in their glare. Tyler ducked his head and shrank closer to her. Breanna held her breath as Morrow's pickup passed them. Then it braked and began backing toward them, coming fast.

"Oh, Lord. Cross the road to the creek, Bree, quick."

A shot whizzed past them. Tyler clasped her arm, dragging her to her feet, then they dashed across the asphalt, Tyler firing off shots to cover them. The next second, Breanna felt open air under her feet, then she was falling. When she hit ground, she landed on her back and slid until her hip collided with a tree trunk. At least the truck couldn't follow them here.

"Damn, it's straight down," he whispered. "Hold on to me."

The rest of the descent was fast and scary. It was so dark that Breanna couldn't see the trees that loomed ahead. She ran into her share of them, scraping her extended arms, and so did Tyler. It was no consolation to hear sharp barks of pain coming from the men who pursued them.

"Who are they? How many are there? It's not just Morrow."

"Counterfeiters, a bunch of them. Dammit, I can't see."

A bunch of them? How many is a bunch?

They broke out of the trees. It was lighter along the creek. Hand in hand, they forded a shallow spot in the stream and raced into the pines on the adjacent hillside. Behind them she heard voices raised in argument, then the splashing of feet following their trail.

Breanna's lungs felt as if they might burst. She had run almost a mile on the road and now they were lunging up a steep hillside. *I can do it,* she told herself. *I can't let him know I'm tiring.* Tyler was getting ahead of her. His arm was outstretched behind him to keep hold of her hand. A couple of times, she felt him slow down so she could catch up. Behind them, she could hear brush cracking. They were losing ground; the men chasing them were getting closer and closer.

Tyler pitched forward. "Oh, damn!" She heard him fall into the brush. Then he bit back a moan of pain.

Frantic, Breanna dropped to her knees, groping blindly to find him. She ran into a tree, bruising her shoulder. She slid down a slight decline into a growth of vines. "Tyler...?"

Her pulse slammed with fear. Where was he? She heard him moan again. She clawed her way on her belly, slapping the air ahead of her with her hands until she touched his boot.

"Bree...my leg...it's bad. Can you find your way out alone?"

Alone? Without him? "No, I..."

"Go to my cabin. Stay in the woods until you're sure you've lost them. You know how to take care of yourself in the brush. You have to get me help."

"But..."

"Get to my cabin and radio for help," he commanded her. "Go! I'm counting on you, Breanna. You've got to make it."

The men below them were drawing closer. She could see the beam of a flashlight bobbing. Tyler squeezed her hand a moment, then gave her a little push. "Go."

Breanna crawled backward. As much as she hated leaving him, if he couldn't run, she had no choice. She sprang to her feet. "Tyler, I—I love you."

"I never doubted it."

CHAPTER FIFTEEN

BREANNA BACKTRACKED AND crossed the creek about a quarter mile above Tyler's cabin, then cut into the heavy brush that lined the road. She'd managed to lose her pursuers, but there were lights glowing in the cabin windows, so she hid behind the woodpile. A blond man stood in the kitchen. She could see him over the top tier of logs, pouring a cup of coffee. His shoulder holster, which was similar to Tyler's, and his nonchalant air convinced her he belonged there. She ran to the front door. Glancing behind her, she rapped softly. A moment later she heard footsteps inside.

"Who is it?" a deep voice demanded.

"Breanna Morgan. Let me in, please, let me in."

The door opened a fraction, then swung wide, but there was no one standing there. That struck her as odd. She stepped cautiously across the threshold.

"Freeze!"

The harshly barked order stopped her dead and buckled her knees with fright. The door hit the wall behind her, and movement flashed on both sides. So tense that her neck creaked, she looked first to the right, then to the left. In both directions she gazed into the snubbed barrel of a gun. She had walked right into a trap.

The two men who flanked her crouched in a ready-to-fire stance that made her skin crawl. Their fingers were curled around the triggers of their weapons. She might be shot if she made a wrong move.

"Arms up," the blond man ordered. "That's good. Now step on inside, lady, real slow and easy like."

Breanna's legs felt like wobbly rubber. She moved forward, praying she wouldn't fall. The blond man inched around her, his pistol trained on her chest.

"Frisk her," he told the other man.

Palms slid beneath her arms, moving in a quick motion downward. "I don't like this, Brent, not with a woman."

"Yeah, well, I'd rather be a live bastard than a dead gentleman."

"She's clean."

The fair-haired man still didn't lower his gun. "Start talking, lady, and fast. Name first."

"Breanna Morgan." Her gaze landed on the gun again. It was exactly like Tyler's. *Agents. Thank God.* "Please, you've got to listen…."

"Don't move," he barked. "I mean it, lady."

"Please. We're wasting time. Tyler needs help."

"Ross?" the other man asked.

Breanna turned to look at him, taking in his brown hair and features. *The man in the manzanita?* So it *had* been Tyler she had seen that night. "Yes. They have him holed up about a mile from here. He's hurt. He fell on a—"

The back door burst open. A tall, dark man rushed inside. "Ross is in trouble. I just heard gunfire. Sounded like all hell broke loose." His brown eyes riveted on Breanna. "My God, Falson, put your weapon away! That's the Van Patten girl."

"She didn't say Van Patten, she said Morgan." Falson lowered his gun. "I wasn't taking any chances."

The older man strode across the room, jabbing his thumb at the pictures on the closet door. "If you'd done your homework, you'd have known her on sight. I told you to study the layouts."

Breanna's attention flew to the photographs of herself and Coaly, then returned to the older man.

"What's going on with Ross?" he asked her. "Do you know?"

"He's hurt. The counterfeiters were chasing us and he fell. He's on a hillside, and he sent me for help. I only heard gunfire for a while. He either ran out of ammunition or they—"

"Okay, slow down. Can you tell me where he is? I'm Jack Jones, his friend. You can trust me."

A vision of the woods slipped into her mind. Setting them an accurate course through the forest at night would be impossible. "No, but I can take you."

"Too dangerous," he countered.

"Too dangerous? Tyler needs help, don't you understand? I don't care if it's dangerous. Besides, it's my land. I've every right to be in on this."

Jones met her gaze. She had the feeling he was sizing her up. "All right." He stepped to the table, picking up an extra box of ammunition. "Jacobsen, you come with me. Falson, you man the radio. Get more lookouts posted around the entrance to the mine. Call Simonson and Miller and get the roadblocks up. This sucker's coming down tonight."

Both Jones and Jacobsen withdrew their guns from their holsters and ejected the clips to check for bullets. When they shoved them home, the rasp of metal filled the room. Breanna flinched.

Jones glanced up. "You sure you're up to this?"

"I'm sure."

"I won't paint a rosy picture. If there's a confrontation, it could be dangerous. We won't have time to be worrying about you." They were already moving toward the door.

"I can take care of myself."

He cocked a bushy eyebrow at her.

"I know these mountains," she explained.

"I sure as hell hope so. We don't. That's what Ross was for."

"Tyler said to douse the lantern. I don't think anyone followed me from the creek, but it's better to be safe."

Jones clipped a radio handset to his belt, motioned to Falson to turn down the light, then spun on his heel to leave. Breanna followed him out the door, then Jones slowed his stride, letting her take the lead. "You're running this show," he said.

"Hell," Jacobsen grumbled. "I could get lost out here five feet off the road."

Breanna pointed toward the peak of Hungry Hill behind them. "Keep that mountain in sight. If something happens and we get separated, head directly for it and you'll eventually hit the road."

Both men pinpointed the location of the hilltop.

"This way," she called over her shoulder, crossing the road. Jones leaped down the bank behind her. "It gets so dark down here, you can't see anything," she warned. "Feel your way and be careful. A sharp branch can go clear through you."

The descent here wasn't as steep as the one she and Tyler had tumbled down earlier, but it was every bit as dark. Breanna heard Jones grunt and knew that he had run headlong into a tree. Jacobsen swore a second later and brush snapped. When they reached the creek, she turned to wait for them.

"How far from here?" Jones asked.

"About a half mile. It would be easier to see if we walked along the creek. Is it safe, do you think?"

"Let's keep in the brush," he decided. "If we stay close to the open, we'll have enough light."

Breanna wove her way into the trees. She picked up her pace to match her heartbeat, thud-thud-thud-thud, begrudg-

ing every minute, every second that kept them from Tyler.
There was no sound ahead of them, only deathly stillness.

"Mr. Jones, do you think...they'll kill him?"

"It depends on how much they know."

"Meaning?"

"If they realize who he is, they'll probably hold him as
a hostage. If they think he's a civilian who's discovered
their operation, they'll dispose of him."

Her throat felt as though a baseball was stuck in it. "Will
Tyler tell them, do you think?"

There was a long pause before he replied. "No, he won't
tell them."

Now her heart was pounding even faster than her feet
could hit the ground. The sound of it filled her head. Was
Tyler's still beating? Her breathing became shallow, fast.

"I can't understand what they were doing in my barn,"
she said, holding back a limb for them.

"Dammit, Jacobsen, keep up with us. *Under* your barn,"
he corrected, sweeping past her so that Jacobsen could get
through. "Ingenious, isn't it? An abandoned mine that isn't
even documented." He grunted and she heard a branch
crack. "Careful, it's a sharp one."

"So there's a shaft under there? I suspected that! But the
entrance has caved in. How do they get in?"

"They boxed in a stairway between the tack room and
the next stall. You probably didn't notice, but the interior
has been altered. Are we nearly there?"

"A little farther. So that's why the barn seemed smaller,"
she exclaimed. "They're actually making counterfeit
money in *The Crescent Moon*?"

"Enough to break Fort Knox. They have a press run by
a portable generator, with a gas motor. How far is it now?"

"We're almost there. It's about five hundred yards upstream. I left him on the hillside."

Breanna's mind reeled. Suddenly so many things made

sense, the footsteps she had heard that afternoon in the stall and the low hum of an engine the other night. No wonder each noise had ceased the moment she spoke. They had heard her and shut down until she left.

Jones grasped her arm to stop her, then took his radio from his belt. She saw a tiny red indicator light blinking. He pulled the antenna and flipped a switch. Soft static buzzed. "Yeah, Jones here."

"We got trouble, boss. Ross is down in the mine. And they didn't take him in through the entrance."

"Damn!" Jack grimaced. "What the hell do you mean, Falson?"

"There must be another entrance," was Falson's reply. "Has to be. They have him down in there and they didn't go through the barn."

Breanna turned to Jacobsen and whispered, "How do they know Tyler's in there?"

Jacobsen replied, "Bugs. You know, listening devices?"

"Oh." Breanna squeezed her eyes shut for a moment. Of course. The tiny microphone she had found in the blind! Piece by piece, it was all fitting together. The man in the manzanita, wearing the headphones. Why hadn't she guessed immediately? She remembered Tyler saying her suspicions of counterfeiting were clear into the twilight zone. How true that was. A tremulous smile touched her mouth, and tears brimmed in her eyes. Would she ever laugh like that with Tyler again?

"Son of a…" Jones keyed his mike. "Is Ross okay?"

"Sounded okay."

"All right, over and out." Jack clipped the radio back to his belt and put his hands on his hips. "What the hell do we do now? There's another entrance. Morgan, you sure that old entrance is completely closed off?"

"Positive." Fear inched up Breanna's spine, fear for Tyler. If there was another entrance, the counterfeiters could come and go without being seen. Which meant they wouldn't hesitate to kill a hostage. They had escape insurance. "Mr. Jones, we have to find that other entrance. Fast."

"Go to the head of the class," he said with a grim laugh. "Where? That's the question." He pivoted, looking at the woods around them. "God, it's so dark, we'll never find it."

"Oh, yes we will. Come on." Breanna elbowed her way past him, aiming for her cabin.

Jones slipped on a rock trying to catch up. "Hey, slow down! How can we find it? Clue me in."

"I've been studying those old maps. I think I can make an educated guess where another entrance might be, that's all."

"It'll be like finding a needle in a haystack," he said with a snort. "I can't waste time on wild-goose chases, lady."

"And neither can I. Everything that matters to me is in that mine, Mr. Jones. My cousin, my dog and—and Tyler. If there's another entrance, I'll find it." Breanna glanced over at him, unashamed of the tears that had spilled onto her cheeks. "It's my fault Tyler's down there in the first place."

Ten minutes later, Breanna and the two agents crawled into Tyler's blind on their bellies, inching up beside a man with a radio set. Jones elbowed his way to the equipment, listening intently to the radio receiver. "What d'ya got, Jackson? Anything new?"

"Not much. Ross is trying to get them to talk."

Jackson. Breanna stared at the younger agent as Jack introduced them. "Breanna, this is Mike."

Jackson nodded, then looked at his boss. "They've been giving him a ration about her. He doesn't know for sure if she's safe."

A grim smile twisted Jack's mouth. "Ross is tough. He won't run at the mouth unless he doesn't see any other way out. Whoa, listen...."

Voices were coming over the main receiver. *Tyler.* Breanna heard him talking and leaned nearer. The agents had done a good job of installing their hidden microphones. The transmission came over the air with very little static. A knifelike pain twisted through her at the sound of Tyler's voice.

"Cue in on this," Jack whispered to her. "Tyler'll try to tell us where they brought him in if he can."

Breanna moved closer to the radio.

"I should have known something like this was going on here," Tyler said. "I never dreamed—"

"Shut up, unless you wanna say something worth hearing. Quit stalling, Ross. Why wait until they drag the girl in here? I'll be in a foul mood by then. And believe me, you don't want me in a foul mood with your lady."

Jones took Breanna's hand and squeezed it. She clasped his fingers. *Chuck.* Just the thought that Tyler was at Morrow's mercy made her cringe.

"I told you, she's not my lady. How do you think I stayed single all these years? Love 'em and leave 'em, that's my motto."

"Yeah? That's not what it sounded like in town the other day. We'll see what you say when she's here."

Tyler laughed. "I got no beef with you fellas, really I don't. You do your thing and I do mine. Live and let live, you know? I'm telling you, I'm just a photographer. I carry a gun in the woods to protect myself."

"Sure, a nine millimeter semiautomatic? Right, Ross. Got any used cars you wanna sell me?"

"I tell you, Morrow," Tyler said, "you're dead wrong. I gotta hand it to you, though, that back door down there is really something. I'll bet we passed it a dozen times and never even guessed it was there. I should have known…."

"I thought I told you to shut up. You got a bug down here? Is that it?" The click of a gun hammer came over the air. The sound was unmistakable and Breanna stiffened.

"You rotten son of a bitch. Answer me! If I find a mike in here, you're gonna be one sorry bastard."

"Hey, easy…easy…"

There was the sound of a scuffle. Breanna's heart shot clear up into her throat and stopped beating. Air came out in a gush when she heard Tyler say, "Whoa…hey, let's not play so rough. I won't say another word."

"Where's Breanna?" Morrow demanded. "I should've known it meant trouble when the little bitch wouldn't leave. Her and that damned dog of hers, sniffing around. It attacked Dane twice, one time in the barn, then out in the drive after that. Smart little sucker. I'm glad Rawlins bashed his skull in. He's been nothing but a thorn in my side ever since he got here. Where is she, Ross? It'll go easier on her if you talk."

There was another scuffle. "Now talk, Ross. Where's that cute little friend of yours, huh? I'll bet you tell me anything I want to know once I've got this gun held to *her* head."

Breanna was shaking. Not even Jones's tight grip was a comfort. *Oh, God, Tyler.* Did Morrow intend to shoot him?

"I don't know where she is. I lost her in the woods. How many times do I have to tell you?"

A long silence followed and then Morrow's low chuckle came over the air, distorted by a spurt of static. "Tell me something. She good in the sack?"

Breanna's stomach heaved. She heard Tyler reply, "What makes you think I've slept with her?"

"You think I was born yesterday?"

"Let's put it this way. If I had slept with her, I sure as hell wouldn't discuss it with scum like you."

"I'll bet she's a firecracker," Morrow mused.

"Just in case you're thinking she means something to me, Morrow, think again. I haven't known her that long. She's a nice woman, but not leverage."

"So you *do* admit you're a Fed."

"I didn't say that."

Morrow snorted. "You don't have to. So…she was just part of your job, huh. Didn't mean a thing to you?"

"She's a nice lady," Tyler repeated. "And I wouldn't want to see her hurt."

"Yeah, yeah, you talk a good game. We'll see if you mean it when they drag her in here. They'll find her, you know. And then you'll talk, Ross, you'll talk." Morrow laughed again. "Maybe we'll all have a little fun. A party. You wanna watch us have a party, man? Rawlins here, he's the slickest fella with a knife you've ever seen."

There was a long silence and then Tyler snarled, "Touch her, Morrow, and there won't be a prison on earth that'll keep me from killing you."

"Oh-ho-ho, so the cool cop loses his temper?" Morrow clucked his tongue. "You threatening me, Ross?"

"I'm promising you."

"And the lady means nothing to you? That's interesting."

"It's called common decency. Something a horse's ass like you wouldn't understand."

"Sure is a pretty little gal. Be a shame if her face got all messed up, now wouldn't it? You wouldn't like that, would you?"

Their voices seemed to be getting farther away. Breanna glanced at Jack. "They left the mike," Jack explained. "Damn, I wish he could have said more. The back door down where?"

They had passed it a dozen times, and never even guessed it was there? *Where, Tyler? What were you trying to tell us?*

"Down," she whispered. "Jones, he said *down* there. That means below the barn!"

"But where?" he challenged.

Her pulse was hammering so fast and hard that her

ears rang with it. The copse? It had to be. Breanna turned to stare at Jack. "Of course! Down by the bathing hole. It would explain everything. How that man appeared, then vanished into thin air. The footprints in the brush, with none going in or out. Coaly having such a fit every time I went there alone."

Jones looked at her as if she had lost her mind.

"I know where it is. Come on, Jones. Bring a flashlight."

"No flashlights. Jacobsen, you and Jackson stay here while we check this out."

Jones dogged her heels down to the stream, then stood back with a puzzled look on his face while Breanna strode purposefully into the brush. *The grassy bank.* It was dead ahead of her, silvery with patchy moonlight. A chill of understanding shivered into her mind. She remembered how Coaly had sniffed the sharp incline after her clothes had been stolen.

"So that's why there weren't any footprints. *My* feet sank into the grass. Don't you see? If someone had climbed that bank, he would have left tracks! And tonight, when I was talking to Dane. Morrow came from this direction."

"Would you try to make some sense, please? What are you talking about?"

Breanna took a halting step toward the bank. "It's here. The door, Jones, it has to be here." She extended her arms, searching the tall grass with a patting motion. "Come on, help me. There has to be a…"

Her fingers ran into cold, smooth metal and she froze. Taking a deep, steadying breath, she tried to pry it up. It moved.

"I knew it," she whispered raggedly.

She turned to grin at Jones, so excited that she wanted to shout. Her smile froze on her lips. A man stood behind Jack, moonlight reflecting off the gun he held in his hand.

CHAPTER SIXTEEN

"DON'T MOVE, MISTER," the gunman snarled. "So much as twitch and the woman gets it. Understand?"

Jack stiffened and slowly raised his arms. "Hands coming up, friend. Don't get trigger-happy."

"Open the hatch," the man ordered Breanna. "You just couldn't let it be, could you? You should've got the hell outa here while the gettin' was good. But, oh, no, you had to keep snooping around."

Breanna curled her fingers around the metal once more and pulled. A familiar creaking sound filled the air, then a black opening yawned at her feet.

"Three steps," the counterfeiter said. "Fall and you're dead."

Her legs felt quivery and she sent up a silent prayer that they wouldn't give out under her. One…. She groped for something solid to hang on to and her palms met with damp earth walls on either side. Two…. She heard Jack's boot settle on the step behind her. Three….

Searching with her sneakered foot, she found the dirt floor and moved forward. The floor of the tunnel sloped sharply. She felt Jack grip her shoulders. His fingers bit into her flesh. Before her was a blackness so impenetrable that it was like walking into death's arms.

No, Jack, no, she prayed. *No heroics. Just do what he says.* But even as she thought that, she knew Jack would make his move. He was a federal agent. She was a citizen.

It was his job to protect her and if they once got down into this shaft, he'd never get her back out of it, not alive.

Breanna expected it when Jack shoved her forward, so she was ready for a headlong dive. She hunched her shoulders for the impact and rolled. She slithered on her belly a few more feet, then sprang into a crouch, staring back at the shaft of moonlight and the silhouettes that were struggling for the gun.

For the life of her, she couldn't tell which figure was Jack. One man grunted and doubled over. The other one dived for him. Their arms were extended upward, etched in stark relief against the silvery backdrop of light. The shape of the revolver wove to and fro as their hands fought for its butt.

In horror, Breanna watched as one combatant slowly gained control, forcing the pistol down. Then the muzzle exploded with a darting tongue of orange fire. The shot reverberated in the tunnel, each echo louder than the last.

"Oh, God…" a voice croaked.

Breanna's stomach lurched. *Jack!*

"Run…Morgan," he moaned. "Oh, Lord…"

Breanna coiled on the balls of her feet to leap forward. She bit back a scream. Jack was sliding down the wall, holding his stomach, his head lolling forward on his chest. And the other man was raising the gun, pointing the barrel at Jack's head.

"No!" Breanna reached out a hand.

"Run!" Jack cried. "Ru—"

A second shot rang out. The timbers above Breanna groaned. Dust and small clods of dirt pelted her face. Then there followed a silence so eerie that the air pulsated. She froze, arm still extended, her lips parted in denial. Jack's silhouette slid to the floor, completely motionless.

The counterfeiter whipped around and ascended the steps to jerk the door shut. Breanna crouched there, too stunned to think. The hinges creaked and total backness swooped over her. She heard the rasp of metal. Dear God, was he locking her in?

Run! her brain commanded. She whirled and stared into the nothingness behind her. She had no idea where the tunnel led, but terror made her legs move. With her arms held wide, she groped blindly, bouncing off one wall, staggering to find the other. It got bigger once you descended the steps, then? Six feet wide, she guessed, more than her arm span. She would have to stay on one side and feel her way along. She chose the left.

Stay calm. Think! Don't run in a panic. Use your head.

Breanna closed her eyes, summoning all her senses. She counted every step she took, forcing herself to measure the length of her stride. She had to know how many paces she took and exactly how long they were.

He knows his way, she thought, *but you have the advantage, Breanna. Keep your head. This is just a mining tunnel, like any of a dozen you've been inside.*

Her left hand met open air. She fanned her arm. It was an opening, about three feet wide. A passage off the main shaft? She felt ahead. Yes, the main corridor that she was in stretched on ahead. Her heart slamming, she turned, praying that she hadn't stepped into a dead-end chamber.

A bright beam of light bounced off the earthen walls of the main passage seconds after she left it. Her knees wobbled with relief. *One, two, three, four...* She hurled herself along the narrow hall, going as fast as she dared, clicking off her steps, trying to keep track. She had gone fourteen strides in the main tunnel; now she had gone sixteen in this one. Seventeen, eighteen, nineteen...

"You can't get out of here!" the man yelled. "There's no sense hiding! I locked the door. We'll find you!"

Breanna blocked him out, counting as she ran. *Twenty-three.* A faint sliver of light glowed above her and she stopped, throwing back her head. Moonlight. Her eyes focused. An airway?

Her pulse accelerated. She threw up her arms and felt a hole about two and a half feet square. Could she get a grip on the supporting timbers and lift herself into it? Her vision grew more accustomed to the light. Yes, it was an air hole, a vertical tunnel going straight up to ground level, with a grate at the top.

Bending her knees, Breanna tensed her legs. She leaped upward, flailing her arms. Her right palm struck wood and she homed in on its position, dropping back to the ground. The light beam was coming closer and closer....

She hunkered down again. One more try. If she didn't get a handhold this time, she wouldn't have another chance. With all her strength, she pushed off in a desperate leap. Her fingertips grazed wood, curled, gripped frantically. The weight of her body pried her fingernails away from the quick, but she gritted her teeth and didn't let go.

She had never been very good at climbing. That handicap, coupled with near blindness, made her ascent into the air shaft all the more difficult. She pumped her legs to swing, using the momentum of her body to help lift herself. Flinging up her free arm and groping with her palm she found a cross section of wood along one side of the opening. Repeating the pendulum motion, she found another, a rung higher, and pulled herself up until she could get a toehold.

The hole was high and narrow, but it was wide enough for her to fold her body into it, bracing her shoulders against one side and her knees on the other. She leaned her head back, willing her heart to stop pounding.

"You're locked in, lady," the man roared. "I don't have time to play games with you. Come out and save us both a lot of trouble."

Breanna saw the beam of light bouncing around on the

floor beneath her. She dropped her chin to her chest. The illuminated figure of the man came into view between her spread legs and she stared at the top of his bald head. *Don't look up.*

"Dammit," he snarled. "Where the hell could she go?"

He turned and stepped out of sight. Breanna felt sweat trickling between her breasts. She waited for total darkness, straining her ears. A cough sounded some distance away. Was he going for help?

She stared down at the blackness under her. It was safe here. She could probably stick tight and never be discovered. The agents outside wouldn't expect any heroics from her. Neither would Tyler. They would want her to hide, wouldn't they?

Perspiration beaded on her forehead now and ran into her eyes. She blinked and swallowed. What could she do to help? Risking her life for no good reason was stupid.

Coward! Think! There has to be something that you can do.

Had the man taken Jack's radio? Breanna mentally replayed the sounds she had heard when she was running. No, surely he hadn't. Right after the gun had gone off, he had closed the door and locked it. He had followed her almost immediately after that. With the radio, she could call the agents aboveground, tell them where the back entrance was, and get help for Jack.

With her heart drumming in her chest, Breanna slid down the air shaft and dropped to the ground. She counted her steps as she ran back up the passage and slowed on twenty-two, feeling for the intersecting corridor. One more step and her hand met nothingness. A right turn and fourteen steps. Jack had to be just ahead of her.

She stooped, searching with her arms. Her fingertips ran into something warm and sticky. She gasped and recoiled, then forced herself to reach out again. His midriff. Sliding her hands downward, she found the radio, unclipped it from his belt and keyed the mike. Nothing. With trembling fingers she searched for an on-off switch, and as she traced the outline of the handset, she felt shattered plastic. Jack must have broken it when he fell.

She stood there for a moment at a loss. With no radio, she couldn't contact anyone aboveground. She was locked in. The only other way out was through the main chamber. Her own life, as well as Jack's and Tyler's, depended on her, and she didn't know what to do. *Jack's gun.* The thought slid into her mind and crystallized. Oh, God, she knew nothing about guns. Could she even fire one? And if she could, would she be able to hit her target? There wasn't much time to think about it.

Tossing the radio aside, she ran her hands over Jack's chest, found his gun and pulled it from the holster. Just as she slipped the weapon into the waistband of her jeans, Jack moaned. Breanna dropped to her knees, scarcely believing her own ears. He wasn't dead? Pressing her palms to his midsection, she found one wound. Nausea rolled up her throat when her hand came away wet with his blood.

Moving quickly, she grabbed the hem of her shirt and tried to rip it. It wouldn't tear. She sank her teeth into it and yanked until the cloth split, thanking God it was a T-shirt, so it would stretch to provide double thickness. As soon as she'd wrapped Jack's middle, she tore another strip for his head. It wasn't much in the way of first aid, but it was all that she could do in the dark. She frisked him, finding his extra bullets and stowing them in the pocket of her jeans.

Oh, Jack, hang on. Knowing how badly a head wound could bleed, Breanna propped him in the corner so that the steps and wall braced him in a sitting position to restrict the blood flow. If he fell sideways… No, she wouldn't think about that, couldn't think about that. She rose to her feet, hating to leave him. *Tyler.* He was down here somewhere.

He needed help, too. She had to go…. She heard a sound down the corridor.

Fourteen paces back the way she had come, a left turn and twenty-three more. Breanna ran until she stood beneath the air hole again. By the time she had shimmied back up into the narrow space and wedged herself there, she was exhausted.

Only moments later, the main passage was echoing with shouts, and lights were bobbing everywhere. Breanna held her breath, so scared that her whole body quivered.

"Well, she didn't get out. Look at this," Morrow exclaimed.

The familiar rasp of the bald man's voice reverberated in the tunnel. "I'll be damned. Is he alive? Maybe I won't get a murder rap out of this, after all."

"He's a goner," Morrow replied. "You're in up to the neck."

The bald man grunted. "Might as well finish him then."

Breanna clamped a hand over her mouth. *No, no, don't.* She tensed for another shot, smothering sobs. *Animals, nothing but animals.* She envisioned cold metal pressing against Jack's forehead. Hot tears slid down her cheeks.

"You moron, don't fire that thing down here again. You want the whole place caving in?" Morrow gave a snort. "Use your head, man. He's history. Forget him. Help me find the woman."

Moments later, the men shone their flashlights down the corridor Breanna was in, but didn't enter it, which confirmed that it was a dead end. The sound of their voices passed her.

"Well, if she hits the main chambers, Rawlins and Pope will nail her," Chuck speculated. "I say we try these. I'd bet money she's in one of them. Damn, she's at home in tunnels."

More passageways? Breanna shivered. It was so cold.

She had forgotten how chilly it was underground. Where the perspiration was drying, her bare midriff felt icy.

"I'll go left, you go right," she heard them agree.

When their footfalls had died away, Breanna lowered herself from her hiding place. Just in case she needed it, she pulled the gun from her waistband and searched for the safety. Right behind the trigger guard she felt a small, round button. She pressed it. Metal rasped, something hit her stomach, and bounced down her leg. *Thunk.* She cocked her head, running her hands over the weapon. Horror raced through her when her fingers found a square hole in the butt.

She had ejected the ammunition clip.

Frantic, Breanna dropped to her knees, patting the ground all around her. Her breath came in quick little gasps. *Oh, God, please.* Her hand bumped against metal. The clip. With a sob, she picked it up. In one end she felt an inch-long bullet, on the other a sloping surface. She knew the bullet end went first, that the tip of the bullet had to point forward so it could be ejected into the chamber. She squeezed her eyes closed, gritted her teeth and shoved the metal cylinder into the hole, hoping the sound wouldn't carry. The clip grated, hit home and stayed.

She knelt there, holding the gun in her hand, pointed away from her. If it had a safety, she didn't know where it was. She curled her finger around the trigger. She had to see if it would move without pulling it far enough to activate the firing mechanism. Easy, easy. She tightened her grip, pulling back. Nothing. The trigger wouldn't move. It was on safety, and she didn't know how to get it off.

A shudder ran through her. She blinked, gulped air and swallowed, then stood up. She had to find Tyler. There was no choice. And if she had to bluff her way with a gun that didn't work, she'd do that, too. If she could get the gun to him, they had a fighting chance. *Rawlins and Pope.* That gave her two more men to contend with in the main chamber, which she assumed was under her barn. If they had Tyler in there under guard, how would she ever reach him?

Driving all doubts from her mind, Breanna elbowed her way along the wall and turned left into the main corridor. Twenty paces farther, she felt another doorway. One of those being searched?

It seemed to her that she walked at least a mile, even though she knew the barn wasn't that far from the creek bank. One hundred and eleven steps had registered in her mind when she walked face-first into dirt. With her right arm extended, she groped until she felt a door. She pressed her ear against it and heard muffled conversation. Gingerly she tried the knob. The door wasn't locked.

Breanna had never jumped into a den of criminals with a gun before, but she had seen how Tyler and the other agents had held theirs and had also watched enough television drama to hope she could do it convincingly. The counterfeiters wouldn't be too frightened of her if they knew she'd never shot a pistol. Especially if they guessed the trigger was locked.

She closed her eyes for a moment, saying a quick prayer, then tried to remember the most recent detective movie that she had watched. One thing she knew for sure, cops always entered rooms with a bang. She was no policewoman, but maybe if she yelled loud enough, no one would notice her knees knocking.

She turned the handle again and eased the door forward so that the latch was free, then stepped back. Raising her left leg, she kicked as hard as she could and jumped into the opening, slapping her gun hand onto her other palm and locking her elbows.

"Freeze!" she yelled.

The sudden pool of bright light blinded her. She blinked to clear her vision, inching sideways, keeping her back protected by the wall. One man was so taken by surprise that he nearly fell off his stool. Another was lounging against the wall to her left, sipping coffee. He slopped the liquid all over his blue shirt and flinched.

Never in all her life had Breanna been so scared. She hoped her voice would stay steady. "One false move, just one, and I'll blast you where you stand."

The man on the stool made a move toward his revolver, which rested on his hip.

"Don't do it, mister."

Their eyes filled with fear.

Breanna shut the door with her foot. "Okay, fellas, real slow and real easy, put your weapons on the floor."

"Lady, be careful with that thing," the man in the blue shirt pleaded. "You might shoot somebody."

"Yes, indeed." Breanna kept the gun weaving from one man to the other. "Fact is, I might shoot *two* somebodies."

"Just stay calm," the man near the stool said smoothly. "We'll do what you say. Just don't accidentally pull that trigger."

Breanna realized her acting hadn't been very convincing, but they seemed frightened of her this way, so that was okay. She didn't care, as long as she got the job done. They put their weapons on the floor. "That's good, very good. Now turn around and step against the wall. Arms up, legs apart. That's the way. Move and you're going to be exceedingly sorry."

Glancing uneasily around her, she got her bearings. It was a large room, filled with machinery. Copying equipment? A press? She spied the huge generator in one corner and marveled that they had ever gotten something that large down here.

With her peripheral vision she saw jean-clad legs stretched out on the floor to her left, bound with rope at the ankles. She whipped her head around and her heart soared with joy. Tyler's slate-blue eyes stared back at her over a band of white cloth. She couldn't see much of his expression, but guessed he was horrified. He wasn't the only one. She hurried over to him, keeping the gun aimed at the other men while she struggled to untie his feet. He leaned forward so she could reach his wrists.

As soon as he could, he ripped off the gag and scrambled for the weapons on the floor, stowing one in his belt, keeping one in his hand. Leaning against a wall, Breanna sighed with relief, more than happy to let him take over. *His leg? He isn't limping!*

"Keep the door covered," he instructed her.

She jerked erect and gave him a bewildered look. He flashed her a quick grin. "Don't quit when you're on a roll, Bree. We've still got the other two to worry about." He kept his gun trained on their prisoners and stepped back, glancing at the paneled ceiling. "Hey, fellas? Coffee break's over up there. We need some help. Send someone down to the creek, too. There's a back exit there, right up from the bathing hole. A sod door in a bank, right there in the brush."

Breanna watched Tyler tie their prisoners with the ropes that had bound him, then edge his way to the opposite side of the door. She remembered how the agents had flanked her earlier when she had entered Tyler's cabin. She could handle that, she thought. All she had to do was keep her arms locked, her gun steady and look shifty-eyed. She took her position, thought of asking Tyler about the gun safety, then discarded the idea. Just in case the criminals got brave, she couldn't risk them knowing she had a weapon that wouldn't fire.

"Bree, don't point it at me!" Tyler snapped.

She moved the barrel tip, shrugging one shoulder. If he expected perfection her first time at this, he could think again. "Sorry."

Just then the door opened. The bald-headed man looked

so big when he stepped into the room that she decided to let Tyler take the lead. Her knees were shaking too hard. Morrow walked in and froze. His brown eyes met Breanna's, and he smiled a smile that turned her skin to ice.

"Come on in, gentlemen," Tyler said calmly, motioning them forward. "Guns on the floor, please."

Breanna watched the barrel of her pistol shake and thanked God Tyler had this mess under control. If she could have pulled the trigger, chances were she would have shot her foot off.

"Shut the door, Bree."

Tyler slid the guns out of the criminals' reach with his foot and instructed them to join their cohorts along the wall. His voice was disappointingly conversational, not rough and tough as she'd imagined federal agents would talk. No wonder the counterfeiters hadn't been convinced by her acting. She was lucky she hadn't botched the whole thing.

"Real good. Keep your arms reaching and don't move." Tyler looked totally relaxed, his eyes deadly calm.

Thumping sounds filled the room and Breanna jerked her head around to stare at the closed door to their right. It flew open and three men entered, Jacobsen coming in last. His eyes landed on Breanna and widened in amazement. She dropped her chin and stared. What was left of her blouse was smeared with blood. Her hands were bright red. No wonder Tyler had looked so horrified. She stooped and let the gun slip from her fingers to the floor.

She fixed her gaze on Tyler. He was already shrugging off his jacket, stepping toward her. Smiling, he holstered his gun, stuffed her arms down the overly long sleeves of his windbreaker, zipped it up and hugged her. It wasn't just an ordinary hug, but a tight squeeze; his arms were trembling.

"What happened to your shirt? Are you bleeding? I'm so glad you're safe."

He leaned over and picked up Jack's gun, stared at it for a moment, then flipped a lever on the left side of the hammer. His face grew pale when he pulled back the slide to check for a bullet in the chamber. "My God, you didn't have a bul—" His eyes flew to hers. They stared at one another for a long moment, then he smiled, hefting the weapon on his palm. "You are one helluva lady, Miss Morgan. Who gave you this?"

Breanna's mind froze. *Jack.* Here she was, feeling so relieved, and Jack Jones was badly injured, maybe bleeding to death. "Jack, he's been shot. Oh, Tyler, hurry. Get a light. We have to help him."

Jacobsen heard her and left the prisoners with the other two agents. "I've got a light," he said, flipping it on as he left the room with them, "but the agents coming in the back way should be there by now."

Breanna cried, "Oh, hurry, hurry…!"

To her relief, the wounded man was surrounded by other agents when they reached him. "She got the bleeding slowed down," one said, "…did a fine job of this, for working in the dark. Excellent…."

Tyler's arm tightened around Breanna's shoulders. Someone shouted behind them. "We've got Van Patten back here! Stomach wound. He's bad, real bad." Breanna turned, staggering down the tunnel. There was a lighted opening ahead. She reached it, braced her hands on each side and leaned in. Flashlight beams bounced. She glimpsed blond hair, a gray T-shirt, sprawled legs. *Dane.* Breanna stepped into the room. She felt Tyler grasp her shoulder, give her a pat. Then he was gone.

Confusion broke out. Voices bounced off the walls around her. Men dashed back and forth. She was trapped in a nightmare of blackness and sporadic light, alone, unable to help, numb. She leaned against a wall, registering bits and pieces of what she heard said.

"Lost a lot of blood."

"Get them to a hospital."

"The dog's a goner. Should I finish him off?"

Tyler's voice rang out. "No! Get him to a vet. That mutt's a good buddy of mine."

Silence. Then, "You gonna foot the bill? His head's bashed in."

Tyler swearing. "Yes, I'll foot the bill, Falson. *Take him to a vet, stat.*"

"Okay, okay, don't get so touchy."

Breanna lifted her head. Tyler's silhouette appeared in the doorway. "Bree?"

She tried to speak, but her throat wouldn't work. There was a terrible emptiness inside her. He came to her, his shoulders blocking out the flickers of light behind him. Breanna finally found her voice, but somehow the words evaporated as they hit the air, coming out in soft sobs, soundless, broken. Tyler clasped her behind the head and pulled her snugly against him. "Shh, Breanna, it's all over."

She closed her eyes. Yes, it was all over. Everything. Dane, Coaly, Jack, Tyler, everything.

"Let's get you out of here. Somebody'll give you a lift to town. You'll want to be at the hospital with Dane, won't you?"

She felt his hands massaging her back. The temptation to lean against him, to need him was great. But her pride was greater. He had said *somebody* would drive her to town, not that he would. And he hadn't used "we" refer-ring to the hospital. It was over, just as he had said. She straightened, pressing her palms against his chest to lever her body away from his.

"Yes...yes, I'll want to be with Dane."

In a fog, Breanna left the mine with him, gazing sightlessly at the steep stairwell as they ascended into the barn. Agents crowded the corridors. Flashlight beams revealed tall stacks of currency. Exclamations erupted around her. She stepped outdoors and down the ramp, taking deep breaths of fresh air. It helped to clear her head. Several pairs of headlights were bouncing along her drive. Car doors slammed. Feet thudded on the ground.

She turned, arching her neck to see Tyler's shadowy face. "Your leg. It's better? I was afraid you'd broken it or something."

He laughed softly. "Let's just say it mended pretty fast after I knew you were gone."

A smile touched her mouth. "You didn't…"

"I had to do something, Bree. They were right behind us and you were exhausted. We had to split up so I could draw their fire, so I tricked you."

She glanced up the ramp at the men in the corridor who were taking the illegal currency as evidence. "All of this was why you wouldn't let me go to the police?"

"You can see how big an operation this has been. Jack didn't want local authorities messing up the bust."

She nodded.

"They wheeled carts right up the ramp, loaded the cash for transport and circulated it, all right from here. One of the most sophisticated operations we've ever run across. Slick, too. Who'd ever guess this ramshackle old barn was being used for something of this scale? Or suspect that the production was all done underground? It took forever to figure it all out."

"No wonder the barn seemed smaller to me. Fake walls. I can't believe it, Tyler. That twenty I found. All of that was on the other side of the wall?"

"These boys are big-time," he assured her. "Your arrival threw a wrench in their fan blades. That's why they tried so hard to scare you off. Given time, they would have gotten mean about it, which was why we put you under protection. The barn is wired with electronic audio devices that are strong enough to pick up conversations in the main chamber below. That's how I knew when you were in the barn that night and got here so fast. I guess they figured we were on to them tonight when they chased us."

"The night I saw the man and followed him in here? It wasn't you? You were in the blind, listening over the transmitter?"

He sighed, hunching his shoulders against the night air. "After that scenario in Wolf Creek, I had proof you weren't involved. I went down to see Jack to get permission to get you out of here. I'm so sorry for all the lies, but I didn't have any choice. Jack had a fit every time I approached him about leveling with you."

"You mean you did talk to him about telling me?"

Tyler smiled. "When I was sure you weren't involved. I thought I might persuade you to leave until we cleaned things up. But Jack was never sure about you. That's why we staged all the treasure hunting, so my hanging around wouldn't make you suspicious."

Breanna glanced up at him. Why was he looking at her with so much wanting in his eyes? He stepped closer, closer. His hand touched her cheek. His eyes caught hers, hungry, full of need.

Breanna stepped quickly away. "Do you think—Dane will be okay?" She closed her eyes for an instant, bracing herself.

"He's pretty bad. All we can do is hope. I'm sorry."

"He made his choice, I guess, a long time ago." Breanna shoved her hands into her pants pockets. "The wrong one."

"If he pulls through...well, I—uh—can't make any promises, but I think they'll go easy on him when all the facts come out. Especially if he turns federal witness. We still haven't found the plates. Dane probably knows where they are. We were waiting until we were sure those had been brought in to close the trap. Breanna, can't you look at me? Please don't turn away."

She forced herself to face him. "Tyler, I don't want you to feel obligated to—"

"Hey, Ross! We need you down here!" Jacobsen roared from the corridor.

Tyler swore under his breath, then sighed. "I have to get back down there. Breanna, we have to—"

"Ross, dammit, we need help with Jones. What's keeping you?"

Breanna looked at Tyler through a blur of tears. "Go on, Tyler. Do your job."

"I don't want you thinking like you're thinking."

"I'll be fine."

"It'll be a couple of days. We've got the loose ends to tie up. Reports to file." He stepped toward her. "I'd like to come back, Bree, to explain, to talk. I've told you so many half-truths, trying not to lie to you. There's so much left unsaid."

"Sure," she agreed. "We'll talk."

"Ross!" Jacobsen leaned out the barn door. "You comin', or what?"

She dragged a hand out of her pocket to give Tyler a shove. "Would you go?"

He stopped at the ramp to look back at her, his face in shadow. "I'll be back," he promised. Then he disappeared. Breanna waited there for a moment, staring into the darkness, then turned on her heel. An agent stepped out from a nearby vehicle. "Miss Morgan, I'm supposed to give you a ride to town. Do you need anything here before we leave?"

Breanna glanced back at the barn, then shook her head. "No, there's nothing."

She climbed into the back seat of the car and slammed her door, resting her forehead against the glass. Her eyes stayed on the barn as the agent maneuvered the vehicle up the drive. She hoped for one last glimpse of Tyler. Oh, he might come back. She didn't doubt his word. But talking could never put things right between them. A federal agent and a wildlife writer? It seemed such a shame. Apart from their professions, they had been so right for one another. A sad smile touched her mouth. As Gran would have said, better to have loved and lost than never to have— She broke off the thought without finishing it. Gran was wrong. It wasn't better. The losing hurt too much.

Trees whipped by her window. Patches of moonlight fell across her face. Breanna gazed through the trees at the silver ribbon of water that snaked beside the road. She had been right about Tyler from the first. His identity, at least where it involved her, had begun and ended down Graves Creek.

CHAPTER SEVENTEEN

The sun inched slowly downward, and the soft, subtle whispers of another summer evening settled over Graves Creek. As Breanna walked to the orchard, carrying a shovel, she tipped back her head to gaze at the distant horizon above Mount Reuben. A smile curved her mouth. At last she could look toward *the California mine* with a sense of peace. Rob Thatcher's ghost was finally laid to rest, his murderer incarcerated. And nicest of all, she and Dane were becoming close again, as they had been as children, no secrets dividing them.

All had ended well....

Sadness caught at her heart. *Almost all.* A week had passed, and there hadn't been a sign of Tyler. He hadn't kept his promise to return. She had narrowly missed seeing him at the hospital a few times when she went to visit Dane. Other than that, there had been no word, nothing.

Sighing, Breanna slowed her pace, approaching the hole she and Tyler had dug to unearth the old water trough. It was too deep to leave. Someone might fall into it. Glancing down at Coaly, she said, "I don't suppose we could reprogram you to dig in reverse, could we?"

The black dog cocked his bandaged head, eyeing the mound of dirt. A single "Woof" and a wag of his tail later, he was in the hole, digging furiously. Breanna groaned, dropped her shovel and leaped in after him.

"You silly old mutt, you. You'll get dirt in your gauze. Out! Out you go." Breanna half lifted her pet from the hole, giving his rump a fond pat as she put a leg up to climb out after him. "Quiet, the vet said, rest and quiet. You can't act like a puppy."

She grabbed the shovel, filled it with dirt, then sighed. Coaly had again descended into the pit. Down she went once more to drag him out.

"I said no, Coaly. Be a good do—" Breanna froze, staring at her dog's dirt-encrusted muzzle. He held something between his teeth. A very dusty something. A leather pouch? She seized it, prying it from his mouth. "What on earth have y—?"

A tingle of premonition zigzagged up her spine. With tense fingers she loosened the drawstring, opened the bag and stuck her hand inside. More leather? Breanna slowly withdrew a folded piece of parchment-dry doeskin. Carefully she opened it—and gaped. It was a note, the letters inscribed with some sort of leather-burning tool so they wouldn't fade. And it was signed and dated: *John Gregor Van Patten, 1903*.

Scarcely able to believe her eyes, Breanna leaned against the wall of dirt behind her, smoothing the leather. The note read: *Below lies my life's work, unearthed and brought forth from The Crescent Moon. Let no man who does not hail to the name Van Patten lay hands upon it.*

The soles of Breanna's feet tingled. She glanced down to see Coaly busily throwing dirt all over her sneakers. His claws scraped metal.

"I don't believe it." Picking up her dog, Breanna lifted him out of the hole, then grabbed her shovel. "It existed. All these years, it really existed. Dane was right."

Bending over the shovel, she began to dig....

One hour and several blisters later, Breanna knelt, holding a rock in her hand, next to the large chest she had unearthed a foot or so below the old trough. With a mighty swing, she clunked the stone against the rusty lock, breaking the hasp. Her arms trembled as she pried open the lid. Then she could only stare. The chest was brimming with nuggets and leather pouches, a horde larger than her wildest imaginings. *John Van Patten's hidden gold.*

She was so excited that she didn't notice the red pickup that had pulled into her driveway behind her Honda, but the slamming of its door woke her from her reverie. She glanced up, did a double take—and again did nothing but stare. Something far more important to her than gold now held her attention. *Tyler.* She abandoned her newly discovered treasure trove, scrambling gracelessly from the hole.

"Tyler?" Her voice squeaked, and she immediately wanted to kick herself. He had probably only come to say goodbye. "Hi there. Long time, no see."

He looked so good, just as she remembered him, comfortably dressed in jeans, an open-necked red shirt and hiking boots. This last week she had envisioned him in a business suit, with a beeper attached to his belt and a gun strapped beneath his arm. Instead, the closest thing to a weapon he carried was a black puppy, which was biting his wrist and squirming, trying to get free.

"This is Snoopy," he said, leaning down to let the pup go. "He's a peace offering. When the prognosis for Coaly didn't look too bright, I stopped by the pound." Straightening, Tyler shrugged. "He looked so much like him, I couldn't resist. Now that Coaly's better, he's sort of surplus, but he grows on you. Maybe he'll keep the old man company?"

Breanna dropped to one knee to rescue her sneaker, which the puppy had attacked with razor-sharp teeth. Laughing, she stroked his wavy black fur. "Oh, Tyler, he's darling. And he *does* look like Coaly. What a stroke of luck that you found him."

"Say that in about a week." Tyler folded his arms over

his chest. "He doesn't eat paper like Coaly. He goes for socks and boots."

Her eyes flew to his frayed shoelaces and she burst out laughing. Looking up, she saw a twinkle of humor in Tyler's eyes. Giving the pup a final pat, she stood. Silence settled. An uncomfortable silence. She glanced one way, Tyler another. Then they both looked at each other, their eyes locking.

"I—um—" Breanna shifted her weight from one foot to the other, folding her arms over her chest, too. "I was hoping you'd stop by. Was the puppy your only reason for coming?"

"Yes." His mouth twisted in a grin. "Only it was more like an excuse, not a reason. I'm a devious fellow, you know."

"Yes, I know."

"I figure that Coaly is all the dog you can handle. Two of him, well—that'd be a bit much without someone around to help corral them. Any openings?"

Breanna's face felt stiff. "Oh, Tyler…how can *you* apply for the job? Your commitment to the department—well, that's all-consuming. How could we ever make it work?"

"I'm a little disappointed in you. Seems to me, no matter what my job, if you love me, it wouldn't matter."

"Ah, but you forget, I have a profession, too. And that's a two-way street. You didn't come back, so I figured you couldn't see how your job and mine could mix. Besides, you never asked for a compromise. You just disappea—"

"I'm asking now," he interrupted. "And I didn't disappear. I've been doing my job and Jack's, too, getting the loose ends tied up for him. It'll be awhile before he's back on his feet."

Breanna glanced at Hungry Hill, blinking back tears. "And just what is it you're asking?"

"If I had to go to D.C., would you go with me? If I had

to live in some city surrounded by miles of concrete, would you live there with me?"

"And give up my work?"

"No. We'd always come back here. You could do your research, then write wherever I'm assigned, couldn't you?"

Breanna looked into his eyes. New York, Chicago, Los Angeles, Washington, D.C., concrete and skyscrapers and smog. It wasn't what she had planned for herself. But without Tyler, all the forests and mountains in the world wouldn't fulfill her. "Yes, I think I could do that. I've done a lot of thinking about my promise to Gran, and I believe her biggest reason for insisting I come here was to force me to face the past. She was a very wise old lady. I think she knew I was running, and it was her way of making me stop." Breanna smiled. "I think she even suspected what Morrow had done. I found the news story about Joe Darren circled. She had to have done that. And she must have felt his death was significant, or she wouldn't have. As long as I keep the assessments done and the claim stays in the Van Patten family, she'll be content."

"We'd have to make sacrifices. Both of us would."

"Yes, both of us. I'm a simple person, Tyler, with plain tastes. Glitz just isn't in me. Putting on airs isn't in me. I'm afraid I'll be a hindrance rather than a help if you're trying to impress your superiors."

He stepped slowly toward her, then cupped her cheek in his hand. Love shone in his eyes as he smiled. "Breanna, you may not be fancy, but you're more beautiful with dirt to your elbows than other women in chiffon and diamonds. To me, anyway. I'm not asking you to be anything but what you are. I just need to know you'll stick with me, no matter what, that's all."

"Because of Karen?" She turned her face to press her lips against his palm, her arms still crossed over her chest. "Oh, Tyler. I won't do what Karen did. If you go away, I'll manage. I'll worry, but I have my own thing to do, my own career. And if we have to live in cities sometimes, I'll tough it out until we can come back to the mountains."

He lifted her chin. "You're sure? You and I are on, no matter what? Even though you hate guns and know what my life can be like?"

"I'm sure."

He gave a whoop and imprisoned her in a bear hug, lifting her off her feet. "That's the right answer, lady, the only right answer. I love you. Did you know that? I love you so much."

Breanna wrapped her arms around his neck, pressing her face into the hollow of his shoulder. "And I love you."

He swung her in a circle, then lowered her feet to the ground. "Lady, I've got news for you. You see that mountain? We don't have to leave it. See that cabin? That's home. No concrete, period. No guns. No job taking me away."

"What do you mean?"

He set her away from him. "Breanna, remember when I told you I tried never to lie you? Didn't I say that I'd changed professions? I'm not with the department anymore. I helped out with the Graves Creek investigation because I know the terrain so well. I've been retired for almost four years." He lifted an eyebrow. "'Investigation,' look it up. Webster's definition is 'systematic inquiries.' That's what I used to do. Now I'm a photographer."

"Oh."

"Oh? That's all you can say?"

"I could say you're rotten for putting me through all that."

"Not rotten, just wanting to be sure." He ran his fingers into her hair. "I'm a little insecure, I guess. I had to know you'd take me however you could get me."

"As long as it's mutual."

"You're a little dirty. But I'll toss you into the creek later."

Breanna broke off in the middle of a laugh, her eyes widening. "Tyler, the dirt. Oh, my, I got so wrapped up in us, I totally forgot to tell you."

"Tell me what?"

"The trough! Coaly dug up a bag in the hole we dug. And then—Tyler, I found the Van Patten gold!"

"The Van Patten gold..." He stared down at her with a blank expression on his face. "What gold?"

"*The* gold." She seized his hand and tugged him along behind her. "See? Isn't it incredible?"

Tyler gaped at the chest, then began to laugh. "Won't Dane do a jig when he sees this? Gosh, it's a shame he can't be here to see it."

"Oh, I wish he could. He'd be over the moon."

"A picture! I'll take a picture so we can give it to him up at the hospital. One of you, standing beside it. Good idea?"

"A great idea!"

He started for his truck, stopped and snapped his fingers. "Damn! My camera's in town at my folks' house."

"I've got one of those instant jobs. We could use that."

Tyler rolled his eyes. "I suppose I can condescend to use it for one picture. Go get it."

A few minutes later, Breanna posed beside the chest, smiling up at Tyler.

"Lift one of the bags and hold it open." He stepped sideways and clicked the shutter. "Another big smile, Bree."

"Get the picture, moron. You're not using your Leica."

Tyler tugged the photo from the slot, tossing it onto the ground. The puppy bounded up. "Nah, get back, you snoopy little mutt." Tyler rescued the picture and held it between his thumb and forefinger while he snapped another. "Okay, lady, climb out and watch yourself appear."

Breanna scrambled from the hole to stand beside him.

Peering over his arm, she watched the images darken. "Oh, it's good, don't you think? Not bad for this light."

"An expert took it." Tyler turned the photo, his smile fading. "A little foggy in one corner." He held up the other, handing her the first. "Oh, this one's clear. Dane'll love it. That smile on your face says it all, sweetheart."

Breanna wasn't looking at her smile. She stared at the corner of the picture, at the foggy spot Tyler had seen, which was now becoming more sharply defined. A frown pleated her brow. "Tyler, who's that man?"

"What man?"

"This man, the one behind me in the picture!"

He glanced over, then did a double take. His eyes riveted on the corner of the photo. "That isn't—well, it *looks* sort of like a man, but it's just a bad exposure."

Breanna's mouth went dry. "It looks like a—" She licked her lips. "It's a miner, Tyler. You can see his slickers. And his headlamp."

Tyler leaned closer. "Sure can, can't you?" His gaze moved to her pale face. "Honey, it's just a trick of the light. You know how you can see things in clouds if you look? It's the same principle."

Breanna studied the blurred image for a long moment, then lifted her gaze to the treasure chest. Coaly was off to the right, sniffing the foundation of the barn, the puppy on his heels. A shiver ran up her spine. "Tyler, you don't think it could be—?"

"No, ma'am, I don't." He took her firmly by the arm. "Talk about clear out into the twilight zone! That's crazy. John Van Patten's ghost? Come on, get real."

"Nobody believed in his treasure, either. And there it is!"

"It's just a bad photo, taken with a cheap camera. Come on, let's get that gold stowed someplace and take the pictures in to Dane."

Breanna took one more look at the photo, then sighed. "It *is* just a patch of blur when you look close, isn't it?"

"Yup, and that's all it is."

As the words trailed off Tyler's lips, he glanced at the barn. Coaly barked, wagged his tail, then sat on his haunches to emit a long, mournful howl.

* * * * *

WITHOUT A TRACE

To the three men in my life: my husband, Sid, and our sons, Andy and John, for their unfailing love and support. And also to my precious sister, Darlene Christean, and to her husband, Gerald.

Special thanks to Betty and Tammi White for their help in researching the setting of this book.

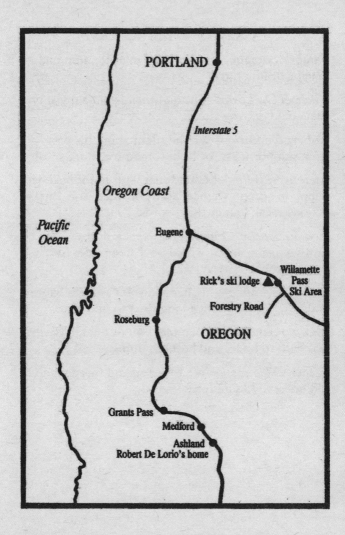

CAST OF CHARACTERS

Sarah Montague—Her routine investigation had taken a deadly turn.

Michael De Lorio—His nightmares hid a mystery that could destroy them.

Robert De Lorio—Was he silent about his past from stubbornness, or from something more sinister?

Marcus St. John—He said that with proof he'd be happy to accept Michael as his brother's son, but actions speak louder than words.

Angelo Santini—He'd never expected to see his brother again, and it would have been safer for everyone if he'd been right.

Brian La Grande—He had plans for Angelo Santini, and he'd been waiting a long time to find him.

Giorgio Santini—His connection to the De Lorios was hard to trace, and best left undisturbed.

Father O'Connell—What secrets did this amiable old priest hold safe for Robert?

PROLOGUE

BLOOD DRIPPED OFF the fringed edge of the chenille spread, splattering in soft plops on the floor tiles. The small boy cowering beneath the bed stared at it, watching as the dark red pools ran into the cracks between the yellow squares. The smell of the blood was sticky in his nostrils, a heavy sweet scent that made him feel sick. *Splat…splat…splat.* He counted the wet plops, *one, two, three,* then started over because three was as high as he knew his numbers. Tears stung his eyelids. He took a big breath and held it until his eyeballs burned dry and felt too large for their sockets. Slowly, afraid to make the tiniest noise, he expelled the air from his lungs.

The silence in the room seemed loud now that the popping sounds had stopped. Where was Helen? Why didn't she say something? He stared through the fringe of the bedspread, trying to see if the men were still in the room. Had Helen left him all alone? His gaze riveted on his teddy bear where it lay on the floor just beyond his reach. One of its ears was turning red. A sudden ache of longing swept through him for the soft, nubby warmth of the bear's fur against his face. The floor pressed hard against his bare arm, cold and gritty. The fuzz balls tickled when he breathed. His bottom lip quivered, and a stinging sensation crept up the back of his throat. He swallowed and blinked. They'd find him if he cried. He inched his fingers across the tiles toward the stuffed toy.

Soft footsteps approached the bed. The boy jerked his

hand back and again held his breath. *Helen?* Was she coming back for him? Through the chenille fringe, he saw a man's shiny black shoes step through the blood and leave red smears on the tile. His heart pounded. His cheek muscle twitched. Papa wore brown shoes with brown-black laces.

"Gino?" a deep voice called softly. "Gino? Are you in here, son?"

No, no. Go away, go away.

The shiny shoes stopped. The boy saw a gray pinstriped pant leg bending, the knee touching the floor, soaking up the spatters of crimson. And then a hand fanned under the bed, the fingers reaching like claws. The child shrank into himself, trying to be small so that the hand wouldn't find him.

"Gino? Don't be afraid. I'm your papa's friend. Gino? Gino, are you under there?"

The fingers were almost touching him. The child couldn't hold his breath any longer, and it gushed from his lungs on the crest of a scream. "No. Go away. Go away."

MICHAEL DE LORIO sat bolt upright in bed, his throat taut as a hoarse scream erupted from his chest. For a moment, he was trapped in a limbo between nightmare and reality, unsure who he was or where he was. The tenor of his own voice and the cries of the child in his dream seemed blended into one.

Throwing back the covers, he lunged from the bed to his feet. The carpet tufts felt soft between his toes—soft and nubby like the teddy bear's fur. He shot searching glances around him, so terrified his skin quivered. Slowly the room began to take shape, cast in shadow and pools of moonlight. He could see an oak dresser against the wall, a cushioned rocking chair in the reading corner. His bedroom. He glanced at the luminous face of his windup alarm. *One o'clock.*

His cotton pajama bottoms clung to his sweat-soaked legs. Running his palm over his bare chest, he traced the muscular contours of his flesh, shuddering as he dragged air into his lungs. He was Michael, Michael De Lorio, thirty-five years old, six foot one, a hundred and ninety-five pounds, a grown man standing beside his own bed inside his own home on City View Drive in Eugene, Oregon.

Gino? Gino? The man's voice from his dream still echoed in his head, and for at least the thousandth time, he wondered who in hell Gino was? Why did he dream of him, over and over and over again? It was a question Michael had asked himself all his life.

He went to the adjoining bathroom and wrenched the faucet on, splashing his face. His hands trembled as he lifted his cupped palms. The *whish* of the water drowned out the voices that whispered in his mind. *Voices.* God, how many of his patients would stay with him if they knew their shrink heard voices?

Grabbing a towel off the rack, he strode back to the bedroom. Blotting his face, he tossed the towel aside as he walked over to the open window. The September night breeze shifted the curtains. Bracing his hands against the sill, he bent one knee and leaned forward so the air could cool his body. The moonlight bathed the trees, turning the flickering leaves to silver. The neighbor's basset hound was baying three houses down, his cries long and forlorn. A cat squalled. A garbage can lid clanked. The normal sounds of night calmed Michael, and he closed his eyes.

Why he dreamed something so crazy, he didn't know. It seemed so real, so god-awful real—as if he had actually lived through it.

Perhaps he had....

Michael opened his eyes, staring out the window at

nothing. Then, with slow, mechanical precision, he walked to the nightstand, flipped on the light and opened his closet. Far back on the top shelf rested an old hatbox. He seized it with trembling hands and went to sit on the bed. It had been years since he had looked inside—so many years, in fact, that he paused a moment, deafened by the rhythmic pounding of his own heart. Then, with teeth clenched and shoulders erect, he lifted the lid. Inside, swathed in yellowed tissue paper, lay the cream-colored teddy bear.

Michael didn't know what he expected to see, but he had to look, regardless. He had done this at least a dozen times over the years, only to find nothing and then he would put the bear back in its box, his doubts put to rest with it. He picked up the stuffed toy and closely examined its left ear, parting the fuzzy nap to see the cloth. *Nothing.* No matter how closely he looked, he couldn't detect a speck of discolored fabric. He tightened his grip on the bear, sinking his fingers deep into the stuffing, his eyes fastened relentlessly on the seam that outlined the ear. It was unthinkable to take the toy apart. His mother had supposedly made it for him before he was born. Since her death, even though he was no longer sure she had done the stitching, it had become one of his most prized possessions, a keepsake that conjured sweet memories of his childhood.

As well as horrible ones....

Dreading what he must do, Michael took his penknife off his nightstand. What if he destroyed the toy and found nothing? He hesitated, holding the knife in an unsteady hand. Then he pried open the small blade. With grim determination, he cut the threads in the ear seam. As the aged cloth parted, a lump of dread lodged in his throat. *Oh, God, there it is.* A dark stain on the inner edge of the seam. Almost anything could have left the brown discoloration. After so many years, it was impossible to say for sure. Cola, maybe? Root beer. Coffee.

Or blood....

His shoulders slumped and he squeezed his eyes closed. He could probably get the stain analyzed, but how would he explain it if it did turn out to be blood? Was that what his father had been hiding from him all these years? Had his nightmare actually happened?

Michael had to find out. If his father wouldn't talk, he'd hire another investigator. And this time, no matter how many dead ends he ran into, nothing would stop him. He had to know the truth before the nightmare drove him insane.

CHAPTER ONE

SUNSHINE GLINTED OFF the gold lettering on the window. Michael paused on the sidewalk for a moment before entering the office. Roots. Good choice of name, short and catchy. He could only hope Sarah Montague lived up to her reputation as a genealogist and proved to be as clever.

The interior of the office was refreshingly cool on such a warm afternoon. He closed the door behind him, stretching his neck against the stiff band of his shirt collar. He stood on a half-moon of shale-colored tile that led to pale gray carpet. To his right and left, brass-framed end tables flanked identical black sofas. His gaze riveted on the detested black color a moment, then circled and came to rest on the young woman in the reception area. She sat hunched forward at her desk, peering in puzzlement at a computer screen. Michael's high hopes sank. This girl didn't match the self-assured voice he had heard on the phone this morning. He stepped onto the rug. "Excuse me, I'm Michael De Lorio."

The girl lifted her dark head and fastened a vague blue gaze on him. "Oh...hello! I'm Molly Harmon, the secretary."

"I'm here to see Sarah Montague?"

"Just a sec. She's in back. I lost a file and she's been looking and looking..." She rose from the desk, took three wobbly steps on white stiletto heels and then paused to ask, "What did you say your name was again?"

"De Lorio, Michael De Lorio. I have an appointment."

She walked to a rear doorway, repeating his name under her breath. "Sarah? A Mr. De Lorio is here to see you."

Michael watched the doorway as Molly teetered back to her desk. The dark-haired woman who emerged a moment later reassured him. She was tall, slender and professional looking in a lightweight white skirt and blazer-style jacket. Her rose-colored silk blouse added just the right touch of feminine softness. As she walked toward him, he noted that her burgundy pumps had practical two-inch heels. From the way she moved, though, he imagined she would glide just as smoothly in Molly's spikes. *Yes, she definitely had nice movement...nice everything.*

"Hello, Mr. De Lorio. I've been expecting you." Lifting intelligent, sherry-brown eyes to his, she gave him a firm handshake, then led him into an office to his left. Nodding toward a leather-cushioned chair in front of her desk, she said, "Please have a seat."

As Michael lowered himself into the chair, he flexed his shoulders, trying to relax. He had been dreading this appointment all morning. While she opened a side drawer and sifted through a pile of papers, he studied a picture that sat catty-corner on her desk: a close-up of her holding a gray striped cat. She wore an overlarge sweatshirt in the photo, her sable hair tousled in soft curls across her cheek. *Beautiful.* Not in the classic sense, more sultry and mysterious with those irregular features and dark eyes, but lovely just the same.

"Here we are." She slid some forms toward him. "You can fill these out here, if you like, or bring them back at your convenience."

He withdrew his pen from inside his smoke-blue suit jacket, angling the papers across the corner of her desk. "I'll do them here if you don't mind."

Sarah swiveled on her chair to face her computer, intending to continue as usual while he filled out the necessary paperwork, but he seemed so nervous and pensive, she sneaked a glance at him. He wasn't at all what she had expected. Hiding a smile, she forced her attention back to her keyboard and began typing. Was it his nervousness that intrigued her? Or those dreamy brown eyes and that wavy black hair? Most of her male clients weren't tall Mediterranean types with broad shoulders.

A frown settled on her brow. Handsome or not, the tension that radiated from him was almost palpable. She struck a wrong key and reversed her cursor. The back of her neck began to ache. Something about him—she had no idea what—didn't feel right. Her skin began to prickle with uneasiness. The stiff way he held himself, the grim set of his mouth, the quick shifting of his eyes. The word *desperate* sprang to mind.

About twenty minutes passed before she heard him shuffling the forms into a pile. She turned her chair, reaching for the papers he extended. Giving them a quick check, she said, "You mentioned on the phone that you want to find your birth parents?"

"Yes."

She nibbled on the end of her pen for a moment, skimming his history. "It looks as if you've already tried several other agencies. How long have you been searching?"

"Four years. You see, I didn't know I was adopted until my mother died of ovarian cancer. Her physician told me that instead of having a partial hysterectomy thirty-two years before, she should have had her ovaries removed as well. I was only thirty-one then."

"So you couldn't have been her natural child. Tell me, Mr. De Lorio, what makes you think my agency may succeed where so many others have failed? Most states are closed, you know. One can't review adoption records in closed states without a court order."

"Yes, I understand that."

"You've left a lot of blank spots here, very little info on your adoptive parents. You've listed their birthplaces in California, then there's nothing else on them until their move to Oregon. Have you filled in everything that you can?"

"No, not everything." His hand tightened on his pen. In the bright light, she could see a sheen of perspiration on the scythe-like bridge of his nose. "I've come up with some new information the other agencies didn't have— my birth name."

Sarah brightened. "Very good. That would at least give me something concrete to go on. How did you come by it?"

He glanced over his shoulder, a flush darkening his neck above the edge of his light blue shirt collar. "It's sort of personal. Do you mind?" Pushing up from the chair, he leaned sideways to shut the door. After he sat back down, he raked his fingers through his hair, shifting his gaze to the papers in her hands. "I don't know quite how to start."

"Try the beginning."

"That's usually my line. I never realized how hard it is to do. I'm a psychiatrist, you know." Pressing his fist to his mouth, he cleared his throat. "I, um, have this recurring dream. I've had it all my life. Before I discovered I was adopted, I thought it was just that, a troublesome dream. Now I believe it may be the manifestation of a forgotten traumatic experience that occurred in early childhood. It's not uncommon in cases of childhood trauma for a person to bury memories in his subconscious, then remember years later when he's better able to cope."

"What kind of dream?"

"A nightmare, actually, about a small boy under a bed. For years it was the same dream, over and over. But lately, it's becoming more and more detailed." His eyes lifted to hers, haunted, aching. "I know this probably sounds crazy."

"Extraordinary, perhaps, but not crazy. Please, go on."

"It's, um, hard to explain, but the name Gino Santini has come to me in my sleep." He leaned forward in his chair. "Please, I know this sounds farfetched, and you're probably thinking I'm some sort of kook, but at least hear me out."

Sarah studied his face, touched beyond words by the desperation she saw stamped upon his features. Settling back in his chair, he heaved a sigh and tugged the sleeves of his jacket down over his blue cuffs. His hands were trembling—large, broad hands that should have been rock steady. She couldn't recall ever having seen someone so reluctant to impart information. When at last he began describing his dream, her stomach lurched.

As he drew to a close, he said, "It's difficult to describe. It's almost as if there's something in my subconscious that's trying to—" He broke off and passed a hand over his eyes. "It's so real. So detailed. I can actually hear the blood dripping on the floor, smell it, feel the cold tiles against my skin."

Sarah licked her lips with a cottony tongue. "A-and you say the man calls you Gino?"

"Yes. The name Santini is sort of—" He cleared his throat again. "When I think of the name Gino, I hear this—" He broke off and gnawed his bottom lip, clearly uncomfortable. "I hate to say little voice—more like a whisper in my mind—Santini. It has to be a memory."

Sarah could hear the clock ticking and tried to focus her attention on its soothing, predictable cadence. Despite the bright fluorescent lighting, she had envisioned his nightmare clearly, and the horror of it still surrounded her. "Have you asked your adoptive father about this?"

"Yes. He not only grew angry, but refused to tell me anything." A muscle in his cheek rippled as he clenched and unclenched his teeth. "He's not well—his heart is bad—so that makes it difficult for me to insist he discuss it. However, from the way he acted…well, I think he's hiding something."

"Something horrible?" She couldn't miss the uncertainty in his eyes. "You're not the first person to go through this, you know. Though I'll admit, you seem to have far more reason than most, but we all wonder about something…if our parents were crazy, if they loved us, if maybe they had two heads, or a hereditary, terminal disease that strikes unexpectedly at twenty-five and kills you within days. It's normal to be curious. If it weren't, I'd still be doing secretarial work at my old law firm, and Roots wouldn't exist."

"You were adopted?"

"That's how I got started with Roots. I, um, lost my adoptive parents seven years ago when I was twenty-two, so I decided to find my real family. I couldn't afford professional help, so I did it by trial and error. After a year's work, I managed to locate my mom and a passel of brothers and sisters. Happy ending. Except that by then I was hooked, so I started to help other adoptees. Before I knew it, I was working at it full-time."

"So you really do understand?"

"I really do."

He visibly relaxed. "Given my father's reaction when I've tried to question him, I think he knows something about my real parents, something he considers so awful that he's gone to great lengths to hide it from me all these years. And the other agencies became evasive and dropped my case a few days after they began investigating my adoptive parents' background. They claimed there was nothing to be found on them before they moved to Oregon. I can't help but think my father deliberately altered his personal records so I could never trace him back to my place of birth. That's possible, isn't it?"

"I suppose."

"So why couldn't you do an investigation on the name Santini? Could you find my biological parents doing the search backward like that?"

"Actually that's not doing it backward. In closed states, getting an adoptee's birth name is quite often the hardest nut to crack."

He leaned forward again, drawing so close she could see amber flecks in his brown eyes. "Will you help me?"

Sarah longed to say yes. There was something about Michael De Lorio that attracted her, not just physically but emotionally as well. The torment on his face reached clear down inside her. "It isn't much to go on. If we had a vicinity to work in—the first and middle name of one or both birth parents... Do you know how many Santinis there might be in the United States?"

"Hundreds, probably. That's why I've come to you. This is important to me—damned important. I can't live the rest of my life like this. It's driving me crazy."

"The question is *how* important. I network with researchers all over the country, which eliminates long waiting periods getting information, but they charge me from twenty-five to sixty-five dollars an hour." She flashed him a smile. "You can run up a tab fast. A wild-goose chase could be extremely expensive. I'm not sure your adoptive parents' records can't be found. A simple error, such as inverted initials, can throw a data search way off track."

"Money isn't an issue. Whatever it costs, I'm willing to pay. But I'm telling you, I've been through this enough times to know, you won't find anything on my folks before they lived in Ashland—nothing."

"Perhaps." Sarah paused to lend the word emphasis. "If that *does* prove to be so, could you approach your father again? Some adoptive parents resent it very much when a child wants to find his birth parents. He may reconsid—"

"Impossible. He comes unglued every time the subject

is broached, and he has a bad heart. I spoke with him on the phone just this morning. Same old story. He refuses to discuss it."

"I see." Sarah straightened the papers on her desk, smoothing the edges where her nervous fingers had dog-eared them. "Is there anyone else who might know where they lived before moving into the state? The reason I ask is that I might be able to pick up a lead if I had a general vicinity to work on."

Michael shook his head, his expression defeated. Then he brightened. "Wait a minute. Father O'Connell down in Ashland might know. I was confirmed there when I was twelve. The church must have had proof of my baptism or I couldn't have received the sacrament."

Sarah scribbled the priest's name on her notepad. "You don't think you were baptized in Ashland?"

"It's unlikely. There's no record of my adoption in Oregon, and my folks, being Catholic, would have had me baptized immediately after."

"I tell you what, Mr. De Lorio—"

"Michael, please...."

"Michael." She felt her cheeks grow warm as she met his gaze; she had no idea why. He was simply dispensing with unnecessary formality. "Let me call this Father O'Connell and do a preliminary data request on the name De Lorio. If *that's* a lost cause, then I'll start looking under the name Santini. Sound fair?"

"Then you'll take my case?"

"It sounds like a challenge, and I've never turned my back on one yet."

"I was afraid...well, what with the dream and all, I thought you might not want to get involved. When you add everything up—the blood, my father's reaction, the life-long secrecy, the agencies dropping my case—it's not so farfetched to think one of my natural parents might have been another Jack the Ripper or something."

Rising from her desk, she extended her hand to him in farewell, repressing an amused smile. "I've had a number of clients, Michael, and I've never yet discovered anything sinister. Let me run a few preliminary tracers, then get back to you."

His warm fingers tightened around hers, sending a warm shock of awareness up her arm. "If there are any unexpected costs your office can't handle, you have my home and business numbers listed on the forms."

After he left her office, Sarah gathered the papers he had filled out, fully intending to stow them in a file until she had time to work on them. Her stomach growled with hunger from missing lunch, and her peach yogurt beckoned to her from its hiding place in the file cabinet. She also needed to make an appointment with the vet to have her tomcat, Moses, neutered before he single-handedly caused a feline population explosion. No two ways about it, she didn't have time to start on a new case today.

But still she hesitated. In all her years working as a genealogist, she'd never before encountered a client who'd had this sort of trouble finding his biological parents. There'd been failures, yes. But she'd never heard of agencies dropping a case a few days after beginning an investigation. Using normal channels and the mail, dead ends usually took weeks or months to detect. That intrigued her.

Was there something extraordinary about the De Lorio case? Had the other agencies found something confidential? Better left unsaid? *Blood on the floor.* Could it be an actual memory?

Sitting down at her desk, she leafed through the papers. Michael De Lorio's address was in one of the nicer sections of town. She ran a finger down the list of schools he had attended, then studied the information on his parents.

Since their move to Oregon, there was nothing odd, nothing that could be considered a red flag.

Sarah sighed and turned toward her telephone. There was no help for it. Moses was going to enjoy a few more nights on the prowl before Mom spoiled his fun. She had to get the preliminaries on this case out of the way or it'd be on her mind constantly. *Jack the Ripper?* Michael De Lorio had quite an imagination. A grin quirked the corners of her mouth as she dialed the number of the Catholic church in Ashland.

A lilting Irish brogue boomed over the wire. "St. Jude's, Father O'Connell speakin'."

Sarah tipped her head and smiled, immediately warming to the priest's friendly voice. "Hello, Father O'Connell, my name is Sarah Montague. I'm a genealogist working out of Eugene. I'm trying to assist one of your former parishioners in tracing his family tree. I was hoping you might help me?"

"Genealogy, ye say? We-l-ll-ll, isn't that grand? Ah, what an interestin' field ye've chosen for yerself, lass. I've a keen yen to do some of that myself. I'm from Ireland, ye know. It's a fascinatin' place, to be sure."

"So you'll help me?"

"But of course! What is it I can do for ye?"

"I was hoping you might have a record of my client's baptism. The man was adopted, you see, and we thought his records might give us some clue as to what part of the country he lived in at the time. The sacrament probably wasn't administered in your church, but he was confirmed there as a boy."

"Then I'll have a record of his baptismal certificate, to be sure. He couldn't have been confirmed without it. What's the name, and I'll be lookin' it up for ye?"

"De Lorio, Michael Robert De Lorio, son of Robert and Maria. It probably dates back thirty to thirty-five years."

Dead silence resounded on the line for a moment. When Father O'Connell spoke again, his friendly voice had taken on a definite chill factor. "De Lorio, ye say?"

"Yes, that's right, De Lorio."

"Thirty to thirty-five years ago? Hmm, that's a long time, lass. It'll take me a wee while to find it."

Sarah gripped the phone more tightly. "How long do you estimate?"

"Well, that'd be hard to say. Why don't ye give me yer name and number, and I'll be gettin' back to ye with it, eh?"

Sarah gave him the requested information. "I'd really appreciate a speedy reply."

"Ah, yes. And I'll be gettin' back to ye, Miss Montague, that I will. Goodbye. God be with ye."

The line clicked and went dead. She lowered the phone receiver to its cradle, realizing the Irishman's sudden reticence was an unmistakable don't-call-me-I'll-call-you stall tactic. Suspicion mushroomed inside her. What the hell was going on? Had she said something wrong? Offended the priest somehow? Or had it been the name De Lorio that had brought on the cold shoulder? Adding all the facts together, Sarah knew it was the latter. Father O'Connell had been more than eager to help her. And he *would* have if she had asked questions about any other person than Michael De Lorio. That could only mean one thing: whatever it was Michael's father, Robert De Lorio, was hiding, it probably wasn't about Michael's birth parents, but about Robert himself. Otherwise, why would the priest have clammed up?

She sighed and rubbed her forehead with tense fingers, staring at the forms Michael had filled out. He had hired many other investigators, from as far north as Seattle clear down to Los Angeles. She underlined the one from Washington, a place called Finders Keepers, then dialed the telephone number. A second later, a man named Paul Rafael answered.

After introducing herself and briefing Mr. Rafael on her involvement with the De Lorio investigation, Sarah said, "I was hoping you could pull the De Lorio file and tell me why your agency dropped his case, whether it was because you hit a snag or if it was for some other less obvious reason."

Rafael sighed. "I don't need to pull Dr. De Lorio's file to give you an answer, Ms. Montague. I handled that case, and I recall my reason for dropping it quite clearly."

"Which was?"

"I was told to back off."

Sarah's scalp prickled. "By whom?"

"I don't feel at liberty to tell you that. Suffice it to say that I had very good reason for agreeing and leave it at that. If you're smart, you'll do the same."

"I see."

"Probably not yet, but you will."

THAT EVENING AFTER work, Sarah parked her ten-speed in her driveway at the end of the cul-de-sac and shrugged out of her backpack, rubbing her neck and sighing. It was going to be a TV-dinner night; she was too tired to cook.

As she climbed the three steps to her secluded front porch, which was bordered on the street side by tall shrubs, she spied a note taped to her front door. *Not another complaint about Moses, please?* She rolled her eyes heavenward. Stupid cat. He'd probably been in Mr. Hansen's garbage can again. Or serenading the Siamese down the street at four o'clock in the morning.

Sarah snatched the note off the door, expecting a long, heated description of Moses's latest offense. Instead, the message was a brief four words: CURIOSITY KILLED

THE CAT. Her stomach dropped. Whirling, she flung her backpack onto the porch and ran back down the steps.

"Mosie? Mosie, love? Pretty cat, where are you?" Visions of her pet lying dead in the shrubs assailed Sarah. His neck broken. Shot. Poisoned. Fear swelled in her throat. This morning, she'd let him out for a bit and, typical of Moses, he hadn't come back. Now she wished she'd been late to work and gone out to find him. "Moses? Moses, dinnertime."

"Rrr-rrhow?"

Sarah whipped around. Her tattered gray tomcat emerged from his favorite hideout in the shrubs, arching his back against the low-hung boughs, his green eyes slitted from sleep. Sarah's breath caught and she scooped him into her arms, giving him a fierce hug. "Oh, you miserable, ugly, immoral rounder you. I don't know why I love you. All you are is trouble."

"Rrrhow?"

"You're going directly in the house. And tomorrow you're paying a visit to the vet. That note scared me silly."

As Sarah carried the cat to the front door, she gazed at the yellow piece of paper clutched in her hand. Why would anyone write something so deliberately cruel? To frighten her? Some of her neighbors had been upset by Moses's escapades, but never *that* upset. Furthermore, curiosity wasn't one of Moses's downfalls. His two greatest sins were a big appetite, which led him unerringly to loose garbage-can lids, and female felines, whom he pursued in the wee hours of the morning—nine times out of ten under a neighbor's bedroom window.

Unlocking the front door, she tossed the overweight tomcat into the entry, grabbed her backpack, then hesitated with one foot on the threshold to study the note more closely. Block printing, extremely sloppy, as if the writer had gone to great pains to disguise the handwriting. That struck her as odd. Her neighbors weren't usually shy when they complained about Moses.

Curiosity killed the cat. Sarah's mother must have said that to her a thousand times when she was a kid, usually when Sarah was poking her nose where it didn't belong. It was an old adage, and when people used it, they usually directed it at others as a warning. *Mind your own business, or you'll be sorry.*

She glanced uneasily over her shoulder, remembering Paul Rafael's vague warning. Suddenly she wasn't so certain this note was about Moses. She hurried into the house and bolted the front door. As she walked into her living room, she recalled the strange phone conversation she'd had with Father O'Connell in Ashland. Had the priest told Michael's father, Robert De Lorio, about her call? Had the older De Lorio driven to Eugene, looked up her address in the phone book and left this note on her door to scare her off? Sarah froze midstride on the pale blue carpet.

Am I jumping to crazy conclusions? She sighed and pressed the fingers of one hand to her throbbing temple. At this point, her instincts told her this case spelled trouble in capital letters. What was it Paul Rafael at Finders Keepers had said? *Suffice it to say that I had very good reason for agreeing and leave it at that. If you're smart, you'll do the same.* Should she tell Michael she'd changed her mind? She envisioned his haunted eyes. How could she jump ship when she knew how important this was to him? The answer to that one was easy; she couldn't. Not after having agreed to take the case and getting his hopes up. Nothing had actually happened, after all. And one thing she didn't do was renege on a deal.

Dumping her backpack on a chair, she strode into the kitchen and rifled the cupboard for some ready-to-eat spaghetti, too drained since finding the note to even bother with a TV dinner. After opening the can and dumping the contents into a microwave-safe bowl, Sarah grabbed the dishcloth to wipe up the mess she'd made. As she made a swipe at the drops of tomato sauce on the yellow countertop, she hesitated, remembering Michael's description of his dream. Blood dripping on yellow tile... A shiver ran over her as she recalled his words.

It's so real. So detailed. I can actually hear the blood dripping on the floor, smell it, feel the cold tiles against my skin.

Her throat tightened. There was a key phrase in there she hadn't picked up on earlier. A person couldn't *smell* the blood in a dream. See it, hear it, yes. But actually smell it?

A chill slithered up her spine. If Father O'Connell was Robert De Lorio's confessor, which he probably was, he'd be bound by his vow of silence. He wouldn't divulge the confidences of one of his parishioners.

A little boy hiding under a bed. Blood on the floor. The recollection of another name. Had Michael witnessed a violent crime? And worse yet, had Robert De Lorio committed it? *Oh, Sarah, what have you gotten yourself into this time?*

CHAPTER TWO

AS THE SUN sank behind the mountains, the room grew dark. Michael changed positions in the vinyl recliner, his mind drifting between consciousness and sleep as he nestled his cheek against the cool plastic upholstery. At first he could still feel the evening newspaper loosely grasped in his hands, hear it rustling when he moved, but second by second, he slipped deeper into slumber, losing touch with the room around him. As he did, his surroundings subtly altered. The cool vinyl pressing against his cheek changed to yellow tile—and he was afraid, afraid to move, to cry, to breathe. He peered out at a room through the blood-soaked fringe of his bedspread.

"Gino, come on, son. Don't be afraid. We must say goodbye to Helen, eh?"

Michael shook his head, shrinking away from the hand that reached under the bed for him. He didn't want to see Helen, didn't want to say goodbye. Through the fringe of the bedspread, he could see people in black clothing. They were standing in a line, shuffling slowly forward, taking turns—one by one—to look inside a long box. Michael didn't want a turn, didn't want to look. The hand grasped him by the arm and pulled him from beneath the bed. He wanted to scream, to fight, but he was too frightened.

Suddenly the scene changed and he found himself outside, walking on a sidewalk. He clung to the hand as he hurried to keep pace with legs much longer than his own. The city street had huge piles of dirty snow down its center where snowplows had made way for traffic. A string of black cars drove up, parking beside the curb. The car doors opened and people in black clothing piled out, walking up steep steps to join a line that trailed into a tall building. Glancing down at himself, Michael saw that he, too, was wearing black. The hand drew him relentlessly forward. Michael knew why. He had to go look in the box.

"It is okay, Gino. It is only Helen, eh? Nothing to be afraid of."

Michael shook his head, struggling to escape the hand as it pulled him inside the building, up a narrow aisle, closer to the box. It wasn't Helen in there. He knew it wasn't. He tried to say so, but no sound would come from his throat. He stared at the box, his heart pounding harder and harder when he saw blood running in streams down its sides. *They had to run. They had to get away.*

With all his might, Michael tugged free of the hand and escaped, running out the doors and down the steep steps. He looked back over his shoulder to see if anyone had chased him. His horror increased when he saw that blood oozed from under the doors, spilling in scarlet rivers down the steps after him.

Run, he had to run. His legs felt heavy and slow. Looking down, he saw the snow was so deep it reached to his hips. The farther he ran, the deeper it got, reaching to his waist, then to his chest. And behind him, drawing ever closer, was the blood.

He flailed his arms to keep from sinking, knowing if he sank he'd never resurface. Bright lights flashed in his eyes, blinding him. The hand, where was the hand? He scrambled for safety, turning, searching. *Help me. Someone, please, help me.*

"Michael?" a soft voice called. *"I'll help you."*

He whirled to see Sarah Montague standing above him, strangely untouched by the blood and snow that engulfed him. Her pretty face softened in a serene, reassuring smile, and she leaned forward, stretching out her palm to him. Michael windmilled his arms, trying desperately to get to her. She looked so beautiful, so comforting, so safe. She would help him. He reached up, catching hold of her fingertips. Could she pull him out or was he too heavy? After all, he was no longer a small boy but a full-grown man, much too heavy for such a slender woman to lift. He tried desperately to get a better grip on her, but her small hand slipped slowly from his. He felt himself falling, and the sensation so terrified him, he woke up with a start. "No!"

He jerked upright in the recliner, scattering the pages of the paper. His breath came in shallow, painful gasps that whined from his chest into the darkness around him. He leaped to his feet, and staggered across the carpet to grope for the electric switch next to the sliding glass door. Light flooded the room, blinding him just as the lights in his dream had. He threw an arm up to shield his eyes and leaned weakly against the wall.

"A dream, just a crazy dream," he whispered.

Even as he said the words, though, he knew it was much more than that. Emotionally he *was* sinking, and Sarah Montague was his only lifeline. Remembering the strong attraction he had felt toward her that morning, he now had cause to question his motives. Was it Sarah herself who appealed so strongly to him? Or was it the fact that he subconsciously saw her as his last hope?

RIGHT BEFORE LUNCH three days later, Sarah's office phone rang. With Robert De Lorio's name hovering foremost in her thoughts, she was taken aback to lift the receiver and hear him introduce himself. She knew Michael hadn't given his dad her number, so only one other person could have: Father O'Connell. By the time she realized that and gathered her wits, De Lorio had been talking a full thirty seconds, sometimes in emphatic Italian, sometimes in English, with her not registering a word.

"I'm asking you—please—don't continue with this craziness. For Michael's sake. And for your own."

Sarah stiffened at the ominous tone of his voice. "Mr. De Lorio, since your son's retained my services, I'm not at liberty to dis—"

"Parla inglese?" he yelled. "You have an obligation to watch out for your client's best interest, do you not?"

She held the phone away from her ear. "Yes, of course, b—"

"Then don't go any further with this investigation on Michael's background. *Mi lasci in pace!*"

Sarah rolled her eyes in exasperation. "Mr. De Lorio, you're talking to the wrong person, here. If you have a quarrel with your son over his hiring me, perhaps it would be more expedient to discuss it with him."

"I'm asking *you*, Miss Montague. I'll pay you. More than my son has offered. Name a price."

"I, um, couldn't accept money from y—"

"Haven't you heard anything I said?" The pathetic pleading note in De Lorio's voice altered, growing high-pitched with anger or panic, she wasn't sure which. "You keep on, and both of you may be sorry. *Capisce?* You understand, lady? Some things are better left buried. This is one of them."

After that proclamation, Sarah found herself on the frustrating end of a dead phone line. She sat there a moment, their conversation reeling through her mind like a poorly spliced recording. De Lorio's intimations were too alarming to ignore, not so much for her own sake as Michael's.

"I got it!" The door to Sarah's office swung wide, hitting the file cabinet with a loud thunk. Molly dashed in, waving a piece of paper. "Robert De Lorio, born in San

Francisco, California. And then I went one step further. I ran a search for Maria De Lorio's record of birth, too. Her maiden name was Ames. Got them both. Bet you can't believe it, huh? That guy you told me to call is really good. I didn't expect results this fast."

Sarah was indeed amazed, not so much over the speedy comeback but because Molly had gotten the information on her own. Sarah had hired the girl as a favor to her adoptive aunt, Janelle Montague, and had been kicking herself ever since. She reached for the computer readout, dubious but hopeful, scanning the information. Just as Michael had said, both his parents had been born in California.

"Well, did I do great or what?"

"Really great, Molly. I don't suppose you found any other records on the De Lorios prior to their moving to Ashland? Records of employment, taxes, education, anything?"

"Nope. Weird, huh?"

"To put it mildly." Sarah worried the end of her pen, staring at the paper she held. The government might lose files, but it was stretching credibility to the maximum to believe it could occur to two people in the same household. This whole mess stank to high heaven. It was time to talk to Michael De Lorio. He needed to be told about his father's phone call. Unless he gave her the go-ahead, she would have no choice but to abort her investigation and mark this case closed.

Glancing at her watch, Sarah reached for the phone book. After dialing Michael's office number and speaking with the receptionist, his deep voice came over the wire, crisp and businesslike. "Hello, Michael? Sarah Montague here. We need to talk."

She heard pages rustling. "My calendar's clear after two."

"Unfortunately mine's not. My mom and sister are stopping off for the night en route to an art exhibit in Portland and I have to pick them up at the airport. I could probably sneak away for a few minutes after five. Could you stop by then?"

"Five-thirty okay?"

"Perfect. I'll leave them to browse at the city mall and come back here to meet you. Try not to be late?"

"I'll be there."

MICHAEL ARRIVED AT the office at five-thirty on the dot. Molly was already gone, which was probably just as well. What Sarah had to say was for Michael's ears only, and she wasn't too sure telling *him* was such a good idea.

He looked just as she had described him to her sister, Beth, a few minutes ago—tall, dark, a little too intense. Today he wore a light brown sports coat over a cream-colored shirt and camel slacks. Gazing up at him, Sarah realized he'd been so much in her thoughts these past few days that she felt as if she'd known him much longer than she actually had. The shiver of excitement she felt at seeing him again set off warning bells in her mind. It wasn't like her to have this strong of a reaction to a man she barely knew.

"Have a seat, Michael."

"What's up?" He sank into the chair, his smile hesitant.

As quickly as she could, she explained that she'd had no luck tracing his folks before their move to Ashland. Then she recounted her phone conversation with Father O'Connell. "To say the temperature dropped when I said your name would be a gross understatement."

"I can tell by your face, there's more. What is it?"

It was on the tip of her tongue to tell him about the note that had been left on her door, but she stifled the urge. She had no positive proof, and it went against her grain to make wild accusations. "Your father called me this morning, pleading with me to stop working on your case."

"Papa? How the hell did he get—"

"It's obvious, isn't it? Father O'Connell called him. Michael, I'm not a Catholic, but I do know a priest doesn't repeat or inadvertently reveal what he's been told in the confessional. Whatever it is your dad's covering up, I think it's about himself, not about your natural parents."

"About himself?"

With a determined lift of her chin, Sarah looked him dead in the eye. "When I was talking with your father, I had the distinct impression he was threatening me."

For the space of several unnaturally quiet seconds, he stared at her, and then without warning, burst into laughter. Sarah could only gape at him. As his mirth ebbed, he angled forward in the chair, his eyes searching hers. "He threatened you? My dad? You're sure it is *my* dad we're talking about?"

"I'm positive. And I fail to see the humor in this."

"Papa's a plump little baker. When he gets mad, he pulverizes bread dough, not people."

Tension tied the muscles along each side of Sarah's neck into painful knots. "I know you love your father, but—"

He held up a hand to indicate the older De Lorio stood less than shoulder high, his smile broadening. "If you could have seen him while you were talking to him, I think your impression of him would have been completely different. I tell you, Sarah—it is okay if I call you Sarah—my dad's harmless."

"Let's put it this way. He talks seven feet tall." She lifted an eyebrow. "What does *Mi lasci in pace!* mean?"

He winced at her pronunciation and laughed again. "It means leave me alone. I'm really sorry he called you. As for Father O'Connell, the two of them are like this." He held up two tightly pressed fingers. "Father O'Connell was our pastor when I was a kid. He and Papa became best friends. In all the years since, they've kept in touch, and now Father's back on limited duty at St. Jude's until he retires. I should have known this would happen."

Seeing Michael's reaction to the scenario she had built up in her mind, Sarah was beginning to wonder if she'd overreacted. "I guess that crack you made about Jack the Ripper made my imagination run away with me. When the priest was so evasive, I thought it could only mean that—" Heat spiraled to her face. "Oh, well, it doesn't matter now what I thought."

He sighed. "Ignore my dad, Sarah. He tends to get a little carried away. As for Father O'Connell, why don't we run down tomorrow and see him? He won't find it so easy to be evasive if we're standing right there, requesting documents I've every right to see. I have a few patients scheduled, but none I can't reschedule. Will your relatives be gone by morning? We could make a day of it, have lunch, then drive back. The grounds are gorgeous."

Her family was leaving right after breakfast. Though she didn't have much hope that a visit with Father O'Connell would prove worthwhile, she couldn't resist the temptation of an entire day in Michael's company. She tried to keep her voice crisp and impersonal as she replied, "Yes, that might be a good idea if you're sure you want to continue with the search."

"Do I detect some hesitancy?"

"A little. Your father's dead set against us doing this."

He rose from the chair. "I'm not backing off, Sarah, not as long as you're still game. Papa must have really laid it on thick. He didn't get too nasty, I hope?"

She pushed up from the desk and reached for her purse. It would be simple to recount the conversation word for word, but not so easy to impart what had been said between the lines. "Well, he didn't come right out and *say* anything. It was more insinuation than anything."

Michael arched an eyebrow but didn't press her for details, for which she was grateful. Glancing down at the handbag she held in the crook of her arm, he said, "If you're leaving now, I'll see you to your car."

She checked to be sure her computer was off, then went to the fireproof file cabinet to give the top drawer a tug to make sure it was locked. Sidestepping Michael to exit her office, she fished in her bag for her keys as she walked. "I appreciate your waiting. I wouldn't want to get waylaid by a little baker on the way out."

His response to that was a low laugh. As they walked across the waiting area, his sleeve brushed hers. The contact set her skin to tingling. Though he was longer of leg, he matched his stride to hers. The breadth of his shoulders and the masculine way he swung his arms made her feel small and feminine. Sarah tried to imagine what her sister Beth might say if she could meet Michael and decided that the seventeen-year-old would probably sigh and call him *a hunk*, a fitting description if Sarah's racing pulse was an indication.

He waited outside on the sidewalk while she locked the front door. The back of her neck prickled because she knew he was studying her. She was glad she hadn't ridden her bike to work this morning. Michael De Lorio was one fellow she didn't want seeing her in riding tights—not that she looked *that* bad in them, but a knockout, she wasn't.

As she turned in the direction of her car, he stepped to the outside of the sidewalk to take her arm. It was an old-fashioned, gentlemanly gesture and apparently as instinctive to him as breathing. The light touch of his fingertips told her a great deal about the kind of man he was, and a great deal about herself. Her insides rippled with excitement. *Careful, Sarah.*

Standing at the curb, he watched while she unlocked the car door. "About your dad, Michael, I hope I didn't—"

"You didn't." His smile tipped up one corner of his

mouth, giving his expression a wry twist. His gaze met hers, soft as a caress. "What time would you like to leave tomorrow?"

For a fleeting instant, Sarah wished the day they had planned wasn't solely for business. "How's nine sound? I have a few things to take care of first, so could you pick me up here?"

He nodded, his eyes never leaving hers. She forced herself to look away and climbed into the car to start the engine. As she let out the clutch and eased away from the curb into the light traffic, his image was caught in her rearview mirror. She heaved a regretful sigh. It was just her luck, wasn't it? A good-looking man like Michael De Lorio, and he had to be a client.

Michael shoved his hands into his slacks pockets and gazed after the Fiero as it rounded the corner, remembering his recent nightmare and his fear that Sarah's appeal to him was fostered more by emotional need than genuine attraction. He smiled to himself. Seeing her a second time had dispelled his anxiety on that score. She was a beautiful woman, no doubt about it; only a blind man could remain unaffected by her. Even though he knew he shouldn't, he looked forward to spending time with her tomorrow. It was a business trip, after all, not a date. How much trouble could he possibly get into?

ST. JUDE'S WAS a beautiful old church of dark stone with velvety green lawns sweeping from its foundations out to the street. As Sarah and Michael walked up the cement path to the rectory, she slowed her pace, smoothing the wrinkles that sitting so long in the car had creased in her skirt. Michael preceded her up the steps to ring the bell, and a moment later, an older woman answered the door, directing them into a sitting room to wait while she went to find Father O'Connell.

Sarah lowered herself into an ancient but presentable chair, flashing a tense smile at Michael. The delicious aroma of fresh-baked bread permeated the room. Though she and Michael had just finished lunch, her mouth watered; bread hot from the oven was one of her weaknesses.

Michael took a seat on the sofa, and his gaze drifted thoughtfully around the room. "I always waited in here for Father when I was a kid so I could walk over to the sacristy with him to dress for Mass. Funny how some things never change."

Sarah looked at the Spartan furnishings through new eyes, trying to envision Michael as a small boy. His tone when he spoke of Father O'Connell was filled with warmth and fondness. Moments later, the priest stepped across the threshold. He was a tall, heavyset man with bushy gray eyebrows, lively blue eyes and a broad smile that looked so sincere Sarah couldn't help responding in kind. In a booming, melodious brogue, he cried, "Michael, me boy, it's a pleasure to be seein' ye, it is. How've ye been?"

Michael leaped to his feet to receive a quick hug from the older man. "Pretty good, Father. And you?"

"Fit as a fiddle. I wish ye'd called and I'd have changed into street clothes. I know how ye hate the black."

"Don't worry about it. We can't stay that long."

O'Connell directed his attention to Sarah. "And who might this fair lass be? Ah, Michael, it's clear ye've not lost yer eye for the ladies."

Sarah felt a flush rise to her cheeks as she stood and extended her hand. "Hello, Father."

Father O'Connell noted her pink cheeks and gave her a sly wink. "Even starvation diets don't deny ye a look at the menu."

Michael's eyes twinkled with laughter, resting warmly on Sarah as he went through the formal introductions.

"Sarah's a genealogist, Father. She's trying to help me find my parents."

"We spoke on the phone a few days back," Sarah inserted.

The priest's grasp on her fingers tightened. She flashed him a glance, noting that his glorious smile suddenly seemed strained. "Ah, yes, I remember. Ye were wantin' Michael's baptismal certificate, weren't ye?" A frown creased his forehead. "Ye know, I can't seem to come up with it for ye."

Michael's eyebrows lifted. "It's lost?"

"Oh, certainly not that." Father O'Connell released his grip on Sarah's hand. "It'd be unheard-of for the church to lose a document. No, Michael, I just can't come up with it. I'll be givin' it to ye, but as I explained to your friend days back, it may take me a wee while."

Michael's brown eyes shifted to catch Sarah's gaze, transmitting a message she couldn't quite read. "A week, a month? You wouldn't be waiting until my father is no longer around to object?"

Father O'Connell clasped his hands together in a gesture of delightful anticipation. "Tell me, have ye had yer lunch? Bessie makes sauerbraten that's the closest thing to heaven this side of the hereafter. And she always makes enough for me and ten others." He gestured toward the door. "Shall we? It'll be gettin' cold, and there's no wrath on earth comparin' to Bessie's if ye're late to her table."

Sarah fought to keep her grin hidden as she watched Michael's expressions, bewilderment and disbelief giving way to discomfiture. He had just been told, ever so politely, to eat or leave. He clearly respected the old man far too much to press him. "Um, we've eaten, thank you."

"Oh, what a shame." Placing his left hand on Sarah's shoulder to give her an affectionate squeeze, Father proffered his right to Michael. "Ye'll come again soon? It's been a disgracefully long while since I've seen ye. Ye're attendin' Mass regularly?"

Michael pumped his hand, smiling stiffly. "Yes, Father."

"There's a good boy. And volunteerin' yer time, of course, and goin' to confession as ye should?"

"Yes, Father." Glancing at Sarah, Michael said, "Well, we'd better get going before Bessie skins him alive."

With a theatrical sigh, the priest escorted them to the front door. "She has no reverence, does Bessie, not when it comes to runnin' her kitchen. Goodbye now, God be with ye."

As the door of the rectory closed behind them, Sarah couldn't suppress a giggle. She touched her fingers to her lips, glancing apologetically at Michael, not at all sure he'd take kindly to being laughed at. For a moment, he scowled darkly. Then a grin crept across his face. "Not very masterful, am I?"

"Not very. I'm afraid confronting him didn't work."

Michael sighed and draped his arm across her shoulders, shaking his head as they walked down the steps. "Any second, I expected him to quiz me on my catechism. Childhood conditioning. You'd think that I, of all people, would be able to overcome it, but it's easier said than done."

Sarah chuckled. "Give yourself a break. You love him; it's as clear as the nose on your face."

He gave the appendage in question a swipe with his knuckles. "That's pretty darned clear with a honker like mine." He groaned. "I can't believe I let him get away with that."

"No big deal. We'll simply proceed with the search using the name Santini."

His fingers curled on her upper arm, his thumb making tiny, maddening circles on the sleeve of her jacket. "A name isn't much for you to go on."

"Think positive." Casting him a quizzical glance as

they drew up at the car, she said, "Can I ask a question I've no right asking? How can a born and raised Catholic hate black?"

"It's a phobia of mine." A distant look clouded his eyes as he released her to open the passenger door. "You know, that's the first time Father's ever lied to me."

She placed her hand on his arm. "Don't be so hard on him. He didn't actually say he couldn't *find* the record, he said he couldn't come up with it. That could have meant something or someone prevented him from handing it over. Like your father, perhaps?"

He rasped his finger along her cheek, his eyes softening with some emotion she couldn't define. "You're a very special lady to understand that, you know it?" Running his finger under her chin, he raised her face, a smile quirking his mouth as he whispered, "And as usual, Father's right. *Molto bella!*"

Not sure what he had just said, she slid into the car, choosing to ignore his comment. "You agree? It was probably your dad."

His expression grew serious. "I'm afraid so. The question is why? What is it my father is so afraid I'll discover?"

"I don't know the answer to that yet, but give me a few days."

He snapped his fingers, leaning down to poke his head inside the car so she could hear him above the sounds of passing traffic. "Which reminds me, I had another dream. Wherever I came from, I think it was a large city that got heavy snowfall."

As he circled the car to climb in on the driver's side, Sarah jotted that bit of information in her notebook so it wouldn't slip her mind, then she glanced at her watch. It was nearly two o'clock. By the time they made the three-and-a-half hour drive to Eugene, it would be early evening. She'd just have enough time to run downtown for an Italian dictionary, get dinner, do the dishes and wade through some paperwork before she crawled into bed. Ah, yes, an Italian dictionary. If her experiences thus far with the De Lorio men were any indication, she was going to need one. *Molto bella?* She hoped the meaning of those two words was as romantic as Michael's deep voice had made it sound.

THE FLASHLIGHT FLICKERED unsteadily on the pale gray carpet as the man pressed the office door of Roots closed behind him. Wheezing for air after his sprint up the sidewalk, he shoved his pry bar into the deep pocket of his raincoat and switched the flashlight off to peer out the window into the street. He half expected a patrol car to round the corner. *Nothing. Not a soul in sight this hour of the morning.* Broken glass crunched beneath the soles of his shoes as he stepped across the entry onto the rug. It was so dark, he couldn't see two feet ahead of him.

Flipping the light back on, he fanned the beam along the walls. Brass end tables. A desk. He strode swiftly across the room and sat in the desk chair to drag open the top left drawer. He found a half-eaten candy bar, three bottles of fingernail polish and a wire brush with wads of dark brown hair caught in the bristles. With a muffled curse, he slammed the drawer closed and quickly searched the others. Nothing. On the desktop, he noticed a sheaf of papers. Pulling them toward him, he spotlighted the top page. Cartoon sketches?

Rolling the chair back on its castors, he rose and trailed the light around the room again, starting to feel panicky. If he couldn't find the files this would all be for nothing. Spying another door, he hurried toward it and entered a small interior office. His light beam bathed the gray-green side of a metal cabinet. *Pay dirt.*

His lungs still whining, he seized the top drawer handle

and pulled. *Locked.* Cursing again, he laid the flashlight on the cabinet and retrieved the pry bar from his pocket. The light beam shining in his eyes blinded him. He had to feel with his fingertips to insert the bar into the crack above the drawer. Then it took all his weight as leverage to break the catch. Metal groaned. The lock finally gave with a resounding pop. He froze for a second, listening. Except for the irregular pounding of his heart, the place was as quiet as a tomb. He jerked the drawer open and grabbed his light, scanning the alphabetical letter tabs until he came to the *D*. And there it was—the De Lorio file. He smiled and lifted it from the runners.

Losing *this* would stop her dead. Tugging a large plastic bag from his pocket, he began pulling all the files from the top drawer. When those were in the bag, he opened the second drawer and took several others at random. There'd be no way for the cops to trace him with so many names missing.

Satisfied, he stepped away, searching the rest of the room to be sure there wasn't another file cabinet. His light reflected off what appeared to be a television screen. *One of those word processors. Damned newfangled gadgets.*

Going back into the front office, he placed his bag and light on the desk. Montague would probably guess who had done this. That suited him just fine. He had to show her he meant business. If this didn't stop her, he'd think of something that would....

CHAPTER THREE

MICHAEL TURNED HIS face into his pillow, frowning at the steady, monotonous pitter-patter of raindrops hitting glass. Or was it rain? Maybe it was snow. He decided to get out of bed and look. Running to the window, he put his hands on the sill and stood on his tiptoes, straining to see out. His nose pressed against the cold glass, his breath steaming an aureole around his face. Yes, it was snow. Big, fat flakes. Tonight, Papa would help him roll a snowball.

His heart skipped with excitement. There came Papa now, pulling up in front of the house in a very long, black car, the same kind of car he and Mamma had been driven away in that morning. Michael gripped the windowsill, his mouth spreading in a gigantic grin that soon turned to a frown. None of those men were his papa. And his mamma wasn't there, either.

"Gino! Holy Mother, protect us."

Michael turned to stare at the woman who came running up behind him, her black rubber-soled shoes going *squeak-squeak* with every step she took. As she swooped down on him, she looked so huge in her black dress and frilly white apron that he fell back to gape at her. Before he could move, she grabbed him, knocking the wind out of him as her fat arms cinched tight around his tummy.

"Under the bed, Gino, you hear? You are not to make a sound, not a single sound until Helen tells you."

"No! It's dark under there. I want my mamma. *Mi lasci in pace. Vada via!*"

Helen gave him a shake that snapped his head back so hard it hurt his neck. Her blue eyes looked wild and scary. "You will mind me, Gino. Not a sound! One whimper and I'll spank you."

The floor beneath the bed was cold and hard. Michael rubbed his eyes, then blinked. He could see Helen's black shoes through the bedspread fringe at the foot of his bed. *Silence.* The room was so quiet, he could even hear Helen breathing. Then a crashing sound startled him. Footsteps thundered, shaking the floor. Another crash. He heard Helen whimper, a soft, uneven sound that turned his skin to ice. Then she whispered, "Oh, my God, I am heartily sorry f—"

A loud popping sound erupted and Helen gave a strange grunt. Then his bed went *boom* above him, the metal spring supports smacking his shoulder. He saw his teddy bear fall on the floor. Footsteps, everywhere footsteps. Doors crashed open. Something popped again, ugly sounds followed by hard thunks hitting the walls. Michael stared out at the room through the border of his bedspread. Helen's shoes were gone.

And then he saw it. Something thick and red, running down a strand of the yellow bedspread fringe. Blood....

With a scream, Michael jolted awake, jackknifing into a sitting position. His throat convulsed around a single word. "Helen! Helen…"

Sweat ran down his face in rivers and his chest heaved for air. With bulging eyes, he stared into the darkness around him, his heart slamming. Inside his head, a terrified woman's voice whispered, "Oh, my God, I am heartily sorry…" He clamped his hands over his ears, lunging to his feet.

"Oh, Lord, please…" The sound of his own voice reverberated around him, hoarse, ragged, a man's voice. Only a moment ago, he had been a child. Groping for the wall switch, he threw the lights on and stared at his bedroom window, relieved to see a modern metal frame instead of an old-fashioned wooden sash. Rain pelted the glass. Leaning against the wall, he squeezed his eyes closed, forcing himself to breathe deeply and evenly. He was Michael, not Gino. It had only been a nightmare.

THE ELECTRONIC BEEP of the alarm clock badgered the edges of Sarah's consciousness until she stirred and threw out an arm to grope for the nightstand, slapping the beeper off. Throwing her legs over the edge of the bed, she felt with her feet for her fuzzy slippers. Once those were on, she rose and wove her way from the bedroom to the kitchen, palms skimming along the white enamel walls to keep her on course. *Coffee.*

Just as she reached the automatic coffee maker, which had been preset the night before, the phone had the audacity to ring. She groped her way down the cupboards, blinking to see. Her ankle bumped Moses's dish as she grabbed the receiver, and the next instant, she felt cold water slosh onto her foot and trickle between her toes. "Hello?"

"Sarah, we've been robbed! Oh, God, I can't believe it."

Prying her eyelids open, Sarah blinked three more times in rapid succession, focusing on the refrigerator magnets. The fake fried egg her little sister, Beth, had sent her for her birthday last year stared back at her. "Molly? That you?"

"Who d'ya think? Dammit, Sarah, I could get murdered standing here! They could still be—oh, God—what do I do?"

Numb, her brain was numb. Sarah dragged her hair back from her face. "Did you say a robbery? There's no money."

"They broke in. Broke the door glass, tore the place up."

Sarah finally came awake enough to think. Fright zigzagged through her. "Get outside, Molly, on the sidewalk where people can see you. I'll phone the cops."

DAMN, DAMN, DAMN. Why, when there was an emergency, did she hit every red light in town and then not find a single parking place? *And no Molly out front.* Frantic, Sarah scanned the street. A bubble top, thank God. The police were here. After double-parking, too frightened about Molly to care if she got a ticket, Sarah threw open the door of her Fiero and dashed between the parked cars onto the sidewalk. Shards of glass littered the shale-colored tiles inside the doorway of Roots. She sprinted through it, braking to a halt when she reached the rug.

Disaster. It was the only word to describe the cyclone effect that greeted her. The broken glass in the door was only a preview. Papers were strewn, tables overturned, garbage dumped, manila envelopes thrown helter-skelter. And poor Molly! Hair awry, mascara running down her cheeks in black rivers, her bottom lip quivering as she responded to a bored police officer's rapid-fire questions. Sarah straightened her windbreaker to conceal her pajama top and stepped forward, shoving her tangled hair from her eyes. "Excuse me. I'm Sarah Montague, the owner. Perhaps I can tell you what you need to know."

The officer skimmed a blue-eyed gaze over her, taking in her water-matted pink fuzzy slippers, her faded blue jeans and the Oregon Ducks windbreaker she hugged around herself. "Did you discover the break-in?"

"No."

"Then I'll speak with you in a moment."

Sarah turned to stare in shock at the mess around her. Why would anyone— She broke off midthought, her gaze riveted to her office door. Placing one numb foot before the other, she walked toward it. *Robert De Lorio.* He had done this; she was sure of it. Fury kindled in the pit of her stomach, flashing outward like jags of lightning to make her whole body tingle. She threw open the door, made a sharp right and stood staring at the empty top drawer of her file. It had been forced open and the *D* file was gone.

Returning to the destroyed waiting area, Sarah said, "I think I know who did this."

The policeman regarded her with solemn-faced curiosity. "Who would that be, ma'am?"

"A man named Robert De Lorio. He called me the day before yesterday making vague threats. I'm working with his son, trying to find his natural parents. De Lorio objects. I think that—"

"It looks like kids, ma'am. No serious damage. I see prank written all over it."

He called this a prank? It'd take an entire day to clean it up, another day to create new hard-copy files, not to mention getting someone in to fix the door. Her spine stiffened. *Hard copy!* Some of it had been stolen. What if...

With her heart in her throat, Sarah ran back to her office and flipped on her computer, praying her documents hadn't been erased. She called up the De Lorio file, holding her breath, expecting the computer to tell her no such document existed.

"Everything okay with the computer?"

She glanced up, focusing on the officer's crisp blue shirt. "Yes, thank God. He didn't think to sabotage my master files."

"Trust me, lady, if it had been an adult out to steal information or *sabotage* you, as you put it, the computer would have been the first thing to get it. It was kids. Last week, we had fourteen taillights busted out in one night. Weekend before, the city mall windows got soaped. Three days before that—"

"I'm convinced." Sarah held up her hands in surrender.

What point was there in arguing? She knew what she knew. "I've got enough troubles without hearing a crime report."

For the first time, he smiled. "Try a cup of coffee. You'll feel a little more oriented once you wake up." He pulled his clipboard from his belt, jotted something down, then tipped his hat to her. "I'll make out a report. Don't hold your breath for results, though. Finding the kids who do these things is nigh unto impossible. We try but…" With a shrug, he turned on his heel and left.

Balling her hands into fists, she turned her head to glare at her rifled file cabinet. *Kids, my foot.* Fiery anger inched up her spine. It might take her two days to get back on track, but back on track she would be. And when she was, she wouldn't waste a second before trying to find something under the name Santini in major cities that experienced heavy snowfall. Robert De Lorio was going to find out what *war* tactics were. He'd probably counted on her running straight to Michael. And of course Michael would call the investigation off, not because he wanted to but because he wasn't the type of man to let someone else take the heat for him. Well, Sarah wasn't going to play according to that game plan. She'd taken this case with the intention of seeing it through to the end, and that was exactly what she would do.

FIVE DAYS LATER, Sarah had cause to wonder if sticking with the De Lorio case had been such a great idea. She didn't know whether to smile or frown when she saw Michael standing outside the door of her office. When he hadn't shown up by closing time, as he'd promised, she had convinced herself he wasn't coming. And she had been *relieved.*

"Hello, Michael."

"Sorry I'm late. I had a heavy patient load this afternoon." He stepped inside, closed the door and lowered himself into the chair across from her, propping his arms loosely on the rests, one foot on his knee. "So what's up?"

For an instant, she thought about lying, saying she had found nothing. "Um, I think I've found your mother."

His hands curled around the ends of the armrests, his knuckles turning white. "My mother?"

Sarah felt her mouth curving in a smile. This was the *good* part, the easy part. "I put out feelers on the name Santini in several large cities that experience heavy snowfall. Three days ago, I finally located a Giorgio Santini in the Chicago area whose brother, Angelo, adopted an infant boy whose birth date matches yours." His throat tightened. "His adoptive parents named him Gino." So far, so good. He hadn't made the connection yet. "Giorgio said the birth mother was a sixteen-year-old girl named Eleanora Pierce, the father a boy named Adam St. John. A teenage pregnancy, from what he said, which is probably why your mother gave you up." The metallic taste of dread shriveled the back of her tongue. "I called and checked county records and found a marriage license on Eleanora Pierce to a Darrell Miller."

"Hold a sec. My folks were named De Lorio, not Santini."

He had finally clued in. "De Lorio's their name now."

"What d'you mean, now?"

"The Santinis that adopted Eleanora Pierce's child disappeared without a trace when the boy was about three years old. Giorgio Santini hasn't seen his brother since. Add it up."

Michael leaned forward in his chair. "What in hell are you saying? You add it up. That *is* what I'm paying you to do."

The tension in the room made the air seem to crackle between them. Sarah licked her bottom lip, then looked

Michael directly in the eye. "If you're going to hold this against me, then let's just drop it right here, shall we?"

A muscle in his jaw flickered. "You know I won't."

"Then why are you angry before I even get started?"

Sarah could hear the clock ticking on the wall, the low hum of her computer terminal, the ragged edge of Michael's breathing. His eyes were black with emotion.

At last he replied, "Because I love my dad."

It was so simple an answer, but it revealed his feelings much more clearly than eloquence might have. A part of him didn't want to hear what she had to say, had probably been blind to the truth for years rather than accept it. She not only couldn't blame him for that, but she admired him for it. This was his *father* she was talking about.

A gray line etched his full lips. "Just what the hell did you find?"

"I just told you. And you're pretending not to hear. I don't think De Lorio was your parents' real name."

"Of course it was."

"Are you certain of that?"

He sprang from his chair to rest his hands on her desk, his face scant inches from hers. "What possible motivation could two people have for moving to a new place and living a lie?"

"Your father might have had a criminal record or something that he was trying to hide."

Incredulity lined his face. He wheeled away from her, took two paces, then rounded for a verbal attack. "My dad is a baker, for heaven's sake, not a criminal. He's a little man with a great big grin who goes to Mass every Sunday and confession every Saturday night. As far as I know, he's never even had a traffic ticket. Why do you persist in painting him the bad guy?"

"How am *I* supposed to know why they did it? He could have gotten in trouble. Way back when he was young. It's been years. People *do* change. Or it might have been a scandal they ran from, family trouble, a jealous ex-wife or husband." She threw up her hands. "Look, you hired me to do this."

He stood there, jacket lapels swept back, squared chin jutting, his eyes aflame with anger. Sarah wanted to scream to end the silence. She was glad now that she had chosen not to mention the note and break-in. Blaming his father for that on top of everything else would have made things even worse.

"Perhaps it would be better if you hired another agency to finish this investigation," she said with deceptive calm.

His face, chiseled like granite one moment, crumpled the next. His shoulders slumped, and he returned to his chair, sinking into it as if his strength had failed him. Bending forward, he dropped his head in his hands. Sarah stared at him, not knowing what to say, what to do.

"It isn't a nightmare, is it, Sarah? The little boy under the bed, the blood. It's a memory."

It was more statement than question. She realized she was shaking. "I—I could be wrong. Maybe you're not the Santini child after all. It's sheer supposition at this point."

"Now I know why the other agencies petered out on me, why everybody looked at me so strangely. They suspected my dad had changed his identity." He lifted his head. Moisture glistened in his eyes. "Is there any way it's a mistake? Did you check to see if you could find death certificates on the De Lorios?"

"Not yet. I wanted to tell you first. We both know what I'll find, Michael. People who assume new identities quite often borrow the identity of a deceased person who was born the same year and then died at an early age."

"I know all that."

Sarah forced her fist open and dropped her pen onto her desk. "I think you need to have a long talk with your father. He deserves that much. No telling why he fled Chicago. It'd be a shame to bring the past crashing down around his head."

"He's got a bad heart."

Sarah didn't see how Robert De Lorio's health had a bearing on the matter. He'd have heart failure for sure if the law, rather than his son, showed up on his doorstep. Of course, she didn't dare say that—not straight out.

"He gets so upset, so angry, when I talk to him about this. I have to do this on my own. Sarah…am I doing the wrong thing? Should I just let it go?"

"Can you?"

Seconds ticked by. "No."

"You've answered your own question then. But you're going to have to be extremely cautious. While speaking to Giorgio Santini yesterday morning, I got the distinct impression he was anxious to know where his brother might be, but at the same time, he seemed to have some reservations about seeing you. I didn't give your name to him—didn't give it to anyone—just mine and the agency's, for fear of repercussions." Sarah picked up a paper with the names, addresses and phone numbers she had written down for him. She handed it to Michael. "You'll need your mother's number off there. What you do about the other two names I've listed is up to you. I would hope that you'll respect your father's right to anonymity, though."

"You really believe my dad ran from something in Chicago?"

"Yes. And I think it's something nasty. Considering your dream, Michael. What *should* I think? If you want to see your natural mother, that should be safe enough. I doubt your biological relatives are ever in contact with your adoptive father's family. I'd steer clear of the Santinis, though. Just in case."

"My mom—this Pierce woman—she agreed to see me?"

"She was thrilled. Couldn't believe I'd found her. She sounded like a lovely person. I did detect a certain hesitancy in her voice at first, as if… Well, I think there's a possibility your existence is something she's kept secret from her family. But in my experience, unless there are extenuating circumstances, that should iron itself out. She'll get around to telling her loved ones in time. Until then, you'll have to be discreet."

Michael's expression looked a little vague. Sarah realized he was reeling from shock. "And she lives in Chicago?"

"On the outskirts."

"And my dad? Did you find my real dad?"

"He's…" The word *dead* seemed so cold. "He's gone, Michael. I did get in touch with his brother the day before yesterday, a man named Marcus St. John, but he was none too encouraging. In fact, he was rather testy. His name and address are on the list I just gave you, but I wouldn't recommend you go see him. He claimed his brother never fathered an illegitimate child, and I didn't get the impression he'd welcome you." Sarah paused. "But your mom was really excited when I finally located her this morning. Just think, after thirty-five years, you'll finally meet her. I'll bet you've got brothers and sisters you never knew you had. They might even look like you. Wouldn't that be something? I have a little sister named Beth who's almost my double. You can't imagine how good that feels."

She saw his throat work, saw him searching for words. "I…uh…apologize for yelling at you. I shouldn't have."

Sarah's chest felt tight. "I don't think it was me you were yelling at."

"No, I guess it wasn't." He rose from his chair, paced a moment, then paused to look at her, leaning his arm against the file cabinet. He glanced at the paper he held in his hand, then folded it and tucked it inside his jacket. Studiously avoiding her gaze, he spied the gouges above the file cabinet's top drawer. "What happened? Molly lose the keys?"

Sarah knew the only reason he was asking was that he needed breathing space for a second, time to collect himself. "Yeah, something like that. It's not important. What counts is how you're feeling. I almost wish I hadn't—"

"No, don't." He held up a hand. "You did what you were hired to do. I'm just not handling the outcome very well. Not that I didn't always suspect… I just didn't figure my dad was involved. I assumed he was protecting *me*, not himself." With a shrug of one shoulder, he closed his eyes for an instant. "He's like that—or at least I thought he was."

"In his way, perhaps he *was* protecting you."

He sighed. "When you're a kid growing up, your mother hugs you and says she loves you, and it never occurs to you that it's a lie. You look in the mirror and you convince yourself you have your dad's big nose and your mom's mouth and you're just tall by accident."

"Oh, Michael…." Even from across the room, she could see the pain in his expression. "Don't throw everything away because of one deception. I'm sure your mother *did* love you. And your father still does."

"Does he? There are some things you owe to people when you love them, like honesty. I don't know who I am anymore." His voice was ragged, pitched so low she almost couldn't catch the words. "According to you, Michael De Lorio is a lie from start to finish. My whole life…everything about me, even my degree is in the wrong name. I feel like a kid who's been stacking blocks, only to have someone come along and kick them over. It was bad enough when I found out I was adopted. But this? How do I pick up the pieces and make sense of anything?"

With that, he jerked the door open and went out into

the main office. Sarah could see the front exit from where she stood. He never broke stride until he was outside on the sidewalk. She watched him through the gold lettering on the glass as he hunched his shoulders, not against the wind, but against the pain.

Feeling numb, she walked out to the window, watching him as he struck off up the street. She understood exactly what he was doing. She liked to walk when she felt upset, too. *Oh, Michael, I'm so sorry.* Finding his mother with so little to go on was one of the highlights of her career. So why did she feel so miserable? *Some things are better left buried.* Perhaps Robert De Lorio had been right.

CHAPTER FOUR

MICHAEL STOOD ON the bridge, staring into the swirling green depths of the Willamette River, scarcely aware of the traffic sounds all around him. He had been walking nonstop for half an hour, but his head still swam with confusion. In his mind's eye, he was picturing the teddy bear on his closet shelf, the stain on the inner edge of the ear seam. Scenes from his nightmare eddied on the surface of the water. *Helen.* Had she really existed then? And died to protect the child, Gino? The thought made him feel sick. What parts of the dream were real, what parts conjured? He'd never know for sure unless he went to Chicago.

He couldn't fathom why his father had fled to Oregon and changed his identity. All he knew was he'd never be free of the dream, never be absolutely certain of his own sanity, never be free to love and be loved, until he found out what had caused his dreams to be so violent and he could put them to rest.

THE OUTER OFFICE DOOR opened. Sarah leaned sideways in her desk chair. She had been waiting for Michael to come back from his walk for over an hour. He stood just inside the entry. His hair brushed his forehead in wind-whipped, glistening black curls. She pushed up from her desk. The emotion radiating from him drew her gaze to his like a magnet. He took one step toward her. Then another.

When he reached her office doorway, he said, "Sarah, I'm sorry for unloading on you like that. I shouldn't have."

Stepping around the corner of her desk, she paused, drawn to him yet hesitant. "I understood, Michael. I laid a lot on you. I'm sorry it had to be that way."

He shook his head, his expression a mix of incredulity and relief. "Oh, I admit, it threw me. But after I walked the shock of it off, it was easier to think. You're right. It's been a long time. People change. My dad is a good man—that doesn't mean he has to be perfect." A slow smile curved his mouth. "You know, when I first heard about you, I knew you were a damn good genealogist. But deep down, even though you were my last hope, I never let myself count too much on you finding anything. After so many failures… I hired agencies as far away as Los Angeles, you know, right in the same state where my folks were supposedly born. I guess I thought a metropolitan area would have more advanced technology, an edge over a small-town office. I can't thank you enough."

"There's no need for thanks. I just did what you hired me to do. And let it be a lesson to you, bigger isn't always better."

His eyes met hers, delving deep, at odds with the teasing smile he flashed as he moved closer. "No need for thanks? Do you know how many times I've tried this and come up against a dead end?" He raised an eyebrow. "Sarah, this might make all the difference in the world for me. If I paid you triple your usual fee, it still wouldn't be enough." With an incredibly light touch, he brushed a stray curl from her temple. Then, with a low laugh, he said, "Why not?"

The next moment, she found herself caught in his arms, receiving a breathtaking bear hug. He did a half turn with her, lifting her off her feet. She braced her hands on his shoulders, leaning back to see his face, unable to conceal her surprise or her discomfiture. He was a strong man. His hand on her back felt large and warm. Awareness of his muscular body coursed through her. Instinctively she levered herself away, her only self-defense against the way-ward, inexplicable emotions pelting her.

As if he suddenly realized he'd overstepped his bounds, he lowered her until her feet reached the floor and then dropped his arms from around her. "Uh…sorry, I guess I—" A blush rode high on his cheeks and he stepped back, smoothing his hair.

Sarah tucked her blouse more snugly into the waistband of her skirt, straightened her jacket, gave her own hair a pat and then just…stared at him. She dated pretty regu-larly—at least a couple of times a month—and, the dating game being what it was, finding herself in a clinch now and then was pretty par for the course. But a racing pulse wasn't, and neither were hot cheeks. She felt as unsettled as a schoolgirl and twice as graceless. The feeling hit her like an ocean wave, leaving her with the same unbalanced sensation she got when the beach sand shifted under her feet. That was bad enough. But even worse was the un-deniable fact that she could see no reciprocative gleam in Michael's eyes. Affection? Yes. Gratitude? Unquestion-ably. But no sign of the same caliber of fondness that was washing over her. Since meeting him her emotions had gone topsy-turvy.

Placing a hand on her shoulder, he gave her a quick squeeze. "Thanks, Sarah. It doesn't begin to say what I'm feeling, but thanks. This kid's on his way to Chicago." He stepped over to her desk and grabbed up her phone. "Mind? I wanna make reservations."

"No—no, not at all."

It was a lie. She did mind. Her business relationship with Michael De Lorio was very nearly over. Once he went to Chicago and the case was closed, it wasn't likely she'd see him again. *Molto bella.* According to her new dictionary, that meant *very beautiful.* Confusion clouded Sarah's mind. It wasn't like her to fall for a man easily, and she didn't know Michael De Lorio all that well. She should be relieved to have this case off her hands after the note on her door and the burglary. Instead she was wishing... She caught her bottom lip between her teeth. *Wishing what, Sarah?*

He punched out the number to information, then called the airport to book a flight to Chicago. While he made the arrangements, Sarah pretended to be putting things in order in her newly repaired file cabinet. Way deep inside, she'd been hoping their relationship might develop into something much more meaningful.

"Well, I'm on my way at seven-thirty-five in the morning. I'll be there late in the afternoon. Just in case of layovers, though, I'll wait to call Eleanora Miller until I'm checked into the hotel."

Sarah closed the file drawer, flashing him a smile that felt as stiff as a dried facial mask. She walked with him from her office, standing near the door to bid him goodbye. "You'll be cautious? Don't give anyone information about your dad."

He paused with his hand on the doorknob. "I'm not stupid, Sarah. I realize what the implications are. You're not the only one who can make inquiries without giving much away. I just won't use my real last name."

She shrugged. "I'm sorry if I sound like a broken record. It's just that I'd hate to see you do anything you might regret."

"I won't. I'm aiming for a clean slate, not regrets." His mouth twisted into a smile and he lifted a hand as if to touch her hair. At the last second, he hesitated and dropped his arm. "I'll be in touch."

"You do that."

He opened the door and stepped outside, letting it swing closed behind him. Again Sarah went over to the window to watch him. There was a dark green sedan parked a short distance up the street in front of an office space that was currently up for lease. After business hours, very few cars parked along this section of Thirteenth Avenue because everything was closed. She peered through the gold lettering on her window at the automobile. The dark silhouette of a man sat on the driver's side. Probably a Realtor waiting to show the offices to a potential client, she decided. Why else would someone be sitting there at six-thirty in the evening?

THE NEXT MORNING at 7:38, the tail of the Boeing 737 sank lower to the ground as the engines revved up to full power for takeoff. Weary from a sleepless night due to a recurrence of his nightmare, Michael leaned his head back against the seat and closed his eyes. Was it cold in Chicago in early September? When he arrived there, would his memory be jogged? Would he unlock the secrets of his past? God, he hoped so. He didn't want to spend the rest of his life waking from a dead sleep in an empty bed, terrified and drenched in sweat.

Forcing his eyes open, Michael leaned forward. At his feet sat the hatbox from his closet shelf. The teddy bear inside was his one concrete link to the past. He'd feel like a damned fool carrying it around, showing it to everyone. But it was something he had to do. Reading the reactions on people's faces was his expertise, a talent he had honed during counseling sessions. If he flashed that bear and rattled someone's cage, he'd know he was one step closer to solving the mystery of his nightmare.

The bear had a bloodstain on its ear. He felt certain of that now. Whose blood, though? In a few hours, he'd be able to call Eleanora Miller and make an appointment to see her. Perhaps she'd tell him something to shed some light on everything. It would be so much easier to accept if his nightmare stemmed from before his adoption. So much easier to discover his dad was uninvolved.

ELEANORA MILLER ANSWERED the telephone with her usual cheerful hello, expecting her husband, Darrell, to be on the line. Instead an unfamiliar male voice rasped in her ear. "Hello, Nora. It's been a long time."

A shiver raised gooseflesh on her arms. "Who is this?"

"An echo from your past. I'm only going to say this once, so you'd better listen close. Years ago, you had an illegitimate son, a son you've kept secret from everyone. If he should contact you, or if anyone should do so in his behalf to set up a meeting, do it at your own risk. You *do* love your husband, don't you, Nora?"

"Who the hell are you?"

"Your conscience, Nora. I wonder what your hubby would say if I sent him a long letter and accompanying evidence that you weren't quite as lily white when he married you as you led him to believe?"

Nora squeezed her eyes closed and leaned against the wall. "What are you getting at? My husband is— You can't do this. It'd break his heart. How did you find out? Who are you? What is it you want?"

"Ah, you're quick. I like that."

"Damn you, stop playing with me! What do you want? Money?"

"Nora, Nora, you insult me. Money is the last thing on my mind. All I want is a favor. Nothing big, love. Just your cooperation in a small matter. Are you game? Or should I put this little packet in the mail to your hubby's office?"

"My husband isn't well. A shock like that could kill him. I—I was only sixteen, for heaven's sake. It was a stupid mistake—nothing more—just *one* stupid mistake."

"We have to pay for our mistakes, though, don't we, Nora?"

MICHAEL TOOK A CAB directly from O'Hare International to the Chicago Hilton and Towers on Michigan Avenue. Immediately after checking in, he took an elevator to the eighth floor and followed the numbered arrows to his room. As he let himself in the door, he was vaguely aware that he'd chosen his accommodations well. It was a beautiful place, tastefully decorated, with luxurious carpeting. He tested the mattress on one queen-sized bed as he set the hatbox and his suitcase on it. Then he strode across the sitting room to gaze out the window at Grant Park and the lakeshore. Images of Sarah's face drifted through his mind.

Nothing seemed familiar to him. Ever since getting off the plane, he'd felt like one insignificant speck in a tumultuous sea of bodies. Eugene wasn't that small a place, but it was miniscule compared to Chicago. From his window seat on the 737, Michael had had an aerial view of some of the downtown area as the plane came in for its landing. He had half expected something to strike a chord in his memory, but nothing had.

Sighing, he turned from the window to eye the telephone on the nightstand. After thirty-five years, he was finally going to hear his mother's voice. Fear coiled in his gut, a cold irrational fear that made it feel like his legs had turned to water. What forgotten memories lurked in his subconscious that he could feel so terrified about dialing a phone number? When he finally recalled those memories, would the fear subside? Or would it be worse?

Striding over to the nightstand, he lifted the phone receiver, dialed to get an outside line and pulled the paper Sarah had given him from his jacket pocket. With a trembling finger, he pressed the digits of Eleanora Miller's number, then held his breath, waiting. A second later, a woman's tremulous voice came over the wire.

"Hello, is this Eleanora Miller?" Michael heard the

quiver in his own voice and swallowed, trying to regain his composure.

"Who is this?"

"My name is Michael—um, Michael Smith. I, um, I was given your number by Sarah Montague, the genealogist."

There followed a long and heavy silence.

"You *are* Eleanora Miller?"

"Yes."

"Then I think I may be your son."

Another silence. "I doubt that."

Those three words hit Michael like a well-placed blow in the pit of his stomach. "I—I'm sorry. I was under the impression you wanted me to contact you."

The woman cleared her throat. "At first, maybe I did. But once I had time to think about it, I realized it'd just complicate my life, open me up to a lot of questions. The past is over. I want to keep it that way."

"Would you at least see me?"

"No, I'm sorry." Her voice rang with tension. "If you had definite proof, maybe I'd risk it, but you don't. The Montague woman admitted it herself. My child dropped out of sight. There's no way to be positive where he is. You're grasping at straws."

"I think I can get the proof. If we both request it, I believe we can review the adoption records. Won't you at least listen to what I've got to say?"

"No. Just…just leave me alone, okay? It's been too many years, Michael, far too many. You understand? I have other children, a husband who doesn't know I had an illegitimate child, a life that can't include you. Please, don't rip it apart. Even if you *were* my boy, the cost of seeing you would be too dear. Stay away from me. Please."

Just before the phone clicked and went dead, Michael heard Eleanora Miller sob. He sat there on the bed, staring at the variegated carpet, letting the phone receiver dangle between his knees. If his mother had been thrilled at the thought of seeing him when she talked to Sarah, she'd had a drastic change of heart. As hard as it was to accept, though, he understood. He didn't want to rip her life apart. He just wanted to fit the pieces of his together.

Sighing, he dialed to get an outside line again and punched the number for Roots in Eugene. After four rings, the message recorder answered. Michael listened to the greeting, waited for the beep and then said, "Just Michael. I'll get back to you."

Hanging up the phone, he glanced at his watch. It would be three minutes after five in Oregon. Sarah must have left the office already. She was probably on her way home. He'd give her half an hour and then call her at her house.

FIVE-TWENTY. SARAH COASTED her ten-speed around the corner onto Elm, a tree-lined residential street. Leaning her head back to catch the breeze, she took a deep breath and exhaled. Since saying goodbye to Michael last night, he'd been constantly in her thoughts. She could only hope a strenuous bike ride home would clear her head so she'd get a decent night's sleep.

A dark green car passed. Sarah hugged the curb to get out of its path, then lifted her hand to wave at a little boy who was racing down his driveway on a shiny new two-wheeler with training wheels. He looked so proud. His bike wobbled dangerously when he attempted to wave back, causing Sarah to smile. She could still remember the rush of excitement she had felt when she finally learned to balance her Schwinn without her dad holding her steady.

"Hi, lady!" the child called.

Sarah grinned as she steered around a Honda parked at the curb and turned to wave at the little boy again. She didn't see the green car make a U-turn at the corner. "Hi. Wow, those are fancy wheels. Are they brand-new?"

"Yup. My dad got it for me yester—"

The boy broke off and swung down from his bike, turning his head to look up the street. Sarah saw a startled expression cross his freckled face. His mouth twisted to yell something, but his words were drowned out by the acceleration of a car engine. Sarah caught movement out of the corner of her eye, whipped her head back around to look and saw a...

Her mind froze before she could register the message her eyes transmitted to her brain. From that split second on, she saw and heard everything as though it were a videotape being played in freeze-frames: a car coming at her, driving in the wrong lane, a pair of headlights. The *click-click* of radial tires gripping the asphalt for traction. A whoosh of air gusting against her face.

Sarah's muscles tensed. She tried to steer her bike out of the car's path, but there wasn't time. She saw it coming one moment and then it was right on top of her. A loud crash filled her head. She felt the jarring impact of a much larger vehicle colliding with hers. And then all she was conscious of was a deluge of pain and a strange cartwheeling sensation as her body pitched skyward.

Sarah felt herself flying end over end. Then a mind-shattering impact brought her to a dead halt. Her body felt too heavy to respond to the panic nipping at the edges of her consciousness. Blackness, everywhere blackness. Pain jumbled her memory. *A little boy,* she thought, *a little boy, a green car and a loud noise*.

Far, far ahead was a pinpoint of light. Ah, she was in a tunnel. She tried to feel the walls on each side of her, but her arms wouldn't move. She could see the opening ahead, broadening, becoming brighter as she moved toward it. Images spun—sky, grass, people's legs. She moaned.

Voices ricocheted within her mind like tennis balls bouncing off concrete. "Don't move her! Haven't you had any first aid?" "Oh my God, is she dead?" "Did you see that? He drove right for her." "Don't just stand here. Somebody call an ambulance."

Sarah licked her lips. *I'm okay,* she said. Or did she just think it? A hysterical urge to laugh hit her. She really was okay. She just couldn't tell them so. Hands slid up her legs, a man's hands. She tried to push them aside.

"Just lie still, ma'am. Don't move. Does that hurt? If you feel pain anywhere, just blink your eyes."

Sarah blinked, not as a signal but to clear her vision. She rolled onto her side. Something prickled her cheek, and she inhaled the sweet, heavy smell of freshly cut grass.

"No, lady, don't try to move."

She pushed herself to a sitting position, shaking her head. Everywhere she looked she saw people's legs. "Where's my bike?"

"Honey, your bike's ruined," a grandmotherly voice crooned. "There, there, you really mustn't be getting up. Ah, that's a girl, just be still."

Plump, gentle arms encircled Sarah's shoulders, and a kindly hand pressed her face against the bodice of a crisp cotton housedress. She relaxed, vaguely aware of an approaching siren. "I'm really okay. Just get me my bike? Do you have my bike?"

Tires skidded to a stop next to the curb. Through the fringe of her dark eyelashes, Sarah saw the back doors of a white ambulance fly open. Metal clanked. A deep, commanding voice said, "Just get back, folks. We'll take it from here."

She felt herself being lifted, then lowered onto something crisp and firm. A stretcher? "No, wait. I don't need—"

"It's okay, ma'am. Just relax. You're in good hands."

The voice was deep and gentle. It reminded her of...?

A smile touched her mouth. *Michael.* Ah, yes, it would be okay if she was with Michael....

SARAH SAT ON THE EDGE of the examining table and stared at the striped privacy curtain that surrounded her, watching the emergency room doctor jot notes on his clipboard. Beyond the curtain, Sacred Heart Hospital bustled with activity. Phones rang. People scurried, barking orders. She imagined the policemen who had just been in to question her had caused part of the stir.

Lowering her gaze to her ripped bicycling tights, she touched the ragged edges of the tear to examine the red marks on her thigh. Tomorrow she'd be a mass of bruises and sore as the dickens. Even so, she'd been lucky. According to the police, all that had saved her from being killed was a freak flip of her bike upon impact that had thrown her clear of the car.

"You're an extremely fortunate woman. You realize that, don't you?" The doctor studied her over the dark rims of his glasses, his blue eyes solemn. "We don't see many people walk away from accidents like that. I understand the police think the driver was drunk?"

"He must have been. I was over by the opposite curb, and he came clear across the centerline. It was almost as if—" She broke off and frowned, wincing as she shrugged one shoulder. "Oh, well, all's well that ends well."

"Just stay off bikes for a few days, okay?" He tore a slip of paper from his pad and extended it to her. "This is for codeine. You might need it later. Get plenty of rest, take it easy, see your regular doctor if anything unusual crops up. Other than that, I guess you're free to go if you're sure you don't want to stay overnight for observation."

She shook her head. "I'll rest better at home." I'll also spend less money at home, she thought.

"If you have any problems during the night, come back in."

"Mmm, yes, I'll do that."

Sliding down from the table, she placed a hand at the small of her back and straightened, following the doctor from the curtained area. Parting company with him as they entered the hall, she angled left for the lobby, pushed out through the door and glanced around for a pay phone. She'd have to call a cab. Her three-hundred-dollar bike was totaled.

Beyond the windows, she could see university students hustling along the sidewalks, heads bent against the swiftly falling darkness, their book bags bulging. They all had places to go, people to meet. Everyone but her. The thought made her inexplicably afraid. She kept remembering that green car, the sound of its revved engine, the click of its tires grabbing asphalt as it swerved straight toward her.

A green car. She had seen a sedan like it somewhere just recently, but when and where escaped her. In the cul-de-sac where she lived? Near the office? Downtown someplace? Where had she been? Why couldn't she remember? Hysterical laughter gathered in her throat, and it took all her self-control to stifle it. It was so insane. Who would want to harm her? She had no enemies, certainly not any who'd wish her dead.

Taking a deep breath, she leaned her shoulder against the wall and closed her eyes. She should probably call her aunt Janelle or a friend, but until she got her head cleared, she hated to. She'd sound crazy if she started ranting about someone trying to kill her, and right now, she wasn't sure she could trust herself not to express the suspicions screaming through her mind. If only Michael weren't out of town, she'd call him for a lift home. She missed him. Raising her lashes, she threw another panicked glance out the windows at the swiftly falling darkness, wishing her mother lived in Eugene. She didn't want to be alone, not tonight....

CHAPTER FIVE

MICHAEL DROPPED THE phone into its cradle and sighed, flopping back onto his bed to stare at the sterile white ceiling. How he hated hotels. They were so impersonal, so cold, so *lonely*. Where *was* Sarah? He threw his arm over his eyes to shut out the light. *She's probably out on a dinner date, you moron. Do you think she's got your name branded on her forehead or something?* The feeling that something was wrong niggled at his mind, refusing to be silenced. He rolled onto his side and stared at the telephone. He'd try her one more time in twenty minutes, and if she didn't answer then, he'd quit. He had to get some rest. Last night he'd awakened from a nightmare around one o'clock and paced the floor most of the night.

Glancing at his watch, he resigned himself to an eternity of waiting. Funny how long a minute seemed when you were counting the seconds. *So you're getting serious about her, are you, old man? Well, you sure picked one hell of a time for it.* Images swirled in his mind of blood dripping from a yellow bedspread. That much blood meant *murder*. He had no business dragging Sarah into his life right now, no business even thinking about her.

To distract himself, he went back over his conversation with Eleanora Miller. Another dead end after traveling so far? Not that he blamed the woman. She had her own life to live, after all, a life that didn't include her adult bastard son.

He heaved a long, draining sigh. Tomorrow he would visit Giorgio Santini and Marcus St. John. If he gave minimal information about himself and used a fake last name, no one would be able to trace Robert De Lorio through him. He had a right to answers, didn't he? A right to a normal life, knowing who he was and where he came from. If he returned to Eugene too soon, he'd never know the truth and the nightmare would haunt him the rest of his life.

Slowly Michael relaxed and let his eyes drift closed. The bed cradled him in warmth. *Sarah.* What was he going to do about her? So much depended on the outcome of this trip, his whole future. He wished this journey into his past was over—over and done with, forever buried.

Buried....

Michael's thoughts gradually became disjointed, floating in a thick, swirling mist. He felt his muscles relaxing, and for an instant, he resisted. Then he deliberately let go. In the far reaches of his mind, he knew there were secrets awaiting him if only he had the courage to face them. *Secrets.* The mist around him reminded him of the fog in an old London horror movie, constantly moving, heavy, impenetrable. He slipped through it, straining to see, afraid something would leap out at him.

"Little boy!" a man's voice called. "Over here, kiddo. Look this way!"

Michael spun around. A man's distorted face loomed above him, half his features hidden behind a black box with a silver circle attached to its top. Light exploded in Michael's eyes. Blinded, he fell back, blinking to see. Then another man leaped from the mist, and another black box exploded light in Michael's face. Panicked, he tried to run, but everywhere he turned, men with black boxes emerged from the fog....

AT EIGHT O'CLOCK the next morning, Sarah lowered herself gingerly onto her office chair, holding a mug in one hand and a portfolio in the other. Her bottom panged as it touched the chair cushion, making her wonder if she hadn't landed rump first last night when the car hit her. Taking a careful sip of coffee, she pressed the surge-control switch with her toe to turn on her computer terminal and typed in the call letters of a file. The computer screen flashed, *No such file exists. Would you like to open a new one?*

She choked, staring incredulously. "What do you mean, no such file exists? Of course it exists." The words had no sooner left her mouth than she rolled her eyes. Since when had she begun talking to inanimate objects and expecting replies?

Retyping the call letters, she hit return, quite sure she'd hear the usual *ker-whunk* and *clickety-click* as a file was pulled from a hard disk. *Nothing?* She froze with her mug halfway to her mouth. There it was again. *No such file exists.* She no longer needed caffeine to stimulate her: panic did the job. She requested the computer directory to review her files. There *weren't* any files? The hard disk was empty? A tingle of alarm ran up her spine.

She flew from her chair. "Molly!"

"Yes?" Molly appeared in the doorway with record speed, waving her freshly painted fingernails. "What's the matter?"

"My computer's been erased."

"I didn't do it." Molly's pencil-lined eyes widened with alarm. "Honest, Sarah, this time I'm innocent."

"I wasn't accusing you. Just bring me the back-up disks." Sarah noticed Molly's face go pale. Suddenly worried, Sarah asked, "What do you mean, *this* time?"

Molly gnawed her bottom lip, looking nervous. "I, um, I was going to tell you Sarah—honest, I was—just as soon as I replaced everything."

"Tell me what?" Sarah asked. "What do you have to replace?"

Molly replied. "I spilled a soft drink yesterday."

Sarah frowned. "What does that have to do with—"

"Into one of my drawers," Molly interjected. "The drawer was stuck. I was jerking on it, and when it came open the cup toppled. Cola got all over the back-up disks."

Sarah felt her stomach twist into knots. It took all her self-control to keep from saying something she would regret. After a long, unnaturally quiet moment, she heaved a sigh. "I don't believe this. We're talking major disaster. I can't run this place without my files."

"I did use the computer late yesterday, just for a few minutes," Molly admitted. "But I was *super* careful. I've learned my lesson."

Sarah certainly hoped so. "Now all we have to work with is hard copy, and half that's gone since the burglary." Turning to glare at the scarred file cabinet, Sarah tapped her front teeth with her fingertip. "Wait a minute, wait just one damned minute. Think, Molly. What's all this point to?"

Molly lifted one shoulder, her expression vague. "That I'm incompetent?"

"No, the break-in! Don't you get the connection? The burglar only took hard copy the first time. He must have realized how futile that was, so he came back and finished the job."

"Last night? But nobody broke in last night."

"Wanna bet." Sarah swept past Molly into the main office, making a beeline for the windows on the left side of the room. "Check on that side. Look for gouges in the paint where someone might have used a crowbar."

The windows on Sarah's side of the office showed no sign of tampering. She circled Molly's desk and went to the back door, opening it to examine both sides of the door frame for any telltale scratches.

"I don't see anything," Molly called.

"Me neither." Sarah stepped across the carpet, nibbling

thoughtfully on the end piece of her reading glasses. "Well, if no one broke in, there's only one other possibility."

"Me?" Molly forgot her wet nails and wrung her hands. "I should have known not to major in secretarial science. Why did my mom insist I be a secretary, anyway? I'm no good at this stuff, no good at all."

The distress in Molly's voice caught at Sarah's heart. As incompetent as the girl was, Sarah knew she tried. "Nonsense, it takes a string command to erase the main terminal."

"If it wasn't me, then what?"

"I'll bet you ten bucks it's the computer. Electronic wonders do screw up on occasion."

Two hours later, Sarah owed Molly ten dollars. According to the repairman, there was nothing wrong with the computer.

"I can't believe it."

The repairman smiled down at her. "You just punched a series of wrong buttons, the way it looks. Have you taken your free classes to learn how to operate your computer?"

"No, I didn't need them."

His eyebrows lifted a fraction. "Yes, well, they certainly can't hurt, you know. It'd save you having to go through retrieving all your data when an erasure occurs."

Her mind stuck on the word *retrieve*. "You mean I can get it back?"

"With the proper software. It's tedious, but it works. Come out to the shop and we'll get you fixed up in no time."

She walked the repairman to the door, still dubious. "You're positive it wasn't a malfunction?"

"Not a mechanical one." His blue eyes twinkled into hers. "Take the computer classes. They're great."

The bell jangled as he let himself out onto the sidewalk. She stood there a moment, staring at the door handle. No break-in, no computer malfunction, which left only one possibility. Either she or Molly had made a fatal keyboard error.

"I knew it," Molly moaned. "It was me, wasn't it?"

Sarah turned on her heel to stare at Molly's angelic features. It was frightening to think anyone who looked so harmless could be so catastrophic. By all rights, Sarah knew what she should do, but knowing and doing it were two different things. Molly truly did mean well. And she needed this job. No one else was likely to give her one, after all.

"All's well that ends well. It just means extra work."

Molly sprang from her desk. "I'll do it, Sarah. I'll even work overtime for free."

Sarah cringed at the thought of Molly fiddling with the computer. She pasted a smile on her face and headed for her office. "Nonsense. Who's to say *I* didn't erase the files? I'll go get the necessary software and you man the phone. Sound fair? We're at a standstill for a couple of days, that's all. I'm sure it won't be fun trying to retrieve the files, but it could have been far worse."

Molly tagged along to Sarah's desk. "I can go get the software if you have things to do."

"I can't *do* anything until I get the files back," Sarah reminded her. "I won't be long." On the way out the door, she paused and glanced over her shoulder. "By the way, Molly, the repairman spoke to me about some free computer classes. They're one night a week, I think. It wouldn't be a bad idea for you to take them."

"See? You *do* think it was me that messed up. You won't say it, but you're thinking it just the same. Oh, Sarah, why don't you just get it over with and fire me?"

Sarah rolled her eyes rather than answer, but Molly's question couldn't be put to rest quite that easily. All the way to the computer shop, she skirted the issue. Why did she keep Molly when the girl was so completely incompetent? Not even her aunt Janelle would blame Sarah if she let Molly go after this fiasco. It took a string of commands to erase the computer hard disk. Surely Molly hadn't done it deliberately. But how else could it have happened?

MICHAEL'S LEGS QUIVERED as he studied the ornate brass chime beside Giorgio Santini's front door. After spending four years of his life searching, he knew he should be delighted to be here, moments away from speaking to a man who claimed to be the brother of Angelo Santini. So why wasn't he?

He depressed the door chime button with his thumb and took a step back, tightening his arm around the box he carried and shoving his other hand into his slacks pocket. He gave the front of the house a quick once-over. The massive brick exterior was impressive. He knew money when he saw it and this house oozed greenbacks from its mortar.

Glancing at the paned windows to his left, Michael searched for any sign of movement beyond the squares of glass. Was that a footstep approaching? A low cough? He swallowed and lifted his chin. The door swung inward with an accompanying squeak, and a small, dark man stepped into view. He looked so much like Robert De Lorio that Michael blinked. Not a double of his dad, but close. His hair was a little thinner, his brown eyes were more serious and scrutinizing, and he looked a tad younger, but he was undeniably a De Lorio. Or rather a Santini. Michael's stomach tightened. How long would it take before he grew accustomed to his legal last name? If Santini *was* his last name.

"You are Michael?"

Even Santini's voice reminded him of his father's. "Yes, Michael Smith."

Santini smiled. He obviously didn't believe Michael went by Smith, but he wasn't going to argue the point.

"I, um, appreciate you seeing me, Mr. Santini. It's very kind of you."

Giorgio Santini threw the door open wide, gazing up at Michael with a distant expression on his squared, wrinkled face. An ache of sadness crept into his eyes as he regarded each of Michael's features as if comparing them to some long forgotten memory. He lifted one shoulder in a shrug of resigned acceptance. "I cannot say I am glad you came." In a louder voice, he added, "You are our Gino, there is no doubt."

With a sweep of his arm, he beckoned Michael into a stately foyer, which presented a spiral staircase that stretched to an upstairs landing. The slate floor reminded Michael of Sarah's office entry. A flash vision of her oval face crossed his mind, and a warm, comfortable glow eased the ache of tension in his gut. He wished she were here with him. He could have used a hearty dose of her sense of humor.

Following Santini through a tasteful gallery into an enormous living room, Michael took a seat on the burnt gold sofa, deflecting Santini's speculative look with a smile.

"Does your papa know you have come?"

Setting the teddy-bear box on the carpet next to his feet, Michael glanced up at the older man. Genuine affection glowed in Santini's eyes, but displeasure was etched upon his features as well. "No, I'm afraid not."

Santini darted a quick look toward the foyer, then met Michael's gaze. "So what is it my brother is doing, hmm? His arm is broken, yes? That is why he has never written a letter to his family, why our poor mamma died not knowing where he had gone away to?" Giorgio lowered himself into a wing chair, waving both hands in agitation as he spoke, another trait Michael recognized as exclusively De Lorio. "You will tell me this is so? I can forgive the scoundrel if his arm is broken."

"I was hoping you could answer those questions, Mr. Santini. I've no idea why my father left here, why he hasn't kept in touch."

"Hmph! Uncle Giorgio, that is my name. You are not sure yet, eh? Well, I may be hitting sixty, but my eyesight is not that bad, my boy. You are our Gino. I would know you anywhere. You used to sit on my knee, making a fine mess with red licorice. You loved it in those days. Do you still?"

Michael couldn't suppress a grin. "As a matter of fact, I do."

"Yes, you are our Gino. You have your papa's nose. Strange, that, don't you think? We used to admire you and brag how much you resembled our family, even though you weren't born to us. 'That boy is a Santini.' That is what we used to say."

Not a De Lorio? Michael tried to get his sense of identity on track. He was Gino Santini, the terrified child in his nightmare. If he broached the subject, would this friendly little man tell him what had happened in his past to cause such a haunting dream? "You're that positive?"

Santini's reply was to bounce from his chair and step to the coffee table to lift a family album from its surface. He offered it to Michael. "You will decide for yourself, no? Come, come, take it, Gino. Look at the pictures."

Michael's hands turned slippery with sweat as he propped the album on his knees and opened it. His head spun. He didn't want to see these pictures. He didn't want to talk any longer with Giorgio Santini. He wanted to run....

The inclination felt foreign. All his life, he'd been taught to face his troubles. Yet here he sat, escape foremost in his mind. And he didn't know why. The first familiar face to stare up at him from the album was that of a slender young woman with dark hair and a gentle smile. "Mamma…." The word trailed from his lips like a caress.

Giorgio craned his neck to see, then nodded. "Ah, yes, that is Marcia at your first birthday party. You made a fine mess that day, too. Cake in your hair and everyone else's. Flip the page. There you are. A fine boy, eh? Smart, too. You took after our mamma."

Michael stared at the child in the photo. The features were blurred with baby plumpness, but the nose and mouth were undeniable. In the background, Robert De Lorio stood poised with a cake knife, his face creased in a gigantic grin. A proud young father, Angelo Santini, Robert De Lorio, one and the same.

"Now you will call me Uncle Giorgio, no? It is so. You can see the truth for yourself." Giorgio returned to his chair, planting his hands on his knees. He glanced toward the foyer again as he leaned forward. "Where is my brother, Gino?"

"I'm afraid I can't tell you that."

Something flickered in Santini's eyes. Relief? Sadness? "I am an old man. We don't have many years left. You wouldn't deny me the chance to see him just one more time, my brother, my flesh and blood?"

Michael closed the album and returned it to the coffee table. "That must be my father's decision. I'm sorry but his health is bad. The shock of hearing from you, if he were unprepared, could kill him. Let me go home. I'll talk to him, break it to him gently. Then if he wants to call you, he can."

Again something indefinable flickered in Giorgio's eyes. "You plan to walk out the door without giving me a clue where you came from? Out of the blue you call me. I invite you into my home. I welcome you and call you nephew. It is a fine way to repay me. Do you know what it's like to believe your brother is dead, then find out he isn't? I want to see him, Gino. I want to be with him. You can't be so cruel, not to your uncle who loves you."

"I swear to you, I'll try to convince my dad to get in touch. It's all I can do." Michael felt like a heel. Giorgio clearly loved his brother. "Papa's heart, you understand? After all these years, it'd give him a terrible shock to hear from you if he weren't forewarned. I don't know why he left here, what he was running from, but whatever the reason, he has to be the one to make contact. Please, try to understand that. I owe him that much."

Giorgio's shoulders slumped and he dropped his head to gaze at the carpet. After a long silence, he said, "I suppose you must do what you feel you must."

"Uncle Giorgio…" The name caught in Michael's throat. "I know I've already asked a lot of you, giving nothing in return, but I have one more thing I need to know."

"And what is that?"

Michael lifted the box onto his knees, tossed off the lid and pulled out the teddy bear. Not a muscle in Giorgio's face moved, but Michael felt sure his color faded. "Do you recognize this toy?"

"No. Should I?"

"I have a recurring dream." Tension electrified the air as Michael described the horrible nightmare. Giorgio's features settled into a stony mask. "Do you know why I remember something so awful? Did it actually happen? There's a stain on the inner seam of this bear's ear. It could be blood. Who was Helen? Why was I hiding under a bed? Whose blood was on the floor?"

"It sounds like a crazy nightmare to me, nothing more. I don't know any Helen. Blood, you say?" Santini snorted with laughter. "It is a child's bad dream, eh? And you've turned it into a mystery." He shrugged and smiled. "There is nothing, Gino. We are a loving family, the Santinis. If you have come here to slay some sort of dragon, you've wasted your time."

"Then why did my father leave here? Why did he change his name?"

Settling back in his chair, Giorgio fixed his gaze on the wall above Michael's head. "That I cannot answer. You ask your papa, no? You tell him Giorgio loves him. You tell him blood is thicker than water. I swear it on our mamma's grave."

Michael returned the bear to its box and rose from the sofa, clasping the container in his arms. "I'll do that. Thank you for seeing me."

"I could do nothing else."

There was an air of resignation in the old man's tone. Extending his hand, Michael forced a smile. "Goodbye, Uncle Giorgio. I'll be in touch. That's a promise."

Giorgio gave his fingers an affectionate squeeze. "And I will be waiting. You can see yourself out? Like your papa, I am not in good health. This has tired me."

"I—" Michael searched for words. "Thank you. I'll call or write soon."

As Michael started from the room, he heard Giorgio Santini whisper, "It might be best if you do not."

Turning, Michael stared at the old man. Not even by the flicker of an eyelid did Santini indicate that he'd whispered the warning. After a long moment, he nodded toward the door and said, "Go, Gino, go with God's blessing."

GIORGIO SANTINI WAITED until he heard the front door shut, then he sprang from the chair and hurried through the gallery. As he stepped into the foyer, a man came forward out of the shadows and followed Giorgio to the door of his office, watching him closely. In three strides, Giorgio arrived at his desk and reached across it to punch the intercom button. Static crackled.

"Yeah, Mr. Santini?"

"Tail him," Giorgio barked. "And don't let him see you. Lose him and you're fired."

"I'm already gone."

Circling the desk, Giorgio grabbed the phone and jabbed out a number. One ring, two. On the third, a deep voice answered with a brisk "Yes?" Giorgio licked his lips, dragged in a raspy breath and said, "It was Gino, no question about it. I've got a tail on him. Now what?"

"We follow him and we wait. Relax, old friend. Angelo will come out of the woodwork, you'll see. And he will collect what's due him, right?"

"Right."

Giorgio dropped the receiver back into its cradle and sank onto the desk chair, gazing at the portrait of his mother that stood next to his paperweight. Moisture glistened in his eyes and a tremor twisted his mouth.

"So blood is thicker than water?" The man who had followed Giorgio now sauntered into the room, flashing an insolent grin. "I hope you didn't mean that, boss. It could mean big trouble."

"There is no question of my loyalty. I am doing all that can be expected, no?"

"Yeah, but your heart's not in it. I heard you whispering something to that Smith fellow. Not a warning, was it?"

"Did he act as if I'd warned him? Use your head, Pascal. I knew you could hear my every word. Would I be so stupid? If I were going to betray our employer, I wouldn't do it when there was a witness, would I?"

"Only if you thought you could get away with it. Angelo's your brother. You must feel something for him."

"I feel nothing. It has been too many years."

Not caring if his employee watched him, Giorgio lifted a shaky hand and turned the picture of his mother facedown. The die had been cast long ago. He had to do what he had to do, but he couldn't go through with it if he looked at his sweet mamma's face.

CHAPTER SIX

IT SEEMED TO be Michael's day for meeting uncles, first adoptive, now biological. As his cab swept through the remote-controlled gates to the St. John estate in Lake Forest, he peeled two antacid tablets off the roll and popped them into his mouth, scarcely tasting the minty chalk as he chewed and swallowed them.

Five Doberman pinschers circled the taxi, their white teeth flashing like sabers as they snarled and barked. Michael peered through the trees at the elegant North Shore mansion and wondered if he was visiting a residence or a minimum-security prison. A six-foot brick wall hemmed the grounds. Nobody could get in the gate without admittance and nobody would dare try to leave without permission, not with those dogs running loose.

As the cab drew up in front of the house, Michael saw a tall, dark-haired man step off the porch onto the brick walkway. Michael's initial relief turned to distaste the moment his gaze touched on the man's clothes. He was dressed from head to foot in black, a color that invariably made Michael feel as if he might suffocate if he didn't keep a firm rein on his emotions. The man yelled something that brought the Dobermans to heel. Then he bent to stroke their sleek heads, eyeing the cab with suspicious brown eyes. Michael could see he bore a marked resemblance to the man, not just in body build but in his features. The Santinis weren't the only family that had large noses.

He tucked the teddy-bear box under his left arm and

climbed out of the car, keeping a watchful eye on the dogs. "Hello, Mr. St. John? Michael Smith. I have an appointment?"

St. John's gaze slid to the cabbie. "Tell the driver to wait, please. I don't think this should take long."

So that was how the wind blew. Well, Sarah had warned him. Michael asked the cabdriver to wait and then threaded his way through the milling dogs to follow St. John into the house. His host strode across the lofty foyer to a doorway beneath a curving stairway, leaving Michael to shut the front door after himself. St. John paused to look back over his shoulder, then opened the door and disappeared into the room beyond.

Arrogant ass, Michael thought. Tipping his head back, he looked up three stories to a vaulted ceiling with the most gorgeous chandelier he'd ever seen hanging from its apex. Open French doors to his right revealed an expansive room with an elaborate marble fireplace and intricate fixtures of brass. The affluence surprised him. He had never envisioned either of his parents as coming from wealthy families.

Marcus St. John poked his head around the door. "Do you mind, Mr. Smith? This isn't my only appointment of the day."

Crossing the gleaming floor, Michael pushed the thick walnut door open with his palm and stepped into a library. Floor-to-ceiling shelves of leather-bound books flanked another marble fireplace to his right. An impressive mahogany desk graced a window alcove ahead of him. It was a charming room, tastefully opulent, with an air of old money.

"Shall we get this over with?" St. John settled himself in the chair behind his desk like a general preparing to discuss war strategy. Placing both elbows on the desktop, he steepled his fingers, pressing his fingertips against his pursed lips. Michael sat down across from him and put the box he carried down on the floor. "You are a client of—" St. John shuffled through the pages of a notepad "—ah, yes—Roots?—run by a woman named Sarah Montague?"

"That's correct."

"And she's given you reason to believe you're my nephew?"

"She traced my adoptive parents to Chicago. The infant they adopted was born to a girl named Eleanora Pierce and a boy named Adam St. John."

Marcus lifted a dubious eyebrow, then sighed. "Don't misunderstand me, Mr. Smith. I would be overjoyed to discover my brother had a son."

Michael leaned forward. "Look at me. Are you denying the family resemblance? That alone should make you wonder."

"It's true, you do resemble me. But I could stand on any corner in Chicago and count fifty other men with your coloring, build and features in the space of an hour, perhaps less."

"Adam St. John was named as my father."

"By Nora Pierce?" St. John smiled. "How do I put this delicately? The Pierce girl had a questionable reputation. Perhaps she did name my brother as your father, but the truth is, the sire could have been one of any number of boys."

Michael's face felt stiff from the effort it took to keep his expression carefully blank. "I see."

St. John's shrewd brown eyes clouded and softened. "No, I'm afraid you don't. I'm handling this poorly. Heaven knows, if you're truly Adam's son, why I—" He lifted his hands in supplication. "I'd kill the fatted calf, welcoming you into the family. I'm not denying you, Mr. Smith—far from it. Nor do I mean to offend you. I'm simply stating facts. Adam and I were very close. He never once intimated that he had a son."

It was Michael's turn to smile. "I hope you don't think I came here to be *welcomed* into the family. It's obvious you have money, but that's inconsequential to me. I'm a successful psychiatrist with my own practice. I merely want to know who my parents were, what my background is, that's all."

"At the same time, you can appreciate my concern?" St. John waved his hand, indicating the palatial home that surrounded them. "You're not the first person to claim kinship. I've even had alleged illegitimate children of my own knocking on the door. And yours isn't the first convincing story. I can only say that I wish I'd had as much fun in my youth as the string of illegitimate children I supposedly left behind would indicate." He cleared his throat. "Forgive me, that was an insensitive—"

"I'm not at all offended, Mr. St. John. I grew up in a loving home with wonderful parents. And as I said, money isn't the issue here. It matters very little to me what my parents' circumstances were. I just want to know who they were. I came here to learn about my father; what he looked like, what he was like as a person, how it came about that I was given up for adoption. You understand?"

"Yes, I think I do. If I were in your position, I'd feel the same."

Michael leaned over to lift the lid from the box near his feet. Watching St. John's face for a reaction, he pulled out the bear. "Do you happen to recognize this?"

St. John fastened puzzled eyes on the stuffed toy. "No, should I?"

Michael grinned and returned the toy to its box. "No, I really didn't expect you to, but I wanted to be certain."

"I assume it's a toy from your childhood?"

"Something like that."

St. John glanced at his watch. "What exactly is the purpose of this visit?"

"I was hoping you might give me information about my past." As briefly as he could, Michael recounted his dream. "Is there any light you can shed on such a memory?"

"I'm afraid not. If you are my brother's child, you were never acknowledged. Eleanora Pierce must have given you up for adoption at birth. Any memories you have would stem from your adoptive relatives."

Michael sighed. "It would seem my trip has been for nothing."

St. John rose from his chair, extending his hand to Michael. "I appreciate the distance you've traveled, but I have another meeting I must attend. If it's any comfort, you're one young man I wouldn't mind claiming as a nephew, should things turn out that way. But I must have documented proof, notarized so I'm assured my copies are authentic. And even then, I must question Nora's word regarding the sire of her child. Perhaps there are blood tests that can be run?"

Michael gave him a firm handshake, liking him far more now than he had at first. "Perhaps. I haven't checked into that sort of thing as yet. But it's certainly a consideration."

St. John came out from behind his desk, leading the way from the room. "It's one I hope you pursue. As I said, nothing could make me happier than to discover I had a nephew. My son, Tim, would be elated. He's an only child, and there are no cousins. Please, get back in touch soon. I'll be looking forward to hearing from you."

"I'll do that. I think I can find my own way out as long as the dogs don't mind."

"Ah, yes, the dogs. Beautiful animals, aren't they? Unfortunately I'm afraid they're rather unruly without a word from me." He led the way to the door, opening it and stepping aside to allow Michael to exit. The Dobermans came up off the porch simultaneously, lips curling to reveal sharp white teeth. "*Guten tag*, Mr. Smith."

The moment St. John spoke, the dogs backed off to let Michael pass. He strode directly to the cab. "Good day to you as well, Mr. St. John. I'll be in touch."

Michael slid into the back seat of the car, throwing an anxious look at the taxi meter. He punctuated a low curse by slamming the door. "Back to the hotel, please. I need to make plane reservations."

"Oh, yeah? Where ya off to?"

"Oregon."

Michael stared out the window at the blur of passing trees, his mind conjuring pictures of blood on yellow tile, of a man's hand stretching toward a cowering child. He had been so hopeful he'd learn something from Santini or St. John. He'd even been entertaining thoughts of a future with Sarah once he had his past settled. Now the burning excitement he had felt over this trip had turned to ashes. Unless he learned the truth, he'd never banish the nightmare from his life.

WITH AN ECONOMY of movement, Sarah unlocked her front door, stepped into the foyer and put her grocery bags on the hall table, emptying her arms just in time to catch Moses, who came rushing at her in a flying leap. Twenty pounds of plump fur hit her square in the chest, setting her back a step. Her shoulder blades connected with the door, slamming it shut. She winced, then giggled and buried her nose in her tomcat's ruff, avoiding the wet push of his eager nose as he tried to kiss her hello. It felt so good to be home. After her paranoia last night and this morning, a good dose of Moses was just what she needed to get her head straight. She hugged the cat tight, absorbing his warmth.

"Hi, Mosey. I'm far too sore for this kind of exuberance, you know."

"Rrrow?"

"Dinner? Moses, I'm scarcely in the door."

"Rrrow?" The cat rammed his nose in her ear and let loose with a rumbling purr. When that didn't serve to make her move, he nipped her earlobe with sharp teeth. *"Rrrow?"*

"All right already, one dinner coming up. But don't blame me when the vet puts you on a diet." She tossed her pet onto the carpet, turned to lock the door and scooped the grocery bags back into her arms. "And no ankle rubbing. You'll trip me. One more bruise and I'll be a candidate for body art without paint."

Walking left through the den and into the kitchen, she unloaded the groceries onto the counter, then opened a tin of tuna packed in spring water. Emptying the fish into Moses's bowl, she gave it a quick turn in the microwave and then set it before the feline, smiling at the satisfied rumbles coming from his chest as he began eating.

The telephone rang as she turned back to sort through the collection of food to look for something for her own dinner. She leaned sideways to snag the receiver and greet her caller.

"Hello, Sarah."

She immediately recognized that smooth-as-honey baritone. "Michael, how nice to hear from you."

There was a long silence at his end. "Is something wrong?"

"No, nothing." She worried her bottom lip. She'd ruin his impression of her forever if she began ranting like a crazy woman about green cars, hit-and-runs and renegade computers. "Where are you? In Eugene?"

"No, but I'm flying out in the morning."

An inexplicable wave of relief rushed over her. "How has your trip gone? Productively, I hope."

"It's a long story. As soon as I get back there tomorrow, I'm driving down to Ashland."

"To see your father?"

"Yes. How's it going on your end?"

"Oh, not too badly. A few equipment problems, nothing serious. I plan to put out more feelers on your folks in California tomorrow afternoon."

"You didn't sound like yourself when you answered. Am I interrupting something?"

"Nothing important. Just throwing supper at my roommate. He started complaining for dinner the minute I got home."

Another very long silence. "Your roommate?"

The thinly veiled animosity that laced his voice was unmistakable. "Didn't I ever mention the man in my life? I'll introduce you sometime. Just don't wear black. He sheds." She leaned against the counter and winced when the formica pressed into a sore spot.

"I never wear black, remember. What do you mean he sheds?"

"Sheds, as in hair rubbing off on your slacks." Stifling a giggle, she added, "He's a cat. His name is Moses. You do like cats, don't you?"

"I, uh, yes, of course, cats are okay." He laughed, then cleared his throat. "Cats are fantastic. You had me going there a minute. I thought you—" He broke off and heaved a sigh. "Listen, the reason I called was to ask you to dinner the evening after next. I thought it might be a good time to share notes and update each other."

She wished he wanted to see her for some other reason. "Dinner sounds great. Is seven too late?"

"Not at all. I'll stay tomorrow night in Ashland and leave after lunch the next day. I'll pick you up at your place if that's okay. Your address is in the phone book." He hesitated a moment. "Well, until then?"

"Yes, until then. Goodbye." A sudden jolt of anxiety ran through her. "Uh, Michael?" She stared at Moses's twitching tail, trying to think how she might phrase this without sounding foolish. "Um...be careful, won't you?"

"Are you sure you're all right?"

"Yes—yes, I'm fine. Just take care. There are muggers in Chicago, you know."

"After the cab fares I've been paying, I'd make a very poor hit, believe me." He chuckled. "You take care, too, okay? *Arrivederci.*"

After hanging up the phone, she hurried putting away the groceries, then strode purposefully toward the bedroom, unbuttoning her blouse. As she stepped over to her bed, she kicked off her high-heeled shoes and undressed. *Ah.* Clothes were sheer torture with all the bruises.

Grabbing her robe off a closet hook, she slipped it on and walked across the room, leaning a shoulder against the sliding glass door to gaze out at her small deck. The surrounding six-foot hedge provided solitude she treasured. The whiskey-barrel waterfalls she had built last summer gurgled softly, as a spray of frothy water cascaded into an ivy-enrobed goldfish pond. Resting her forehead against the glass, Sarah watched the mesmerizing movement of water, letting it relax her.

Several seconds passed before her skin began to prickle. She shifted and scanned the hedge. It was silly, but... She stiffened and reached for the door lever to make sure it was locked. Was that a man peering at her through the foliage? She focused on the spot. The hedge swayed slightly, possibly from the breeze. Or was it from someone moving? The man's face had disappeared. *If it had even been there.* She stepped away from the window, reaching for the traverse-rod cord to close the drapes. Why would anyone be lurking in her hedge to spy on her?

Her hand trembled as she nudged the curtain aside to peek out at the deck. *Nothing.* She had probably imagined that she saw someone. It wasn't even dark yet. No Peeping Tom in his right mind would stand on the sidewalk of a cul-de-sac at dusk and peer through a single woman's hedge. He'd be seen by neighbors and end up with the cops breathing down his neck.

Even so, she felt uneasy. Before taking her shower, she systematically checked every door and window in the house to be sure they were locked, chiding herself the entire time for being ridiculous. Then, as she stood under the jet spray of her shower, she remembered the charming little bathroom scene in the movie *Psycho.* She made short work of bathing and swathed herself in her towel before creeping to her bedroom door to peer down the hall. *Anyone out there?* Moses came around the corner from the living room, arching his back against the wall to rub. His lazy *rrrow* reassured her. The cat didn't take well to strangers. If anyone were in the house, he'd be ruffled and slitty eyed. She raked her hair back from her eyes and laughed at herself.

Still uneasy, she walked up the hall, stepping inside each bedroom to glance around. What she would do if she found someone, she didn't know. As she entered the last room, she went to the window and lifted the pink chiffon curtain to peer out at the street. *No bogeyman.* Passing a hand over her eyes, she sank onto the edge of the bed, wondering what on earth had gotten into her. She'd been living alone for years and never behaved like this.

Perhaps she was having a delayed reaction from the accident. She *had* received a nasty bump on the head, enough to knock her out. That could account for why she felt so jumpy. She sighed and smiled. Michael would be home tomorrow. When she told him about all this, he'd probably laugh. And if she had any sense, she'd laugh with him.

MICHAEL SAT AT his father's kitchen table sipping a freshly brewed cup of coffee, trying to think of a tactful way to bring up his trip to Chicago. Since his arrival last night, an opportune moment hadn't come up, and time was running out. No matter how he broached the subject, the older De Lorio would be upset.

Robert leaned over his open oven door, checking a tray of cinnamon rolls. As he straightened, he kissed the tips of his fingers with a loud smacking of his lips, then threw the kiss into the air, grinning. "*Perfetto*, eh, Michael? That aroma. It is *profumo*." He rolled his eyes and sighed theatrically as he closed the stove door. "Sheer heaven, no? Your papa, he has not lost his touch. There is snow on the roof, but the fire still burns in the oven."

Michael chuckled. "Papa, I think that expression was meant for the libido, not yeast rolls."

"Oh, yes?" Robert's brown eyes twinkled. "At my age, yeast rolls are the only game in town." He brushed his palms on his bib apron as he strode back to the table. "A few more minutes and we shall have piping hot rolls to go with our coffee. You will stay for lunch?"

"Sure. I can stay until three if you don't have other plans."

"Other plans!" Robert's hands went into action as he spoke. "My only son comes to stay and me have other plans? I will cancel. You are more important, no? It is a rare treat that you come to see me."

"It's not that seldom that I come. You make it sound as if I neglect you."

"No, Michael. You are a good boy."

The love shining in his dad's eyes made Michael's throat ache with guilt. There were thousands of people who would give anything to have a father like Robert De Lorio, but Michael couldn't be content with that. Instead he drove himself crazy trying to unlock the secrets of a past he wasn't even sure existed. Glancing around the cozy kitchen, he could almost see his mother bustling from cupboard to cupboard. He'd grown up with all the love and attention and warmth a kid could ask for, so why couldn't he just let it go at that?

"Papa, I have something I must tell you."

"Uh-oh, this sounds serious." Robert arched an eyebrow. "*Mamma mia!* You are getting married? It's finally happened. This dried-up old man will have grandchildren to spoil after all. *Si figuri!*"

"No, I'm not getting married. It's something more serious than that."

"More serious? More serious, he says?" Robert glanced toward the ceiling as if some unseen spectator floated above them, listening to the conversation. "Do you hear this, Mamma? Where did we go wrong raising this boy? Something more serious than grandbabies? Hmmph."

"Papa, I——" Michael shook his head. "You're impossible."

Pulling a straight face, Robert folded his hands and rested them on the tabletop. "Okay, you have my undivided attention. What is this serious thing you must tell me?"

"I'm afraid you may feel angry."

"You forewarn me so I can work up a temper? Spit it out, Michael. I can get plenty mad without your help, you know this well."

"I, um, just got home yesterday from a visit to Chicago."

The kitchen went so quiet Michael could hear the defroster inside the refrigerator dripping ice water into the pan. His father stared at him, his face so still it looked lifeless.

"Papa, try to under——"

"Chicago? Chicago you say?" Robert's voice lifted to a yell on the last syllable. He closed his eyes and with a swift motion of his hand, he crossed himself. "How dare you do something like this without speaking to me first? How dare you? I have given you all the love a man can give and this is how you repay me?"

"Papa, I had a right to meet my real father and mother."

Robert opened his eyes and shot from his chair, leaning across the table to slam his fist down next to Michael's coffee mug. "Rights? Don't speak to me of *your* rights. Honor your father and mother! It is your duty. *I* am your father, not some stranger in Chicago. I raised you. I fed you. I—" His voice cracked and tears glistened in his eyes. "I am the one who loves you, yet you set out to destroy me."

Spilled coffee dripped off the edge of the table onto Michael's legs. Scalding, searing drops. His eyes stung from staring but he couldn't blink, couldn't drag his gaze away from his father's. *Splat, splat, splat,* just like in his nightmare. The sound seemed to intensify, echoing inside his mind until he wanted to scream. Finally he did. "Destroy *you*? I'm the one going crazy, not you! Do you hear me, Papa? The dream is driving me insane! I've asked you who Gino was a thousand times! And you lied to me. You lied! *I* am Gino!"

With a sweep of his arm, Michael sent the coffee mug skittering across the table and crashing into the wall. The sound of ceramic striking plaster froze both men, Michael with his arm still outstretched, Robert with his white-knuckled fist on the tabletop. Their faces were a scant inch apart. The coffee splattered the white paint and ran in rivulets toward the floor.

"Who did you see there?" Robert asked in a soft voice.

"Even now you won't admit it, will you?" Michael sighed and put a trembling hand over his eyes. "I called my mother and went to see my uncle, Marcus St. John."

After Robert's violent reaction, Michael was afraid to tell him he'd also visited Giorgio Santini. He had to remember the old man's bad heart. "My real father is dead."

"*I* am your real father."

Michael felt nauseous. "Papa, I never meant to hurt you. Try to understand that."

"I forbid you to make any further contact with those people. Do you hear me? I forbid it."

It seemed to Michael that his every childhood memory crowded into his mind at that moment. He loved this old man. Nothing was worth hurting him like this. "Papa, please, I'm a grown-up, not a child."

"Grown or no, I forbid it. I mean it. If you disobey me, you are no longer welcome in this house."

Robert straightened, and as he did, Michael sat back in his chair, looking up at him. In that instant, as he studied his father's ashen face, Michael knew the game was up. He couldn't risk his dad's health. Robert was old; his years were numbered. There would be plenty of time after his father passed away for Michael to dig up the past. Some sacrifices were too great, and hurting his father like this, just to satisfy his own curiosity, was one of them.

"All right, Papa. You win."

Robert sank back onto his chair. "I am sorry, Michael. I didn't mean it. This is your home always."

"I know that." Grabbing a towel off the counter, Michael got out of his chair and hunkered down to clean up the mess he had made. "You don't have to apologize to me, Papa."

Leaning his head back, Robert closed his eyes. "You will go now, eh? This has exhausted me. I need to rest."

The ache of guilt in Michael's throat swelled, spreading to his chest. "I could read or something while you take a nap. Then maybe we could go see Father O'Connell and take him out for pie and coffee."

"Not today, Michael, not today." Opening his eyes, Robert flashed a weak smile. "You come another time, no? We will·do it then."

Michael rose to his feet, running a shaky hand over his hair as he tossed the towel on the table. "Okay, another day." Grasping his dad's shoulder, he said, "Papa, you know you can trust me, don't you? That I'll always love you, no matter what. If there's something troubling you, something about Chicago, you can tell me. It won't make a difference."

Patting Michael's hand, Robert nodded. "I know you love me, Michael. It isn't that. You go, eh? We will talk of this another time."

Michael started to leave the kitchen. As he drew near the door, he looked back over his shoulder. "Are you going to be okay?"

"Oh, yes. Go on with you. I am only very tired."

Robert didn't move from his chair until Michael had retrieved his things from the bedroom and shut the front door behind him on his way out. Then he jumped to his feet and sprang for the telephone on the counter, punching out a well-memorized number. A moment later, a woman answered.

"I need to speak to Bronson. This is Robert De Lorio calling."

"One moment, please."

The phone clicked and rang three times. Then a deep voice cut in. "Bronson here."

"Don, this is Robert De Lorio. I—I'm in serious trouble. There's been a security break."

Bronson's voice sharpened. "You're sure? When?"

"This past couple of days. Michael flew to Chicago and saw his biological uncle and spoke with his mother on the phone."

"Why in hell didn't you stop him?"

"I didn't know he was going. And how could I stop him without telling him the truth?"

Bronson sighed. "You don't want to do that. You tell one person and pretty soon it's the best kept secret in town."

Robert breathed in short, wheezy little gasps, pressing a hand to his chest as he stretched the phone cord to reach his bottle of nitroglycerin tablets on the kitchen window-sill. "I—I'm scared."

"Listen, Robert, this may not be as serious as it sounds."

"Not as serious—" Robert's hand was shaking as he placed a pill under his tongue, struggling for air. "You know La Grande's never stopped looking for me. Remember a few years back when he sent someone to ask questions at the Chicago offices? He's just biding his time, waiting for me to make a slip, and you know it."

"Biological families seldom know adoptive relatives. I doubt there was any contact made with the Santinis, and unless there was, you're safe."

"You think so?"

"I'll have men standing by. We're just a phone call away if anything else develops. There's no point in panic."

Robert skimmed his face with the palm of his hand, wiping away beads of sweat. "I think I should tell Michael the truth."

"Let me make the decision on that."

"Yes, but this changes things, doesn't it? He could talk to the wrong people, leave a trail back to me. We could both end up dead."

CHAPTER SEVEN

THE RESTAURANT AT the Valley River Inn was crowded as usual, but the candlelight and strategically placed foliage around the circular booths lent an illusion of intimacy. Sarah chewed a bite of halibut smothered in sour cream and lemon, watching Michael's face. He looked wonderful, dark and breathtakingly attractive in a white jacket over a light blue shirt and navy slacks. But ever since he had picked her up two hours earlier, Sarah had sensed a brittle tension in him. There were shadows under his eyes that hadn't been there before his trip to Chicago.

She hoped the news she had just imparted hadn't added to his stress. Though she had warned him to expect the worst, it still must have been a shock to learn that the real Robert De Lorio had died at three months of age and Maria Ames De Lorio before her twelfth birthday. It looked as if Michael's adoptive parents, Angelo and Marcia Santini, had taken the names of dead children whose years of birth matched their own.

She lifted her goblet, taking a sip of Chablis. "Well, I've briefed you on my progress. Your turn. How did your trip go?"

He lifted one shoulder in a shrug. "It went all right."

Turning her glass, she watched the wine shimmer in the flickering light. "Something's wrong, Michael. Won't you tell me about it? You surprised me by arriving at my place early. It isn't something that happened during your visit with your dad?"

"Am I that transparent?"

"Like a window."

He chuckled and shook his head. "I'm sorry. I planned for this dinner to be a special thank-you. Now here I am pulling a grim face and ruining the atmosphere."

She glanced out at the city lights reflecting off the river. "It is a beautiful view."

"Yes, it certainly is."

Something in his tone told her he wasn't talking about the water. She turned to find his gaze lingering on her. A self-conscious flush crept up her neck, and she turned her attention back to her plate, disconcerted by the inexplicable wave of pleasure that ran through her. She had worn a cream-colored blouson dress of fluid georgette with a shimmering lace peplum over the pleated skirt. With gold heels, it was elegant enough to go anywhere but not so dressy that she would have looked overdone if he had taken her to a less prestigious restaurant. Her only other evening dress was black, which was definitely out of the question, considering Michael's dislike of the color.

"Did you see your mother? I'm dying to hear."

He reached for his wineglass with a sigh. "There's no way to get around it, is there? Business first." He gave her a quick rundown on his trip to Chicago and the later visit with his father. "It was a pretty nasty scene with Papa," he concluded. "He was so upset, I didn't dare tell him I'd seen Giorgio Santini. After all your hard work, I hate to tell you this, but I've decided to drop the whole issue. No more investigation, at least not while Papa's alive. I owe him that."

She reached across the table to touch his hand. The white around his mouth told her just how taxing the confrontation with his father had been. "Oh, Michael, I am sorry. I know what this investigation meant to you."

Did she know? Michael doubted it. He looked into her

shimmering eyes, searching for any indication that she understood just how much this would affect his relationship with her. He had told her about his nightmare, how he had hoped to stop having it by discovering its cause. But he'd never mentioned how frequently the dreams plagued him.

"At least you know for certain your dad used to be Angelo Santini. You spoke to Marcus St. John and he's receptive to considering proof. And you found your mother. That's better than nothing."

"I guess I did accomplish quite a lot. I was surprised St. John was fairly open with me after he was so testy to you."

"After he had a chance to think it over, he must have realized there was no point in being difficult." With a shrug of one shoulder, Sarah gave his hand another quick squeeze, hoping to comfort him. "As for your dad's reaction, Michael, I'm sorry. But he's obviously left something unpleasant behind him and doesn't want it dug up. One can't condemn him for that. I know it's a big sacrifice, but there's some comfort in knowing you're making the right choice."

"You really think so?" He speared a piece of prime rib, dipped it in horseradish, then eyed it as if it were shoe leather. With a clink of silver against china, he dropped his fork and leaned back in his seat, gazing at her over the candle flame. "I suppose I'll learn to accept it. Someday, when Papa won't be hurt by it, perhaps I'll pursue it again."

Shadows shifted in his dark eyes. Watching him, she wished there were some way that she could make him forget his nightmare and erase the tormenting questions from his mind. With a slight toss of her head, she brushed an annoying lock of hair from her cheek, then reached for her fork.

"Sarah...what happened?" He reached across the table to grasp her chin, tipping her face to the light. Too late, she remembered why she'd worn her hair brushed forward. Now he had seen the nasty bruise along the curve of her cheek from her biking accident. "You've been hurt."

"I had a biking accident, Michael. Nothing serious."

His grip relaxed. "It sure looks serious."

She smiled. "Well, actually, it felt a little more serious when it happened. From the feel of things, I'm still not sure if I hit my head first or my other end."

He touched the contour of her jaw with a gentle fingertip. "Are you okay?"

"I'm fine." Taking a deep breath, she took refuge behind a dazzling smile. "I just crammed a year's bad luck into twenty-four hours, that's all. You know, if anything could go wrong, it did?"

He looked unconvinced. "Such as?"

"Such as getting hit by a drunk driver when I was riding home on my ten-speed? Losing all the files on my computer's hard disk because of an operator error? I even had a Peeping Tom. It's been one crazy week."

"Are you serious? You were hit by a car?"

"Amazing, isn't it?"

"Sarah, are you sure you're not seriously hurt?"

"My dignity was destroyed, but other than that, it's just bruises. The police think the man driving was intoxicated. I can only hope he had a hangover the next day. He left the scene of the accident."

"Hit-and-run? No wonder you sounded strange on the phone."

"Strange? Yes, I suppose you could say that. If you told me the sky was about to fall, I'd dive under the table."

He laughed. "Who could blame you? Rest assured, I'm an excellent driver. You'll get home in one piece and feel much better after a good night's sleep."

She dropped her napkin on her plate to hide the large portion of food she'd left uneaten. "Ah, yes, a full eight hours sounds heavenly."

The night air was cool as they exited the inn twenty minutes later. Michael led Sarah to the right, circling behind the building to reach the cement footpath along the river. "A meal here isn't complete without a stroll in the moonlight afterward."

They walked downstream beyond view of the restaurant. Releasing her arm, he leaned his elbows on the top rung of the safety railing, bending one knee. Lifting his face to the breeze, he took a deep breath. She joined him with a sigh of pleasure. Glancing sideways, she wasn't surprised to find he was watching her. His gaze was intent, thoughtful, his smile mysterious and perhaps a little sad. It was as if... Her breath caught. He looked at her as if he were trying to memorize her face.

Turning toward her, he placed his hands on her shoulders, drawing her to him. Her heartbeat accelerated. She placed her palms against his chest, raising her gaze to meet his. A muscle ticked along his jaw as he studied her. With a gentle hand, he gently traced the bruise again.

"You're lovely in moonlight, so very lovely."

She closed her eyes. There was a note of goodbye in his tone. He felt so big and warm and solid, she wished she could stand there in his arms forever. He crooked a finger beneath her chin, tilting her face farther back, and she lifted her gaze to meet his. Dipping his head, he kissed her, so softly, so carefully that her breath caught again. She savored the silken pressure of his lips, sensing as only a woman can that this man was someone extremely special. In sudden desperation, she clung to him, treasuring the moment, knowing without being told it would be the last.

Slipping her arms around his neck, she pressed her body closer to his and parted her lips, surrendering more completely to his kiss than she had done with any other man, tasting the sweetness of his mouth, sharing the secrets of hers. A warm tendril of heat ribboned through her belly, pooling in a molten shimmer of sensation in the pit of her stomach. *Michael.* The sound of his name was a song inside her.

When he drew away, he took a deep, shaky breath and exhaled slowly. The glimmer in his eyes told her he'd been as affected by the kiss as she, despite the frown that settled on his brow. "I'm sorry, Sarah. I didn't intend to do that. It was selfish, but I wanted this one time to remember."

Upon hearing the goodbye put into words, a wave of pain washed over her, so all-encompassing it took her completely off guard. How could he apologize for something so perfect, so right? She averted her face, staring blindly at the river. The only explanation was that he hadn't felt what she had; she'd only imagined it.

"Sarah...." There was a note of concern in his voice.

"No—don't say anything more, please." Squaring her shoulders, she forced an impersonal smile. "Let's call it an evening, shall we? I'm terribly tired."

She thought she heard him mutter a curse, but he didn't argue. With a heavy sigh, he touched his hand to her arm, guiding her up the footpath, back the way they had come.

EN ROUTE HOME an hour later, Michael thought of little else but Sarah. He had only scratched the surface of his past. No matter what Giorgio Santini claimed, there *was* a dragon to slay. For his father's sake, Michael couldn't dig any deeper now. And until he knew the truth, he had no right to become involved with a woman.

How many Vietnam veterans had he treated whose marriages had been destroyed by frequent, violent nightmares? Dozens. He wasn't a war veteran, but his dreams were every bit as horrible as theirs, affecting every facet of his life. What point was there in fooling himself? Sighing, he crooked a finger under the knot of his tie and worked it loose. There was something special developing between him and Sarah; he couldn't deny it. But how would she or any woman feel about him when she'd lost sleep night after night because of his screams? How would she like waking up in a sweat-soaked bed, smelling his fear and panic? For that matter, how would it make him feel? Michael clenched his teeth. He couldn't put someone he cared about through that.

He wouldn't.

An ache rose in his throat as he thought of all the empty tomorrows that stretched ahead of him. He'd get up in the morning, go to work, come home. The same thing, day in and day out, week after week, month after month, year after year. It presented a gloomy picture, but what real choice did he have? He didn't wish his father dead.

MICHAEL FINISHED BREAKFAST at the Shilo the next morning, pulled out of the parking lot and exited south onto Interstate 5, heading toward his office. As he switched lanes, he braked once behind a station wagon, signaled, accelerated and moved over one more lane to a position behind a semitruck. When he glanced at his speedometer, he noticed he was doing sixty miles an hour. The semi downshifted for a snag in traffic. Michael touched his brake. Nothing happened. His foot went clear to the floor.

And his stomach followed....

For a split second, Michael froze, staring at the eighteen wheeler in front of him. Then he tromped on the brake pedal again. *Nothing*. His brakes were gone? Riveting his gaze on the silver trailer doors of the truck, he watched in horrified fascination as the embossed diamond pattern in the metal became clearer and larger. Then his eyes dropped to the clearance under the vehicle, and he remembered reading stories about cars driving right under semitrucks, sheering the passengers' heads off. He threw a frantic glance at his rearview mirror, hoping he could move over into the next lane, but traffic blocked him in both directions. He was boxed in with no place to go, no way to stop. With a curse, he again pumped wildly at the brake pedal. He was going to crash if he didn't do something.

Leaning forward, he grabbed the emergency brake handle and jerked on it with all his might. The Mercedes was still gaining on the truck. Sweat sprang to his forehead. With a shaking hand, he turned off the ignition key. His car radio blipped into silence. His power steering stopped working, and the car listed heavily to one side. The Dodge beside him blared its horn and its driver roared obscenities out his window. Michael swallowed, wrenching with all his weight to correct the drift, watching the remaining few feet of space between his front bumper and the truck trailer disappearing. Fear made his mouth feel filled with cotton.

Then he saw the distance between his car and the truck gradually widening. He slumped in the seat, letting out a pent-up breath. Checking to his right, he saw a gap in traffic and heaved on the steering wheel to turn into the next lane. He was trembling by the time he could pull off onto the shoulder of the road.

After the Mercedes coasted to a stop, he climbed from the car to thumb down a motorist. His legs felt as wobbly as half-set Jell-O. A battered blue pickup pulled over behind him and a farmer piled out, hooking his thumbs in the straps of his overalls.

"Trouble, partner?"

Michael gave a weak laugh. "You could say that, yes. Thanks for stopping. My brakes went out."

The older man averted his face and spewed a brown stream of tobacco juice onto the gravel. "Did ya pull yer emergency?"

"Uh, yes, as a matter of fact, but the damned thing didn't work."

The farmer squinted at the car, noted its make and said, "Hmmph. Well, lock 'er up. I'll give ya a lift to town."

While Michael leaned inside the car to pull his keys from the ignition and lock the doors, the farmer took two pieces of wood from the bed of his truck and blocked the Mercedes's tires so it wouldn't roll.

"I really appreciate this," Michael told him as he climbed into the pickup cab. "If you can let me off at the nearest service station, I'll call a tow company and cab."

"Better git them brakes fixed, sonny. Or a decent car, one 'r tuther. Man could git killed out here on this freeway without no brakes."

Michael nearly choked at the derogatory remark about his Mercedes. Taking a deep breath, he said, "Yes, that thought occurred to me a couple of times."

The farmer exited the freeway and drove to a gas station. Michael laid twenty dollars on the seat as he left the truck, hoping the old man wouldn't notice the money until he was back on the freeway. Lifting his arm to wave, he strode to the phone booth. After calling a tow truck, he dialed Pete's Auto Repair, where he was a regular customer. "Hey, Pete, this is Michael De Lorio."

"Hi, Michael. What'cha got for me?"

"A brake job. Lost all but my pedal out on the highway a few minutes ago. A tow company's hauling her out to you." Michael turned his back to the freeway as a semi-truck passed, blowing its air horn. Raising his voice to be heard, he asked, "Can you give me a call at the office when you've got her fixed?"

"Sure." Pete was silent a moment. "I would've sworn we just did a brake job for you a couple of months back."

Michael sighed. "I thought you did, too."

At FOUR-THIRTY, MICHAEL'S receptionist buzzed him, saying he had a phone call from Pete's Auto Repair. Michael picked up the phone. "Yeah, Pete, how's it looking? Do you have her fixed already?"

"It's not lookin' too good. And I haven't touched a thing. I think you'd better call the cops."

Michael lifted an eyebrow. He'd never heard Pete sound so solemn. "The cops?"

"Some so-and-so cut your brake lines."

"You're kidding."

"I'm sure not, buddy. Somebody's out to get you."

A chill ran up the center of Michael's back. He'd known Pete Bakker a long time and trusted the man implicitly. Glancing at his watch, he said, "I'm with a patient right now. I'll be there in about forty minutes."

THE UNDERBODY OF THE MERCEDES was dirty and complicated looking. Beyond that, Michael understood very little of what Pete was pointing to and jabbering about as he stepped beneath the power lift and explained the damage to a policeman. "See there? That line was nicked just enough to spill fluid when the pedal was pumped."

The policeman craned his neck to look upward, nodding and frowning. Michael's stomach knotted. Who would have cut his brake lines? The question ricocheted inside his head, filling his entire mind. Who? And why? The lines had to have been cut while he was eating breakfast at the Shilo. Someone must have followed him there. There were only a couple of stops between the restaurant and Interstate 5. Whoever had cut the lines had taken a gamble, counting on Michael to take the highway route to reach his office. Fast traffic and failed brakes were a deadly combination. Someone had tried to kill him.

Pete pointed at a severed cable, his expression grim. "And there you can see where the emergency brake cable was cut. This wasn't any accident, buddy. Somebody who knew what he was doing did his damnedest to kill this fella."

Michael silently seconded that. The Shilo parking lot was always packed with vehicles, and he had only been inside eating a few minutes. Only an expert could have slipped under his car and sliced his brake lines so quickly with such deadly precision.

The policeman examined the severed cable, then gave his soiled fingers a cursory wipe on his dark slacks. "In other words, the lines were cut that way so the fluid wouldn't spill out immediately?"

Pete nodded. "That's right. Just a big enough cut that the hydraulic system would work two, maybe three times, then go kaput. Every time Dr. De Lorio hit his brakes, he squirted more fluid. And these babies don't work without fluid."

The policeman jotted notes for several minutes, then lifted curious gray eyes to scan Michael's face. "Dr. De Lorio, do you have any idea who might have done this?"

"None at all."

Pete stepped out from under the car, wiping his hands on a rag.

"Can I get this fixed now and out of the shop?" Michael asked.

The *tatti-tat-tat* of an air-powered drill drowned out the police officer's reply. All three men left the garage area to escape the noise the other mechanics were making. "I think it would be a good idea to leave the car as it is until we can investigate this further," the officer repeated.

"No problem, Michael my man, you can take my loaner." Turning toward the garage, Pete cupped his hands around his mouth and yelled, "Hey, Jimmy, take the Mercedes down and push it around to the parking area. Then take the LTD up and give her a quick check. Dr. De Lorio is going to borrow her for a few days."

The policeman stepped closer to Michael. "Dr. De Lorio, can you come to the station so we can make a full report on this?"

"Certainly."

"On the way, try to figure out who could have done this. My bet is it's one of your patients. In your line of work, you never know when one of those people might go off the deep end."

One of those people? Why did everyone always assume his patients were crazy? They were just average people with stressful lives and more than their share of problems. "I'll certainly think about it as I drive over."

Fastening his pen to the clipboard, the officer frowned. "Another possibility is a jilted girlfriend. Anyone like that in your life? Someone who might have hired this done?"

Michael immediately envisioned Sarah's upturned face from last night. Her lips had shimmered in the moonlight, her large brown eyes searching his, the curve of her cheek shadowed by a nasty bruise. His heart lurched as he recalled her story about being hit by a car. Had it really been a drunk driver? Or was it a deliberate attempt on her life? He glanced at his watch. It was almost six.

"Could you excuse me a moment, officer? I have an urgent call I need to make."

Stepping into Pete's small office, Michael dialed Sarah's business number. Her answering machine took his call. Not wanting his message to be recorded in case Molly played it first, he hung up and tried Sarah at home. No answer. He glanced at his watch again. He'd call her again from the police station.

SARAH LOCKED THE OFFICE DOOR and pocketed the key, pivoting on the shadowy sidewalk. She had eaten dinner with an important prospective client at a nearby restaurant, then returned to the office to work late retrieving computer files.

It was now well after seven. The bright amber halos around the streetlights shimmered against the black sky. With her bike out of commission and her Fiero in the shop for a scheduled lube job she hadn't wanted to cancel, she had no choice but to walk to the bus stop. It was only three blocks, but she was running late and wearing the most impractical shoes she owned. Why hadn't she thought to bring a pair of comfortable shoes to change into? She'd known she wouldn't have the car tonight. A wry grin curved her mouth. A lot of good it had done her to dress up. Her important prospective client hadn't panned out, and now all she'd get for her trouble was blistered feet from wearing these silly spikes.

Through the window of her office, she heard the phone ringing. Hesitating, she started to turn back, then changed her mind. As it was, she had barely enough time to catch the bus. Her answering machine could take the call.

Tucking her purse under her arm, she set off at a brisk pace. At this time of evening, the business offices along this part of the street were all deserted. The night air was crisp and cold on her cheeks. She shivered, watching the darkened doorways ahead of her. Too bad cab fare from here to home cost an arm and leg. She felt uneasy out here this late. Just that morning, Molly had read a news story aloud about a rapist who broke into a house over on Eleventh night before last. That wasn't far from here, she realized. A woman couldn't be too cautious walking alone after dusk.

Sarah had no sooner thought that than she heard footsteps on the concrete behind her. She lengthened her stride, holding her head high, looking both right and left. She had read that alert people were far less likely to be attacked than those who ambled along, watching their feet. Her heels made sharp and precise clicks on the cement. The shoes behind her were much more quiet and seemed to be getting closer. A man, she guessed, wearing street shoes.

The hairs at her nape tingled. She could feel eyes watching her. Catching her lip between her teeth, she veered left across the street, glancing back over her shoulder. There was no one there. She hesitated, straining to see. The streetlights illuminated the sidewalk, but it was shadowy next to the buildings. She knew she had heard someone. Had he hidden so she wouldn't see him?

She hurried to reach the opposite sidewalk, picking up her pace. Her heart started to slam when she heard running footsteps cross the street and fall in behind her. She began walking even faster. The footsteps picked up speed, too, coming closer and closer. Sarah whirled to look. *No one?* Her mouth went dry and the metallic taste of fear slithered up her throat. She hadn't imagined the footsteps. Someone *was* there; he was just hiding.

Tightening her arm around her purse, she walked backward several steps, hoping to spot him. *There!* She saw the dark, hulking outline of a man step out of a shadowed doorway, then step quickly back. A tremor ran the length of her legs, making her stride unsteady. If only there were a lighted office nearby she could go to. *Don't panic, Sarah. Just get rid of those high heels and outrun him.* Keeping her eye on the doorway, she stepped out of one shoe, then the other. The cement felt cold and rough under her nylon-clad feet. Stooping over, she picked up her shoes with her right hand. The sharp spike heels might end up being the only weapon she had. Taking three steps backward, she watched the doorway a moment longer, then whirled to flee.

As soon as she bolted, Sarah heard the man leap out to follow her. The hem of her skirt snapped taut around her legs as she bounded for the corner. A pebble cut into the ball of her right foot and sent a streak of pain clear to her knee. She kept running, forcing herself to breathe in a deep, regular rhythm, knowing she could keep going much longer if she conserved her strength and paced herself. She knew she was a fast runner, she just hoped the man chasing her wasn't faster.

At the corner, Sarah saw headlights coming from her left. She plunged off the curb, dashing into the car's path. "Help me!"

Brakes screeched as the car slid to a stop. She skirted the front bumper, peering in the driver's window at an elderly woman who looked as frightened as she was.

"Help me! Please! A man's chasing me!"

Shaking her white head, the old woman gunned her accelerator. Her car lurched forward into the intersection.

Sarah staggered backward, staring at the man running toward her. She had managed to get some distance ahead of him, but he was coming up quickly. He was nearly to the corner now, the tails of his long black coat flying behind him, his hat pulled low to conceal his face. Terror made her breath come in shivery little gasps. She lunged for the opposite curb, running as fast as she could. Shoe leather slapped the asphalt behind her, the sound growing louder and louder.

CHAPTER EIGHT

As SARAH DREW close to an alleyway, something brushed the back of her suit jacket. A hand? Oh, God, he was grabbing for her. She could hear him breathing, almost feel the steamy heat of his expelled air on the back of her neck. She tried for another burst of speed, but she was extended to full stride now. Her lungs ached, feeling as if they might burst. She couldn't run much farther. Glancing frantically right and left, she tried to recognize something. In her panic, she had turned down another street to lose him, and now *she* was lost instead.

In a last desperate attempt to save herself, she tightened her grip on her shoes and swung around, smacking her pursuer in the face with the sharp spikes of her stiletto heels.

He doubled over, pressing his hands to his eyes. "Ahhh."

His hat tumbled off and rolled on its brim into the gutter. A sob welled up in her throat, threatening to choke her and she ran, not looking back. Seconds later, feet again thudded behind her, at a slower pace now, but still following. Building fronts blurred in her peripheral vision. Each breath she took knifed into her ribs, whistling back up her throat and out her mouth in puffs of steam. Where was she? Her legs grew heavy. The bottoms of her feet felt raw. Then she saw a more brightly lit block of buildings up ahead of her.

The city mall. People. She cannoned across the intersection, not even looking for cars, and threw herself against the door of a busy ice-cream parlor. The overhead bell clanged to announce her arrival, and several young people turned curious stares on her. She backed away from the parlor windows, clutching her shoes to her chest, fighting to get her breath.

"You okay, ma'am?" the girl behind the counter asked.

Sarah swallowed, nodding her head. "C-can you call the police? A man's chasing me."

A brawny young fellow, who looked like a university football player, swaggered over to the window. "Where is he? I'll take care of the jerk."

He pushed open the door and stepped out onto the side-walk, walking first in one direction, then the other. Saun-tering back inside, he said, "If he was out there, he's long gone now, lady. Did you know him?"

"I don't think so. It was so dark, I can't be sure."

"Wouldn't do any good to call the cops then. Did he hurt you?"

Sarah sank onto a wrought-iron chair, shaking her head. "No, I'm fine. I think I should report this, though."

"Be my guest if you wanna waste two hours of your time for nothing. Won't do any good unless you can give a description."

"I suppose you're right." Pressing a hand over her eyes, Sarah took a deep, steadying breath. "Could you call me a cab?"

SARAH ADJUSTED THE SHOWER nozzle to the massage setting and turned her back to the pelting water, pressing her fore-head against the shower stall wall. Her arms and legs felt like they weighed a hundred pounds each, hanging off her body like pieces of clay. Every time she closed her eyes, she envisioned that man in the long black coat, his legs scissoring, his stride outdistancing hers.

Hot, throbbing spurts of spray hit the sore places on her back, kneading, soothing. She closed her eyes and took a deep breath of steam, relaxing her shoulders. Tonight she wouldn't bother with soap. Just standing here to get the aches out of her body would be enough. A distant ringing sound caught her attention. She lifted her head, listening. "Oh, damn."

She shifted the faucet handle to Off with the heel of her hand and shoved open the stall door. Shivering, she snagged a towel from the rack as she raced for the bedside telephone. She grabbed the receiver and snapped, "Hello."

"Sarah? Thank goodness you're finally home. It's Michael."

Wrapping the towel around herself, she tucked an end between her breasts to secure it and sank onto the bed.

"This may sound a little peculiar, but hear me out, okay?"

She pressed the phone closer to her ear. "I'm listening."

"I'm on my way to Ashland to see my dad. I'll be back sometime tomorrow. While I'm gone, I want you to be extremely careful. If there's any way you can, just stay home with your doors locked until I get there."

An icy tendril of fear slithered up her back. "Michael, I can't stay home. I have a business to run."

He was silent for a moment. "Then call a cab to take you to and from, and don't leave the office or house until you see the cabbie pull up out front. Fact is, you should stay around people as much as you can."

"You're frightening me."

"Good."

"What d'you mean, good?"

He sighed. "Look, I know this may sound a little crazy, but, uh, someone tried to kill me this morning. The brake lines on my car were cut. The cops think it was one of my patients but I don't buy it. I immediately thought of *your* accident. Isn't this a bit much to be coincidence?"

Sarah ran her tongue over her lips, glancing toward the

sliding glass door. "Michael, tonight when I left the office, a man chased me. I got away, but just barely."

"Did you call the police?"

"Uh, no. I ducked into an ice-cream parlor and he disappeared. There wasn't anything the police could have done. It was too dark for me to describe him."

"As soon as we hang up, call them. Tell them we have reason to suspect a connection between your accident and my brake lines being cut, and get a patrol watching your house for the night."

"Are you all right? You weren't in a wreck?"

"Just an extremely close call. Listen, write down my father's number. If you need me—if anything suspicious happens, anything at all, no matter how silly it seems—you call me, understand? And call the police."

She grabbed a pen and notepad off her nightstand, jotting down the number he gave her. "You'll be careful, won't you?"

"*You* be careful. I can take care of myself."

She sighed as she depressed the phone button. If that wasn't a typically male response, she had never heard one. But it didn't really annoy her. His concern told her better than words that at least he cared about her as a friend, even if she had struck out with him romantically. With the end of her pen, she punched out the number for the police station.

It was twelve-thirty when Michael pulled into his father's driveway in Ashland. A golden sphere of light reflected against the living-room drapes, which told him his dad was sitting in his favorite chair reading, as was his habit late at night. Climbing out of the car, Michael ran his fingers over the door panel to find the lock button. Slamming the door, he tossed the keys and caught them, gazing up the street. No sign of anyone following.

He strode up the front walk and onto the porch, ringing

the doorbell. His throat ached with tension. This was one conversation he wasn't looking forward to. When Robert answered the bell, he looked older than he had yesterday. Older and more tired. Michael gave him a hug, enduring the cheek pinching that was as much a part of Robert De Lorio's greetings as the loud, wet kisses he showered on people's faces.

After the initial embrace, Robert grasped Michael by the arms and stood back to look up at him. "This is a wonderful surprise."

"Hello, Papa." He couldn't put much enthusiasm into his voice. "I need to talk to you."

Robert's smile faded. "It is bad news, eh?"

"I'm afraid it's not good." Michael glanced around the room, remembering how upset his father had become yesterday, during their conversation about Chicago. As a precautionary measure, he strode into the kitchen to get the older man's heart pills, returning to the living room with the bottle clasped in his right hand. "Sit down, Papa."

"No. You tell me what is wrong."

Michael tightened his grip on the bottle. "Papa, someone cut the brake lines on my car this morning."

All the color washed from Robert's face, leaving his skin gray as cement. "What is this craziness? Who would want to kill you?"

"That's what I'm hoping you can tell me."

"How should I know?"

Meeting his father's gaze, Michael said, "Papa, please, no lies this time. Too much is at stake. Why did you leave Chicago and change your name?"

Robert's breath quickened and a sickly blue line etched the edges of his white lips. "Who told you such a thing?"

"I know who you really are. I saw pictures of you and Mamma and myself that were taken when I was a baby." Michael took a step forward. "Don't you realize how much

I love you? Whatever it is you're hiding, it won't matter to me. You're my father."

"Pictures? Where? How?"

Michael hesitated, then decided this was no time for half-truths. "I visited Giorgio Santini."

Robert's eyes widened and the black of his pupils flared until the brown of his eyes disappeared. He swallowed convulsively, staring up at Michael as if he were a ghost. "G-Giorgio?"

"Yes, Papa."

Swaying on his feet, Robert clamped a hand to the center of his chest. For a moment, Michael thought it was yet another attempt on his father's part to forestall this long overdue conversation, but when Robert's throat began rattling for air, he knew it was no act. He popped the lid off the medicine bottle and shook some pills onto his palm. Grabbing one, he shoved it under his father's tongue. "Papa, please, calm down—just calm down. It'll be okay. Don't you see? There's nothing we can't handle together."

Robert sucked in another tortured breath. His eyes bulged and he made a feeble grab for Michael's jacket. The next second, his knees buckled and he hit the floor like a felled tree. Michael dropped beside him, ripping open Robert's shirt. His father's face was turning blue. Tearing to the kitchen, Michael grabbed the phone and called for an ambulance, then ran back to the living room.

"Papa, please… Oh, God, don't let this happen." Pressing his fingers to the vein in his father's throat, Michael checked his pulse. It was faint and irregular. Sweat filmed Michael's face. Though his father was still breathing, it was clear he was growing steadily weaker. His eyes were rolling back into his head. His lips were turning a frightening bluish black. Michael was well trained in CPR, but his knowledge was useless unless Robert's heart went into complete arrest. He wished he could do something, anything to help him. "Oh, Papa, forgive me, forgive me."

It seemed to Michael that an eternity went by before the ambulance arrived. He stood back, watching in numb disbelief as attendants worked desperately over his father's unconscious body. One thought echoed in his mind like a litany. *It'll be my fault if he dies.*

Michael drove behind the ambulance to the hospital. When he entered the building, he wandered around in the halls as if in a trance for several minutes, then collapsed on a vinyl chair and buried his face in his hands. More time passed. He had no idea how much. He sat and stared blindly at a potted philodendron, seeing nothing, hearing nothing.

"Mr. De Lorio? Are you Mr. De Lorio?"

The man's voice seemed to come from miles away. Michael focused on brown pant cuffs, lifting his eyes to the tail of a white coat, then to a blurry face. "Yes?"

"I think your father is going to make it."

Michael closed his eyes.

"It's a shaky situation. It's not uncommon for a second, more severe attack to follow the first, but if his condition stays stable until tomorrow noon, I think we can relax a little. We'll have to watch him closely for a week or so, but it looks good. He was lucky. The damage wasn't as serious as we first thought."

Lifting his lashes, Michael said, "He was extremely upset when it happened. If he's conscious now, he may still be upset. I gave him some bad news. I guess I shouldn't have."

The doctor nodded. "Yes, he's been muttering and calling out, so I assumed there had been some sort of emotional upheaval. We're doing our best to keep him calm. I, uh, think it might be wise if you didn't see him this first twenty-four hours. You understand?"

"Yes. You'll keep me posted? I'll be staying until you feel he's out of danger."

"Someone will try to keep you updated. I'll leave a note on his chart so they won't forget you in case I'm not around."

As soon as the doctor walked away, Michael sank back in his chair, gazing at the opposite wall. A hairline crack zigzagged from the baseboard to the ceiling. He had a feeling he'd know every twist and turn in that fissure by the time his father's condition stabilized enough to risk leaving him to return to Eugene. *Sarah.* It was going to take him much longer to get back to her than he had estimated.

He pushed up from the chair, balancing on wobbly legs. A pay phone. He had to phone Sarah so she'd know where she could get in touch with him. Then he should call Father O'Connell. Just in case his father took a turn for the worse, there should be a priest nearby.

AT FIVE-THIRTY THE next afternoon, Michael left the hospital, assured by the doctor that his father's condition had stabilized enough for him to leave for a few hours. It was a comfort knowing that Father O'Connell would be readily available should anything go wrong. The church was only a few minutes away, and the priest had promised to spend his every spare minute that evening at Robert's bedside. Michael drove directly for Eugene, his only thought that he must reach Sarah.

About an hour after Michael left the hospital, Robert De Lorio regained enough strength to demand to see his son. After he was told that Michael had left for Eugene, Robert asked that a telephone be hooked up beside his bed. The nurse dialed the phone number Robert gave her, then handed him the receiver.

When a man answered, Robert said, "Mr. Bronson,

please. This is Robert De Lorio." He closed his eyes, already short of breath. "Hurry. It's urgent."

"Bronson here."

Robert licked his lips, keeping his eyes squeezed shut. A tear escaped from beneath his lashes, slipping silently down his pale cheek. "They have tried to kill Michael. He told me last night that he saw Giorgio Santini when he was in Chicago."

Bronson let loose with a string of curses. "Where are you?"

Robert told him, then added, "You'd better hurry. And get to Michael first. He's on his way to Eugene. He is most important. You understand?"

"Don't you worry about Michael. I'll have men on the way to both of you right after we hang up."

SARAH HEARD A FLAT RAP on the office window and leaped with a start. Ever since Michael's second phone call last night after his father's collapse, her nerves had been shot. Glancing up from her desk, she was relieved to see it was Michael outside the front door. Who else it might have been, she didn't know, but the entire day, a heavy feeling of foreboding had clung to her. Probably just concern over Robert De Lorio's condition, she assured herself, but unsettling just the same.

Despite her gloomy mood, excitement fluttered in her stomach as she hurried for the door. Michael looked so handsome standing out there, stooped slightly to see between the gold letters on the glass, his jacket collar turned up against the wind, the fluorescent light from inside bathing his face. As she let him in, she cried, "Michael, I was worried about you."

"What do you think you're doing here this late?"

She lifted an eyebrow at his tone. "Working. I figured it was safer than being home alone. Molly was driving me crazy so I let her off early to go shopping. I had extra stuff to do before I could close." Glancing at her watch, she added, "I didn't expect to be this late, if you want the truth, but some information for a client came in over the modem right before closing and I've been going over it."

He shut the door behind him. "I'm sorry, Sarah, I didn't mean to snap."

"You look tired." Relocking the door, she stepped closer to study his face, then touched his arm, not sure what to say. His eyes met hers, so filled with pain, she blinked back tears. "Oh, Michael."

She couldn't be sure who made the first move, but the next instant, she was in his arms, hugging his neck, pressing her face into the hollow of his shoulder. He tightened his hold on her, squeezing until she could scarcely breath, his body taut. It felt so right, so wonderfully right, being close to him like this. Sarah closed her eyes, willing the moment to never end.

"I shouldn't be doing this," he whispered. "It's not fair to you. But I—" He took a ragged breath. "I need you right now, Sarah."

She pressed closer. "And that's all that counts. We'll worry about tomorrow later. How's he doing?"

"Better. It looks like he'll make it."

"That's wonderful."

He ran a trembling hand up and down her back, then pulled away. "We need to talk."

The phone rang just then. Sarah sighed. "That's probably Molly. Her roommate called here, worried about her. She hadn't come home." She ran to the secretary's cluttered desk. "Roots. Sarah Montague speaking. May I help you?"

A hollow buzzing crackled over the line, and then a man said, "Yes, is Dr. De Lorio there?"

"Uh, one moment please." Sarah shrugged and held out the phone. "For you."

Michael walked over and leaned against the desk, taking the receiver. "Hello?" A frown creased his dark face. Hanging up, he said, "Nobody there. We must have gotten disconnected." Concern flickered in his eyes. "I wonder if it might have been the hospital."

"How would they get this number?"

A relieved smile touched his mouth. "Good question. Oh, well, whoever it was will call back." His lips immediately thinned into a somber line. He sighed, tugging the cuffs of his shirt down to a precise inch below the sleeves of his jacket. She studied his bent head, wondering what she could say that might comfort him. As if of its own volition, her hand reached up to smooth his hair. Touching him filled her with an ache of longing, but she was too concerned about him at this point to care about the cost to herself.

He caught her hand and lifted his brown eyes to hers, his expression rather dazed as he brushed her knuckles along his cheek. "I've been doing a lot of thinking since my brake lines were cut. About my father, about the peculiarities you found in his background. Remember when you mentioned he might have some kind of criminal record? Well, I think maybe you were right. Someone from Chicago is trying to kill us. That hit-and-run wasn't any accident. I had my suspicions last night when I called you, but after seeing my dad's reaction when he heard I'd seen Giorgio Santini, I'm almost positive."

She pulled her hand from his, staring at him. "But why? Why would anyone—"

"When my brake lines were cut, the emergency brake cable was severed as well. It's an entirely different mechanism from the hydraulic system. It couldn't have been an accident."

"There's no way the mechanic could have been mistaken?"

"None. He's one of the best in town. Put two and two together. Someone runs into you and drives off? My brake lines get cut?"

With a troubled frown, she turned on her heel to pace, remembering the man who had chased her last night. Murder was something that happened in Hitchcock movies, not in real life, not to people like her and Michael. As she pivoted to walk back toward him, she saw headlights round the corner. "So you really believe we're in danger?"

"I don't see what other explanation there is."

She paused within three feet of him. "It's so outlandish. Who could it possib—" A series of muffled pops interrupted her. She heard a musical tinkling sound and glanced toward the window. A car was coasting past out front. "What on earth was th—"

Another staccato burst of pops sounded, and there followed an explosion of noise as the window glass shattered. Split seconds seemed to stretch into eternity as the room around her disintegrated, first a vase, then a lamp, then an end table. Sarah froze. A horrible feeling of déjà vu washed over her. The window glass separated into hundreds of sparkling shards, spewing toward her like shimmering rain as they pelted the gray carpet. She threw up an arm to shield her face, turning as she did to scream at Michael. She didn't identify the popping sounds, didn't give them a name, but deep within her, she knew what made the rapid-fire noise and felt incredulous terror rushing through her.

Michael's left shoulder jerked backward as if an invisible hand shoved him. His feet lifted clear off the floor from the force of the impact and he did a half spin in the air, landing facedown in a sprawl over Molly's desk. The computer monitor crashed to the floor.

"Michael." She reached for him, moving like animated sketches in slow motion, each action broken into jerky segments. Her eyes widened in horror as he rolled off the desk onto the floor. For an instant, he lay there stunned, but then he struggled to his knees and lunged at her. As he knocked her to the rug, she saw blood spattered all over Molly's desktop. "M-Michael, you've b-been shot."

"Shut up! Keep down!" Michael slithered backward across the carpet like a crab, dragging her behind him in the crook of his arm. "The lights. Where's the switch? Sarah, answer me."

Blood. The small hole in his jacket held her gaze riveted. Memories spun in her mind, mingling with the present. There was another volley of shots. Bullets impacted against the walls so loudly they sounded like cannonballs. Particles of plaster puffed into the air above their heads. They were going to die. Sarah worked her mouth, but no sound would come out. Blood. Blood on the side of the desk, on the rug, on her hand as she drew it away from Michael's arm. She studied the crimson smears on her spread fingers, only vaguely aware of Michael's voice calling her name.

He shook her. "The breaker box, Sarah. We've gotta douse the lights."

She heard the car's brakes squeal, saw headlights still glowing out front for all the world to see. She knew without being told why he wanted darkness. "T-the bathroom." She wriggled out of his grasp, clawing her way on hands and knees to the back of the office. "Oh, God, Michael, you're shot, you're shot."

"Keep down, don't talk," he implored behind her.

Sarah crawled into the bathroom, slamming her hip against the doorjamb as she hurled herself through the door. Stretching her arm up the wall to the metal breaker box, she opened the cover. She had no idea what switches supplied what, so she hit them all. Blackness swooped over her—complete, utter blackness. She heard ragged, shallow breathing next to her.

"Run, Sarah. You have to hide. I can't make it."

She reached out, homing in on his voice to grasp the front of his jacket. Lunging to her feet, she ground her teeth and strained with all her might to haul him up with her. *The broom closet.* It was deep enough to hide them, but was it wide enough? She helped him across the bathroom, propping him up by pressing her shoulder into his underarm. She groped with her other hand for the wood panel that opened into the wall. Her fingers touched a crack. Frantic, she patted her way down it. *The handle.* She seized it and jerked the door open.

She remembered there was a box of eight-foot fluorescent tubes leaning against the back wall inside the closet. She had bought it just last week. She groped for the box, slid it from the closet and leaned it against the wall. Michael was slumped against her, standing, but only barely. Sarah wrapped both arms around his waist, squeezed with all her might and lifted, shoving him into the narrow opening. He grunted with pain as his shoulders were compressed to fit between the walls.

Shoes crunched glass and loud voices echoed in the front of the office. Throwing all her weight against Michael, she stuffed him farther back into the enclosure. Easing herself in behind him, she pulled the box of fluorescent tubes in after her and closed the door. There was room, barely. Michael's knees buckled, bumping her leg, and he slid partway down the closet wall. She caught his waist in a bear hug, heaving all her weight against him to keep him standing. Burying her face in his chest, she stifled her labored breathing, praying he stayed conscious and didn't betray their hiding place by moaning. The light box pressed against her back, moving every time she did, the tubes clinking. She held herself rigid.

"Quiet, Michael, quiet."

The sound of voices had ceased. Footsteps scuffled,

so soft now she could scarcely hear them. She craned her neck to look around the box. Faint light glowed through the crack of the door, bobbing crazily, growing brighter.

"We got 'em!" barked a voice on the other side of the door.

She pressed her quivering knees together. *Oh, please, if he opens the closet, don't let him look behind the box. Please, don't let him look.* She heard the door creak open. Holding her breath, she moved closer to Michael. The *thud-thud-thud* of his heart beneath her ear almost deafened her. A flashlight beam played over the box of light tubes. The man was so close she could smell his after-shave, a sweet lemony scent.

"Nope. They're not here after all. They in there?"

"No," yelled a man from the storage room.

"Dammit!" The closet door slammed shut. "Find the lights. They have to be here somewhere."

"Come on, we're wasting time. They're in the alley."

She estimated by his voice that the man who had opened the closet door was walking toward the storage area. The back door opened. Feet hit the alley, crunching in gravel. Her breath gushed out of her. Michael slumped against the wall, trembling. The small space afforded little air.

"You okay?" he whispered.

"I'm fine." Her fingers touched something warm and sticky. "Oh, Michael, you're bleeding so bad. Your jacket's soaked."

"D-don't talk about it." He swallowed and dragged in air. "I feel like I might pass out."

"Don't you dare, not yet. We've got to get out of here and you're too heavy for me to carry." She shifted, her hand sliding down his chest. "Oh, Michael, your shirt is sopped."

"I said don't talk about it. Sarah, run—you have to ru—"

He went limp. She tightened her arms around his waist.

His head flopped forward, his forehead smacking hers. She blinked, seeing stars for a moment. She peered up into the blackness, pressing her temple against his cheek to support his head. Cold sweat filmed his skin.

"Michael?" No answer. "Michael?" She shoved him harder against the wall and lifted her hand to his face. She couldn't feel any breath coming from his nose or mouth, couldn't feel his chest rising or falling. A shock of fear coursed through her. "Oh, my God! Michael...?"

CHAPTER NINE

CONCERN FOR MICHAEL made Sarah forget all about the possible danger to herself if the men out in the alley heard noise in the office. All she could think of was getting Michael to a hospital. He wasn't dead. He *couldn't* be dead.

She fought to get him out of the closet. The blackness around her was so thick, she felt as though she could reach out and grab a handful of it. As she set the box of light tubes outside the enclosure, the container toppled and hit the opposite wall with a deafening crash. Meanwhile Michael slumped on top of her, doubling her over at the waist. She stepped forward and her shoe slipped out from under her. Falling to one knee, she slid from the closet with Michael's weight shoving her from behind. The air whooshed out of her lungs as he landed on top of her. Then he rolled off, hitting the floor with a sickening thud.

Sarah slipped an arm under his neck and cradled his head. Now that they were out of the closet, she could see the outline of his face in the dim moonlight coming through the window. Pressing her fingers to his throat, she felt for his pulse. Her own heart was pounding so hard, it was impossible to tell if his was beating. She prodded the wet front of his jacket. How badly was he bleeding?

"Ouch! Take it easy."

Sarah started. "Michael?"

He pushed feebly at her arms. "Who else?"

"Oh, Michael, I thought you were dead. You scared the living daylights out of me."

With a groan, he managed to sit up. In the darkness, his features were indiscernible, but she could see him swaying. She knew he was clinging to consciousness by sheer force of will.

"Where did they go? We have to get out of here."

"They went down the alley looking for us."

He struggled to his feet, bumping into the box of light tubes. Broken glass tinkled. His legs nearly gave out. He stumbled to the wall, and used it to hold himself erect. "Come on. They could show up any second."

Fear shot through her, but it quickly faded, chased away by a strange feeling of detachment. Rising to her feet, she draped his arm over her shoulders, guiding him out to the lobby. Their shoes crunched glass as she steered him to the front door. The car the gunmen had come in still sat in the street, engine running, headlights bathing the asphalt with yellow light. Sarah stared for an instant at the dark green automobile's front fender, her mind frozen with incredulity. The night of the hit-and-run, she hadn't been able to remember where she had seen the other green car. Now it all came flooding back to her. The evening before Michael left for Chicago, when she had walked him to the door! The Realtor's car! Only, of course, it hadn't been a Realtor in the car at all—but a murderer.

This was a nightmare. That was why her legs felt numb, why her feet dragged like lead weights. It was always like this in bad dreams, as if she were walking through hip-deep molasses. No one was really trying to kill them.

It seemed to Sarah they moved a fraction of an inch at a time toward the brown Ford Michael was driving. Her scalp tingled. She expected shots to ring out at any second as she stuffed him into the car and took the keys he proffered. Fear niggled its way up from the numbness inside her chest, coiling at the base of her throat. Throwing a dazed glance over her shoulder, she slammed the passenger door shut and ran around to the driver's side. Leaping in, she started the engine. She shoved the shift into drive and the car lurched away from the curb.

"Don't use the lights," he hissed. "They'll see 'em."

Her eyes widened and the last traces of shocked numbness fled. Clutching the steering wheel tightly, she screeched, "They've already seen us. Oh, God, Michael, what do I do?"

He stiffened when he saw the two men who had jumped out from the buildings ahead of them. "Turn on the lights and step on it, Sarah! They'll get out of the way." When she hesitated, he roared, "Do it!"

Knowing she had no choice, Sarah flipped on the headlights and shoved the gas pedal hard against the floorboard. The men brought up their guns, taking steady aim at the windshield. Michael cursed. Grabbing for the wheel, he yelled, "Get down!"

"No, you get down. I'm the one driving." Sudden anger shot through her. The men had cleared a path for the car, one on each side of the road. If they thought she would drive between them and make a target of herself, they had another think coming. Wrenching on the wheel, she drove straight for the man on the left. He froze for a moment, then dived for the curb to get out of her way. He no sooner did so than she gave the wheel another vicious twist, careening in the opposite direction. The second man scrambled backward, the snubbed barrel of his weapon spitting white flame as he took several haphazard shots. Then his nerve seemed to fail and he threw himself sideways, rolling into the gutter.

Sarah managed to avoid hitting the man, but couldn't correct her steering soon enough to miss the curb. The Ford bounced onto the sidewalk and swerved wildly, sideswiping a parking meter before veering back onto the street. She glanced toward Michael, who was still clinging to the dash, his face ashen. "Are you all right?"

He sank back in his seat, slanting his right arm over his eyes. "I'm fine. And you're doing great. Now hit I-5 and head for Ashland. And step on it or they'll be on our tail."

She hit the gas, taking a corner on two wheels. No lights appeared behind them. "Ashland? Are you crazy?"

"Sarah, I've got to get to my dad." He dropped his arm to read the street signs as she took an erratic route through an older residential section of the city. "Where are you going?"

"The hospital." Her tires grabbed traction on a turn and burned rubber with a squeal. Still no lights behind them. She slowed a bit and relaxed her grip on the wheel. "We've got to get that shoulder tended and call the police."

"No hospital. They know they got me. That's the first place they'll look." He leaned his head back against the rest, swallowing convulsively. "I'll be okay, Sarah. I think the bullet went clear through. I've got to get to my dad— before they do."

Gnawing on her bottom lip, she threw a worried glance at the side mirror. "You won't be any help to your father dead. We'll call the cops, Michael. They'll take care of him. And us."

"You think they'll believe a story like this?"

"You don't think that hole in your shoulder might convince them?"

He groaned. "And how long can they protect us? For the night? A couple of days? Then what? Those fellows aren't amateurs. We've got to find someplace for the three of us to hide until we can think what to do."

"And where might that be?"

"A friend of mine has a ski lodge up Highway 58. I know where he keeps the key. No one could find us there."

Sarah's mind felt like fried mush. She was too confused to make sense of anything, too numb to argue with him. Maybe hiding someplace until they could sort things out wasn't such a bad idea. The police might not believe them at first if they went to them with a story like this. Michael was right about that. And they didn't dare stand around making long explanations. She gave a brisk nod. "All right, Michael, but first we go to my house and take care of that shoulder."

"And get blown away? You think they don't know where we live?"

She slammed her hand against the steering wheel and shot him a glare. "Well, what do you suggest? Letting you bleed to death? Call it cowardice if you like, but I don't want you dying on me."

Her voice rose to a shrill pitch on the last word. He squeezed the bridge of his nose between his thumb and forefinger, closing his eyes. "Okay, okay, point taken. We have to go someplace. One house is as bad as the other, so make it mine. It's south of town and we won't waste time that way."

As SARAH PULLED into Michael's driveway, the Ford's headlights washed over the contemporary, shake-roofed house from end to end. She parked by the front entrance and hurried around the car to help Michael out. The moment he climbed from the car, he laid his arm across her shoulders and leaned most of his weight on her.

"I'm sorry, Sarah."

"Hey, not to worry." His pallor frightened her. A lump rose in her throat and she blinked away tears. Seeing him like this drove home how very much she had come to care for him. If something happened to him, she didn't know what she'd do. She slipped an arm around his waist, tipping her head to smile up at him. The moon was so bright, she could see the beads of sweat on his brow. If only she were strong enough to carry him. "Ready?"

He eyed the porch as if it were a mile away. They walked toward it. "You've got the key there on the chain." He sagged against the house while she unlocked the door. When she turned back to him, he was clutching his injured shoulder with his right hand, his face twisted in pain. She helped him inside and groped for a light switch. A series of clear globes above them sprang to life.

"The family room," he whispered hoarsely, inclining his head toward the rear of the house. "It's got a sink in the wet bar."

She blinked, adjusting her eyes to the sudden brightness as she helped him circle the fountain in the atrium entry. He nearly fell as they stepped down into the living room. She steadied him, straining under his weight as they passed through the formal dining area to reach the family room. After lowering him onto a natural tweed sofa before a fireplace with a stone hearth, she paused, gasping for breath. Light shone through the glass wall of the atrium. Hurrying to the wet bar in the corner, she found a cloth in the top drawer and dampened it under the faucet.

"There are sheets in my laundry, right there off the kitchen. Get one and we'll cut it into strips to use as bandages."

She forced another smile, trying to hide her anxiety over his shoulder as best she could. She wiped his pale face with the cool cloth, then pressed it to his brow, forcing his head back. "Just relax here, hmm? I can find what I need."

He closed his eyes, too weak to argue. She dropped her gaze to his shoulder. The dark weave of his wool jacket was soaked black with blood around a jagged hole. A red splotch was spreading on the light upholstery of the sofa behind his shoulder. How much blood could a person safely lose? Could she staunch the flow with pressure? Panic fluttered in her chest. She hurried toward the kitchen, making a mental note to gather some food together to take to the lodge before they left.

Halfway across the dimly lit family room, Sarah halted midstride. Her eyes widened as she saw the built-in roll-top desk along one wall. The drawers on either side had been jerked from their runners and dumped on the floor. The overhead cupboard doors stood open, the contents of the shelves littering the work areas below them. The hair on her nape tingled and she hugged her arms around herself, doing a full turn to give the room a careful once-over. There was no question. Someone had been in here. She strained her ears for the slightest sound. What if they hadn't left? What if they were still here, waiting in the dark recesses of the house?

Nonsense, she scolded herself. *If they were still here, you'd be dead. But they might be driving by now and again, watching the windows for lights.* Sarah's heart began to pound as she ran back to the atrium. She hit the electric switch, blanketing the house in darkness.

"Sarah? Sarah!"

The hysteria in Michael's voice lent wings to her feet as she scurried through the house to him. "I'm all right, Michael. Don't get up." Moonlight gilded the room with silver. She sank to one knee by the arm of the sofa, bringing her face close to his. "Someone's been in the house. I cut the lights just in case they come back or drive by again."

"Oh, no..."

He started to get up, but she stopped him, gripping his uninjured shoulder with a firm hand. "No. Stay put. With the lights out, they won't know we're here. We have to bandage that shoulder. You're losing too much blood."

"The car, they'll see it."

"I'm going to move it into the garage. While I'm gone,

you stay put. The less you move around, the better. Do you have a flashlight?"

"Under the kitchen sink." He lifted his hand to cup the side of her face. His teeth flashed in a weak smile, luminescent against the shadowed planes of his face. "Sarah, I hate this. It should be me taking care of you."

"Nonsense. What are you, a chauvinist?"

He leaned his head back. She saw his eyes drift closed as he grinned. "Be careful. And if you need me, scream."

She rose to her feet, knowing full well as she walked away from him that if something happened, she was on her own. It would have been wonderful to be able to dump her problems on a big brawny hero right then. But her hero was injured, and it was sink or swim.

She felt her way into the dark kitchen and found the sink, then rummaged beneath it until her fingers curled around the handle of the flashlight. "Where's the garage, Michael?"

"Through the laundry."

Sarah let herself out and paused on the garage steps, waiting until her eyes grew accustomed to the meager shaft of moonlight shining through the small window across from her. With a brief flick of the flashlight, she located the garage-door opener and hit the button, cringing at the noise when the mechanism rumbled into action. As the doors lifted, she ducked out into the driveway and ran to the car, fishing in her jacket pocket for the keys.

It seemed like hours passed before she had the car parked in the garage and the doors lowered to hide it. Before she went back inside the house, she leaned against the fender and took several deep, bracing breaths. She couldn't let Michael see how terrified she was. He'd become upset. That would accelerate his heartbeat and make him lose twice as much blood.

"How you doin'?" she called as she stepped into the laundry room.

"Fine. You?"

"I'm great." Sarah flashed the light and tugged a sheet from the laundry closet. Moving quickly into the kitchen, she withdrew a small butcher knife from a rack above the sink. "Where's your medicine cabinet?"

He gave her directions to the bathroom. *No outside windows.* Sarah shut the door and flipped on the light so she could see to tear the sheet into strips. She found a bottle of alcohol in the cabinet over the lemon-yellow sink. There were also two prescription bottles, one of Percodan, the other penicillin. It was just like a doctor not to finish his antibiotics. She took two tablets from each, then set the containers on the counter to take along with them to the ski lodge.

It wouldn't be a very professional nursing job, but at least she could get the wound clean, give him antibiotics to prevent infection and slow the bleeding by applying pressure. The Percodan would help ease his pain. She darted out of the bathroom into the hall, shutting the door so the light wouldn't be visible to anyone outside the house. Patting her palms along the walls, she moved back toward Michael.

"Find everything?"

"Enough to do us. I hope you have a high pain tolerance." She helped him off the sofa. "All I could find was alcohol. Cleaning that wound is going to burn like fire."

"Just get the job done."

He slitted his eyes when she opened the brightly lit bathroom and helped him inside. Sinking onto the commode, he lifted his good arm, wincing as she peeled his jacket off him. When he saw his scarlet-soaked shirt, he swayed slightly and looked away. "Sorry, but blood makes me woozy."

It was Sarah's turn to feel woozy as she cut away the garment with the knife. The hole in his shoulder where the bullet had entered wasn't large, but the exit wound above his shoulder blade was gaping and jagged. She swallowed down wave after wave of throat-convulsing nausea, her gaze riveted on the sheen of his dark skin. Muscle played on his back with his slightest movement. Such a beautiful body…so male, so strong. In the back of her mind, she had envisioned the wound, but she'd never pictured this— never dreamed a bullet would make such a yawning hole where it exited.

She pulled a paper cup from the dispenser on the wall and filled it with water, trying to keep her hand steady as she offered it to him. "Here, Michael, take these pills."

"What are they?"

"Antibiotics I found in the cabinet." She watched him take a mouthful of water. Then she popped four pills into his mouth before he could count them. She knew he'd refuse to take the painkiller for fear it would make him rummy, so she made the decision for him. She couldn't bear to see him suffering like this, and the pain was only going to get worse. "More water?"

"No."

Picking up the bottle of alcohol, she clenched her teeth and grasped the cap, giving it a twist. Her eyes fell to the torn flesh on his back. As she tipped the bottle, her stomach lurched. He jerked when the liquid spilled into his wound. With a muffled curse, he stiffened and hissed air as the alcohol ran in watery red rivulets down his back. His face, already pale, went sickly white.

Sarah's hands shook as she pressed pads of gauze over the bullet holes. As quickly as she could, she wrapped him, encircling his chest several times, then angling up over his shoulder. Around, over, around, over. When she was finished, she was so weak-kneed she could scarcely stand. "Is that tight enough?"

"Plenty."

"Too much?"

He shook his head and rose to his feet, swaying as he exited the bathroom into the hall. "I'm going to get a fresh shirt. Bring what's left of the sheet and the alcohol. We may need it later."

Sarah glanced down at her own smeared clothing. She thought about borrowing something clean, but there wasn't time. When he emerged from a doorway a moment later, wearing a dark shirt, she assisted him into the family room. He paused, staring at the strewn papers by the desk that glowed blue-white in the moonlight. "I wonder what they were looking for?"

"I don't know and I don't care. Let's just get out of here."

"The letter from my dad!" He jerked free of her grasp and staggered to the wall, hitting the electric switch. Light flooded the room. Casting a frantic glance across the floor, his gaze riveted on a piece of folded yellow stationery. "My God, they found it and took the envelope."

"Michael, what are you—" Sarah ran to catch his arm, holding him up as his knees gave way. "Michael?"

He continued to stare at the yellow stationery. "It's a letter from my dad. The envelope with his return address is gone. That's what they came for. Don't you see? Now they know where to find him."

His voice rang in the quiet room like a death knell. Sarah fought off panic. She didn't know Robert De Lorio, had never even seen him, but Michael loved him and that was all that mattered. "What are we going to do?"

He walked unsteadily to the desk and dropped onto the chair. "The hospital, I'll call the hospital and warn them not to let anyone but me into his room. No telling what time they broke into the house. They could already be in Ashland."

She shoved the phone toward him.

He grabbed the receiver, dialed information, then placed the long-distance call. A moment later, he said, "Yes, my name is Michael De Lorio. I'm calling in regards to a patient of yours, a Robert De Lorio?" He listened for a moment. "What do you mean, he's been released?" Lunging unsteadily to his feet, he roared, "What two men? Who were they? Look, lady. This is his son calling. Don't talk to me about privileged information. I want to know where he's at and I want to know now." He paused a moment, gripping the phone so hard that Sarah could see his knuckles turning white. "You're sorry? You're sorry!"

Slamming the phone down, Michael stared at her. She took a step toward him. "Where is he? What men took him? Michael, what did she say?"

The blank, numbing terror she felt was mirrored in Michael's eyes. "Two men checked him out a little while ago. She wouldn't give me any more information than that over the phone."

Her heart pounded, each beat seeming louder than the last until the thrumming in her temples nearly deafened her. "Wh-what are we going to do, Michael?"

He reached out and touched her cheek. She leaned toward the warmth of his hand. "Save our own hides. What else can we do?" His gaze rested on her face for a long moment, his eyes cloudy with pain, confusion and concern. "I don't know where they took him. I can't even begin to guess." He threaded his fingers through her hair and pressed her head forward to rest against his chest. Then he whispered, "I'm so sorry, Sarah. If it weren't for my stupidity, you wouldn't be involved in this mess. I wish I'd never called Roots, never met you."

She wrapped both arms around his waist, fighting back

tears. As crazy as it was, she couldn't imagine not being with him right now, letting him go through this alone. She knew she would opt to stay even if she had a choice, and that confused her even more. Nothing made sense to her, nothing but the feel of him in her arms. "Michael, neither of us had any idea something like this might happen."

"No. I've gone over it and over it, my trip to Chicago, the people I saw there, my dad, and everything I know about him. It's insane, Sarah. Someone's trying to murder us and I don't even know why."

She tipped her head back. "I'm glad I'm here with you, Michael, really I am."

He slid his hand down to her shoulder. "Can you drive?"

"I even promise to stay off the sidewalks."

"Then let's get to that ski lodge where we'll be halfway safe. I'll think what to do about Papa from there."

"Just give me two seconds. I thought I'd round up stuff from the kitchen to take along."

NERVOUS SWEAT FILMED Sarah's palms as she steered the Ford around a sharp turn. She had never driven Highway 58 at night and now she knew why—*curves and steep grades*. On a nice, sunny day, this was a gorgeous drive, the asphalt shaded by towering pines, the roadside lakes shimmering like sapphires through the trees. But this wasn't a sunny day. It was pitch-black, and on every curve, she played a guessing game, trying to figure where the road went next. In many spots, there were no guard-rails and, therefore, no reflectors. The centerline had been all but obliterated by sand dumped from snowplows last winter. She sat hunched forward, peering over the dash to see where she was going. Her neck ached, and if her hands ever came unglued from the steering wheel, it would be a miracle.

She glanced over at Michael, who had long since

slumped against his door, his head lolling against the window. Passed out or asleep, she wasn't sure which. She hoped it was just the Percodan doing its job. He'd spoken to her back at Oak Ridge when she'd stopped, so he was probably just asleep.

Two foam cups of coffee from the restaurant sat untouched on the console tray. They'd both be cold soon, but she couldn't risk even a sip for fear she'd go off the road. She darted another look at Michael. If he was unconscious, what was she going to do? She had no idea where his friend's ski lodge was. A couple of miles this side of the summit, he'd said. That didn't tell her a lot. She was driving toward Willamette Pass. That was all she knew.

Bright headlights washed her back window with a silver glare, reflecting off her rearview mirror and into her eyes. Instant wariness assailed her. She'd tried to be certain no cars had tailed her out of Eugene, but with city traffic coming and going, it had been impossible. She squinted, tapping her brake to signal to the other driver to lower his beams. He didn't take the hint and was soon practically on her back bumper. She edged the Ford toward the shoulder of the road to let him pass. But he slowed down to stay behind her. *Don't jump to conclusions, Sarah. A lot of people have poor night vision.* She couldn't blame someone for using her taillights to blaze a trail. She'd do the same if she could.

"Get off my bumper," she muttered.

Tapping her brakes again, she slowed down even more to force the car to pass her. The twin orbs of the other vehicle's headlights grew larger in her mirror. Her breath caught. Before she could hit the gas pedal for a burst of speed, the other car plowed into her back bumper, throwing her forward against the steering wheel. Her horn blared. She straightened and stomped her foot on the accelerator, spinning her right rear tire in gravel as she fishtailed onto the asphalt. Michael moaned and stirred.

Sarah glanced frantically over her shoulder at the other car. It had backed off a bit. She tapped her brakes again so she could see it better. The rosy glow of her taillights splashed on green paint. Fear made her heart skip a beat and she reached sideways to release Michael's seat belt. Sliding her hand between the seat and his back, she shoved him forward, cringing when his head cracked on the dash. He moaned, legs folding as he slid to the floorboard. Leaning his head back, he muttered under his breath.

All thought for the treacherous curves fled Sarah's mind. She clenched her hands on the steering wheel as the speedometer crept toward seventy. The other car stuck to her like glue. She saw it swerve into the oncoming lane to pull up beside her. Terror struck her mouth dry as she imagined a bullet plowing into her skull. She longed to be on the floor with Michael.

Without warning, the green car swerved into Sarah's lane and crashed against her door. The force of the impact threw her sideways in the seat. Her breath came in ragged gasps as she fought to regain control of the car. She felt the car leave the road and a helpless scream tore from her throat as her headlights fanned over stout tree trunks and huge boulders. Then the car's front bumper pitched downward into a swath of blackness.

CHAPTER TEN

THE CAR LANDED with a jolt, metal crunching metal as the body slammed into the frame. *A ditch?* Sarah's stomach knotted. She heard Michael moan, but the sound barely registered. Brush and trees loomed in her bouncing headlights, tilting at crazy angles. Then a gigantic boulder appeared. She screamed and jerked the steering wheel hard to the left. The undercarriage dragged over rock and dirt. Michael moaned again, stirring and mumbling as she maneuvered the car out of the ditch and back onto the pavement.

She glanced in her mirror. There was only one way out of this situation. She held her breath and watched the green car's headlights inch closer. She tensed her arms. She would only get one chance. Her temples began to throb from not breathing.

Now! With all her might, Sarah wrenched on her steering wheel. A shuddering crunch of metal reverberated through her own vehicle, as it hit the other car's front fender, but this time she was prepared for the jolt and kept a tight grip on the wheel. Rubber squealed. The other car's headlights wobbled crazily as it bounced into the oncoming lane and plunged into the opposite ditch.

Letting her breath out in a rush, Sarah careened around the next curve. This was a game of kill or be killed. There were no rules. She couldn't allow herself to think of anything but survival. *Now what?* She had no way of knowing if she had put the other car out of commission. She needed a plan of action, and she needed one fast.

"Michael?" She reached sideways until she touched his hair. A lump of anxiety choked her. "Michael?"

"Hmm?" He stirred and then groaned. "Wha'ya want?"

"Where's the ski lodge?"

He mumbled something unintelligible. Maybe she could hide on a forestry road until he came around. How long would the effects of the painkiller last? Four hours? Six? She speeded up. She had to outdistance the other car so her headlights wouldn't be seen if she made a turn.

She drove past the ski area, never slowing down. The lodge was back there somewhere, but she didn't dare to try to find it as long as those men might be following her. As if on cue, lights appeared again behind her, flickering in her rearview mirror. Her mouth went dry, and she licked her lips with a cottony tongue. There weren't many cars on Highway 58 at this time of night. She increased her speed and sat more erect.

Green road signs peppered the side of the highway. Watching her mirror, she waited until she couldn't see the car behind her, then turned off the highway, dousing her headlights immediately. Complete darkness swooped over her.

Her teeth snapped together as the Ford lurched from one chuckhole to another. She cringed with every jolt, afraid of what the rough ride might do to Michael. She heard his jagged moan, but she couldn't stop. Headlights from the highway flashed through the trees. If she touched her brakes, their pursuers would see the red flare of her taillights.

Reaching under the dash, she felt for the emergency brake. She found a small handle far to the left and jerked on it. A thunk resounded through the car. Horror swamped her. Had she pulled the wrong release and popped open the hood? Where was the damned emergency brake? With her left foot, she searched the floorboard until she found a pedal. She slammed it home, locking her rear tires. The car fishtailed into a skid. All she could do was hold tight to the steering wheel and pray nothing stood in her path.

The Ford finally rocked to a stop. She killed the engine and rolled down her window. The night breeze rustled the foliage. She heard the soft crackles and pops of the car motor as it cooled. Otherwise there was nothing but an eerie silence. Had the men stayed on the highway then? Hot tears ran down her cheeks. She stared at her side mirror, her hand poised over the ignition key, ready for a quick getaway. Who was she kidding? If they had seen her turn off, she and Michael were history. This road probably wound through the woods to a dead end, a *very* dead end in this instance.

Twisting sideways in her seat, she groped for Michael, calling his name. He shifted his position and hissed air through his teeth. She slid a hand down the neck of his shirt to check his bandages for wetness. What if the jostling had made him start bleeding again? The cloth felt dry. Relief flooded through her.

Folding her arms across the steering wheel, she dropped her head onto her hands. Her thoughts flitted aimlessly. Only one thing seemed clear: they were safe....

Or were they?

She lifted her head. Dear God, what was she doing sitting here? It wouldn't take the killers long to realize she'd left the highway. As soon as they did, they would turn around and start searching for her. She had to get out of here. To the ski lodge, if possible, where she could care for Michael.

"Michael? Michael, wake up!" Leaning over him, Sarah caught his head between her hands and slapped his cheeks. "You have to tell me where Rick's lodge is."

He grunted and turned his face aside.

"Michael, wake up!" She slapped his jaw harder. "Wake up! Now!"

"What the—"

She peered down, trying to see if his eyes were open. It was too dark. "The ski lodge, where is it?"

"Mmm-hmm."

"Don't you dare go back to sleep." Grasping his uninjured shoulder, she gave him an urgent shake. "The lodge, tell me how to get there."

"—the ski area. Turn right at the store, then right—first road. It's the place—" he broke off to yawn "—at the end."

She felt his head loll to one side and knew he'd gone back to sleep. What if she got lost out here? What if the men doubled back and saw tire tracks where she'd turned off? What if...

Throwing open her door, she leaped out and slammed the hood of the car closed. There was no time to worry about what ifs. She had to get back on the highway and find the ski lodge before those men turned around and came hunting for her. She *wouldn't* get lost. She couldn't.

FLAMES RUSHED AT Sarah's face when she lifted the lid on the cookstove to peer at the fire. She reared back, blinking and waving her hand before her eyes. The unmistakable smell of singed hair assailed her nostrils and she glanced down to check the drape of dark hair on her shoulder for scorched ends. A pioneer type, she wasn't.

Replacing the iron stove lid, she hung the pot holder on its hook and propped her shoulder against the cedar wall. Weakness attacked her legs. She pressed a hand over her eyes, willing the memories away. *Singed hair, burning flesh.* Those were two smells a person never forgot. It had been years since she had allowed herself to think of that day. Now she had done it twice in one night. The exploding window glass earlier must have unnerved her even more than she'd realized.

Pushing away from the wall, she stepped across the

shadowy kitchen into the adjoining living room. She couldn't risk using the lamps for fear of drawing unwanted attention to the lodge. The only light came from the moss-rock fireplace. She sat on the hearth and stared into the flames, congratulating herself for starting not one but two roaring blazes. In the hour since their arrival, she had helped Michael inside and put him to bed, hidden the car by the creek under a bunch of dead brush and packed in enough wood to last the night. And she'd accomplished all of that in a straight skirt and high heels. She deserved a merit badge. Crossing her arms over her chest and rubbing her shoulders, she shivered and lowered her lashes.

Through her eyelids, she could still see the amber glow of flames. Pitch ignited and sputtered. She listened for any strange sounds in the silence that lay so heavily over the house. Surely no one could find them here. So why did her nerves leap at every sound?

Opening her eyes, she heaved a sigh. She'd never relax enough to sleep. Rising from the hearth, she crossed over to the bottom of the rustic stairway, lifting the drape to peer out the window. A tangled oak loomed black against the midnight sky, its twisted branches reaching toward the anemic moonlight like gnarled witch's fingers. Dark clumps of manzanita swayed in the wind. Every movement sent prickles of alarm over her skin. If anyone had followed them....

Throwing an anxious glance toward the bedroom where Michael slept, she spied a gun cabinet she hadn't noticed earlier. Sweat gathered in her armpits and trickled in icy rivulets down the sides of her breasts. She approached the cabinet, looking through the glass at the rifles perched in their slots. Years ago, her dad had taken her to the rifle range. She'd learned how to load and shoot. With any luck, there was a rifle in there similar to the kind she had used. Opening the door, she reached for a pump action 30.06, and slid open the ammo drawer. Her fingers shook as she fitted bullets into the magazine.

When the gun was loaded, she hefted it in her hands, then peered down its barrel to check the sights. A heavy feeling pooled in her abdomen. Could she shoot someone? She lowered the stock and stepped across the room, leaning the weapon against the wall next to the fireplace. Glancing back at the bedroom, she lifted her chin and squared her shoulders. Yes, she decided, if she had to, she could pull the trigger. She might not like it, and it might haunt her the rest of her life, but she could do it.

She veered away from the hearth and headed for the kitchen. There was only one thing to do when you were going to pace the floors all night, and that was make plenty of strong coffee.

Blood. MICHAEL HELD his breath, staring through the bedspread fringe at a man's pant legs. Where was Helen? His heart slammed, thudding against his ribs, the sound so loud he was sure someone would hear. The man's black shoes stepped ever so softly toward the bathroom. The farther away he walked, the more Michael could see of him. He held something blue-black in one hand that had a funny-looking belt hanging off it.

Pausing outside the bathroom, the man propped the blue-black thing on his hip and reared back on one leg, kicking the door open. A horrible noise rent the air and the man's body started to jerk. White flame spurted from the blue-black thing in his hand. Glass shattered. The shower curtain fluttered and came partway off its hooks. Then silence returned. The man turned from the doorway....

Michael woke from the dream with a jolt, breathing jaggedly. Pain exploded in his shoulder when he tried to sit up and he fell back against the sweat-soaked pillow. Where was he? Panic chewed at him. He stared at the cedar ceiling above him, trying to remember. Pale yellow sunlight spilled across the bed. His head didn't hurt, but he felt terrible otherwise. A hangover? His body ached as though he'd been pummeled by a prize fighter.

He tried to sit up again. The effort sent excruciating pain stabbing through his shoulder and down his back, stealing his breath. He clenched his teeth and closed his eyes. The moment he did, images played behind his eyelids, images of Sarah's office, of the windows vomiting glass. He ran a hand over his chest, feeling the thick swathe of bandages. He remembered now…going to his house, discovering the break-in, calling the hospital in Ashland. But what had happened after?

He rolled onto his right side and pushed himself to a sitting position. Sarah, where was she? Fear clenched his guts. He recognized the house now. Rick's ski lodge.

Staggering to the bedroom door, he leaned against the doorjamb until his head stopped spinning. A fire burned low in the rock fireplace, the flames licking feebly at charred logs. A sofa sat catty-corner to the hearth, facing the fire. At one end he could see the top of Sarah's dark head resting against the cushion. He walked slowly toward her, his legs quivering and unsteady.

A grim smile touched his mouth. She had fallen asleep sitting up. She'd kicked her shoes off and drawn her slender legs up under her. An empty coffee mug lay in her lap. Had she watched over him all night? His recollection of getting here was vague at best, but he remembered her helping him from the car into the house. She must have been terrified.

He glanced uneasily toward the windows. As much as he wanted to know what had happened, he couldn't bear the thought of disturbing her. He couldn't believe he had conked out on her like that, sleeping the whole night through when his father was missing and someone had just tried to kill them.

From the way she hugged herself, he guessed she was cold. Taking care not to jostle his shoulder, he went to get a pillow and blanket from the bedroom.

She murmured something unintelligible, responding like a child to the touch of his hand as he tugged her legs from under her so that she was lying prone. He wished he had two good arms. If he could, he'd carry her to the bedroom and tuck her into bed. The thought made him wince.

He was clumsy getting the pillow under her head. Her eyes opened, confused and bleary. Then she snuggled her cheek into the downy softness, smiling as he unfolded the blanket and tucked it around her. He started to turn away, but the sweet curve of her mouth drew his gaze. Her face fascinated him. Feature by feature, she wasn't a beauty, but blended together, the irregularities in her countenance composed a striking loveliness.

Her lashes fluttered, feathering her cheeks like fringed velvet. His hand was drawn to her hair. The sable strands slid through his fingers like watered silk, curling in warm tendrils around his wrist. Remembering the barrage of gunfire last night, he felt physically ill. It could so easily have been Sarah who'd taken the bullet instead of him.

He rasped the backs of his knuckles along the line of her jaw, and straightened his index finger to trace her lips. Her breath felt warm. How close she had come to never breathing again. What had he gotten her involved in? He wanted to pull her into his arms and hug her tight. He never wanted to let her go.

He stood so fast the blood rushed from his head. He swayed for a moment, then veered from the sofa. No matter how strong his feelings for her grew, he had made his decision regarding Sarah, and he had to stick to it.

His uneasy gaze settled on the fireplace. Leaning

against the wall next to the rock was one of Rick's hunting rifles. Sarah must have taken it from the cabinet in case she needed it during the night. As irrational as it was at a time like this, revulsion swept over him. He knew he could never have done the same for her. He closed his eyes, hating himself for his fear of guns. It should have been him protecting her, not the other way around. If it weren't for him, she wouldn't be in danger at all.

His head swam, whether from seeing the gun or from loss of blood, he didn't know. He licked his dry lips and raked a trembling hand through his hair. In all his life, he'd never felt so helpless. Sarah's life was in danger. His father had been kidnapped. And here he stood, so weak he was quivering. What was he going to do?

SARAH HEARD THE pitter-patter of raindrops, monotonous, faraway, soothing. She also heard a fire crackling. The aroma of bacon and fresh coffee wafted to her nose, a wonderful smell that made her stomach twist with hunger. Something warm and fuzzy pressed against her cheek. Ah, a blanket. She lifted her eyelids, peeking out at the world through the dark sweep of her lashes.

The ski lodge. She bolted upright. "Michael?"

"In here."

Throwing back the cover, she slipped on her shoes. When she reached the kitchen, she halted next to the woodstove. Michael stood before the electric range, cracking eggs into a skillet. He looked wonderfully healthy and uninjured in clean jeans and a red flannel shirt, with his jaw freshly shaved and his dark hair still glistening from a shower. When his brown eyes lifted, her heart skittered in an unwelcome response.

"You didn't get your shoulder wet, did you?"

"I wore a plastic garbage bag."

She blinked and ran a hand over her sleep-tousled hair. "You what?"

"I didn't get it wet." His gaze dropped to the open collar of her blouse, then veered away. "Coffee? It's fresh."

"I, yes, coffee sounds great. Where'd you get the clothes?"

"They're Rick's. And he's got a couple of sisters who come up occasionally. If you rummage, you might find something that'll fit."

Watching him more closely, she could see he favored his left arm, moving it as little as possible. He was also pale, though it was hard to detect because of his dark complexion. "Should you be up doing this?"

He tossed an eggshell into the trash can. "I told you last night it wasn't that bad a wound. People have abdominal surgery and walk the next day, even go home sometimes. The worst danger is infection, and we guarded against that with the antibiotic. I found the pills on the table and took another dose this morning. Which reminds me..." He leveled the spatula at her nose. "That wasn't just penicillin you gave me last night, was it? I thought I had more than two pills in my mouth. You're lucky I've only got one good arm. You deserve a good paddling for pulling a stunt like that. *Capisce?*"

The glimmer of affection in his eyes told her he was teasing about the paddling, so she decided to be gracious and let the comment slide. "I understand, but that doesn't mean I wouldn't do the same thing again if you were in that kind of pain."

He filled a coffee mug and handed it to her. "It was harebrained."

"Necessary."

"Emasculating." His mouth twitched at the corners as he turned the eggs. "Do you know how many movies I've watched where the fellow gets shot and *still* whips the bad guys and saves the lady? My one big chance and you ruined it."

"You were in so much pain you looked green."

"But I was still on my feet."

"You passed out in the broom closet."

"Only a heartless woman would bring that up."

She took a sip of coffee, grinning behind the mug as she swallowed. The glow of happiness she felt at seeing him on his feet again radiated through her whole body. "You were wounded and still dragged me halfway across the lobby to save me. I thought you were wonderful."

"I agree, I was heroic." Lifting the eggs from the skillet onto a plate, he added, "I usually pass out the second I see blood. Making it to the closet was a miracle."

"You're kidding."

"Nope."

"How on earth did you ever make it through med school?"

"That kind of blood doesn't bother me. It's accidents— blood where it shouldn't be—messy stuff. You will also note that I specialized in psychiatry? There was a method to my madness." The laughter left his eyes, replaced by shadows she couldn't fathom. "I, um, think we'd better eat before this gets cold. Hungry?"

"Starved. I'm sure glad we thought to clean out your fridge. Rick doesn't keep much here."

Striding over to the planked table, Michael set the plate of eggs beside a platter of bacon and toast, indicating with a nod of his head that she should sit opposite him. "Coming up as infrequently as he does, he can't keep perishables here. If not for you keeping your head last night, we'd be pretty hungry now. I wish I'd had more in the house but I pretty well emptied my fridge before I went to Chicago."

She took a seat and propped her elbows on the edge of the table. Cupping her mug in her palms, she eyed him through the steam that wafted from her coffee. "I meant it when I said you were wonderful. If it hadn't been for you, I'd have been killed last night. I froze."

"A lot of people freeze in situations like that."

"I, um…" She tried to smile and failed, but she pressed on. He deserved an explanation. "Remember when I told you my adoptive parents were killed? It happened in an explosion. There was a propane leak inside our trailer. We didn't realize it." Memories played through Sarah's mind. They were so vivid she no longer really saw Michael. "My mom was taking a nap. My dad and I had gone down to fish on the lakeshore. When we came back, I stopped at the fish-cleaning station to take care of our catch, and he went on ahead to wake Mom. He was holding a lit cigarette."

"Oh, Sarah…."

"I saw it happen, tried to reach them. The force of the explosions knocked me off my feet and stunned me." She lowered her eyes, staring into her coffee. "Anyway, explosive sounds—they, um, bring it all back. I'm sorry I panicked, but it wasn't something I could really help. I used to have nightmares, too. I'd wake up screaming. Maybe that was why I wanted to help you so badly when you first came to my office and told me about your dream. I knew what it was like."

Emotion clogged Michael's throat. The haunted look in her eyes made him want to take her in his arms. "Sarah, I didn't blame you for freezing. I hadn't even thought of it."

"I almost got us killed."

"And you made up for it a hundred times over later. We all have our weaknesses, which is why team effort works so great. People compensate for one another."

Her smile was tremulous. "We did make a pretty good team, didn't we?"

"Damned good. Not that I contributed my share. You held things together through the worst of it."

She took a deep breath, turning her attention back to the food, desperate for a change of subject before she made a fool of herself and burst into tears. "I should make a trip to the store on Highway 58. It's not that far. We'll need a few supplies."

He seemed to understand her need to switch topics. She was grateful for the easy way he shifted with her, responding to her unspoken cue. "Let's hope they take plastic money. I'm short on cash, and the lady I'm traveling with forgot her purse." His eyes twinkled with teasing laughter. Unable to use his left hand, he chased an egg, trying unsuccessfully to lift it from the serving plate with the spatula.

She set her coffee aside, and took the utensil from his hand. The longer she studied him, the paler he looked. She knew a class act when she saw one. "You should be flat on your back in bed. Here, let me. Two?" She heaped his plate with food, then served herself half as much, taking a bite of crisp bacon. "Mmm, this is wonderful."

He nodded. "Not bad for a one-handed cook."

"I hope you haven't overdone it. I have a vested interest in your health after all I went through to get you here."

"Had to do something useful. Where'd you hide the car?"

"Down by the creek. I covered it with brush."

He cut into his egg, then watched the yolk run onto his plate. A gray pastiness washed over his face and he closed his eyes. She leaned forward.

"Are you all right?"

He nodded. "I'm fine, just woozy."

She started to stand. "You're going directly to bed."

"No, I'm going to eat and then do a little walking to get my legs back under me. I can't take forever getting my strength back. My dad's out there somewhere. He needs me."

She sincerely hoped he was right, that his father wasn't

dead. "You can't rush it. It'll just take you longer to get well if you do."

He filled his mouth with bacon and chewed with all the enthusiasm of a child eating spinach. Swallowing, he said, "Do I remember going off the road last night, or did I dream it?"

"You're changing the subject."

"Did I dream it?" he persisted.

"I wish. They caught up with us and gave me a couple of quick lessons in how to play bumper cars."

He choked and grabbed for his coffee. After a quick swig, he lifted his watery gaze to meet hers. "I slept through *that*? You're incredible. You gave me those pain pills knowing full well I'd conk out on you. Then you stayed up all night with nothing but a gun for company. Most... I'm surprised you can still joke about it."

"I was a quick learner. I ran them off the road. It's over now. That's all that counts."

"And you just apologized to me for freezing?"

She studied his lean, dark-skinned face. He was running on sheer willpower. She wished he'd go lie down and let her serve him breakfast in bed. She jabbed her egg with her fork. Men could be so bullheaded sometimes— for some of the stupidest reasons. As if he'd be less masculine if he complained a little and let her baby him while he was recuperating. An ache of longing assailed her, miniscule at first, increasing to a sharp pain. She *wanted* to pamper him, needed to. He'd almost died last night. Short of drowning him in her tears of relief, touching him and making a fuss over him were the only emotional outlets she had.

"Do you think we'll be safe staying here for a few days?" he asked.

"I don't think they can find us here. The problem is figuring out what to do next. We can't stay here forever."

"No, just long enough for me to get some strength back."

"Then what? We have to do something, call the police, something."

"No police. I'm going back to Chicago."

CHAPTER ELEVEN

SARAH STARED AT him, waiting for him to grin, wink, laugh, do anything to let her know he was kidding. He didn't do any of those things. Fear for him swamped her. "Have you lost your mind? Those men are probably *from* Chicago."

"Exactly. There's no other place to get to the bottom of this."

She wiped her mouth with a paper napkin, her gaze locked to his. "What's wrong with calling the police and letting *them* get to the bottom of this? We're not equipped to handle those men. Do you want to get killed?"

"No. And I don't want you to get killed, either. Sarah, I gave this a lot of thought this morning. When I told my dad I'd seen Giorgio Santini, he wasn't just upset, he was terrified. Thirty years have passed, but he's still living in fear. I think he was involved with the mob in Chicago and fled to Oregon because they threatened him and his family."

"That's sheer supposition. I've never heard such a ridiculous idea. The mob? Come on."

"What about my nightmare? That much blood? Someone must have been murdered. My folks left Chicago and went into hiding, never even telling me they'd changed my name? They must not have been running from a small-time hood, Sarah, but from someone with a very long reach, someone with a reputation for never letting bygones be bygones. Those men who attacked us last night were professionals. Don't you see? The local police can't give us round-the-clock protection, not indefinitely. We have no proof so I doubt we could convince them it was necessary at all. If we leave it to the police we'll be dead within a week."

"If we go to Chicago, we'll be dead within hours. No way, Michael."

"I didn't say *we*. I'm going alone."

"You're what?"

"You heard me."

"You're going to take off and leave me? If it weren't for you, I wouldn't be in this mess."

The hurt that flickered in his eyes made her regret saying it. She knew darned well that the only reason he planned to leave her behind was that he feared for her safety and knew he was going into danger. She rose from the table, tossing her napkin onto her plate. "I'm sorry. I didn't mean that, really I didn't. I think we both need some time to think about this. *Rationally.*"

"Meaning I'm not?" He sighed and passed a hand over his eyes. "Listen to me, Sarah. It's not you I'm angry at. Maybe you're right. We do need to think."

She glanced out the window at the drizzle running from the cabin eaves. The silence seemed heavy. "If you'll give me your charge card, I'll run out to the store while the rain has let up."

He fished in his wallet and extended a gold Visa card to her. When she reached for it, he hesitated and tightened his grip on the plastic. "On second thought, I'll go. You could have problems signing on my account. Besides, look at yourself. You're a mess."

Her appearance wasn't what concerned him, and she knew it. She snatched the card from his hand, glancing down at the dark stains on her lapel as she tucked her blouse into her tweed skirt and straightened her jacket. "You can't tell it's blood," she said. With a smile, she slipped the charge card into her pocket and ran her fingers through her hair. "I'll just say we're newlyweds and I don't have my own card yet. If you move around too much, you'll open that wound and start bleeding again. Right now, that's the last thing we need."

He pushed up from the table when she turned toward the back door. "I don't want you going out alone. Sarah, dammit, come back here!"

She paused with her hand on the doorknob, looking back over her shoulder at him. His gaze met hers, glinting with determination. She stood there for a long moment, then twisted the knob. "Go lie down, Michael."

With that, she left and slammed the door behind her.

THE GROCERY STORE on Highway 58 was small, but its shelves were well stocked for the outdoor sportsmen who flocked into the area. Sarah gathered what supplies she thought she and Michael might need, putting them on the counter next to the register. Her attention wandered to the pay phone outside the window. She should call her mom while she was here. If an account of what had happened last night at the office hit the news, everyone who knew Sarah would be alarmed.

The middle-aged man who was waiting on her didn't hesitate when she handed him Michael's Visa. Just as he was about to run the card through his imprinter, she spied a news rack. Michael might enjoy reading the newspaper. Unless she discovered a way to entertain him while he convalesced, keeping him quiet might be difficult. They could also check the paper for mention of the shooting at her office last night, though she doubted it would have been reported before Molly went to work that morning.

"Put a paper on my bill, too, would you please?"

She stepped over to the rack and took a copy of Eugene's *Register-Guard*, returning to the counter to stuff the paper into one of her bags. As she folded the publication in half, she noted a few of the headlines.

"Sure is nasty out there," the man commented. "Rainin' again. Look at it come down."

She glanced out the window and nodded. "Pretty wet for September."

A woman's photo smiled up at her from the front page of the newspaper. Her hand tightened. Molly? She pulled the *Register-Guard* back out of the sack. Her heart slammed as she read the headline: LOCAL WOMAN LEFT FOR DEAD.

"Ma'am, are you okay?"

The store seemed to swirl around Sarah. She felt as if she might be sick. She grabbed the counter to steady herself. Someone had hurt Molly? It couldn't be true. Not harmless, scatterbrained Molly with the vague blue eyes and the funny little smile. Scanning the print, she read enough to make her legs turn to water. Molly might not live. "The young woman was found at 9:00 p.m. yesterday lying in an alley near her place of work." Near the office? It had probably happened shortly after Molly left Roots then. She had been going to Valley River Center, a shopping mall that was quite some distance from Thirteenth Avenue. "The police have not yet released an official statement, but they suspect Harmon was a random victim of robbery. She suffered multiple knife wounds, one an apparent attempt by her attacker to sever her jugular vein. Harmon remains in critical condition, unable to give the police any information about her attacker."

"Can I get you some water? Are you feeling faint?"

Sarah lifted her gaze to the storekeeper's concerned face, too shocked to reply. She stuffed the newspaper into the bag and scrawled her name across the charge ticket, adding De Lorio as an afterthought. Then she scooped the sacks into her arms and hurried to the door, peering out at the passing cars on the highway.

"Goodbye," the man called. "Thanks for stopping. Come again."

Tears filmed her vision. She staggered out of the building, fighting back sobs as she ran through the rain to the car, panic licking at her heels. She didn't believe Molly had been a robbery victim, not for a second. The attempted murder was somehow connected to Michael. But why? The question echoed in her head.

She unlocked the Ford and tossed the groceries onto the back seat. Another car pulled into the parking lot, splashing through a mud puddle. Fear clawed at her with icy talons. She glanced wildly over her shoulder, afraid to look, afraid not to. A woman with two toddlers in tow climbed out of a Volvo station wagon. Sarah's legs nearly buckled. Shaking, she slid into the driver's seat and struggled to insert her keys into the ignition. She had to get back to Michael, she thought, back to Michael and the safety of the lodge.

SLANTING RAIN PELTED Sarah's face. She held her arm up to shield her eyes while she dragged brush from the creek bank and draped it over the car. By the time she grabbed the bags of groceries from the back seat and made a run for the house, her suit was soaked. Thunder cracked across the sooty sky, reverberating in the air. She leaped with a start, looking back over her shoulder at the shadowy woods.

With every step, her high-heeled shoes sank into the sodden grass, mud sucking at the soles to bog her down. She half expected a killer to jump out at her from the brush, knife upraised. Pictures of Molly lying crumpled in an alley assailed her.

In the back of her mind, she knew she was hysterical; the gnawing, electrical fear she felt was irrational. The assailants didn't know where she and Michael were. But logic played no part in her reactions to the storm and Molly's attack. She sobbed as she ran, angling across the yard and up the steps onto the deck. The grocery bags were soaked and disintegrating. A can of chili dropped and hit the top of her foot. She stooped to pick it up and the sack in her left arm split, scattering groceries onto the rain-drenched planks. The next instant, she felt the bottom of the other bag give way. She cupped her palm under it and managed to slow it down enough to save the eggs, which were on top, but everything else spilled.

Staring down at the array of wet foodstuff, Sarah's fragile hold on her self-control snapped. She sank to her knees and set the two cartons of eggs on the deck with exaggerated care. She hung her head and her hot tears mingled with the raindrops on her cheeks. Molly was lying in a hospital, barely clinging to life. The realization was slowly sinking in, filling her with icy dread. She lifted her face to the angry sky, closing her eyes.

"My God, what's happened?"

She raised her lashes at the sound of Michael's voice. He lunged out the back door and across the deck, sinking to his knees beside her to grasp her shoulders. She worked her mouth, tried to speak, but no sound would come out.

"Sarah?" He caught her face between his hands. Rainwater dripped off his black hair and ran in crooked streams down his forehead and over his cheeks. "Honey, answer me. Are you all right? I knew I shouldn't have let you go by yourself. I knew it."

She caught hold of his shirt, forgetting all about his shoulder. She could feel his heart pounding under the knuckles of her right hand. He felt so strong, so solid and safe and warm. "M-Molly. They tried to k-kill Molly."

His features twisted and his skin lost some of its color. "Oh, no, not Molly."

He echoed her first reaction exactly. Molly was such a lovable girl once you grew accustomed to her scattered, vague way of thinking. So gentle, eager to please. It was inconceivable that someone would hurt her. Of all people, not Molly. A fresh rush of tears spilled from her eyes, and she leaned against him to hold herself erect. The sobs welling felt as if they were ripping out her vocal cords. "They found her in an alley. H-her throat was slit."

A wave of nausea rolled through Michael's stomach. He bent his head, dragging in a breath, his face pressed against her wet hair—dark hair, similar to Molly's. The suspicion that sprang to his mind unnerved him. Molly was about Sarah's height and weight. From a distance or in the dark, could someone have mistaken one woman for the other? He remembered Sarah saying a man had chased her. Now he wondered what might have happened if she had been caught. He lifted his head, checking the shadowy yard for signs of movement. "Come on, let's get you into the house."

Sarah staggered to her feet. "But what about the groceries?"

"Forget the damned groceries. I'll get them later."

He took her hand and tugged her along behind him. Once they were inside with the door locked, he turned and pulled her into his arms. She pressed her face into the hollow of his right shoulder, clinging to him. "M-Michael, hold me. Don't let go. Hold me."

The shrill hysteria in her voice raked down Michael's spine. With his uninjured arm, he squeezed her tightly around the waist. Her suit was so wet that it oozed and dripped under the pressure of his hand. "I won't let go. I'm here, Sarah. It's okay."

Even as he reassured her, he knew it wasn't okay. Right then, it didn't look as if anything would ever be okay again. How easily it might have been Sarah lying half dead in

that alley. Her sobs filled up his mind until there seemed
to be nothing else real around him but her pain and terror.
He felt her tremble and didn't know if it was from cold,
shock or both. He needed to get her out of her wet clothes
and under a pile of warm blankets.

"Michael, please, don't go to Chicago. They'll kill you.
I know they will."

"Shh. Calm down, Sarah. It'll be all right. Calm down."

"What are we g-going to do? They're going to kill us,
aren't they? Even if we go to the police, we w-won't be
safe. There's some sort of vendetta, isn't there? That's
why your father hid all th-these years. Why he broke into
my office—why he threatened me on the phone. He was
d-desperate."

"What do you mean, he broke into your office?"

In between sobs, she told him about the burglary. "I
knew it was your dad. I—I didn't tell you because you
would have d-dropped the case to get him off my back. I
knew how important it was to you to find your parents. I
should have told you, though, shouldn't I? You would have
stopped the investigation. Maybe then none of this would
have happened. Molly might not be—"

"Stop right there. None of this is your fault. Don't even
think that way."

She shrank closer to him. "I let her leave the office and
walk right into a trap. I was so *stupid*. The memory loss
on my computer wasn't an accident. All the information
about you and your father was on there, don't you see?
They erased it. They must have been planning to murder
Molly and me so there'd be no proof of who you really
were. That man who chased me, he was going to kill me,
only I got away. But Molly didn't."

"It's not your fault, sweetheart. Please don't do this to
yourself."

"But she might be dead! The paper said she might not

make it." Her breath caught and she went quiet a moment. "Oh, Michael, please… I couldn't bear it if something happened to you, too."

He stirred and dropped his arm from around her. "Come on." Taking her hand, he led her to the bedroom, halting beside the bed to tug her jacket off. She blinked when he unfastened her skirt and nudged it down her hips.

"What are you—"

"Hush and be still," he whispered, bending his head to kiss the tears from her face as he fumbled with the buttons on her blouse. "I'm having enough trouble doing this with one hand without you fidgeting. You're exhausted and cold. We've got to get you warm." When she was stripped down to her slip and bra, he drew back the covers. "In you go."

She lay down, shuddering and rubbing the gooseflesh on her arms. He sat on the edge of the bed and drew the blankets over her. His touch was incredibly light as he smoothed her wet hair, combing it back from her forehead with his fingertips. Over and over again, he ran his hand from her temple to her nape, mesmerizing her, slowly relaxing her. Gradually her sobbing subsided and her lashes fluttered against her cheeks. "I have to call the hospital," she murmured. "It's my fault this happened to Molly. I have to find out if she's okay. It's my fault, Michael."

"No—no it isn't your fault. Stop it, Sarah. Molly wouldn't want you feeling this way."

Her eyes widened. "Wh-what if they're still after her? What if they try again?"

He pressed her back against the pillow. "She's safe for now. She can identify her attacker, honey. The police will guard her to make sure the killer can't get to her."

She relaxed, realizing that what he said was true. Molly was safe. At least for now….

"It's my turn to stand watch, hmm? You sleep a while. You'll feel much better with some more rest."

She sought his gaze, comforted by the warm assurance that glowed in his eyes. "You won't leave me?"

He touched a finger to her lips. "You know I won't. I'll be right here when you wake up."

She nodded and nestled her cheek into the pillow, her mind already adrift as she slipped into slumber.

SARAH WOKE HOURS LATER. Darkness pressed the window above her head, casting the corners of the room into black shadows. Through the doorway, she could see amber firelight flickering. She sat up and saw a man's terry robe draped over the foot of the bedstead. She leaned forward, grabbed it and slipped her arms into the sleeves as she rose to her feet.

Michael sat on the sofa before the fire, his gaze fixed on the burning logs. He looked up when she approached and patted the cushion next to him, his lips curving in a half smile. "You look much better."

She sank beside him, leaning forward to hold her palms to the heat. "I feel better. I'm sorry I came unglued like that."

"I came a little unglued myself. After everything you've been through, a little hysteria was understandable."

"I can't believe it happened."

He sighed and motioned toward the newspaper where he had spread it near the hearth to dry. "I read about it. I guess the hardest thing is knowing what she's like. Who could hurt someone like her? She's so childlike."

She shivered. "I don't think the men we're dealing with would hesitate killing a child."

"No, I'm afraid not." Scenes from his last nightmare spun through his mind again. As a child, he hadn't recognized the blue-black thing the man in his dream had carried, but now he knew what it had been: a machine gun with an ammunition belt. "Men like that can kill without a thought."

"You are going back to Chicago, aren't you?" Thinking about Michael flying into danger made it hard to breathe. "Oh, Michael."

"I have no choice. The only way to stop all this is to find out who's behind it and sic the law on them." He looked at her, his expression solemn. "There *is* one change in plans. I want you to go with me. I can't risk leaving you here, not since hearing about Molly. Before I figured they were just after me and my dad, that once I was gone, you'd be safe. Now I know better."

She nodded. "I know who you are. Who you *really* are."

"Which explains your computer erasure. Eliminate you, Molly and the computer files, and I'm plain old Michael De Lorio. If my father and I wind up dead, there's no way to trace who did it. It makes sense in a spine chilling sort of way."

"But who? And why?"

"That's what we have to find out. Are you game? Your investigative knowledge may come in handy." He arched an inquisitive brow at her. "I figure we'll have to spend several more days here while I get my strength back. We can call from the store to see how Molly is and make plane reservations."

"There's no way I'd let you leave me behind." She tried to smile and her mouth quivered. "I'm the one who gave Molly a job. No matter what you say, what happened to her is my responsibility. If we don't stop whoever is behind all this, she won't be safe once she leaves the hospital. She knows who you really are, so they can't leave her alive. You have your reasons for going to Chicago; now I have mine. After all, calling the police wouldn't do any good. They're convinced Molly was a random victim. And besides, I've watched too many scary movies to make *that* mistake. The person left behind always gets it."

FEAR AND TERROR and waiting. Sarah learned to live with each as constant companions. Long, quiet days before a warm hearth with only the sounds of the wind whispering through dense woods. Lonely nights in an even lonelier bed, only a few feet away from the man who was slowly becoming the nucleus of her life. They'd made two phone calls: one to Sarah's neighbor, Mrs. Tyson, to ask the woman to care for Moses, the other to the hospital. Molly's condition remained critical, but the prognosis for recovery was now much better. Aside from that, they made contact with no one. Not even with Sarah's birth mother, whom she knew would be frantic with worry by now. Too risky, Michael said. The less the woman knew, the safer she was. As much as Sarah wanted to phone her family, she knew Michael was right.

She lived through the hours as a dying woman might, treasuring every brush of Michael's hand against hers, every smile, every semblance of normalcy, for she knew with dead certainty that each minute, no matter how serene it seemed on the surface, could be their last. With mounting anxiety, she watched Michael regaining his strength. Each milestone he passed toward recovery took them that much closer to Chicago. She understood how frantic he felt. He was worried about his father. But sometimes she wanted to put her fingers on the hands of the clock and physically stop time from ticking away.

The day of departure from their haven in the woods came quickly. Or so it seemed to Sarah. A week of solitude with Michael, when she had longed for a lifetime, seemed pitifully brief. She almost hoped something would go wrong during their drive to Eugene, something that would send them scurrying back to their hiding place.

Nothing did. The quick stop at her house for her clothes went uneventfully. Then they drove to Michael's.

Sarah sat on the hearth, waiting while he packed. She stared at the rifled rolltop desk, wishing they were still back at the ski lodge. The future yawned ahead of them as dark as the soot-blackened firebox behind her. She was afraid for herself and for Michael, and nothing seemed to ease her mind.

Michael emerged from the hall, gripping a brown suitcase. His eyes met hers. "I'm ready."

She rose and wiped her hands on her slacks. She'd changed clothes at her place. "Are you sure you aren't forgetting anything?"

"I even got cash out of the safe. We're all set."

They had left the car parked up the street and sneaked in the back way just in case someone was watching the house. She hoped that the exercise wouldn't sap too much of Michael's newly recovered strength.

He led her through the house to the back door carrying his suitcase with his good arm. She stepped around him to open the door. Just as she touched the knob, a knock sounded out front. She whirled to stare at the atrium. She could see the silhouettes of two men through the sidelights in the entry.

"Mr. De Lorio?" a voice called.

She and Michael bolted outside and dived into the bushes beside the back porch. She worried about Michael. He wasn't up to much running. Luckily the car wasn't far. "You all right?"

He motioned for her to lead the way, glancing back over his shoulder as they went. She circled the garage and eased her head around the corner. She was surprised to see a brown car parked in the driveway instead of the green one she'd expected. "It's not them."

"Wanna bet your life on it? They could have switched

cars." Michael nudged her forward, moving abreast of her so that his body was between her and the men on his front porch. "Go for it."

Darting through the terraced garden that bordered the driveway, she threw a fearful glance at the house. The two men heard them and turned. Her heart skipped a beat.

"Hey!" one of the men barked. "De Lorio! Hey!"

"Don't stop." Michael fell in behind her to shield her as they raced up the street toward the Ford. "Hurry, Sarah, hurry. Get your keys ready."

She dug her hand into her jacket pocket. At any moment, she expected bullets to whiz past her or, worse yet, to thud into Michael's back. She could hear the two men running down the driveway.

"De Lorio, wait!"

She and Michael threw themselves into the car and slammed their doors at precisely the same second. Sarah jammed the key into the ignition; the engine roared to life. She put the car in gear and tromped on the gas pedal. The Ford surged forward into the street.

"If they get in your way, drive right over them."

"Don't worry. I stopped playing nice over a week ago."

They both fully expected the two men to pull guns from beneath their suit jackets and open fire. When the car swept past the house and nothing happened, there was almost a feeling of anticlimax.

"Not to look a gift horse in the mouth, but why didn't they shoot?" She whizzed through a stop sign, screeched around a corner, then sped along a main drag leading to Eighteenth. "We were sitting ducks."

"Too many witnesses. Step on it, Sarah. They'll be on our tail all the way to the airport if we don't lose them."

She flashed him a grin. "Now you see me, now you don't. I am quickly becoming the world's worst driver."

BACK AT MICHAEL'S HOUSE, two U.S. marshals dashed for their car. Peeling out of the driveway, they streaked up the street after the Ford, staying on its tail all the way through Eugene. They knew De Lorio was booked for a flight to Chicago, but they had hoped to head him off before he reached the airport. The man in the passenger seat groaned when it became apparent they couldn't outrace De Lorio's companion. "Now what?"

With a grim scowl, the other man peered through the windshield at the fleeing car. "Why did he run? Doesn't he know we're his only hope?"

"You saw the Montague woman's office. They're probably so panicked, they don't know which end's up."

"We could call in the Feds and have them apprehended at the boarding gate."

"If we let them know where De Lorio's headed, you can bet La Grande will hear. We can't tip him off. He'll have thugs all over the airport. If De Lorio makes it that far, we have to let him board. We'll just notify the Chicago office, and after that, he's not our problem."

"And what if somebody messes up making the pinch?"

"They won't. The idea is to nail La Grande, not the lid of De Lorio's coffin."

CHAPTER TWELVE

SARAH EXITED HIGHWAY 99 onto Airport Road, driving west toward the Mahlon Sweet Airport. Glancing into her rearview mirror, she caught her bottom lip between her teeth. "Michael, there's a green car on our tail."

He twisted in his seat to look out the back window. "Damn! Step on it, Sarah."

His voice sounded unsteady. She looked sideways at him as she accelerated, noting the whiteness of his lips. He couldn't do many more hundred-yard dashes. He had regained a lot of his strength in the week at the cabin, but he wasn't up to this.

A feeling of unreality washed over her. How many men were chasing them? She could see two in the automobile behind them. There had also been two back at Michael's house. They had been hiding an entire week, and they'd been so careful not to be seen when they returned to Eugene. Whoever these men were, they were outguessing her and Michael at every turn. She felt like a dim-witted rat wandering in a researcher's maze.

"Just pull into temporary parking," Michael said when she got to the airport. "The car's in Pete's name. They'll contact him and I'll settle with him later."

If there is a later.

Sarah's eyes burned with tears as she whipped the car into a slot. Glancing back over her shoulder, she saw the green sedan approaching the parking area. A Chrysler, she realized. Being able to identify the automobile's make told her it was dangerously close.

Grabbing their bags, they darted back and forth between parked cars, then made a dash into the building. Unlike large airports, Mahlon Sweet consisted of one central lobby where tickets from various airlines could be purchased. They ran to American Airlines, where they had reservations. Michael guarded Sarah's back while she got their tickets and seat assignments. So far, so good. No sign of anyone suspicious. It was 12:27. Flight 168 should be boarding any second.

Racing across the airport, they joined a line to pass through the metal detector. *Oh, dear God, please hurry,* Sarah prayed as the queue inched forward. A cowboy wearing a gigantic belt buckle set the detector off. Everyone came to a halt. Sarah's heart began to slam. She felt Michael's arm grow tense under her hand. She wanted to shove her way up to the front and rip the stupid belt off the man.

And then it hit her. Even after they passed through the detector and were admitted to the boarding area, they wouldn't be safe. The boarding area was transparent glass on all four sides. Passengers exited from there to cross the blacktop to their planes, all within clear view of nonpassengers inside the airport. She and Michael would be as defenseless as fish in a bowl.

A strange feeling slithered up her back. Glancing uneasily over her shoulder, she saw a man elbowing his way through the crowd toward them. She guessed him to be in his early fifties, medium height with steel-gray hair and hawkish features. The word predatory came to mind. "Michael, they've spotted us."

Sarah crowded in front of a large woman in a blue pantsuit, to put her purse and bag on the conveyor belt to go through the detector.

"Well, I never—" the woman sputtered.

Goose bumps peppered Sarah's arms. Her scalp tingled. Michael placed his suitcase on the conveyor as well and stepped in close behind her, his hands at her waist, his broader frame between her and the man watching them. Once again, moisture filmed Sarah's eyes. Michael might still be weak, but a coward, never. The agent took their tickets, thanking them for flying American.

"Don't look back," Michael whispered. "Keep walking. Get over there in that cluster of people so he can't get a clear shot."

Tension knotted her neck as she stepped through the doorway. The man on the other side of the glass would have an unobstructed view of them until they were inside the plane. "I'm scared."

"Just keep walking."

Sarah slipped into a group of people, Michael right on her heels. Two men broke off talking, staring down at her. "Nice day for flying, isn't it?" she chirped. Neither man made a reply. "We're heading for Chicago. How about you?"

The older man gave a nervous cough. "Dallas."

Sarah could see the gray-haired man staring at them through the glass. "You'll be on our plane then. Do you live there?"

Michael smiled. "My wife's a little nervous about the flight. Her first, you know."

The younger man laughed. "Oh, nothing to it. You'll love it once you're up there. Ah, it's time to board."

Sarah was so frightened she could scarcely breathe as she and Michael walked across the asphalt. At any moment, she expected a bullet to slam into one of them. When at last they were aboard the jet, she heard Michael sigh in relief and knew just how he felt.

"We made it," he whispered.

Her legs felt as if they might dissolve and run into her shoes. "Not all of us. My stomach's still back in the boarding enclosure."

Michael chuckled and took the window seat, asking if she'd mind handing him a pillow from the overhead compartment after she stowed their bags. It wasn't until she sank into the space beside him that she realized they were on the airport side of the plane and that Michael was still a target. He gave her a sly wink and covered his window with the pillow, leaning his head against it.

Her heart gave a peculiar little twist. A hundred thoughts crowded into her mind, foremost the fervent wish that he wouldn't be so noble all the time. If he kept it up, she was going to do something really stupid, like fall in love with him. She stared at the squared heel of his hand against the crisp white pillow, at the fine black hair that dusted his bronze skin. As she well knew, those long fingers had an incredible grip, yet could be soft as down when they brushed her skin. Her throat tightened at the thought.

Dragging her gaze away from him, she riveted her attention on the passengers who were still boarding as she fastened her seat belt. A darling old woman in a prim black suit and pillbox hat made her way down the aisle. Next came a stewardess, leading a small boy by the hand. Then two men boarded, one in a gray suit, the other in blue. *Mutt and Jeff,* she thought, one tall and skinny, the other short and rotund. She could have sworn they stared at her as they passed. She considered telling Michael, but when she glanced over at him, he looked so pale she decided against it. Even if the men *were* staring, what could Michael do, tell them to stop? At least she knew they couldn't have brought weapons on board.

She leaned forward to pull an airlines publication from the pocket in the seat ahead of her. As she leafed through the magazine, she pretended to have a coughing attack.

Turning her head away from Michael, she covered her mouth, darting a look at the men. They were two rows back, one engrossed in a newspaper, the other already napping. She smiled at her own silliness. Her nerves were strung so taut, she would be leaping at her own shadow if she didn't watch it.

AT THE EXACT SAME MOMENT that Sarah settled back in her seat, the hawklike features of the man she'd seen in the airport twisted into an angry snarl. He stepped to a pay phone and punched out a phone number. When the operator broke in to inquire about the charges, he snapped, "Collect, from Shuelle."

While he waited for his call to go through, Shuelle ran his thumb and index finger up and down the armored telephone cord, his touch caressingly light as he imagined it wrapped around the Montague woman's neck. At last a familiar, precise voice came over the wire, saying, "Yes?"

"Yeah, Shuelle here. We followed them clear to the boarding gate, but we didn't dare shoot. They're on flight 168, due at O'Hare about ten-twenty tonight. There's not another flight to Chicago until tomorrow, so we're stuck here."

A long, tension-packed silence ensued. "Did you ever discover where they were hiding out?"

"No. But we heard when they made the plane reservations."

"If you knew they had made reservations, why on Earth didn't you make some as well so we wouldn't have a twenty-four-hour delay?"

"Because we didn't intend for them to get on the plane. We staked out the road coming to the airport. Woulda stopped them, but the Montague woman was drivin' like a bat outa hell. We couldn't catch up."

"I thought I made it clear that I wanted the matter handled on that end?"

"We tried."

"Trying isn't what I'm paying you to do. I want results. I'll arrange for Lund to be at O'Hare when they land and have him follow them so we can keep their whereabouts pinpointed. Meanwhile, get on the first flight back so you can get this job done."

HOURS LATER, SARAH and Michael arrived in Chicago. O'Hare International was so big and busy it boggled her mind. To add to her discomfiture, the two men who had seemed to be staring at them on the airplane had followed them outside. She tried to tell herself she was only imagining that they were watching her every move, but it did little to ease her mind when she turned and caught the thin man's gaze on her again. He looked away immediately, pretending interest in a blond punk rocker stuffed into tight black leather, but Sarah wasn't convinced. He *had* been staring at her; she felt sure of it. She didn't peg him as the black leather type. He looked too grim and straight laced.

She couldn't find a cab fast enough. While the cabbie stowed their luggage in the trunk, she opened the rear door for Michael, stepping back so he could get in first. He was favoring his shoulder again. As Sarah slid onto the seat beside him, she touched her hand to his. "Are you okay?"

He looked past her at the throng of people pouring out the doors. "The worse off they think I am, the sloppier they'll be."

Her heart lifted when she saw how alert and clear his eyes were. "You saw them, too?"

He turned his hand palm up and curled his fingers around hers. "I'm a little weak, Sarah, not blind."

"Have they come out?"

"Not that I've seen." He shrugged one shoulder. "Maybe we're being paranoid."

Glancing over at her, Michael could see tension in every line of her slender body. It amazed him that she was still able to smile. Most of the women he knew would have been hysterical five days back—most of the *men* he knew would have been! She was some special lady. He wished he hadn't involved her in this mess. If something happened to her, he didn't know how he would live with it.

The cabbie climbed into the front seat. Michael leaned forward and gave him the name of a hotel. "There's twenty in it if you make sure no one follows us."

"You got it," the cabbie replied, tromping on the gas pedal.

The tires of the cab squealed, and Sarah grabbed the armrest on her door. Michael turned to see her lift an accusing eyebrow at him. That was another thing he liked about her. She took things in stride.

STEPPING OUT OF the bathroom, Sarah tipped her head to one side, running a brush through her hair. A hot shower and her own cotton nightgown instead of something borrowed gave her a feeling of normalcy. Slipping her feet into her slippers, she went to the dresser to check her watch. She'd ordered room service forty minutes ago. Dinner should be along anytime.

With a heavy sigh, she set the brush on the dresser and stretched her arms high, closing her eyes. In a city the size of Chicago, she and Michael would be as hard to find as fleas on a dog's back. In all that milling traffic, how could anyone possibly have followed them? For tonight, she felt fairly sure they were safe and she intended to enjoy it.

Picking up their room receipt, she studied Michael's signature, grinning. Mr. and Mrs. Lorenzo. It made her think of Lorenzo's Pizza Parlor back home. Of course, right now she was so hungry that anything might make her think of food.

She smiled again when she saw that her mister had already fallen asleep. He was sitting up in bed, propped by both pillows, chin on his chest. Closing the distance between them, she pressed her hand to his forehead. No fever. Just weak and understandably exhausted. He murmured something, frowning at her touch. Then he jerked awake, a wild look in his eyes as he shrank from her hand. She froze, staring down at him.

"Michael?"

At the sound of her voice, the tension seemed to leave him. He laughed softly. "Sarah...you scared me. I must have been dreaming."

Her attention shifted to her outstretched hand, and she recalled him telling her about the clawlike fingers that reached for him in his nightmare. She dropped her arm, doubling her knuckles into a tight fist. Hearing about his dream and actually seeing the expression on his face when the horror of it touched him were two entirely different things. She noticed a flush creeping up his neck beneath the collar of his pajama top.

"I, um, ordered dinner to be brought up."

His gaze fell to her modest gown, then skittered away. "Great. I'm starved." He swung his legs over the side of the bed, propped his elbows on his knees and held his head in his hands. The corded tendons in his tanned forearms looked taut. "Sorry about that, Sarah. I didn't mean to startle you."

She longed to touch his dark hair, to tell him he needn't feel embarrassed. She longed to, and she couldn't. Not once in the past week had he encouraged any sympathy from her.

A light knock sounded. "Ah...dinner."

She went to the door, fitting her eye to the peephole. A uniformed waiter from the downstairs restaurant stood in the hall, one hand on the trolley. As she turned the dead bolt, she heard Michael's change jangling and knew he was getting out a tip.

"Room service," the waiter said in a monotone. He stepped back to push the cart inside. The next second, dishes and silver clattered as the trolley shot forward. Sarah flattened herself against the wall to avoid being hit, her gaze fixed on the two men who had lunged into the room on the waiter's heels. Even before she looked at their faces, she knew who they were by the blue and gray suits they wore. *The men from the airport.* The door shut behind them with a click of finality.

"Freeze!" the hefty man hissed, brandishing a revolver.

Michael stood near the dresser, still holding his pants. She threw a frantic glance his way, then closed her eyes. An almost overpowering rush of fear washed over her as she envisioned bullets plowing into their bodies. Lifting her lashes, she blinked to bring the room into focus.

"Don't get trigger happy," Michael said in a soft, reasonable tone. "It's me you're after, so let the lady go."

"Shut up!" the lean man barked. He stepped across the room, shoving the terrified waiter out of his way. When he reached Michael, he pressed the barrel of the .38 revolver against his jaw. "Get dressed, buddy." Glancing at Sarah, he snarled, "You, too, and hurry up about it."

She pressed her palms against the wall, staring in frozen fascination as the hefty man rifled through her suitcase and threw a purple blouse and burgundy slacks at her. His features were seared on her mind, the crooked bridge of his nose, the squared angle of his chin, the winglike tufts of his silvery brown eyebrows. He looked like a kindly grandfather except for his eyes, a killer's eyes, so flat and hard her skin felt icy everywhere they touched.

"Get dressed." He aimed the black revolver at her fore-head. "Now!"

She leaned forward and gathered her clothes with a quivering hand. As she straightened, it hit her that they expected her to disrobe right there—in front of them all. A tingle of horror crept up her neck.

"Hey, come on, fella," Michael interjected. "At least let her go in the bathroom."

The waiter made a funny little squeaking noise, clearly terrified. The heavy man in blue threw open the bathroom door and gave the room a quick once-over. Motioning to Sarah, he said, "Step on it or strip out here, lady, your choice."

Sarah scurried into the bathroom and pressed the door closed with her back, shaking uncontrollably. She heard Michael's change jingling again and knew he was pulling his slacks on. *Think, Sarah,* she commanded herself. *You've got a few precious seconds and that's it.* Shooting frantic glances around her, she saw nothing she might use as a weapon. She unbuttoned her nightgown and tugged it off over her head. As quickly as she could, she threw on her clothes and cracked the door to peek out.

"Hurry it up!" the thin man ordered when he saw her.

She stepped through the doorway and moved to the closet to grab her running shoes. Michael sat on the bed, pulling on his socks with exaggerated slowness. The waiter grasped the trolley handle as if the cart was all that kept him standing. Michael's eyes met hers as he reached for his loafers. She slipped on her shoes and walked noncha-lantly toward the dresser, picking up her hairbrush with one hand as she opened her overnight case with the other. Giving her hair a quick brushing, she curled her fingers around her can of hair spray.

"Enough!" the thin man snarled.

Sarah watched his approach in the mirror, steeling

herself to act. Even his features were thin and mean. She leaned forward slightly, turning her head as she spotsprayed her hair. *Spiff-spiff.* She saw the man reaching for her. *Not too soon, Sarah,* she cautioned herself. Timing would mean everything.

His fingers bit into her shoulder as he jerked her around. "Enough, I said!"

She lifted her innocent brown eyes to meet his gaze. His gun was pointed in her general direction but not precisely *at* her. It was now or never. With a flick of her wrist, she turned the spray nozzle toward his eyes. The can spewed lacquer. He reared back, gun hand wavering, his other flying to his face.

"Now, Michael!" she cried.

Throwing herself at the thin man's chest, she knocked him off balance. He staggered backward. Michael shot up off the bed and sacked the hefty man in a football tackle, the momentum of his thrust carrying them both across the room to crash into the wall. Drawing back his arm, Michael plowed his fist into the older man's jaw, the force of the blow snapping his head back. The waiter stood there in frozen horror.

Knowing the hair spray would only blind the man for a few seconds, Sarah grabbed his arm and fought with him for possession of the gun. "Help me!" she screamed at the waiter. "Don't just stand there!"

The waiter snatched up the silver coffeepot and swung it in a wide arc, clunking the man on the side of his head. Scalding coffee splattered the back of Sarah's blouse. The man bellowed with pain. Sarah wrenched the gun with all her strength, prying it from his fingers only to lose her grip on it. The weapon fell to the carpet and rolled under the bed.

"Let's go!" Michael cried, seizing her arm.

They hit the hall in a mad dash, the waiter right on their

heels. Careening around the corner to the elevator, both she and Michael dived for the control buttons. *Oh, hurry, hurry,* Sarah pleaded, shifting her weight from one foot to the other, glancing frantically behind them.

"The stairs…come on, we'll take the stairs," the waiter cried.

Michael jerked her half off her feet, lunging after the waiter down the corridor. The next thing Sarah knew, she was plummeting down a metal stairway, her hand in Michael's, the sound of their footsteps thundering inside her head. Running, running, never slowing down. Pain snaked around her ribs, squeezing tighter and tighter until she could scarcely breathe. When they reached the bottom floor, the waiter threw open the stairwell door and the three of them jammed the opening, each trying to spill through it at once.

When they erupted into the lobby, Michael jerked her to a halt near a potted palm, his chest heaving for air. For a moment she thought he was stopping to rest, but when she glanced up, she saw he was staring at the *concierge*'s desk. Two men in dark suits stood at the counter, earnestly questioning the man on duty.

The elevator chimed, announcing its arrival in the lobby. Michael threw a panicked look at the trembling waiter. "A back door! We have to go out another way."

The waiter stood there for an instant, indecisive, his mouth working and no sound coming out. Then he pivoted and ran toward the restaurant, waving at them to follow. Sarah heard the elevator doors open behind them. Footsteps thudded on the rug. A deep voice barked, "There they go!"

The sprint through the restaurant was a blur. The waiter darted around tables, weaving a zigzag path toward the back, Michael and Sarah flying along behind him. The two gunmen careened in their wake, followed by the two

men from the *concierge*'s desk. Dishes clattered. A woman
screeched in dismay. A hotel employee yelled at them to
stop. After they shoved through the double doors into the
kitchen, the waiter whirled to look for something to block
the gunmen's way. Spying a cart of desserts, he shoved it
in front of the doors and took off running again.

He led them through the kitchen to another set of double doors that opened onto an alleyway. Cold air blasted
Sarah's face as she hurtled along behind Michael, her hand
still clasped in his. The waiter angled left. "Get away from
me!" he cried. "You're gonna get me killed!"

Michael obliged and turned right, pulling Sarah along
behind him. Ahead she could see car lights whizzing past
on a main drag. Her heart pounded every time her feet hit
the ground, faster, faster. Michael took a left when they
reached the street. Neon signs blinked above them. The
lines in the sidewalk seemed to blur, they ran so fast. She
lost track of how many intersections they crossed. Her
body became numb with exhaustion, her legs pumping
beneath her from sheer force of will.

When she felt certain she couldn't take another step,
Michael faltered midstride and staggered to a stop, leaning
his back against a building. With a limp arm, he encircled
her shoulders and drew her against his chest, pressing his
face into her hair. She gulped for air, grateful for the lean
length of his body bracing hers.

"T-tired, h-have t'stop," he wheezed.

She swallowed, nodding in mute assent. When at last
they were rested, they drew apart and looked around to
get their bearings. She immediately stiffened. How they
had done it, she didn't know, but they had run from a posh,
upper-class neighborhood into a slum area with drunks
lounging outside doorways. Michael kept his arm around
her as he pushed away from the building, his protective-

ness confirming what she'd already guessed; they could get into trouble here fast.

The smell of food wafted on the damp night air. In spite of herself, she sniffed. When had they eaten last? He started walking, keeping her clamped securely to his side, his hip bumping hers. She sneaked a glance at his face. "How you holding up?"

"Aside from expiring from hunger? Fine." He paused under a quaint sidewalk awning, gazing through a tavern window.

She couldn't see over the café-style curtains. "What's it like?"

"Murky. Just our kind of place." Stepping forward, he pulled open the door for her. "Ladies first."

"Thanks a bunch."

The inside of the tavern was dark and smoky, the air pulsating with jukebox music from the sixties. She gravitated toward the darkest corner and slid into a burgundy vinyl booth. She scratched dried mustard off the tabletop with her fingernail. "This is a class operation if I ever saw one," she whispered.

He leaned forward, giving her the bedroom eye. "Stick with me, baby. This is just for starters."

Catching her lip between her teeth, she met his gaze, wondering how he could find the heart to joke. She wavered between hysterical laughter and tears. He reached across the table and put his warm hand over hers, his gaze shifting to the door.

"I think we'll be safe here for a few minutes. We'll grab something to eat then find a place to stay the night."

"Around here?"

He cocked an eyebrow. "You have to admit, it isn't the first place they'd start looking."

Her heart sank. There wasn't a chin in there, aside from Michael's, that wasn't sporting at least a week's growth of beard. Intermingled with the greasy smell of grilled cube steak, she detected the even less pleasant odor of stinky armpits. "I hate to tell you this, but I've got an aversion to fleas and body odor. If it isn't bug free and clean, this lady doesn't lay her head on it."

His hand tightened around hers. "You can use my shoulder."

CHAPTER THIRTEEN

SARAH WAS NO connoisseur of shoulders, but Michael's was definitely the nicest she had ever come across, solid but not too hard with a hollowed place that seemed carved especially to fit her cheek. Add the wonderfully strong circle of his arm and the heat of his muscular body pressed to hers, and as far as shoulders went, she felt certain his was the ultimate. The dingy hotel room, the lumpy mattress and the squeaky bedsprings didn't bother her at all.

Through the drapes at the window, a neon sign flashed red and pink on the walls. She stared at the play of light, her limbs heavy, the patter of her heart harmonizing with the steady, resonant thud of his beneath her ear. The clean smell of his skin and shirt overcame the foreign odors of the room, making her feel safe and cozy. It wasn't rational, but for this little while, at least, she didn't care that killers chased them. She had Michael beside her, and that seemed enough.

He was still awake. Every few minutes, he ran his hand up and down her back, the touch of his fingertips burning a trail through her thin blouse onto her skin. Each time, she closed her eyes, savoring the moment, filing the memories away so she would always be able to recall the pleasure of his touch. *Michael.* His name whispered through her head like the lyrics to a song, tugging at her heart, bringing tears to her eyes. How had she come to love him so desperately? After this was over, would she see him again?

Would they even have an after?

As if reading her mind, he tightened his arm around her, his hand pressed firmly to the curve of her ribs, his fingertips grazing the beginning swell of her breast. "You know, all this past week, I've avoided sleeping in the same room with you."

She stirred, raising her face to his. In the dim, ever-changing lights, his strong features were etched in shadow, his eyes luminous beneath the thick fringe of his lashes. "Why is that?" Her heart seemed to grow still as she waited for his answer.

"I, um, didn't want you to see me when I had a night-mare."

For a fleeting second, she felt like laughing. It was such a silly thing to worry about. But then she remembered the panic she had seen in his eyes earlier when she had awakened him from a dream. Not a laughing matter, she realized, not to Michael. "Are you self-conscious about going to sleep?"

He hesitated before answering. "Yes."

A dozen words of comfort sprang to her mind. She said none of them. His feelings about this subject ran far too deeply to be assuaged with pat phrases. She closed her eyes, remembering her nightmares after her adoptive parents were killed. "It's not easy, is it? I had dreams for two years after the explosion. It helped when I found my natural mother. The dreams stopped once I developed a strong relationship with her."

"What's she like?" His voice rang taut with emotion. "How did it feel to meet her?"

A smile curved her mouth. "It was like finding a part of myself that had been lost. I was a funny kid, more sensitive than most, and I always felt sort of—" She paused, trying to put her feelings into words. "It was as if I didn't really fit where I was. My mom and dad were blond, I was dark. They were short, I was tall. I loved them dearly, but way deep inside, I knew we were ill matched. I'd sneak off into the bathroom sometimes and look at myself in the mirror, wondering where I had come from.

"I wondered why my mother gave me away, if she ever thought about me. I didn't feel like a complete person. I had the most wonderful adoptive parents in the world. It wasn't anything lacking in them or the life they gave me that made me feel that way. It was me. I don't know why. I never told my folks. But I always felt I had to find my real mother and ask the questions that haunted me."

"And why did she give you up? Did you find out?"

"She was an unmarried teenager, the daughter of a minister in a small town. Her parents threatened to disown her if she kept me."

"And did she ever think about you?"

"When I called her, she cried so hard she couldn't talk. She had tried to find me for years. She had been forced to give me up and it had always *haunted* her. It's different for women who willingly make the choice, feeling in their hearts that it's what's best for the baby." She sighed and rubbed her cheek against his shirt. "From the beginning, she felt coerced into it and resented it all her life. I'm sorry, Michael. You shouldn't have asked me about my mom. I get carried away."

"Nonsense. I wanted to know or I wouldn't have asked." He took a deep breath and let it out very slowly. "I want to know all there is to know about you, Sarah. I just wish—"

"What?"

"That I—" He brushed his fingertips across her lips. "My nights are ugly, Sarah, too ugly to share them with anyone."

She stiffened. "Don't tell me you want separate rooms. I'll have hysterics."

He tucked his chin against his chest to look down at her. "No, I mean on a permanent basis. You understand?"

And suddenly she did. Oddly enough, with understanding came joy because, unlike Michael, she believed there had to be a solution to his problem if only they looked hard enough. He cared for her. If he didn't, he would never have begun this conversation. Knowing that gave her something to hold on to, even if it was fragile. "It's sort of silly to worry about permanent when we can't even count on temporary."

His mouth curved into a half grin. "I prefer to think positively." Touching a hand to her hair, he whispered, "Oh, Sarah, Sarah, what have I gotten you mixed up in?"

"I wish I knew." Snaking her arm around his waist, she gave him a quick hug. His expression, the ache in his voice and the incredibly light way he touched her, all told her how very deeply he cared, how concerned he was for her safety. "It's not your fault, you know."

He sighed and closed his eyes, keeping his hand on her hair. "I can't understand it. That's what bothers me the most. In the beginning, they were trying to kill us. But now, for no apparent reason, they've changed their methods. Those guys at my house this morning could have picked us off easily and they never even went for their guns. Then the men at the hotel tonight—they wanted to take us somewhere."

"The men at the *concierge*'s desk didn't shoot, either."

"Which is another piece to the puzzle. I think half of Chicago's chasing us."

She snuggled as close to his warmth as she could. "Oh, Michael...."

He turned slightly, pressing his lips against her forehead. Silence settled over them. Time drifted by. Her eyelids began to feel heavy. She fought sleep, acutely aware that he was wide awake, but eventually she lost the battle.

When her breathing grew shallow and even, Michael traced the shape of her mouth with his forefinger, remembering the one time he had kissed her and the explosion of feeling that had erupted within him. Not just passion, though of course he had wanted her, but more than that—much more than that. Tenderness. Protectiveness. Longing. He supposed if he had to describe his feelings for her in one word, he'd choose *cherish*. He closed his eyes on that thought. Nightmare or no, he had to get some rest if he planned to get her out of this mess alive.

DOUGHNUTS AND COFFEE were not Sarah's favorite way to wake up, especially not when both were cold and greasy. She'd seen greasy pastry plenty of times but never a cup of Java with oil floating on the surface. *Blue film.* It made her think of polluted bay water. It was particularly irritating to see Michael across the booth from her, sipping, dunking and munching as though he were at the Ritz.

He lifted curious brown eyes to hers, a crescent of doughnut halfway to his mouth. "You're grumpy this morning."

"I'm always grumpy until I've had my two cups of coffee."

His gaze dropped to her foam cup. "That isn't coffee?"

She jabbed an accusing finger downward. "*That* is muck. How can you drink it? Did you see that man's fingernails? He looks like a mechanic, not a cook."

"I thought it tasted pretty good."

She rolled her eyes. "You don't swallow this stuff; it slides down."

The laughter in his eyes encircled her with warmth. "Come on, drink up so I can take you back over to the room. I promise lunch will be better."

She raised an eyebrow. "What d'you mean, so you can take *me* back? You're not going?"

"I'm going to Santini's house."

She leaned forward. "Where you go, I go. This is Sarah the shadow you're talking to."

"No way, not this time. It'll be too dangerous."

Hysterical laughter welled in her throat. What could be more dangerous than staying in this creepy neighborhood by herself? "I'm not staying here alone. End of subject. You leave, I leave, *capisce?* Who knows, maybe I can snag a cup of decent coffee someplace."

His eyes went deadpan. "I don't want you hurt."

"Yeah? Well, I don't want me hurt, either, especially not when I'm alone. If I'm going to get it, I want to have company."

He scowled at her, but if Sarah were one to be intimidated by scowls, she never would have gotten where she was in the business world. She smiled brightly and poured her coffee into his cup. He narrowed his eyes, but she could see by his expression she'd won the argument.

"So…why Santini's?"

He sighed, reaching for another doughnut. She had been counting and that was three, a good sign if increase of appetite was an indication that he was recovering from his wound. "I think he can tell me something. There must have been a reason my dad left here and never once got in touch with his own brother. If I can find out why, we'll be that much closer to finding out who's behind all this."

It sounded reasonable. Unfortunately it also sounded risky. She leaned back in her seat. "We'd better not call him in advance. As it is, we could be walking into a trap."

THE FIRST THING Sarah said when she saw Giorgio's expensive home made Michael recall his first visit there when he'd longed for a dose of her sense of humor. She climbed out of the cab, tipped her head to one side and smiled. "One thing's for sure, he doesn't toss noodles for a living."

"He doesn't make doughnuts, either."

A horrible thought struck her. "Your dad doesn't make *greasy* ones, does he?"

He laughed and slammed the cab door. "I was hungry, okay? Give me a break. I'll take you to the nicest place I can find for dinner and make up for it."

"In our new neighborhood, the nicest place has roaches crawling along the baseboards." She linked her arm in his, walking up Giorgio's walkway with him as if they had been invited for high tea. In burgundy slacks, a purple blouse and sneakers, that was a feat in itself.

"You sure you want to go in? You'd be safer waiting in the cab."

A little quiver at the corners of her mouth told him how tense she really was. "No way. Like I said, if I'm going to die, I want to do it in good company. Besides, he might serve coffee."

He rang the bell, then placed his hand over Sarah's where it rested on his arm. Her small fingers felt fragile beneath his, reminding him how easily she could be injured. His throat tightened around a lump the size of a baseball. He would have given everything he owned right then to have her someplace safe, uninvolved in the circus his life had become.

A man in a gray suit answered the door. His blue eyes flickered with recognition when he saw Michael, then drifted curiously to Sarah. "May I help you?"

"Yes, we're here to see Mr. Santini. I'm Michael Smith. He'll recognize the name."

The man stepped back, motioning them inside. After closing the door, he led the way into the living room and offered them each a seat. "I'll inform Mr. Santini that he has guests. Please, make yourselves comfortable while you wait."

Michael kept hold of Sarah's hand, pulling her down on

the sofa beside him. Moments later, Giorgio appeared in the archway, his brown eyes filled with alarm. "Gino, what brings you here?" Glancing over his shoulder, he snapped his fingers. "Please, Pascal, remain here with us? I may require your presence."

Pascal lingered beside the much shorter Santini, his eyes darting nervously around the room. Michael glanced at Sarah. Pascal didn't seem any too thrilled about staying. Had he hoped to notify someone outside the house of their arrival? Giorgio motioned Pascal to a wing chair, then took a seat opposite him. "This is an unexpected pleasure."

"I came to get some answers," Michael said with a bluntness that made the room grow still. "When I came here before, we both did a lot of hedging. The time for that is over. My father has disappeared. I think you may know who abducted him."

The color washed from Giorgio's face. "Angelo has disappeared? When did this happen?"

Michael leaned forward. "It happened over a week ago, as you probably well know." He gestured toward Sarah. "And after that her secretary was attacked in an alley. What is it, the mob? Some kind of vendetta?"

Pascal settled back in his chair, scratching his chin. Then, ever so nonchalantly, he reached a hand under his lapel. Giorgio's attention shifted immediately to him. "Don't do it, Pascal. You were right, blood is thicker than water. He is my brother's son. I don't have any of my own."

Sarah couldn't breathe. Her gaze was glued to the almost imperceptible lump under Pascal's jacket. She felt Michael's tension. It was so powerful, so electrical, it pulsated around her, tingling on her skin.

"The boss won't like this," Pascal said in a silken voice.

"To whom do you owe your loyalty?" Santini demanded. "Him or me?"

Pascal hesitated and at last dropped his hand to his lap.

Santini visibly relaxed. Only Michael seemed coiled to spring. "The boss? Uncle Giorgio, please level with me. My father's life, as well as mine and Sarah's, depend on my knowing who's behind all this. You're involved with the mob, aren't you?"

Giorgio's mouth twitched as he smiled. "Don't be ridiculous, Gino. The day of the Chicago gangster is over, has been for years. Do I—" He threw back his head and chuckled, lifting his hands in a persuasive way. "Do I look like a mobster to you? I am an old man, no?" His gaze slid to Sarah. "Ms. Montague, I presume? You are a close friend of our Gino's, eh? Perhaps you should persuade him to go home before it's too late. Before you both get hurt."

The threat was unmistakable. Michael stood, pulling Sarah to her feet beside him. Nudging her toward the entry, he turned to face the two men, walking backward so he could watch them while he moved away. "Go to the cab, Sarah. I'll be right there."

"But—"

"Go.... This visit was obviously a waste of our time."

Sarah grasped the door handle, reluctant to leave him, afraid not to for fear she'd get him killed. Escaping onto the front porch, she ran for the cab, not looking back.

When he reached the archway to the gallery, Michael paused to give Sarah time, his gaze leveled on his adoptive uncle. "If you have me tailed, if you let *him* have me tailed, you're signing my death warrant. I'm going to trust you not to let that happen."

Giorgio inclined his head ever so slightly, indicating that he would see to it that Michael left without anyone following. Whether he could trust him or not, Michael didn't know, but it was a chance he had to take. He didn't have any options.

After Michael left the house, Giorgio closed his eyes for a moment, then fastened an understanding look on Pascal.

"I know what you must do. I will not stop you, eh? But out of loyalty to me, wait five minutes. As Gino said, for old times' sake? I will ask nothing else of you."

"You're a dead man. You know that, don't you? When La Grande finds out Gino was here and you didn't grab him, it's wreath time."

Giorgio again inclined his head. "I am an old man, Pascal. Gino has the rest of his life ahead of him. I would die soon anyway, would I not? When I do, I want a clear conscience. My brother is the only family I have left. Because of my connections, I chose never to marry and have children of my own. After Angelo left, I never felt...worthy or safe."

Silence settled over the room. Pascal fastened his attention on the wall, a distant expression on his face. "You could clear out. If I got hit on the head, no one could blame me. You could be long gone by the time I came around. I got Gino's cab number. That'll pacify La Grande."

"If you give it to him, my nephew may be killed once he is no longer useful."

Pascal smiled. "I have a hunch Gino's got more Santini in him than you think. He won't be easy to trace. At least he has a fighting chance. I'll buy him a little time, but I can't make a miracle. Neither can you. Go for it. Get out while you still can. I hate funerals."

"And where would I run?"

Pascal raised an eyebrow. "To the Feds, where else? Who knows, maybe *they* can work a miracle for your Gino, eh?"

Giorgio grinned. "Perhaps. I got the cab number, too."

ANOTHER SEEDY HOTEL in another seedy neighborhood. More greasy coffee, coming up. Sarah plopped on the creaky bed and threw her head back to stare at the smoke stains on the green ceiling. She might not have minded loud bed springs if she and Michael were making some of the right noises with them, but the frown of concentration on his forehead didn't indicate he had any such intention.

She sighed loud and long, casting him an inquisitive glance. "So now what?"

"I'm thinking."

"My vote is Marcus St. John. He might know something."

He shook his head. "No, whatever's going on, it started with my father. St. John wouldn't even know the Santinis, so how could he help us?"

"How about your mother? Her behavior was sort of about-face, suspicious at best."

"Same thing goes for her. She probably never laid eyes on Angelo Santini. No, Sarah, it all leads back to my father, no two ways about it."

She twisted on the bed, snapping her fingers. "Newspapers!"

"What about them?"

"Old ones. I'll bet we could come up with something if we went through old publications. Think about it. In your nightmare, there's blood on the floor. That means someone was badly injured or murdered. That would make the news. Maybe your dad killed someone." She warmed to the idea, rising to her knees on the mattress to wag a finger at him. "Or *finked* on someone! Presto, you've got vendetta."

He turned from the window, his brow creased in a scowl. "Maybe you have something there. Where could we find old news copy?"

"At the library. They keep it on microfilm. And if that fails, most newspapers have morgues."

"Don't say that word. It sends chills up my spine."

Bouncing off the bed, she hurried to the scarred dresser to rummage through the grocery bag sitting there. Pulling out a newly purchased brush, she went to work on her hair, grinning at his reflection in the mottled mirror. "We're on to something this time. I feel it in my bones. With both of us going through film, it shouldn't take us that long."

FOUR HOURS LATER, Sarah would have given almost anything she owned for a good cup of coffee. The viewing room was stuffy and hot, she felt nauseous from staring at blurred pictures and she had eyestrain from reading. And she was getting sleepy. The lack of caffeine in her system was taking its toll. Since Michael was searching for news articles on the Santinis and there were no duplicate films available, she was looking for information on his real father, Adam St. John, trying to find an obituary. So far, no luck. She was beginning to wonder if St. John had died in another city.

Running the film forward, she stifled a yawn and blinked tears from her eyes. What a dull year. She passed a hand over her brow and ran more film. *Wait a minute, was that something?* She reversed, scanning the bold print. And then she realized what had caught her attention. A picture of Michael? A tingle of excitement slithered down her back. No, not of Michael, but a man who was his near double—Adam St. John. Bingo! His obit. Sarah bit her lip, forgetting all about her headache.

The headline read:

COMPUTER MAGNATE DIES

HEIR TO ESTATE CANNOT BE FOUND

Heir? Slowly advancing the film, she scanned the article. She had just begun to read about a clause in St. John's will that provided an inheritance for his illegitimate son when Michael called her name, his tone imperative. Shoving back her chair, she circled to his machine.

"You'll never guess what. Your father *did* have a son. I just found mention of it in his obit." The inanity of that remark hit her and she giggled. "Well, of course, you *knew* he had a son. But this is proof that—" She stared down at his pale face. "What's wrong?"

He stared straight ahead, not moving, not seeming to hear her. She could see that he was stunned. She leaned forward to peer at the newspaper page. SANTINI AGREES TO TESTIFY leaped off the screen at her. Excited, she moved closer, grasping his shoulder. Angelo Santini has agreed to testify against someone named Paul La Grande? La Grande, according to the article, had been charged with several crimes ranging from police bribery, prostitution, illegal gambling and loan sharking to several counts of murder by proxy. Santini's testimony was considered to play a key role in the prosecution's case.

She advanced the film, wondering what had upset Michael so badly. This was no more than they had expected. His dad had finked, just as she had said. She found another article dated three days later that said Santini's life had been threatened by Paul La Grande's father, Brian. As she ran the film forward again, she felt Michael's tension build. And then she saw why:

MOBSTERS HIT SANTINI HOME, MURDER HOUSEKEEPER

Nausea rolled through her stomach, and she knew if the effect on her was that bad, the effect on Michael had been far worse. The mobsters, according to the paper, had swept through the Santini home with machine guns, riddling the walls with bullets. Three-year-old Gino Santini had hidden under his bed and miraculously escaped harm. When federal agents searched the house, the child had been so terrified, he stayed hidden even though agents called his name. The child had to be forcefully removed from his hiding place.

Sarah's heart twisted. Tightening her grip on his shoulder, she started to crouch beside him. He forestalled her by saying, "Advance it. There's more. It says we were taken into protective custody."

She did as he asked, her pulse slamming. A picture came on the screen of Michael, three years old, clinging to his father's leg, attending the highly publicized funeral of the murdered housekeeper. The expression on the little boy's face in the photo was one of shock. Even with the grainy detail, she could see the blank horror and utter confusion in his eyes as he fell back from the cameras. *Michael.* She touched a finger to the child's dark hair, the love she felt for the man beside her stretching back thirty-two years to include the boy he had been.

"I remember," he said hollowly. "I finally remember."

She didn't know what to say, what to do. He was shaking, shaking violently. Propping his elbows on the counter, he dropped his head into his hands.

"It was never a nightmare, Sarah. None of it. Even the parts that never made sense. The long box with the blood dripping down its sides—I dreamed of it with a child's perception, translating my horror into something I could understand." He took a deep, jagged breath. "The lights in my dreams—do you know what they were?—camera flashes. The reporters came at me with cameras, jumping, yelling, trying to make me look at them. I remember it now—how terrified I was. I didn't understand. I was just a kid and they didn't care—not as long as they got their story." He shook his head. "So many things make sense now. No wonder I had phobias about black clothing and guns."

"Oh, Michael...what can I say?"

He shook his head. "Nothing. That's the hell of it. It's

over and done with, has been for over thirty-two years. It's only real inside my head."

If it was real to him, it was real to her. Sarah bit the inside of her cheek, blinking back tears. "Maybe now you can put it to rest."

He lifted his head, staring at the picture. After a long moment, he leaned back in the chair. "Look how young my dad was. And Mamma. She looks scared to death, bless her heart. These past few weeks, I've hated both of them in a way. Now, at least, I can try to forgive them. No wonder my father was so secretive. I was right all along. He *was* protecting me, wasn't he?"

"Yes, I believe he was."

He looked up at her, his face pale. "We're in way over our heads, Sarah. We've got to get help, and we've got to get it fast."

CHAPTER FOURTEEN

SARAH GAZED AT the microfilm screen, studying the stricken look on Marcia Santini's face. Right now, Michael strongly resembled his adoptive mother.

Michael rubbed his eyes, blinking as if he were dazed. "If my dad was a key witness, there should be some kind of agency that helps people like us. Maybe the police will know."

"If your dad's alive, maybe they can find him. The most immediate thing is to get some protection for ourselves until they can get this La Grande character behind bars. Sure wish we could afford a cab. It'd be safer than walking."

"Unfortunately we're on a limited budget." He rose from his chair, grasping his injured shoulder as he carefully rotated his arm to get the kinks out. "Let's get out of here."

Remembering the obituary she had found, she said, "Wait for me at one of the tables. I'll be right along. I want to get a photocopy made."

He didn't ask of what, and Sarah chose not to tell him. He had faced enough truths today to last him awhile. She'd make a copy of his natural father's obituary and give it to him later.

WIND GUSTED AGAINST Sarah's face, and she pressed closer to Michael, longing for a coat as they strode along the sidewalk. He seemed distant, speaking infrequently, his face creased in thought. She maintained the silence, respecting his need to remember and sort things into some sort of rational order so he could deal with them.

Traffic sounds drifted around them. The smell of exhaust permeated the breeze. Pedestrians scurried, each in his own separate world, eager to get somewhere, not noticing the two out-of-towners. She took a deep breath and exhaled, tipping her head back to look at the sky. She felt a hundred percent better now that she and Michael knew who was after them and why. At least now they could fight back. A bird swooped from one building to another, graceful, beautiful, as out of place among the tall buildings as she.

"Finding those news stories and triggering my memory will probably end my nightmares. Once this is all over, I can get counseling if I need it and begin looking forward instead of back." He angled a glance at her upturned face. "The first day of the rest of my life. How's that for trite?"

She smiled. "The reason some sayings become hackneyed is that they're generally so true."

"Will you look forward with me?" His eyes were warm, cloudy with tenderness and questions. "Or am I wishing on rainbows?"

A glow started deep inside her, radiating upward into her chest, as warm as sunshine. She faltered and came to a stop, keeping her head tipped back to see his face. "What are you asking?"

He lifted his hand to touch her cheek, a habit of his she had come to cherish. "You know what I'm asking."

"Maybe, but if you think I'll let you off easy, you've got another think."

He laughed and led her into a recessed doorway so they wouldn't be so easily seen from the street. "Miss Montague, would you consider starting over with me—beginning today?"

She pretended to consider that and then grinned. "Yes, Mr. De Lorio, I might do that if I were asked properly."

"Witch. And my name's not De Lorio, it's Santini." His eyes widened. "My God, come to think of it, it's not even Michael, it's Gino." The corners of his eyes crinkled in a smile. "Somehow, Gino just doesn't cut it."

"I don't care what I call you, just as long as I can call you."

"And I'll take that to mean yes."

"Don't delude yourself. I'll say yes when the question is put to me in a yes or no fashion. Not before."

"Yeah? Well, I'm not asking, not on a smutty sidewalk with a mobster out after my hide." He grabbed her hand, tugging her along behind him. "Let's go to the hotel so we can call the cops."

She skipped to catch up with him, laughing at the grin he flashed her. At just that moment, a cream-colored car swerved into the curb and two men jumped out. She recognized them immediately as the men they had seen at the *concierge*'s desk in the hotel last night.

"Mr. De Lorio?" one of them barked.

Michael whirled, shoving Sarah behind him. "Yes?"

Both men reached inside their jackets. Sarah saw all twenty-nine years of her life flash before her eyes. Then their hands emerged, holding pieces of folded brown leather which they flicked open and shoved toward Michael's face. *Badges.* She nearly collapsed on the sidewalk from sheer relief.

"Dennis Tealson, United States marshal," the shorter man said. "My partner, deputy marshal Sam Paddao."

She felt Michael's body relax. "U.S. marshals? My God, if only we'd known—"

Tealson smiled and motioned toward the car. "Our sentiments exactly. You've led us a merry chase, believe me. Please, let's take a little ride, shall we?"

Sarah felt like singing. United States marshals? It was the most wonderful thing that had happened to her since... She glanced at Michael as he slid into the back seat beside her and bit back a gigantic grin. Nothing, not even rescue, compared to Michael admitting he loved her. Oh, he hadn't said it in so many words, but she'd seen it in his eyes, and that was enough.

"My father must have called you then?" Michael asked.

"He's in our Witness Protection Program. We checked him out of the hospital and took him to a government medical facility. Then we tried to pick you up as well."

Sarah frowned. "I didn't think that program came into existence until the early seventies."

"It didn't, but Robert De Lorio was one of the few we grandfathered in. La Grande never stopped looking for him. A couple of years ago he even tried bribing a deputy in our Chicago office for information, so it was a necessary safeguard."

Tealson drove aimlessly through the city, talking constantly, and with every word, Sarah's heart sank a little more. Giorgio Santini had come forward shortly after their visit to his home. He was now in protective custody with Robert De Lorio, who had been flown to Chicago two days ago. Michael was being offered immediate transport to join his father. From there, the three men would go *under* with new identities, and Sarah would be returned to Eugene. Once La Grande could no longer get at either of the De Lorio men, he would have no use for Sarah, so she would be safe.

Michael raked his hand through his hair. "Uh, whoa—run that by me again. Under? New identities? What exactly does that mean?"

"A new start in a new place with a new name," Tealson explained. "We'll try to fix it so you can practice in your field. No promises, but we'll try."

Michael smiled uncertainly at her. "I like being who I am, thanks. Once is enough, right? I'll stay Michael De Lorio."

Tealson glanced at them in his rearview mirror. "I'm afraid you don't understand, Mr. De Lorio. This isn't an option, it's survival. You have to go under."

Michael's smile vanished. "But I—" he licked his lips "—I have a life of my own, separate from my father."

"Explain that to Brian La Grande. Even if we put him away—which we have plans to do—especially if you'll agree to cooperate, he could still get to you from prison. The heads of these organizations don't relinquish control because of incarceration."

"What do you mean, if I'll cooperate? Cooperate with what?"

Tealson sighed. "We need you as bait to catch him."

Sarah felt sick. Sick and heartbroken. Michael was going away? This couldn't be happening. None of it. And after all they'd been through, how could the marshals ask him to endanger himself again? She listened to Tealson, feeling more numb by the moment. They said they would keep Michael under close surveillance. When La Grande made his move, he'd be arrested.

"But why would Michael make such wonderful bait?" Sarah squeaked.

Michael grasped her hand, giving it a squeeze. Tealson frowned at her in the mirror. "La Grande wants Angelo Santini—Robert De Lorio to you—an eye-for-an-eye kind of thing. If La Grande can get his hands on Michael, he'll have the bargaining power to draw Robert out of hiding and get his revenge. We hope to use Michael to turn the tables and catch La Grande red-handed. As of this afternoon, we also have a contact on the inside."

Sarah lifted an eyebrow. "Who?"

"The man asked that his name be kept confidential. Contacting us could put his life in danger if it leaks."

"I see." Sarah saw all too well. "And what does Michael get out of all this?"

"Satisfaction." Tealson shrugged. "It's not an ultimatum. You don't have to do it, Dr. De Lorio. We just thought you might want your pound of flesh before you went under."

"You thought right." Michael avoided looking at Sarah. "He's messed up half my life. Now it looks like the next half is shot all to hell, too. You bet. If I can do something to put him behind bars, I'll do it."

"It could be dangerous. We aren't infallible, as much as we'd like to be. One mistake and you could be a dead man."

"I'll risk it."

Sarah parted her lips to protest, but she was forestalled when Tealson said, "And how about you, Miss Montague? We can swing it without you, but it'll look less suspicious if you stay in for the duration. La Grande will wonder why you're suddenly out of the picture if you fly back to Oregon."

"Oh, no!" Michael held up his hands. "I agreed to putting *my* neck on the chopping block, not hers."

Sarah leaned forward. "How closely will you be watching us?"

"I won't know if you have your toast with butter or without, but I'll know if you're eating white or wheat."

"I'll do it."

Michael jerked her back against him. "You won't. You're getting on the first flight home. This is my problem, not yours."

"I make my own decisions, Michael. I've got *my* pound of flesh coming, too. For Molly."

"Fine. The deal's off." He met her gaze with steely determination. "It's not a go, Tealson, not with her involved."

She lifted one shoulder in a shrug. "Suits me. I didn't want you getting your head blown off anyway."

"She'll be protected to the fullest extent of our capabilities, De Lorio," Tealson inserted.

Michael rolled his eyes and tried one more time. "Sarah, look, this is my—"

"I'm doing it if you are and I'd do it without you if I could. End of discussion."

He studied her for a long moment. Then at last he nodded his head. "Okay, Tealson, what do you want us to do?"

The marshal took a right turn, glancing at his partner. "Brief them, Paddao."

Paddao twisted in his seat. "Mostly we just want you to be visible, to La Grande and to us. When you went into a less affluent area, it threw everyone a curve. Giorgio Santini helped us trace you. His man, Pascal, will probably tip La Grande with the same information. You need to stick tight in one general area—make it easier for La Grande, stop covering your trail." He shrugged. "What were you doing at the library?"

Michael explained.

Paddao nodded. "It would stand to reason you'd be looking at microfilm trying to find out what's going on. The library's as good a place as any for us. Bear in mind, it could take hours or days for La Grande to make his move. It's a waiting game."

Michael shrugged. "We can always read. We don't have to stay there constantly, I hope?"

"You'll leave for meals, of course, and at night to go to your hotel. At those times, we'll be around, you just won't be able to see us. When La Grande tries to nab you, we'll have his men spotted and move in as soon as we have proof of the La Grande connection."

"What's to stop him from killing us?" Michael asked. "He's tried before."

"Not since your dad was taken into protective custody. He needs you alive to lure your father out of hiding. Before, he probably wanted you out of the way so you couldn't talk." Paddao cocked an eyebrow. "Well, what do you say? Back to the library?"

Michael glanced at Sarah. "Yeah, the library will be fine."

SARAH'S MOOD WAS in a steady decline. She had decided to put their time at the library to good use and look for more articles on Adam St. John. It was unlikely Michael would ever be able to return to Chicago. This way, at least he'd have information about his father to take with him, something he could save and show his children.

His children....

It was that thought that depressed her so badly. He was going away, possibly within hours, certainly within days, to take on a new identity in an unknown town. She wouldn't know who he was or where he was. He would simply disappear without a trace, lost to her forever. As if he had died.

He might ask her to go "under" with him, but the very idea panicked her. All her life, because she had been so dark and her parents so fair, she'd had a feeling of separateness, of being different, of not quite belonging. No matter how dearly she had loved her adoptive parents, her own appearance had made her wonder where she had come from. Now, after sacrificing a year of her life to find them, she had a mother as well as brothers and sisters who looked like her. She even had nieces and nephews, which she could never have had as an only child. It gave her a feeling of roots, of having a niche where she truly belonged. Because she had never had it as a kid, that feeling was doubly important to her now.

To go with Michael, she would have to take a fictitious

name and cut all ties with the people she loved. She stared
at the machine before her, advancing the microfilm without
really seeing it. The overhead lights hit the screen at just
the right angle so she could see her reflection on its surface. How many times as a kid had she stared in a mirror,
asking herself, "Who am I? Who am I really?" A hundred
times? A thousand? And always the same answer. *I am
Sarah from nowhere.* She couldn't go with Michael and
live the rest of her life feeling like that. She just couldn't.

Sighing, she decided she had scanned too many blurred
newspaper articles. She already had several copies of
stories about Adam St. John stuffed in her slacks pocket.
She hadn't taken time as yet to read them, but she hoped
she had accumulated enough information to give Michael
a sense of identity.

She found Michael at a reading table, hunched over a
book. She hesitated behind him, trying to compose her
features. Since her time with him was limited, she wanted
to make the most of every second. Sneaking up on him,
she bent down to blow softly in his ear. He whipped his
head up, focused on her and grinned. "Do that again and
I'll follow you anywhere."

"How about following me to a restaurant? I didn't eat
breakfast. We skipped lunch. And I'm suffering from caffeine withdrawal."

He glanced at his watch. "It's four? I didn't realize."

"It was all those doughnuts you ate. Meanwhile I'm
expiring."

He closed the book and pushed up from his chair, taking hold of her arm. "I saw a café a couple of blocks over."

"Did it look clean?"

"Squeaky."

Sarah fell in beside him, wondering if he sensed how
depressed she was under her facade of cheerfulness. If
he did, he didn't say anything. As they exited the library,

she saw him glancing around as they walked and realized he was searching for the marshals. "Cagey, aren't they?"

He smiled and put his arm around her. "Good at what they do, that's for sure. If they're here, I can't spot them. Kind of gives me chills."

They were nearly to the café when she noticed the arm he held her with was on his injured side. "Hey, you must be getting better."

"Much. Fact is, I'm feeling almost human. Another week and I'll be just like new."

Sarah averted her face. In another week, he'd be gone. She'd never see him again. The bell overhead rang when he pushed open the door. She slipped inside ahead of him, pleased with the café's appearance. Delicious smells wafted to her nose, the most delectable being the rich aroma of freshly brewed coffee. She took a deep breath, glancing back over her shoulder. "Any preference where we sit?"

He guided her to a nearby booth, taking the back side and leaning forward to lift an eyebrow at her. As she sat down across from him, he said, "Earlier, you mentioned something about finding my father's obituary?"

As briefly as she could, she related what she had found. "I found a few other stories about him, too. Quite a prominent citizen, from what I read."

"I'm not surprised. You should have seen Marcus St. John's house. We're talking three or four million on the low side." His eyes began to glow with excitement. "So there was actually mention of my dad having an illegitimate son?"

"According to the article, he even provided for the child in his will but could never locate him."

"Of course he couldn't. My adoptive parents covered their tracks too well."

She frowned. "One thing really bothers me, now that

I've stopped to think about it. Why did Marcus deny the existence of a nephew?"

"If you'd seen his home, you'd know why. With that kind of money and the will being made public, he's probably had hundreds of people lay claim to the inheritance. More than likely, he wanted to do a little detective work before he encouraged me." He shrugged. "I can't say I blame him. I'd do the same, I think."

She nodded. "Yeah, I suppose I would, too. When you visited him, you weren't even positive of the relationship."

"But I am now." He glanced up and smiled at the waitress, taking the two menus she proffered. "We'd like two coffees, please." Returning his gaze to Sarah, he said, "You know, maybe I should call him. After this La Grande thing breaks, I may not have a chance."

She tried her best to share in his enthusiasm. "It would be neat if you could have at least one visit with him as a member of the family." An ache of tears crept up the back of her throat. "Family's important. It would be nice to have some information about your dad—maybe even some family pictures."

Spying a pay phone across the café, he slid out of the booth. "Why not, I'm gonna call him. All he can say is no, right?"

"Right."

His eyes searched hers. "Will you go to his house with me?"

Sarah knew she should say no, but her time with him was running so short, she didn't want to waste any of it. "Sure, if you're not ashamed to take me."

He glanced at her clothes and grinned at the atrocious color combination. "Never. Besides, look at me. I'm not exactly at my best."

She watched him stride away. The waitress brought the coffee, and Sarah took a sip, closing her eyes to savor the taste. When Michael returned, she cracked an eyelid and said, "Now *this* is coffee."

"You won't believe it, but St. John not only agreed to see me, he's been trying to contact me for days. He did some checking and says he's satisfied that I'm his brother's child. Isn't that fantastic?"

She smiled over the rim of her cup. "It's wonderful."

"And not only that, he's sending a car to take us out to his house for dinner."

"Should we do that? What about the marshals?"

"They can tail us. No way was I going to pass up the invitation. Would you? This might be my one and only chance to learn about my real father."

She set her cup in her saucer. "It sounds fun. Better than cockroaches and smoke-stained paint. I've never been in a three-million-dollar house. It'll be an experience." Glancing down at her outfit, she rolled her eyes. "It'd be nice to dress up but I've got nothing to change into."

He checked his watch. "He said the car would be here in twenty minutes or so. That's not enough time to shop so let's go ahead and have a snack. I'm starved."

"Good idea. Otherwise, I may faint before we get there."

Sarah was just finishing a piece of the most delicious lemon meringue pie she had ever tasted when a man in a blue suit slid into the booth beside her. Because she and Michael were expecting Marcus St. John to send someone for them, she wasn't alarmed until she turned her head and recognized her companion as the heavyset gunman who had broken into their hotel room last night.

She froze with her fork suspended halfway to her mouth, her gaze fastened in horrified disbelief on his face. In her peripheral vision, she saw another man slide into the booth beside Michael. It was the other gunman, the tall, thin one who had been clobbered with the coffeepot.

One side of his face was an angry red where he had been scalded.

"Don't make a scene," the heavy man hissed, jabbing something into her ribs.

Her gaze slid to Michael. From the taut set of his features, she knew there was a weapon being poked in his ribs, too. Remembering his gun phobia, she knew his heart was probably slamming even harder than hers. She lowered her fork to her plate, reminding herself that the marshals were right outside. There was no reason for her to feel so frightened.

"This is the plan, people," the thin man sneered. "We're gonna get up, real slow and natural and walk out the door. Do what you're told and you won't get hurt." He rose and motioned them out of the booth with the gun he had hidden under his jacket. "We're just taking you for a nice little drive."

Sure, Sarah thought. After what had happened to Molly, she doubted they were going on a scenic tour of Chicago's Magnificent Mile. Her legs felt like half-cooked noodles. Michael moved close to her, settling his hand at her waist. She was surprised he wasn't shaking. When she looked up at him, she was even more surprised to see him wink at her. That wink meant the world to her. If Michael, who was terrified of guns, could overcome his fear and have faith in the marshals, then so could she.

The heavyset man led the way, the thin man bringing up the rear. She glanced out the window, scanning the building fronts across the street for any sign of the marshals. A man in a gray overcoat leaned against a light pole, reading a newspaper. He wore a hat pulled low over his eyes. Tealson? She couldn't tell. People scurried along the sidewalks, heads bent, shoulders hunched. None of them looked like lawmen. How did the marshals plan to rescue them? Would there be shooting?

The gunman in the lead stepped out onto the sidewalk, holding the door ajar. Michael moved his hand to Sarah's hip, drawing her closer to his side as they stepped across the threshold. His warmth and the strong support of his arm reassured her as the cool breeze touched her face. Out of the corner of her eye, she saw a blue Pontiac parked several spaces up the street. The front doors of the automobile opened and two men climbed out. The next second, the air exploded with gunfire. For a moment, Sarah didn't feel afraid, believing the men to be U.S. marshals. Then she saw the heavyset man grab his stomach and stagger. The next instant, he crumpled onto the sidewalk. Surely the marshals wouldn't shoot a man with no warning.

"Rudd! Are you okay?" the thin man cried.

"They got me," the older man grunted.

The thin man dived forward and flattened himself on the concrete, reaching for his injured partner to drag him back to the door of the café. "Who's shooting?"

Sarah shrank against Michael, her heart slamming. One of the men by the Pontiac had his arms locked in front of him, the Uzi in his hands aimed directly at her. She noted his sharp features and gray hair. *The man she had seen in the Eugene airport?* Michael cursed and jerked her clear off her feet as he dived into the gutter between two parked cars. Sarah's shoulder no sooner hit the asphalt than she felt herself rolling, Michael shoving her from behind. The rough texture of the pavement dug into her back, tearing at her shirt.

"Keep flat, Sarah," he whispered.

Down the street, in the opposite direction from the Pontiac, she heard Tealson yell, "Freeze!" The rat-a-tat-tat of another gun split the air. Everything became disjointed. Footsteps. Men yelling. People screaming. Rubber grabbing pavement. Michael swore and stuffed Sarah under one of the cars, slithering in after her. She lay there on her belly, her mouth pressed to her fists, eyes lifted to peer out from under the car at the street. The blue Pontiac sped past, tires squealing as it rounded the corner.

Michael wasted not a second. Crab walking from under the automobile, dragging Sarah behind him, he staggered to his feet. Throwing a glance both right and left, he lunged across the intersection, angling the opposite direction from the way the Pontiac had gone.

"But, Michael—" She flailed one arm, trying to grab his to make him to stop. "The m-marshals! What about the marshals?"

"Forget the marshals," he yelled over his shoulder, never breaking stride, his arm stretched out behind him to hold her hand. "Come on, Sarah, kick it in gear."

She threw a frantic look behind them. If they ran, they wouldn't have the marshals to protect them. On the other hand, though, if they stayed, they could end up dead. She decided to kick it in gear.

They ran as if a monster breathed down their necks— not normal running, but flat-out, legs extended, heels jarring against the concrete. With her hand in Michael's grip, trying to keep up with his longer stride, there were moments when she felt airborne.

Several blocks later, a black car swerved in at the curb. A man poked his head out the window and yelled, "Hurry! Pile in."

"The marshals," Michael gasped, veering for the limo.

The rear door opened for them as if by magic. She glanced up the street, her heart thudding, then jumped inside the car. Michael flew in behind her and slammed the door. "What took you so long? We almost got our heads blown off!"

The man who had opened the door for them turned sideways in the seat, his knee touching Sarah's thigh. She saw something in his right hand and lowered her gaze. A gun? Her stomach dropped and she glanced at the men up front. The one on the passenger side sat crosswise in his seat, his back to the door, the muzzle of his .38 pointing directly at her head. She recognized him instantly. *Pascal, Giorgio Santini's thug.*

"Don't do anything foolish, Mr. Santini," the man next to Sarah told Michael in a soft, persuasive tone. "Your little friend's life depends on your cooperative behavior." Pulling two black hoods from his pocket, he handed one to each of them. "Please, draw those over your heads. Compliments of your host, Brian La Grande."

CHAPTER FIFTEEN

A HALF AN hour later, Sarah and Michael were dragged out of the car and told to remove their hoods. Sarah withdrew the black cloth from her head and blinked to accustom her eyes to the sudden light. Before her loomed the biggest house she had ever seen, a Spanish design white stucco with a red-tile roof, surrounded by gorgeous terraced gardens.

Pascal grabbed her arm, leading her up a stone path into a courtyard. When she lagged, the cold flash of his blue eyes told her he would just as soon kill her as look at her if she didn't cooperate. She heard Michael shuffling along behind her, offering no resistance. After the threat on her life, she wasn't surprised.

As Pascal pulled her through the front door, the toe of one of her sneakers caught on the threshold, sending her into a headlong sprawl. He pulled on her arm and snarled a curse, but he didn't really hurt her. The moment she regained her footing he drew back his hand and slapped her. The impact of his palm against her cheek carried little force, but as his hand connected, he shoved her, making it look as if the blow had sent her reeling. Again he gave her arm a tug.

Michael jerked away from the men who held him, launching himself at Pascal and knocking him against the balustrade on one side of the hall. Their combined weights broke a baluster.

She clamped a hand over her mouth to keep from

screaming, watching in horror as Michael's hands closed around Pascal's throat. Pascal's face flushed crimson and his eyes began to bulge. Michael didn't seem to feel the other two men pulling at his arms, trying desperately to break his hold.

"Michael! Michael, please!"

One of the men pulled his gun out from under his jacket, raising it high to slam the butt into Michael's skull.

"Meeks!" a commanding voice barked. "Injure him and you're fired."

The stocky blond lowered the gun, his pale blue eyes shifting uncertainly to Pascal's mottled face. "But he's gonna kill him."

"Which he richly deserves for manhandling the woman."

Sarah glanced over her shoulder and spied a tall, white-haired gentleman in a nearby doorway. He inclined his head, his blue eyes alight with laughter. "Please, Ms. Montague, call him off? Pascal is a little rough around the edges, but he's loyal."

She whirled back toward Michael, only to find he had already stopped choking Pascal and now stood with his hands braced on the bottom rail of the balustrade, head dropped. Pascal was crumpled on the floor, holding his throat and gagging.

"Michael?"

He glanced up at her, breathing heavily. "Are you all right?"

She took hold of his arm. "I—I'm fine. He didn't really hurt me."

Shaking free of her grasp, Michael turned to square off with their host. The older man in the doorway chuckled and stepped forward, extending a manicured hand. "Gino, this is a rare pleasure indeed. You are a chip off the old block if ever I saw one. The Santini temper in all its glory."

Swiping his sleeve across his mouth, Michael looked at the man's outstretched palm with ill-concealed distaste. "That wasn't temper, La Grande, that was rage." Reaching for Sarah, Michael pulled her into the protective circle of his arm. "Your man should pick on someone his own size."

"Ah, so you know who I am?"

"I've been reading about you in old newspapers. And your worms used your name a few times during our little ride."

La Grande's lips thinned but he maintained his smile as he lowered his arm. Gesturing toward the room he'd just left, he said, "Please, come in by the fire."

He led the way into a gorgeous sitting room, inclining his head toward a velvet settee. Sarah glanced back to see that two of the men, Meeks and Axtell, had followed and were standing just inside the door, their gun hands under their jackets. The back of her neck crawled as she sat beside Michael. She heard the front door open and then slam closed. Pascal? Judging by the force with which he shut the door, she assumed he had gone outside to walk off his temper. A frown creased her brow. It puzzled her how lightly he had slapped her—almost as if he had been trying not to hurt her.

Her heartbeat provided a steady backdrop for Michael's and La Grande's voices as she scanned the room, looking for an escape route. The only way out, aside from the guarded doorway, was through lace-covered French doors that opened onto a courtyard. She knew the grounds were well guarded. Even blinded by the hood she had been able to tell that. The car they had come in had stopped at a gate and she had heard someone ask the driver to identify himself before they were admitted. Even if she and Michael managed to flee the house, they'd probably be caught.

"So to what do we owe this honor?" Michael asked La Grande sarcastically. "Isn't one Santini enough?"

"I regret inconveniencing you," La Grande replied, "but you are—how shall I put it?—necessary to me. I must make good on an old debt to your father, you see, and I'm hoping he will come forward if you are my houseguest."

"You already have my father," Michael accused. "You abducted him over a week ago."

Sarah entwined her fingers with Michael's, watching him in silent admiration. No one would ever guess that he had already been briefed by Tealson on everything La Grande was telling him.

La Grande frowned. "I had hoped to keep this a pleasant interchange, truly I had. Must we be testy? It was the marshals who took your father, not I."

"I tend to get testy when someone's trying to murder me."

"Come now, a ride in a limousine isn't exactly life threatening."

"And what about the Uzi?"

La Grande's brows drew together in a scowl. "Yes, I was told about that. I assure you, I had nothing to do with it. One of my own men was badly hurt."

Michael snorted with disgust. "Who else would be trying to kill us?"

"A very good question, one that I have my people checking into. But be assured, you are far more useful to me alive. At least for now." La Grande turned to open a brass box on the mantel. Taking out a cigar, he rolled one end in his mouth, biting off the tip. Leaning over to spit it out in the fireplace, he threw Michael a glare. "Your father put my son behind bars. For that, he must pay. It's nothing personal. I will try to make your stay here as pleasant as possible."

"Until you don't need us anymore and decide to kill us?"

A wreath of smoke encircled La Grande's face. "Your fate is as yet undecided."

Sarah tensed, staring out the French doors. What was going on? Pascal was skulking around out there, darting behind lawn furniture as if he didn't want to be seen. Her fingers tightened convulsively on Michael's. Was Pascal the inside contact Tealson had mentioned? Were there marshals out there? A shiver of fear ran over her. She shifted her gaze to La Grande and kept it there, not wanting to give Pascal away by watching his approach. He *had* been trying not to hurt her. When he had slammed out of the house, he must have gone to admit the marshals through the gate, and now he was leading them up to the house.

Michael flicked her a puzzled glance, but she didn't dare respond to the question in his eyes. A second later, she heard the front door burst open. Then the glass in the French doors shattered. She threw herself forward onto the floor, pulling Michael down beside her.

"Freeze! U.S. marshals," Tealson yelled, leaping into the room from the courtyard. When Meeks reached for his gun, Tealson barked, "Don't do it, friend."

Sarah turned her head to see Meeks and Axtell raise their hands high. Michael stared toward the French doors at Pascal, scarcely crediting his eyes as the man stepped into the room in Tealson's wake. Pascal's gaze met his, lighting with laughter. Lifting his hands, he said, "It was a question of loyalty, eh? Giorgio is like a father."

"You betrayed me?" La Grande threw his cigar into the fire, his face contorted. "You'll pay for this, Pascal, that's a promise."

"If you can find me, only if you can find me. After I testify against you, I will disappear, eh?"

Tealson and Paddao frisked Meeks and Axtell, relieving them of their weapons. Sarah and Michael rose from the floor, straightening their clothes. Glancing over her shoulder, Sarah was surprised to see La Grande calmly selecting another cigar, one shoulder propped against the mantel. He was one cool cookie, she'd say that for him. When Tealson approached him with cuffs, La Grande smiled and said, "I had nothing to do with any shooting. It's the truth. One of my own men was hurt. Even Pascal will tell you I just wanted to speak to Santini's son."

Tealson jerked on La Grande's arm, smiling none too pleasantly. "Maybe you've made too many enemies. It wouldn't be the first syndicate killing in Chicago."

La Grande stumbled, shaking his head in disgust as Tealson steered him forward. "I'm telling you, it had nothing to do with me! I have no enemies. You're making a mistake, Tealson. I wanted Santini, not his boy."

"All snakes have enemies, La Grande," Tealson sneered. "Comes with bein' a viper."

Michael stepped toward Pascal. "I think I owe you an apology."

"Not at all. You did exactly what I hoped, just with a little more enthusiasm than expected." Pascal grasped the knot of his tie and stretched his neck, grinning. "I wanted it to look as if I were out of commission for a while, and you played your part almost too well. I suffered no permanent damage, though. I hope your lady can say the same."

Michael glanced at Sarah. From her radiant smile, he knew she was fine. He hesitated a moment, then offered the mobster his hand in friendship. Pascal raised an eyebrow, then shook hands with him, chuckling. "It seems I have changed my colors, eh? It's just as well. Here soon, we'll be like cousins."

Michael lifted a dubious eyebrow. "Pardon?"

"Cousins, you and me. Your uncle Giorgio, he is like my papa. We'll go under with you. During the trial, we'll return here, but otherwise, we'll be starting a new family."

Michael hesitated. "In a limited sense, perhaps. No breaking the law."

Looking at Tealson, Pascal lifted his hands in supplication. "But of course not! Me? I am an upstanding citizen."

Tealson shoved La Grande toward the door, his expression amused. "Just don't forget it, Pascal. I'm grateful, but not *that* grateful."

Sarah grinned up at Michael, hugging his waist, oblivious to the confusion as Tealson joined the other marshals in the entry hall. Michael responded by running his hand up and down her back, caressing her lightly. Tealson returned within moments, a gigantic smile spread across his face.

"Well, we did it. I hope it didn't get too nasty?"

Michael slipped his arm around Sarah's waist. "It was worth it."

Tealson gave Pascal a congratulatory pat on the shoulder. "If it weren't for this fella, we'd have had problems. The guys in the Pontiac were an unexpected complication."

The memory made Michael's body grow taut. As long as he lived, he'd never forget that instant when he'd looked up and seen the Uzi aimed at Sarah. "So now what? Do I have to testify?"

"Thanks to Pascal and Giorgio Santini, I think we'll have enough on La Grande to send him up and keep him there for good. You and your father probably won't be needed."

"Does that mean my dad no longer qualifies for protection?"

"Not at all. He already did his part for society. As long as he's in danger because of it, we'll give him assistance. You should both be able to lead relatively normal lives."

"Normal? Is that what you call it?"

Tealson's smile held a hint of grim resignation. "I know it's not ideal, but it's better than the alternative." He glanced at his watch. "I'll bet you two are tired. Your luggage is being held at our office. It's early evening. I'm sure there's a room available at a suitable hotel with tight security."

"That sounds great," Michael replied. "I feel like I could sleep for a year."

"Mc, too," Sarah agreed.

"Well, let's get you back to the city. You'll need a good night's sleep. Ms. Montague has a flight to catch at ten-thirty in the morning, and you'll be leaving to join your father even earlier. That only gives you a few hours."

SARAH STARED AT her reflection, unable to dispel the ache within her. A few more hours, Tealson had said. That was all she and Michael had. She wanted to scream, to cry, to shatter the mirror. Anything to block out the hurt. It wasn't fair—it just wasn't fair.

Opening the bathroom door, she stepped out and saw Michael standing by the window, gazing out at the swiftly falling darkness. With her heart in her throat, she went to join him. He didn't glance down as he put an arm around her.

"What are you thinking?" she asked.

"About you." At last he looked at her. "About what's best for you. It's selfish, I know, but I want you to go with me."

She couldn't speak; if she did, she would cry.

"You're not going to come, are you?" His eyes searched hers. Then he heaved a sigh. "I guess I don't blame you."

She moistened her lips, fighting to keep tears out of her eyes. "We have tonight, Michael."

"Yes, that's true. We have tonight." He laughed, an empty hollow sound. "It doesn't seem like much."

"You kissed me once and said you wanted that one time to remember. That's how I feel now. Give me tonight?"

"Oh, Sarah." He turned and pulled her against him, lowering his head to press his mouth to the curve of her

neck above the edge of her nightgown. "You might regret it tomorrow. I'll be gone. You'll never see me again.
What kind of—"

"Trust me, I'll never have regrets." She leaned her head
back, placing her palms on his rumpled shirt, lifting her
eyes to his. "There's magic between us. Once in a lifetime magic." Sliding her hands up his chest, she cupped
his face between her palms and rose on her toes to press
her lips to his.

He moaned and crushed her to him, raising her feet
clear off the floor. She felt a pinpoint of warmth kindle
in the hollow of her stomach, a pinpoint that burst into a
searing, licking heat when his lips slanted like silk across
hers. She slipped her arms around his neck.

It seemed to her she had waited a lifetime for this moment. She had yearned for him, tried to imagine what
being with him would be like. But dreams were nothing
compared to reality. When he led her to the bed, she felt
as if she were floating on rainbows. Michael was indeed
magic.

There was no initial feeling of strangeness between
them, no hesitation. She didn't even think about it when she
felt him peeling off her gown. His touch wasn't a physical
thing so much as it was emotional. He was satin, a cradle
of warmth, her love. To share her body with him was ec-
stasy. She arched into his hands, breathless with wonder
as he learned the contours of her flesh, seeking its secrets
with gentle fingers and silken lips.

When at last he came to her, she cried, not with regret,
not with pain, but with an indescribable joy because being
one with him felt so incredibly right. It didn't matter that
his injured shoulder hampered them. It didn't matter that
marshals stood outside their door. Michael was her only
reality for now.

When the last waves of pleasure ebbed slowly from their

bodies, she pressed her cheek against his bandaged shoulder and closed her eyes, not wanting to move away from him. As if he sensed that, he held her close and stroked her hair, not speaking, not moving, letting the minutes slip sweetly past.

After a long while, their surroundings came back into focus. She heard the forced-air heat kick on first. Then she heard traffic sounds outside their window. But the most jarring sound of all was the faint ticking of his watch, measuring off their remaining minutes together.

"I love you. You do know that?" he whispered.

She touched the dark hair that tufted over the wide strip of bandage on his chest. "Yes, I know."

He made a fist in her hair. "Sarah, I realize how important family is to you, but we could start over, have our own family."

She closed her eyes. "Oh, Michael, please, don't make this harder than it has to be. It breaks my heart to say goodbye. But how long would I be happy? I'd never be able to see my mother and sisters and brothers again. I know it sounds selfish but—"

"No—no, it doesn't sound selfish, sweetheart. I understand. Probably better than anyone else possibly could. You've found all the things I've searched for. It wouldn't be fair to ask you to give them all up." He lay quiet for a moment. "I have nothing to offer you, nothing. A fake name in an unknown town, always looking over my shoulder, afraid La Grande might find me. Ten years down the road, I might have to jerk up roots and go under all over again. That's no kind of life. When I think about it, I don't want that for you. I don't even want it for myself."

Sarah bit her lip, holding her breath to keep from sobbing. When she regained her composure, she said, "Maybe if I'd had a different kind of childhood, it'd be easier for me to cut ties. But I used to ask myself who I really was, and there was never an answer. Now I know who I am, where I came from. I can't imagine going back to—"

He rose on one elbow, tracing the contour of her cheek. His eyes were cloudy with tenderness. "You don't have to explain. Even now, I wish I could have seen St. John again, talked to him. At least then I could have taken a piece of myself with me, something to hold on to."

"Then why don't you go? It's still early. Call him. You'll never have another chance, Michael. Once you leave here, you don't dare come back. Not ever."

"I don't want to waste the time I could have with you."

"So we'll stay up all night. You'll regret it forever if you don't go."

He sat up, glancing over his shoulder at her. "You really think I should?"

Sarah replied, "Yes, I do, Michael. Because of La Grande, you'll never have an opportunity to convince your birth mother to meet with you. Marcus St. John is the only blood relative you'll ever be able to see."

"Why don't you come, too?"

She nearly said yes, but then she realized the sooner they grew accustomed to the idea of parting, the easier it would be when the inevitable moment arrived. "I'll wait here. You go. When you get back, we'll order dinner by candlelight."

"It'll be so late. I know you're hungry."

"I'll order a snack. Go. Please? I want you to, really I do."

He hesitated a moment then reached for the phone, dialing out to information. A few minutes later, he said goodbye to Marcus St. John and turned to her with a smile. "He's sending his car to pick me up. He practically insisted you come, but I explained you were too tired. Didn't seem upset that he missed us at the café earlier. I was afraid he might be."

"Did he ask what had happened?"

"No. Maybe there was no sign of trouble when his driver got there."

She sat up, smoothing his hair back from his forehead with trembling fingertips. "Well? What are you waiting for? Get dressed and go downstairs to meet him."

She pulled on her nightgown and propped herself up with pillows, watching him race around the room getting ready. When he stepped over to the dresser to straighten his tie, he glanced back at her, clearly nervous. "Well, how do I look?"

He looked wonderful, heartbreakingly so. "Very nice," she said softly.

He walked over to the bed and pressed a kiss to her forehead, then rushed for the door. When he opened it, Paddao stepped into his path, lifting an inquisitive eyebrow. Michael explained where he was going and started to step around him.

Paddao grabbed Michael's arm. "I'm afraid I can't let you do that. You're in protective custody."

She slid from the bed, approaching the door. She could sense Michael's disappointment.

"This is something I have to do," Michael insisted.

Paddao shook his head. "Let me call and get you an escort."

"How long would it take?" Michael asked, checking his watch.

"A couple of hours, at most."

"That'll be too late." Michael looked at Sarah. The future without her yawned ahead of him like a black abyss. There was only one thing concrete in his life—his true identity. He had already lived half of his life not knowing who he really was. The next half he was going to be someone else. Was it so unreasonable to want something solid to cling to? "I'm going," he whispered to her. "If La

Grande's thugs are out there, then maybe that's how it's meant to be."

Sarah nodded, understanding in a way that another person might not have. He was taking a big risk, but to him, it was worth it.

Paddao stepped into his path. "I'm sorry, but I can't let you leave."

Michael brushed past him. "What are you going to do? Shoot me?"

"You could be kicked off the program for this!" Paddao warned.

Michael turned to walk backward, lifting his hands in a helpless shrug. "You gotta do what you gotta do, man. And I gotta do what I gotta do. Sorry...."

SARAH'S THOUGHTS WERE with Michael. She called room service, ordering dinner to be served at ten, then went over to her suitcase to see what she might wear. *Dinner by candlelight.* Her brushed cotton nightgown was completely unsuitable.

Her soiled clothing lay in a crumpled heap on the floor beneath the suitcase rack. As she rummaged through her case, her foot brushed the garments and she heard a faint crackling sound. Perking her ears, she glanced down and spied the folded photocopies about Adam St. John protruding from the pocket of her slacks. She'd been so anxious to shower earlier, that she'd stripped without a thought for the clothes she shed.

Thankful she had spotted the copies, she picked them up to lay them on top of Michael's suitcase so he wouldn't leave tomorrow without them. Her wish to be close to Michael somehow, along with boredom and curiosity, made her unfold them. She had only skimmed the articles earlier, and so much had happened since, her recollection of them was a blur. Stepping over to the bed, she flopped back against the pillows to read the first news story. A smile curved her mouth. Adam St. John had been touted as a genius in advanced computer technology. It figured. It was no news to her that Michael came from superior stock.

Scanning the next page, her smile faded and her grip tightened on the papers. Adam St. John hadn't just looked halfheartedly for Michael, he'd searched for years. She bolted upright in bed, her trepidation escalating as she read. St. John had put out newspaper feelers and offered rewards to anyone with information that might lead him to his son. The inheritance involved wasn't just a token portion of his estate, but the estate in its entirety. Marcus St. John would have had to relinquish claim to everything if his nephew had ever been found.

Dread filled her. It seemed rather odd that Marcus would welcome his usurper so cordially, even going so far as to send a limousine for him, when he knew Michael's existence would divest him of millions. The man was either a saint or a...

She leaped to her feet, staring at the phone. Should she call St. John's and caution Michael? Or was she jumping to crazy conclusions? Gnawing her lip, she began to pace, rereading the articles. Tension crawled up her neck, tightening her jaws. "Oh, Michael, what should I do? I hate to ruin your visit for nothing."

She thought back to the very beginning. When she'd first begun her investigation under the name Santini, immediately after speaking to Giorgio Santini, she had called Marcus St. John, giving him her name and the name of her agency. He would have had just as much time as La Grande to trace her.

Passing a hand over her eyes, she remembered La Grande's insistence that he'd made no attempts on Michael's life. Had he been telling the truth? Had it been Marcus St. John all along? Had he hired someone to run over her? To break into her office and erase her computer? To attack Molly? It all began to make sense and Sarah's horror mounted. The first break-in had been engineered by an amateur—Robert De Lorio, most likely—but the second had been a professional job. Of course for Marcus's purposes, she and Molly would have to be eliminated as well. They knew who Michael De Lorio really was. Michael had been La Grande's ace in the hole, just as he claimed; a pawn in a game of revenge; more valuable alive than dead. Only St. John would have benefited from Michael's death.

Sarah froze, studying the telephone for a long moment. She should at least call Michael at St. John's and check to see if anything was up before raising an alarm. With a trembling finger, she dialed to get an outside line, called information and acquired St. John's number. While punching the digits and listening to the phone ring she closed her eyes and prayed. A gentleman with a British accent answered.

"Yes, may I speak with Michael De Lorio, please?"

The man asked her to wait and the line rustled. She presumed he had covered the mouthpiece. A moment later, he came back on the phone, saying, "I am sorry, but there's no Mr. De Lorio here, ma'am."

"I see. Thank you."

She hung up, gazing at the wall. Michael would never leave St. John's without notifying her, not when the threat from La Grande still hung over them. He would know how worried she would be. Rising from the bed, she raced for the door, pouncing on Paddao who lounged against the wall outside her room. Talking so fast she tripped over the words, she told him about the news clippings and the sizable inheritance. "Anyway, I just called to check on Michael at St. John's—" she gasped "—and some man with a British accent told me he wasn't there. I'm really frightened."

Paddao frowned, following her into the hotel room. Giving her shoulder a comforting pat, he picked up the phone. "Let me check with the office to see if Mr. De Lorio called in about a change in plans." With a smile, he sat on the bed, propping his elbow on his knee. "Yeah, Tealson? Paddao. Have you had any word from De Lorio? Nothing, hmm? Well, yeah, I am. Ms. Montague has some interesting photocopies here that might shed a different light on things." As briefly as he could, Paddao related the contents of the news stories. He listened for a moment, then nodded. "Okay, will do. If there's anything up, I'll get back to you." Hanging up, he quirked an eyebrow at her. "You got St. John's number? I'll call and check myself."

She pointed to a piece of hotel stationery. Paddao glanced at the number jotted there and made the call. Clearing his throat, he said, "Yes, may I speak to Marcus St. John, please? Sam Paddao here, U.S. deputy marshal."

She leaned against the dresser, wringing her hands. Her stomach tightened when Paddao began speaking again.

"Yes, Mr. St. John, this is Deputy Marshal Sam Paddao. I'm calling to see if Michael De Lorio is there." Paddao listened with a broadening grin. "Ah, the butler was just confused? Then we were alarmed over nothing. May I speak with him, please?" Again Paddao waited, flashing Sarah a reassuring smile. "Yeah, Dr. De Lorio? Paddao here. Everything okay there?"

"I want to talk to him!" she cried. "Please, just for a sec."

"Uh, Mr. De Lorio, Ms. Montague wants to talk to you. Yeah, here you go."

She grabbed the phone. "Michael, are you okay?"

"Yes, fine."

There was a strained edge to his voice, almost undetectable but there. "Are you sure?"

"Except for being stuffed from that dinner we had, I'm great. How 'bout you?"

Her empty stomach knotted. She threw a frightened look at Paddao. "I—I'm fine. You'll be back soon then?"

"The sooner the better," he replied. "I love you."

The line clicked and went dead. Slamming the receiver into its cradle, she whirled to face the deputy. "I knew it. He's in trouble."

Paddao's eyebrows rose toward his hairline and he laughed. "I just spoke to him myself and he said nothing was wrong."

"Yes, but he told me he was full from dinner! Since we haven't eaten, I'd say that's a little strange, wouldn't you?" She ran to the closet, digging through her suitcase. "They were listening, don't you see? He couldn't come right out and say anything. Call Tealson. We've got to get out there."

"Whoa!" Paddao held up his hands, striding loosely toward her, his smile persuasive. "You're jumping the gun here. He could have eaten at St. John's. Ever think of that? Did he or did he not say he was fine?"

"Yes, but—"

He shrugged. "I rest my case. Relax, Ms. Montague. If he isn't back in a couple of hours, we'll go out and check on him."

She grabbed her soiled blouse and slacks from under her suitcase, not bothering to search for a clean outfit. There wasn't time. "He could be dead in two hours. Call Tealson!"

"I just spoke to Mr. De Lorio. He said nothing was up. We can't converge on a private residence without just cause. There are laws, you know?"

Sarah hugged her clothes to her chest. "Maybe you can't, but I can. I had an invitation. I'll just go late."

Paddao stared at her. "I don't think you and Mr. De Lorio understand the gravity of the situation we have here. Have you any idea how powerful a man La Grande is? Without constant protec—" He threw up his hands. "You can't go traipsing all over the city."

She strode toward the bathroom. "Watch me."

CHAPTER SIXTEEN

SARAH STARED OUT the cab window at the wrought-iron gates of the St. John estate. She had never seen so much outdoor lighting at a private residence. Just in case her hunch was wrong, she hated to be seen sneaking onto the property. She'd ruin Michael's one and only chance to visit with his uncle. It would be far better if she could return to the hotel, no one the wiser. And if she was right? Tension knotted her hands into fists. If she was right, she had to slip back out and call Tealson.

There was an intercom panel on the left side of the brick entry arch. The cabdriver gave it a long look, then said, "Lady, you wanna go in or sit out here all night? I charge for sittin', ya know."

Glancing at the fare meter, she cringed. "As a matter of fact, I need you to drive up the road about a block and wait."

"For how long? I want payment in advance."

"How much would thirty minutes run?"

The price he quoted made her teeth ache. She dug into her purse for the fare, muttering under her breath. Shoving the money at him, she said, "Keep the extra. If I don't come back, would you do me a favor and call the—"

"Look, lady, I'm a cabbie, not a messenger service. You want a phone call made, it's an extra fifty."

"I don't have fifty. All I've got is ten."

"Fifty," he insisted.

She rolled her eyes and stuck out her palm. "On second thought, I want my change."

He grumbled about it, but he returned the seven dollars he owed her. Sarah stuffed it into her purse, throwing him a glare as she climbed out of the car and slammed the door. Turning to survey the gate, she slung the strap of her purse over her head so she'd have both hands free to climb. The cab swept away from the shoulder of the road, its tail pipe rattling as the rear tires bumped onto the asphalt. Putting her hands on her hips, she heaved a sigh. She was on her own now. If she took more than thirty minutes, it was a long walk back to town....

She approached the gate, looking up at the three decorative arches across its top. Grasping a vertical bar with both hands, she jumped, getting footholds on the iron with her rubber-soled sneakers. Shinning up to the top crossbar, she grabbed the crown of one arch, swinging a leg around its rise. *So far, so good.* Twisting her body, she straddled the bar, pivoting on her bottom to draw her other leg over. Taking a deep breath, she wriggled forward and jumped to the asphalt below.

Darting off the driveway into the protective shadows of the shrubs, she wove her way toward the house, surprised at how easy trespassing was. She had expected better security—not that she was complaining. She'd just sneak up and peek through a few windows, satisfy herself that Michael was indeed okay, and leave. No fuss, no fanfare.

Three-quarters of the way to the house, she heard something behind her—a low, vicious snarl. The hair on the back of her neck prickled and she paused to look over her shoulder. The first thing she saw was teeth, lots and lots of teeth that glowed blue-white in the artificial light. *A Doberman?* Now she knew why canines were classified as meat eaters.

This was bad....

The dog didn't have Trained to Kill branded on his fore-head, but the message came across loud and clear. *Move, and you're dead.* She tested the animal's intentions by wiggling the fingers of her left hand, an innocuous little movement she hoped looked friendly. "Nice dog."

The canine sprang forward a foot or so, growling with an intake of air through its nostrils that sounded wet, im-patient and deadly. Then he barked. Not an ordinary bark, but a bark interspersed with snarls. Four more Dobermans rose to the hue and cry, springing out at her from the dark shrubbery. She closed her eyes, imagining their teeth tear-ing into her flesh.

To her surprise, the dogs didn't attack. They raised an alarm, barking, lunging and snapping the air, but they didn't bite. Eternity passed—at least it seemed like eter-nity. Then two men appeared on the well-lit front walk-way of the mansion, moving toward her. One wore a blue smoking jacket and looked so much like Michael from a distance that she nearly dissolved with relief until she re-alized it wasn't him. The other was tall, portly and bald, wearing a black suit with tails. *The butler.*

The man who resembled Michael walked into the midst of the snarling dogs with an amused smile creasing his face. "Ms. Montague, I presume?"

She worked her mouth, then stammered, "Y-yes," flinching when the sound of her voice excited the crouched Dobermans.

"Guten tag," he said sharply, snapping his fingers. The Dobermans immediately quieted, circling his legs as he stepped closer to her. "As I'm sure you've guessed, I'm Marcus St. John. This *is* an unexpected pleasure." He pulled a small silvery gun from the pocket of his jacket, aiming the barrel at her chest. "Frisk her, Snider."

The butler ran trembling hands over Sarah's clothes, clearly embarrassed. "She has no weapon, sir."

Extending his hand to her, St. John said, "Your purse, please, and then we'll escort you inside to join my nephew."

"Sir, whatever are we going to do?" the butler asked. "That gentleman, Shuelle, is already gone. I haven't a thought how we might contact him."

"We'll simply wait, Snider," St. John growled with impatience.

At St. John's request she handed over her purse and walked toward the mansion, prodded in the back by his gun. The two men followed her. Once inside the house, they flanked her and seized her arms, hurrying her across a spacious entry hall and up a winding staircase. Three floors up, they paused outside a door. The butler unlocked the portal, then preceded Sarah and St. John into the dark room.

"Tie her," St. John ordered, forcing Sarah to lie face-down on the floor.

Light from the hall spilled across several coils of rope lying on a nearby trunk. With shaking hands, the butler grabbed a length of it and trussed Sarah hand and foot, arms behind her. Then he and St. John stepped out, slammed the door and left her in darkness. She heard a key rasp in the lock.

"Sarah?" She heard a rustle and a thump, then a dragging sound. A warm shoulder bumped hers. "Sarah…" Michael's voice sounded so close and wonderfully dear that tears flooded her eyes. "Are you okay?"

"I—I think so." She swallowed and gave a weak laugh. "For a while, I thought I was gonna be dog food." She told him about the newspaper stories she had read, how she had put two and two together and come out here to check on him. "Paddao wouldn't believe me when I told him something was wrong."

"I can't say I'm sorry you left. I just wish you hadn't

come here. St. John sent Shuelle and two sidekicks to kill you."

"Who's Shuelle?"

"Hired muscle, that creep in the Pontiac who packed the Uzi, the gray-haired, skinny guy? He's got two thugs named Lund and Packer working with him. The three of them make La Grande's boys look like nursemaids."

Dim light shone through an oculus window at the gable end of the room. *An attic?* She sniffed and wrinkled her nose. The mustiness was so strong it nearly made her sick.

Straining her eyes to see, she could barely make out his silhouette. "Have they hurt you?"

"I'm fine. They're saving the fun for later. We've got to get out of here, Sarah. When Shuelle gets back…"

Even though he didn't finish, she knew what he'd been about to say. "He wouldn't dare. Paddao knows we're here."

"They'll just say we left. La Grande will get the blame."

She closed her eyes. Her shoulders felt as though they were being pulled from their sockets. She squirmed, rolling onto her back. Staring blindly at the blackness above her, she said, "What's our plan? In the movies they get back-to-back and untie each other."

After a great deal of thumping and grunting, they managed to touch hands, but the ropes were too tight to work them loose.

"Before they brought you in, I was rubbing my wrists on a wall stud, trying to cut the ropes."

"Was it working?"

"Yeah, but it would take all night. We may only have a few minutes." She saw him struggling to sit up. "The window. If I can get on my feet and break it, maybe we can get some glass to cut the rope."

She craned her neck. "How could you break it?"

"With the back of my head."

"Oh, my God…no way, Michael. You could cut yourself."

Dry humor rasped in his voice. "It'd take me awhile to, uh, well—you know. Before that happens, I'll be long gone and on my way to a doctor."

"*Bleed* to death. Why not just say it?"

"Don't push it, Sarah, or you'll have an unconscious hero on your hands."

"It's a stupid idea."

"Maybe, but it's our *only* idea at present."

She watched him bounce his way toward the window with growing horror. If he hit the glass wrong, he might sever an artery in his neck. Struggling to sit up, she bounced after him. "Michael, wait. We'll think of something else."

"Like what?" He put his back to the wall and shoved with his feet, trying to inch his way up it. "I have to get you out of here."

An ache rose in her chest, crowding into her throat. If ever she had doubted his love for her, she never would again. He finally gained his feet and hopped along the wall to the window. She cringed when she saw the silhouette of his head and shoulders against the glass.

"Hitting it from this side, all the glass will go out on the roof," she protested. "Please, don't—"

She saw his head come forward, then snap back. *Crack*. She cringed and bit down hard on her bottom lip. The glass didn't break. He sighed and tucked his chin on his chest again. The next moment, another loud crack resounded. Glass shattered.

"Michael?" She stared at his silhouette. If he was hurt, she wouldn't be able to help him. The thought petrified her. "Michael, are you all right?"

"Just seeing a few stars. Did all the glass go out?"

She had heard some of it fall inside the room. She tried

to home in on where the sound had come from. Off to her right someplace? "I heard at least one piece."

"Wonderful. That's like a needle—" he dropped bottom first onto the floor "—in a haystack."

"It's over here somewhere," she said with a grunt, pushing with her feet to move her rump sideways, then rocking forward to move her shoulders. When she reached the spot where she thought she had heard the glass fall, she rolled onto her side, stretching her hands out behind her to flick her fingers along the floor.

"Can you feel it?"

"No. You?"

He heaved another long sigh. "No."

A sudden pain shot through her shoulder. She flinched and grew still, twisting her neck to see. "I think I just found it."

"Where?"

"I rolled on it." She pivoted to get her hands near the glass, tucked her bound feet under her and strained to sit up. She rasped her fingers on the dusty floor until her thumb touched something sharp. "I've got it! Get back-to-back with me."

He rolled across the floor and wriggled into a sitting position, pressing his back to hers. "Sarah…" She heard him swallow, a loud plunking sound at the base of his throat. "Need I remind you that wrist arteries—"

"Trust me. I'm very good at feeling my way." She hooked a finger around the hemp between his wrists and began sawing furiously. She felt the rough cording snap in two. "Did I get it?"

The support of his back disappeared and she nearly toppled.

"Yeah, hold on a sec."

She could hear him breathing heavily beside her. A second later, he flipped around and seized the bindings on her hands. She sighed with relief when the ropes fell away. Jackknifing forward, she hurried to free her ankles. "Now what?"

"We—" He broke off and fell silent. "Damn, we don't dare chance the dogs. Our only hope is to overpower St. John and the butler before Shuelle comes back."

"You and me?" she squeaked.

"Got a better idea?"

"That isn't an idea, it's suicide."

He rose to his feet, grabbing her arm to haul her up with him. After shedding his jacket and tie, he tugged her over to the broken window. Her heart started to pound wildly. "Not the roof! I hate heights. Do you know how far up we are?"

"Three stories. But they'll hear us if we bust down the door. It's the roof or nothing, Sarah." He kicked off his shoes and grasped her waist, boosting her to the opening. "Careful, don't cut yourself."

Sharp jags of glass snagged her clothing as she shinned through the hole. The pitch of the roof fell sharply under her. It had begun to sprinkle rain, making the shakes slick. Her head spun with dizziness, and she had to take a deep breath. *Don't look down, Sarah.* On all fours, she turned to the window, offering a hand to Michael. He clasped her wrist and heaved himself up, working his broad shoulders through the narrow passage.

Once he was beside her, he reared back on his knees to scope out the windows in both directions. "If we can sneak back in, maybe we can take them by surprise."

Rising carefully to his feet, he offered her a hand. Moving inch by inch, they worked their way along the steeply slanted shakes toward an old-fashioned double-hung window. Then it happened. She took a step and her foot flew out from under her. When she fell, her momentum jerked Michael off his feet. She saw the edge of the roof coming up fast and clenched her teeth to keep from screaming. *Oh, please, God, no.* She clawed frantically at the shakes with her free hand, and tried to dig in her toes for a foothold, all to no avail.

At the last moment, Michael stopped his own descent by shoving his heel against the drainpipe along the eave. Sarah shot past him, a cry escaping her lips as she felt herself pitching off into nothingness. Michael tightened his grip on her hand, jerking her up short, praying that both the drainpipe and his newly healed shoulder held up under their combined weights. She hung there, the edge of the roof digging into her abdomen, her legs dangling.

"Oh, my God, Michael—"

"I've got you," he grunted. "Swing a leg up."

She hooked a knee over the gutter, sobbing with fear. Her arm felt as if it were being pulled from its socket. The sound of metal tearing from wood filled her with panic. "Michael!"

"It's all right. Slow and easy." He began pulling her upward. The gutter groaned and separated from the eave a little more. "Don't lose your head. Just get your knee on the roof. That's right."

With her right hand, she clawed at the shakes, helping him as much as she could. Slowly, inch by agonizing inch, she got both knees onto the rooftop again. She lay there, panting for air, so terrified she couldn't even think, her fingers vised on the rough wood.

"Don't move," he whispered, prying his hand from hers to get a locked grip on her wrist. "I've got you. Let me get to my feet, then I'll help you up, okay?"

She nodded, pinning her gaze on him to keep from looking down. His hand felt wonderfully strong around hers as he crouched, then slowly stood, teetering to keep his balance.

"Okay, sweetheart, now it's your turn. You can do it."

She *had* to do it. She clutched his hand, her breath coming in shrill, uneven gasps as she rose to her knees. One wrong move, just one, and she knew they'd both slide off and plunge three stories to the driveway below. If the fall didn't kill them, they still had to face the dogs. Her legs shook as she stood.

"Okay, I'll go first, then you." He took a careful step up the roof, paused to get his balance, and then nodded to her. "Your turn."

"I—I can't." She froze.

Michael tightened his hand on her wrist, staring at her pinched features. The outdoor lights reflected off the shakes onto her skin, giving it a cast that was almost green. He'd seen Sarah rally in a lot of terrifying situations, but this time, her fear of heights was undermining her usual gutsiness. He'd never seen that blank look in her eyes or felt her shake like this. As much as he had always admired her spunk, this moment of weakness endeared her to him more than anything.

"Sarah, look at me."

Her wide eyes clung to his, shimmering with tears. Her mouth trembled.

"Do you trust me?" he whispered.

"Y-yes."

"Then look at me—no, not down—look into my eyes. Now step toward me. I've got you."

"M-Michael, I—"

"I won't let you fall." He hoped he could keep that promise. "Come on, Sarah. You've got to do it."

She dug her fingernails into his wrist and took a shaky step. When she didn't slide, she laughed rather hysterically and nodded. "I—I'm okay."

"Sure you are." He moved another pace upward. "Okay, your turn again."

He led her the remainder of the way up the roof. When

they reached the window, he grabbed the sill with one hand and pulled her against him with his other arm. She clung to him, shaking violently until her fear subsided.

"Hold the sill," he whispered.

She didn't need to be told twice. She grabbed the wood in a death grip. Keeping his arm around her, he placed the heel of his other hand on the lower sash bar of the window and shoved upward. A sliding sound filled her with relief. It wasn't locked. Throwing a leg over the sill, he crawled through, never releasing his hold on her. She followed, dropping softly beside him onto thick carpet. Never had she been so glad to feel level floor under her feet.

Tiptoeing across the room, he led her to a door. They eased out into a hall. Ahead of them, she saw the attic room. They passed it and rounded a corner to the stairs, descending one flight. Voices drifted up to them from the entry hall below.

He leaned over the banister, cocking his head. "They're in the library. We need a distraction to draw them out of here so I can jump St. John from behind."

She gave him a thumbs-up. Together they crept down the remaining stairs. Glancing around the entry, she spied an extremely expensive-looking vase perched on an ornate table. Michael pressed his back against the wall next to the library door, nodding his head as she curled her fingers around the porcelain. Lifting her arms high, she heaved the vase at the floor and dived toward Michael. An ear-shattering crash resounded throughout the lofty hall. The murmur of voices within the library stopped. Footsteps thudded. The door opened.

Sarah held her breath, melting against the wall like a pat of butter on a hot roll. The butler charged out, sliding to a halt when he saw the broken vase. No St. John? Blood thundered in her temples. She stared in horror at the butler as he slowly turned toward them. The next sec-

ond, St. John stepped into the doorway, his gun pointed
straight at Michael.

"I see you've saved Shuelle a trip upstairs to get you,"
St. John said softly. "Please, come into the library and
enjoy the fire. Shuelle will be back anytime. He called a
few moments ago to say your marshal friends were guarding Ms. Montague and he couldn't get to her. He was extremely pleased to discover she was here."

"You won't get away with this, you know," Michael
said softly as they entered the library. "The marshals know
we're here, and they have all the photocopies about my father and his will. They know Sarah suspected you of being
the one who tried to kill me."

"I'll say you left. They can't prove otherwise." St. John
waved them toward a sofa adjacent to the hearth, keeping his back to the fire, the gun aimed straight at them as
they sat down. Snider, the butler, stood off to one side.
"Shuelle is very good at what he does. La Grande has the
more obvious reason for wanting you dead. It will be assumed it was him."

"Why?" Michael asked. "All I ever wanted was to know
who my father was. I didn't want your money."

St. John stared at Michael for an endless moment, then
shifted his gaze to Snider. In a conversational tone, he
said, "All my life, my brother Adam was always the one
who got everything. Snider will testify to that. Now that
Adam's dead, it's my turn." Tapping his chest with his finger, he smiled. "My turn."

Sarah had never seen a man who looked more sane, and
somehow that emphasized his madness. What frightened
her most was the look in his eyes that reflected his abso-
lute certainty that he was doing the right thing.

"You'd kill your own flesh and blood for money?" she
whispered.

As if the question had been posed in a foreign language,

St. John frowned down at her, his eyes clouding with confusion. Something flickered in his expression—a moment of sanity, perhaps?—and his mouth twisted.

"I don't want to hurt anyone. But he didn't give me a choice." He slumped against the marble fireplace, the gun wavering. Michael eased forward in his seat, watching him. "I can't let you take it all from me," he continued in a plaintive whine. "I've worked my fingers to the bone, doubled the corporate holdings. Adam always thought he was so smart. Well, I showed him." He fastened glazed eyes on Michael's face. "You're nothing but a worthless bastard. Your own mother didn't even fight for you. One phone call from me, that's all it took, and she backed off. I planned for everything. I couldn't let you come back and take it all. It's mine! I won't hand it over to you, no matter what his will says. What about *my* son, Tim? I suppose he should live a pauper's existence?"

"I don't want your money."

"You're a liar! Of course you do. Who wouldn't?" He made a wild arc with the gun at the richly appointed room. "And even if you didn't, he bequeathed it all to you. It was my sweat that made it what it is—years and years of my life—but he didn't care. Didn't leave me a lousy dime. The only way I stood to inherit was if you never came back."

Sarah's heart was slamming, marking off the seconds. She knew that Shuelle might arrive anytime. She and Michael had to do something, and do it fast. A trickle of cold sweat ran between her breasts. She felt Michael's body coil to spring, saw him ease forward on the sofa.

"So you decided to be sure I didn't come back," Michael said softly.

St. John laughed, making another wild gesture with the gun. "I'd be crazy to just stand by and lose my life's work. Would you?"

With no warning, Michael lunged off the sofa. Crooking one elbow around St. John's neck, he grabbed for the gun. Sarah saw the butler step forward and she jumped up to bar his way. He stopped and blinked, clearly unaccustomed to violence, physical or otherwise. She quickly deduced she had nothing to fear from him and glanced over her shoulder to see Michael slamming St. John's gun hand against the mantel. The weapon flew from St. John's stunned fingers, thudding onto the carpet. Sarah ran to pick it up before Snider could, whirling to aim it at St. John who had crumpled against the fireplace, his face contorted, shoulders shaking.

Michael straightened, breathing heavily. Not taking his eyes off St. John, he said, "We have to get them tied before Shuelle gets here. Find some rope, Sarah."

Running over to the butler, she dug into his jacket pocket to get the attic room key. Giving Michael the gun, she sped from the room. Over her shoulder, she cried, "Call Tealson."

She raced up the stairs, knowing full well Tealson would never get there in time. She and Michael had to save themselves. How? That was the question. She unlocked the attic room and snatched rope off the trunk, returning to the library at breakneck speed. Michael handed her the gun, looking glad to be rid of it, and bound both men, shoving them into the library closet and locking the door.

Turning to look at her, he said, "Now what? Tealson said he'd be at least thirty minutes. We have to think fast. One gun against three won't cut it, that's for sure. Our only chance is to catch them off guard before they know what hits them."

If that was their only chance, they were in trouble. She couldn't envision herself doing a football tackle. And Michael couldn't take three men by himself, especially not with an injured shoulder. With a touch of despair, she said, "We could feed them to the Dobermans."

He snapped his fingers. "Hey, maybe you've got something there. The kitchen! Hurry, Sarah."

"Are you out of your mind? Those dogs will probably tear us up if we go anywhere near them."

He ran down the entry hall, tossing open doors until he spied the dining room. Sarah stuffed the pistol into the waistband of her slacks and raced after him. He pushed through a set of swinging doors into a huge kitchen, then tore from cupboard to cupboard looking for something. At last, he smiled and pulled a can of nonstick spray off a shelf. "Good for zippers that stick, drawers that catch, doors that hang up."

"So?" She threw him an incredulous look. "Michael, those men are killers."

"And this may even the odds a little."

He hurried back to the entry, Sarah right on his heels. Bending at the waist, he began to spray the glossy tile with a sweeping motion of his arm, starting in front of the door, stepping back a pace at a time as he made his way toward the library.

"This will never work!"

He smiled. "Run back to the kitchen and go through the fridge. Find some meat—anything a Doberman might find tasty."

Her eyes widened as she began to see a method to his madness. She did as she was told, returning a moment later with two packages of sirloin steak. He grinned, making one last sweep with the can of nonstick spray, which had covered several square yards of tile. Taking care not to fall, he padded the length of the hall in his stocking feet, closing all the doors.

"Okay, now give me the gun," he said softly.

She handed him the weapon, following him to the library, the cold packs of meat cradled in one arm. He went directly to the closet, unlocking the door to grab St. John and press the tip of the gun to his temple.

"Will the dogs attack without a command?" he asked in a conversational voice.

Sweat trickled down St. John's nose. Casting Michael a horrified glance, he said, "I'm your uncle. You wouldn't kill me."

"Try me." Michael jerked on the man's collar. "Remember that girl you ordered killed in Eugene? She's a friend of mine. You're not related to me, not in any way that counts. My dad is twice the man you are."

"But she didn't die. She's recovering, Michael. I called this evening and checked." As if he sensed Sarah's relief, St. John threw her an imploring glance. "I never meant to hurt anyone. Please believe that. I didn't have a choice."

Michael looked disgusted. "So why did you call the hospital? To see if Shuelle needed to go back and finish his job? Lucky for Molly, that's one order you aren't going to be giving. Just tell me about the dogs, you sniveling coward."

St. John's face paled. "They will attack only if one makes a threatening move. Otherwise they've been taught to hold intruders and not harm them."

Michael gave him another shake. "What constitutes a threatening move. Pulling a gun? Fast!"

"Yes, a gun would incite them. I—I didn't want them to attack unless there was cause. Lawsuits, you know. A man of my means has far too much to lose. Smart of me, don't you think?" He slid his gaze sideways, clearly terrified by the gun. "I'm much smarter than Adam, you know. You can see that, can't you? Our parents never could. It was always Adam this and Adam that. But *I* knew I was better. Why, anyone could see. He had everything—everything a man could want—and he drank himself right into the grave while I kept the company together."

"Save it for the judge." Michael pushed him none too gently into the closet and slammed the door, turning to look at Sarah as he shoved the weapon into his waistband. "You stay in here. If anything goes wrong with the dogs, go out the window and try to make it off the grounds while they're preoccupied."

"But—"

He cut her off by pressing his hand to her lips. "Just do it. For me? Please?"

Though it wasn't what she wanted, she nodded, knowing he would only stand there arguing if she didn't. Taking the meat, he left the library. She followed him, holding the door ajar so she could watch him. Stepping carefully across the oily tile, he opened the front door and whistled for the Dobermans, calling *guten tag* to them and ripping open packages as they scrambled up on the porch. Dangling sirloin before their noses, he coaxed them inside, whispering *guten tag* again and again to keep them calm as they slipped and slid on the slick floor. Sarah was so afraid for Michael that her body quivered as she watched him. When all five dogs had come inside, he threw the meat clear across the hall, then shut the front door and ran for the library. She let him in and slammed the door shut behind him, releasing a pent-up breath.

"Simple as feeding lions," he said with a laugh. "Now we wait for Shuelle."

"You're going to sic the dogs on them?" The thought made her feel sick.

He caught her around the waist, pulling her against him. "You heard St. John. The dogs won't attack unless they pull weapons or do something else threatening. It's them or us. I don't like the thought any more than you do. Maybe less. Remember me, the guy who hates blood?"

She sighed, laying her cheek against his chest. "Did you hear what he said about Molly, Michael? She's recovering."

"I heard," he whispered. "Prayers *do* get answered. I don't think I would have ever stopped blaming myself if she had died."

Sarah knew exactly how he felt. The sound of his heart thrummed softly, soothing her with its even, predictable cadence. The rhythmic ticking of the pendulum clock in one corner of the room mesmerized her as it measured off the minutes. She closed her eyes, wishing she could stay in his arms forever, that Shuelle and his men would never return.

It was a wish that couldn't come true, of course. All too soon the intercom buzzed. Sarah pressed the gate-release control. Moments later, they heard a car drive up out front. Doors slammed. Voices approached the house. The dogs whined and growled, pacing the entry in eager anticipation. Michael cracked the library door to peer out, whispering *guten tag* to the Dobermans to keep them quiet. A knock came, then another. At last, a voice called, "Hey, St. John, it's me, Shuelle. Let us in!" Muffling his voice with a cupped hand, Michael called, "It's unlocked. We're in the library."

The door opened. Shuelle stepped into the entry, completely unconcerned about the presence of the dogs, glancing down in surprise when his shoes slid on the tile. "What the—"

"Welcome, Mr. Shuelle," Michael said, bracing his weight against the door. Shuelle stiffened when he realized it was Michael who had spoken, not St. John. Then he grabbed for his weapon. The Dobermans hesitated for a second, then took offensive stances. Shuelle's attention was on Michael and he failed to notice the warning snarls. He raised his arm, aiming his gun at the library door. That motion was all it took to spur the dogs into an attack.

Shuelle roared with alarm, rearing back when he saw the dogs leaping at him. His feet slipped out from under him on the slick tile and he crashed to the floor, yelling at his companions as he disappeared under a pile of writhing black fur. "Lund, help me!"

Lund jumped into the entry, one leg shooting forward as his shoes slipped on the oil. He yelled, drawing the attention of one of the Dobermans. The animal turned, fangs slashing, saliva frothing its lips. "Down! Down, you stupid—" He threw up an arm to protect his face, reeling backward into the wall as the Doberman hurtled into him. "Packer! Do something!"

Packer, a stocky redhead, drew his weapon and skidded across the tile, staring with indecision at the churning mass of fur. Each time he tried to aim, Lund or Shuelle rolled into his line of fire. It was clear none of the men knew the antiattack command, *guten tag.* Only Michael or Sarah could reverse what Shuelle had set in motion. Sarah closed her eyes, but only for a moment. The report of a gun cracked the air. She peered around Michael's shoulder to see the redhead staggering backward, his arm held by powerful canine jaws. His gun fell clattering to the floor. The shot had gone wild.

Michael stepped out into the hall, skirting the oily area, to retrieve Packer's weapon. Motioning to Sarah, he handed the revolver over to her. "Put your back to the wall," he instructed her. "If they make a wrong move, pull the trigger."

She nodded, retreating slowly, the gun quivering slightly in her hand as she pointed it at the scrambling pile of men. Michael took position on the other side of the melee, yelling, *"Guten tag."* The dogs immediately backed off and three badly lacerated criminals sat up, staring in disbelief at the weapons Sarah and Michael had trained on them.

Michael smiled broadly. "Mr. Lund, Mr. Shuelle, put down your guns and slide them across the floor. Real slow and easy so I don't get nervous."

Lund and Shuelle did as they were told. Michael stepped forward, and pushed the guns with his foot to slide them well beyond the criminals' reach.

"And now we wait," Michael said softly. "The United States marshals will be here anytime."

Sarah stared at Shuelle. She would have recognized his chiseled features anywhere. He was the man she had seen at the Eugene airport. Predatory, she had thought then. And that impression still held true. There was something so cold, so emotionless about his face that it made her blood freeze. Her finger tightened around the trigger of the gun she held. She envisioned Molly's vague smile and blue eyes, knowing beyond a doubt that it had been Shuelle's knife that had slashed her throat.

For the first time in her life, she wanted to kill. The urge was like a fire in her gut, raging out of control. Sweat filmed her face. She no longer saw Shuelle, but visions of Molly as she had looked the last time Sarah had seen her, silly, lovable, harmless Molly. She would have been so frightened right before Shuelle slashed with the knife— frightened and bewildered. No thanks to Shuelle, she was still alive, but she would never be the same naive, trusting girl she had once been. The fearful memories would always haunt her.

"Sarah?" Michael's voice seemed to come from a long way off. "Sarah, look at me."

She dragged her gaze from Shuelle's hated face and fastened her attention on Michael.

"It's over," he whispered. "Don't let him take you down with him."

She nodded and relaxed her finger on the trigger. Even if Molly had died, killing Shuelle wouldn't change what had happened. Shattered innocence, but the outcome could have been far worse. Shuelle might have done a more effective job with his knife and Molly might have died there in that alley after he left her. Sarah lowered her weapon, heading for the attic to get more rope with which to tie their captives. Soon Tealson and the other marshals would come. They would see to it that Shuelle paid dearly for what he had done. For her and Michael, the nightmares were finally over....

CHAPTER SEVENTEEN

DAWN BROKE ACROSS the Illinois sky like a promise, turning the dark horizon cotton-candy pink and rose-red. Sarah and Michael stood at the window watching the new day begin, bodies pressed close, arms cinched tight around each other. It was a moment of sweet sadness, sweet because they had savored every second of the night together, sad because each knew their time was swiftly running out. Paddao had knocked on the door twenty-five minutes ago, saying the government car would arrive for Michael in half an hour, much earlier than they had expected.

"I wish I could say I'll keep in touch," he whispered, "but we both know I won't be able to."

She nodded, nibbling her lip. "Have you any idea where you might go?"

He shrugged one shoulder. "Wherever the mood strikes us, I suppose."

"I wish—" Her eyes filled with tears and her mouth began to tremble.

He pressed his fingers across her lips. "Don't, Sarah. I want to remember you smiling." Moisture crept into his eyes, too, and he blinked, chuckling at himself. "We made it through the night without getting drippy. Let's not blow it the last five minutes."

Sarah nodded and took a deep, bracing breath. Trying desperately to think of something safe to say, she asked, "What about your house and car and office?"

"I don't know. I would think everything would be sold

and the proceeds sent to me, but you never know. I've read about people on the Witness Protection Program who started over in a new city with nothing but a new identity and enough money to set up housekeeping."

"Oh, Michael…everything you've worked for…you'd be starting from scratch."

"Exactly, which is why I'm not arguing with you about your decision to stay behind. I don't even know if I'll be able to practice in my field. I've nothing to offer you. Isn't that ironic. I find I'm the heir to a fortune, but circumstances prevent me from claiming a cent. Marcus's son, Tim, will get it all I suppose. Oh, well. Perhaps that's only fair."

"I wouldn't mind the financial insecurity. It's leaving my real mom, my little sister Beth, all the others. I've become so fond of them. Never seeing them again would be hard enough, but never even writing them a letter? I have to think of the effect on them, too. I don't know, Michael. I love you so much, but—"

"Hush. The decision's been made. Don't agonize over it. I've tried to imagine never seeing Papa again, never hearing from him, never knowing if he was sick or well. I don't think I could willingly cut myself off from him, either. I understand. This is best for you. Ten years down the road, you'll be glad it happened this way."

"And what about you?"

A knock sounded on the door, making both of them jump. Her heart squeezed with pain, and she instinctively hugged his waist more tightly, not certain she could bear having him leave. He bent his head, brushing his lips across her cheek.

"Time to go!" Paddao called.

Michael tensed, vising his arms around her one last time before pulling away. Cupping the side of her face in his hand, he traced her features with shimmering eyes, his smile shaky. "I'll remember you always," he whispered. *"Ti amo."* Touching his mouth to hers, he added, *"Ieri, oggi, domani."*

She caught hold of his hand and clung to his fingers, dreading the moment when the warmth of his touch would be gone. "Goodbye, Michael. God be with you."

He drew back, his eyes riveted to hers. Then he pulled his hand from hers and walked across the room for his suitcase. Turning to look at her, he flashed her one last smile. And then he was gone.

Sarah stood there, so racked with the pain of losing him that she felt numb to everything else. She could hear Paddao outside the room, bidding Michael goodbye. Then Michael called farewell, his voice fading as he walked farther away from the room. She turned to the window, pressing her palms against the glass to look down onto the street. A black limousine was parked at the curb. Tealson stood on the sidewalk, leaning one hip against the front passenger door. He turned his head continuously, looking up and down the street, over his shoulder, alert to everything around him.

It seemed to her an eternity passed before Michael appeared on the sidewalk below, flanked by two security men. Tealson opened the rear door of the limousine, smiling. Michael handed over his suitcase to the man on his left so it could be stowed in the trunk, then strode toward the car. Sarah saw Giorgio Santini lean forward and smile.

Her last look… She moved closer to the glass, gazing down, memorizing every detail of Michael's appearance. In the brown slacks and tweed jacket, he looked so wonderfully handsome, broad shoulders tapering to lean hips and powerful long legs. He placed a hand on the roof of the car to climb in, and then paused, glancing back over his shoulder at the hotel. She saw him searching and tried to smile as his gaze settled on her. His expression was so empty as he lifted his hand to her in a final farewell. She waved back, swallowing down a sob. *Michael, I love you,* her heart cried.

Then he turned away and climbed inside the limousine. Tealson stepped forward, closing the door. She clamped a hand over her eyes, unable to hold back the ragged sobs any longer. Why did it have to be this way? she asked herself. Losing him was like dying. But if she went with him, what kind of life would she have? She dropped her hand, watching the car pull away from the curb, carrying Michael away from her, not just for a month or a year, but forever. He'd disappear and she'd never be able to find him—never. Not even the marshals would tell her where he was.

A small snag in traffic brought the limousine to a halt a half block up the street. She stared at the tinted black window of the car, trying desperately to tell which man within was Michael. And suddenly she saw herself as she would be years from now, walking down city streets, looking at every dark-haired man she passed, at every bronzed face, wondering if it might be him. She heard the voices of her nieces and nephews asking, "Aunt Sarah, why didn't you ever get married and have kids? Weren't you ever in love?" *Yes,* she would say, *I was in love once, a very long time ago.*

The limousine inched forward another car length. Panic rose in her throat as she watched it. Roots were important—she desperately wanted a feeling of family—but was the past that important? Couldn't she begin her own roots, her own family? She stared at her reflection in the window, remembering all the times she'd looked in the mirror as a kid, asking herself who she really was. Could she handle having that feeling the rest of her life?

Indecision held her paralyzed. Wouldn't she always have her family, no matter where she went? Perhaps not in a physical sense, but they would be with her in her heart. Her sense of identity had been what she missed as a child. That couldn't be snatched away from her now. She knew who she was.

She was Sarah—Michael's Sarah.

A knock sounded and she jumped. Paddao, who had a key to the room, opened the door a crack and poked his head inside. "Anything I can get you? Coffee, some breakfast? They have great doughnuts."

She stared at him. *Paddao.* The name had a definite Latin flavor. "Are you Italian?"

He looked nonplussed. "Half."

"What does *ti amo* and *ieri, oggi, domani* mean?"

He frowned, trying to make sense of her clumsy pronunciation, then his mouth quirked in a silly grin. "It means I love you, yesterday, today, tomorrow. Why?"

Sarah smiled through her tears and ran across the room. "I've got to stop that car!"

Paddao fell back to get out of her way, watching incredulously as she sped up the hall. "Hey, wait! You can't leave! They're already gone. Ms. Montague, come back here! You forgot your suitcase!"

Sarah didn't care. She rode the elevator down, feeling as if every second lasted hours, then she burst out into the lobby. *Michael.* Nothing else mattered to her. If people stared, so what. She shoved her way through the revolving doors out onto the sidewalk, whirling in the direction of the limousine. Her throat tightened to call Michael's name so he'd have the driver pull over.

The light had just turned green, and the limousine was third in line to make it through the sluggish intersection. She sprang into a run, waving her arms in the air. "Michael! Michael, stop! I've changed my mind!"

She was still almost a block behind them, too far away for them to hear her voice. Fear clogged her throat. If the car drove out of sight, she doubted the marshals would break security to tell her where Michael had gone. With all the speed she could muster Sarah shoved through the pedestrians who blocked her way, her gaze riveted on the black car as it swung around the corner. *Oh, God, please, don't let them drive off without seeing me.*

"Michael! Michael! Mi—" She watched the black car disappear behind the corner of a building and she staggered to a stop, the rest of his name trailing off her lips in a whisper.

He was gone.

People bumped into her. A few shoved her. A man cursed and called her a name. She just stood there, staring at the traffic, her insides twisting with unbearable pain. The worst part was, she had no one to blame but herself. She could have gone with him. Staying behind had been her own choice.

An irrevocable choice.

She glanced back at the hotel, then closed her eyes. Would Paddao break the rules? Just once? What was she going to do if he wouldn't?

"Sarah?" a faint voice called. For a moment, she thought she'd imagined it and didn't look. "Sarah?"

Her heart caught and her eyes snapped open. She saw a black head bobbing toward her. "Michael?"

Shouldering her way through the crowd, she started to laugh. It was Michael. She could see his face now as he ran toward her, turning sideways to slip by pedestrians, his tie flying in the wind. When he drew close, she launched herself into his arms, hugging him with all her might, forgetting all about his sore shoulder.

"What are you doing out here?" he cried.

"I changed my mind. I don't care where I go or what my name is, just as long as I'm with you!"

His arms tightened around her. "Are you sure?"

"Yes, yes, I'm positive. You're my roots. We'll make our own family."

He lifted her off her feet, swirling her in a circle. "When I saw you running up the sidewalk, I thought I was imagining it. I wanted you to be there so much."

"Oh, Michael, I thought I'd lost you."

He set her on her feet and tugged her toward the limousine. "We can have Moses shipped." He flashed a sheepish grin. "I asked—just in case you decided to come. Tealson says the Portland office can put the cat in a kennel cage and fly it here. He'll send Moses on to us wherever we are."

"Great! Where are we going?"

He drew up beside the limousine, winking at Tealson who stood at the curb, looking none too pleased with their foolishness. "Someplace warm," he answered.

"Sounds wonderful."

As she slid into the rear seat of the limousine, her smile grew tense. Across from her, Paddao sat beside two old men, both of them dead ringers for Giorgio Santini. She wasn't sure which was the real Giorgio. They looked so much alike. Her gaze slid to the one on her left. He looked pale and tired.

Michael climbed in beside her, pulling the door closed. He grinned from ear to ear. "Papa, I want you to meet Sarah. Sarah, my father. Given his predilection for changing his name, you may as well call him Papa from the start and save yourself a lot of trouble."

The man on Sarah's left leaned forward to gaze intently at her face, not smiling, not speaking for an endless moment. She was afraid he disapproved. At last, his brown eyes began to twinkle. Slapping Giorgio on the knee, he said, "*Mamma mia!* It has finally happened. My Michael is getting married. This old man is going to have grandbabies after all."

Sarah smiled and inched closer to Michael, glancing out

the window as they pulled away from the curb. The car picked up speed, taking them she knew not where. But it didn't matter, not if she was with Michael. She knew her mother would understand that.

"Are you sure, Sarah?" he asked.

There was no need to answer. Her kiss said it all. The limousine rounded a corner, merging with the heavy Chicago traffic. Then it disappeared without a trace.

* * * * *

In Hope's Crossing, love knows no season....

**A touching new romance from *USA TODAY*
bestselling author**

RaeAnne Thayne

Spring should bring renewal, but Maura McKnight-Parker cannot escape the past.
Still reeling from the loss of one daughter, the former free spirit is thrown for a
loop by the return of her older daughter, Sage, and the reappearance of her first
love, Sage's father. Jackson Lange doesn't know his daughter—didn't even know
that he'd left the love of his life pregnant when he fled their small town—but he
has never forgotten Maura. Now they are all back, but Sage has her own secret,
one that will test the fragile bonds of a reunited family.

Sweet Laurel Falls

Available everywhere paperbacks are sold!

REQUEST YOUR FREE BOOKS!

2 FREE NOVELS
FROM THE SUSPENSE COLLECTION
PLUS 2 FREE GIFTS!

YES! Please send me 2 FREE novels from the Suspense Collection and my 2 FREE gifts (gifts are worth about $10). After receiving them, if I don't wish to receive any more books, I can return the shipping statement marked "cancel." If I don't cancel, I will receive 4 brand-new novels every month and be billed just $5.99 per book in the U.S. or $6.49 per book in Canada. That's a saving of at least 25% off the cover price. It's quite a bargain! Shipping and handling is just 50¢ per book in the U.S. and 75¢ per book in Canada.* I understand that accepting the 2 free books and gifts places me under no obligation to buy anything. I can always return a shipment and cancel at any time. Even if I never buy another book, the two free books and gifts are mine to keep forever.

191/391 MDN FEME

Name	(PLEASE PRINT)

Address	Apt. #

City	State/Prov.	Zip/Postal Code

Signature (if under 18, a parent or guardian must sign)

Mail to the **Reader Service:**
IN U.S.A.: P.O. Box 1867, Buffalo, NY 14240-1867
IN CANADA: P.O. Box 609, Fort Erie, Ontario L2A 5X3

Not valid for current subscribers to the Suspense Collection
or the Romance/Suspense Collection.

Want to try two free books from another line?
Call 1-800-873-8635 or visit www.ReaderService.com.

* Terms and prices subject to change without notice. Prices do not include applicable taxes. Sales tax applicable in N.Y. Canadian residents will be charged applicable taxes. Offer not valid in Quebec. This offer is limited to one order per household. All orders subject to credit approval. Credit or debit balances in a customer's account(s) may be offset by any other outstanding balance owed by or to the customer. Please allow 4 to 6 weeks for delivery. Offer available while quantities last.

Your Privacy—The Reader Service is committed to protecting your privacy. Our Privacy Policy is available online at www.ReaderService.com or upon request from the Reader Service.

We make a portion of our mailing list available to reputable third parties that offer products we believe may interest you. If you prefer that we not exchange your name with third parties, or if you wish to clarify or modify your communication preferences, please visit us at www.ReaderService.com/consumerschoice or write to us at Reader Service Preference Service, P.O. Box 9062, Buffalo, NY 14269. Include your complete name and address.